Unveiled

The Revealed Series – Book 3

Alice Raine

Published by Accent Press Ltd 2016

ISBN 9781786154460

The story contained within this book is a work of fiction. Names and characters are the product of the author's imagination and any resemblance to actual persons, living or dead, is entirely coincidental.

Accent Press
Octavo House
West Bute Street
Cardiff
CF10 5LJ

Acknowledgements

As always, my first thank you must go to you readers. I can never express in words how grateful I am for the support you give, and I truly hope you enjoy this third instalment of the new series.

Many thanks to my beta readers, Sam Berwitz, Grace Lowrie, and Suzanne LeBrun-Berry. Your input has helped me to carve the direction of the storyline as it develops, and has been so incredibly useful. An especially big thank you to Sam Berwitz, your advice and feedback during the initial editing phase has been invaluable. Thank you for putting up with my constant emails and questions, and also for the assistance with re-wording the vital final line!

A huge thanks also to my advisors: Dr Helen S. for the medical advice, Eve K. for sharing your knowledge on prop making and prosthetics, Joanna R. for the technical advice on film studios and author Laura Carter for the technical advice and support.

Once again I need to extend a huge thank you to everyone at Accent Press for the hard work and dedication that goes into supporting my writing. Especially Alex for your fabulous editing and advice, and Bethan and Kat for all the marketing and promotion work.

This instalment is my favourite so far, I'm really relishing the character development in this series, and I hope you all enjoy it too.

Alice xx

Prologue

Cait

Bursting through the front door into the early summer evening, I felt the breeze on my skin, warm and soft, but instantly blowing my long hair across my face so I couldn't see. A frustrated mewl flew from my lips as I continued to blindly run, raising a hand to drag my hair back from my eyes to clear my vision.

Down the driveway, or through the field? That was my only choice. I barely hesitated, diverting my feet towards the relative safety of the tall wheat crop to my right. At least in the field he wouldn't be able to jump in his car and drive after me.

A loud, furious bellow behind me broke the peace of the evening and made every single hair on my body stand up in fear. *Fuck.* He was coming. I'd hoped it would take him longer to get up and get his trousers back on. I barely had a head start on him, and I knew from experience that he was a fast runner. Too fast.

The cut on my temple from his punch stung, and sweat began to pop on my forehead as I urged my legs to move quicker, my arms pumping desperately at my sides to try and propel me forwards. Usually a good runner, I found that tonight, fear was paralysing my lungs and stopping me from breathing properly. Instead, I was gasping and stuttering, panting so desperately that it seemed to be echoing in my ears.

Finally I reached the edge of the crop, ducking my head

as I began to blast my way through. Pointy ears of wheat stabbed at my arms and face, surprisingly vicious for their small size, but I ignored the scratches and threw my hands out in front to help clear a path through the stems.

My pulse has hammering in my ears and my breathing was ragged and wheezy, but I heard the exact second that Greg joined me in the crop. The crunching and smashing of the wheat stalks behind me was unmistakable.

As was the sound of his heavy, determined breathing as he began to gain on me. Shit, shit, shit. What had I been thinking, coming in the field? I was disorientated and isolated. At least on the driveway I would have stood a chance of making it to the main road and signalling down a car for help.

It was too late now, and as the helplessness of my situation fully dawned on me, panic surged up my spine, making me light-headed.

My feet stumbled on a lumpy root and before I even realised it I was tumbling forwards, my arms flailing as I tried and failed to regain my footing. Given the speed I had been running I hit the ground with considerable force, and any remaining air in my useless lungs was forced from me in a sharp exhalation as my ribs connected with the hard soil.

I saw stars before my eyes, my body shocked and my vision swimming, but my brain was still alert enough to urge me on, and I was up on my knees and crawling almost as soon as I had fallen. The rough ground cut at my hands and knees as I tried to push back to standing while still scrabbling forwards, but then I felt an iron grip on my ankle and knew it was too late.

He'd caught me.

A high-pitched scream left my lungs, but knowing it was useless out here in the middle of nowhere I saved my breath and began to fight. There was a second or two of battling;

my free leg desperately stamped out in an attempt at kicking him to free myself, but gradually his strength overcame me and I felt myself being dragged towards him.

Greg was swearing now. Drops of his spittle landed on my scratched bare arms as he called me all sorts of filthy words and muttered exactly what he was going to do with me now he'd caught me. It made me shudder to my core, silent tears sliding across my cheeks and falling helplessly to the dry ground as his words washed over me in terrifying waves. They were dirty and violent and too much for me to take in, so my mind seemed to switch my hearing off.

For some reason, as I lay there sprawled on my stomach, I noticed just how much dirt was embedded under my fingernails. That would take ages to wash out, and I didn't own a nailbrush. There was blood too. Why such an insignificant detail was stuck in my mind I had no idea, but it was better than listening to his vile words. Perhaps I just needed something mundane to focus on to ground me from my terror.

Strong fingers bit into my shoulders, gripping hard and yanking me over onto my back as he smirked down at me. 'Gotcha. You know I love the thrill of the chase, babe.'

Dropping to his knees, he grabbed my wrists into one of his huge hands and smashed his lips down onto my mouth so violently that I felt my top lip split under the pressure. Blood leaked into my mouth, tangy and coppery as I fought to turn my head away. Greg leant up, a smear of my crimson blood flared across his triumphant face like a proud battle scar.

'I'm really going to enjoy this.'

My body went limp at the determination in his voice. There was no point fighting him; I was pinned below his wiry strength and totally useless without my hands. His free hand skimmed down my arm, across my breast, fondling it so hard I winced, and then it slid down the front of my trousers.

'No!' I sat bolt upright, unsure where I was. As I blinked wildly and took in the calmness of the room I realised I'd been dreaming.

Holy fuck.

I had no clue what had triggered the horrific nightmare, or why my hands were clutching at my mouth until a huge, hiccupy sob ripped from my throat, quickly followed by a hot mouthful of bile. Choking on the acidic burn I flung myself from the bed and ran to the en suite, only just making it to the toilet before the contents of my stomach expelled themselves violently into the bowl.

Staggering to the sink I rinsed my mouth out, brushed my teeth, and splashed several handfuls of water on my face before daring to look in the mirror.

Ugh. I shouldn't have bothered. I looked even worse than I felt. My blotchy cheeks suggested that I had been crying in my sleep, and the bags under my eyes led me to believe that the slumber I had got hadn't been particularly refreshing.

Plonking down onto the toilet seat I tried to get my composure back. That had been one hell of a nightmare. Except it wasn't just a figment of my imagination, was it? It was the reality of my past. My lips twisted as my mind flooded with memories of Greg. Now that I was awake I could only remember parts of the actual dream, the rest of it lost to my sleep, but my cruel mind was more than capable of filling in the blanks.

At least I'd woken up before the worst part.

Shuddering, I raised my hands and rubbed furiously at my face, trying to wipe away the cloying, disgusting memories.

I hadn't had a full nightmare like that for over two years now, but during the months that had immediately followed Greg's final attack I'd had them practically every night.

Letting out a long sigh, I wondered briefly what had prompted it, before shaking my head resolutely. I would not let him fuck up my life any more. I just wouldn't. Full of resolve, I practically leapt from the toilet and headed to the shower, determined to wash the lingering dream down the plughole.

Chapter One

Allie

The mix of emotions swirling in my chest was practically choking as I stared in shock at Savannah's smug and irritatingly beautiful face. The last two minutes left alone with her since Sean had left the room had sent me spiralling out of control. I didn't know what to believe any more, or who to trust. I was so overwhelmed that I could barely think straight, but her words just kept rolling over and over again in my brain until my sensibilities had been drowned out with the pain searing through my heart.

'You're very good for overlooking the fact that Sean and I still fuck ...'

Savannah and Sean *had* slept together? And *still* did? I hadn't believed it initially, but her cruel, malicious confessions were ringing inside my head over and over again like a tuneless record on repeat. Could it be true? Sean *was* an insatiable lover – that much I knew for sure. And Savannah was clearly a temptress with her sultry smiles, touchy-feely fingers, and fluttering eyelashes.

'It's understandable that our sexual urges sometimes get the better of us ...'

The idea of Sean and Savannah rolling together amongst sweat-soaked sheets was enough to turn my stomach almost to the point of retching. But depressingly, I knew how spontaneous Sean was when it came to sex, so her statement could potentially hold some truth. In our time together in England, the relationship between Sean and me had been incredibly sexual and completely impulsive – our liaisons on a bar stool, kitchen counter, and his office desk were a testament to that. In fact, we'd probably had sex out of his bed almost as much as we'd had in it.

The two of us had been drawn together like moths to the flame, and had never gone long without something sexual occurring. Was it possible that he'd given in during our eight weeks separation and slept with her to ease his needs?

'Sean was like a man possessed that night, I don't think he's ever taken me that roughly before, or so many times. It was incredible ...'

The fact that he had obviously told her about our argument, something so personal, only seemed to support her claims that they were indeed close. But were they intimately close? Had he turned to Savannah to release his pent-up anger after our argument with a few rounds of angry, rough sex?

The breath left my lungs as a deflated whisper. It was too much to deal with: my anger at Sean for lying to me, my annoyance at Savannah's irritating smugness, a feeling of complete inadequacy when I compared myself to her beauty, and lastly, a hot coil of jealousy that was working its way up my throat and threatening to erupt as a string of curse words, or worse, a flurry of fists and a flood of tears.

I wouldn't lower myself to hitting her, even though I desperately wanted to slap that look from her face, and I would not let them see me cry. I kicked the stool out of the way and it sailed sideways and crashed into the table, sending the salt and pepper shakers falling to the floor noisily as I staggered away. Tipping my chin back to boost my flagging confidence, I glared at her one final time as I decided that my best hope of escape would be the open patio doors.

'Sounds like a herd of elephants has arrived. What on earth are you two doing?' I heard Sean's joking voice from behind me as he re-entered the room, but I didn't bother to turn around and face him.

Bloody celebrities. Fucking with other people's lives and trampling on their hearts, thinking they can do whatever they like without considering the consequences of their actions or the hurt they might inflict. I'd had enough. I was done with all of them.

Without saying so much as another word to either Sean or Savannah, I side-stepped her false boobs and walked directly out of the back door to find myself on a large deck overlooking the enormous garden.

After the cool interior of the house, the warmth of the day hit me full force, almost knocking the air from my lungs, but I was a woman on a mission – an escape mission – and nothing would stop me getting away.

'Allie?' It's was Sean again, somewhere in the distance and sounding completely confused, but in response I quickened my pace, trotting down the steps towards the lawn.

'Savannah? What the fuck is going on?' His voice had now risen to a yell. My lip curled into a sick grimace – they'd probably be having sweaty, passionate, angry sex on the kitchen counter in less than two minutes.

I was running now, so desperate to get away that my legs were working on autopilot as my eyes tried to seek out the best route to help me escape. Flipping hell, this garden was immense. There was even a statue and a fountain in the middle of the lawn. How the other half lived, eh? How on earth had I ever considered that I could fit in with someone like Sean? We might have been sexually compatible, but apart from that we lived completely different lives, and clearly finding willing sexual partners wasn't an issue Sean struggled with.

Rolling my brimming eyes at my naïvety, I charged down a path that seemed to lead towards the side of the house before groaning as I saw how far I had to go. I hadn't realised how ridiculously big the bloody house was. It might be mostly on one level, but it was gargantuan. Grimacing, I shook my head angrily as I jogged along the side of the property and finally rounded the corner to the front driveway.

I didn't know who I was more annoyed with – Savannah for her crude words and bitchy, mocking face, Sean for outright lying to me, or myself for believing a man as handsome, charismatic, and famous as Sean Phillips could be monogamous, truthful, and seriously interested in me.

What an idiot I was!

A multitude of colourful swear words slid from my tongue as I realised to my horror, that as much as I wanted to leave, I wasn't going anywhere.

The gates.

The fucking, stupid, fancy, electronic gates were looming ahead, but they were shut tight. With a defeated groan, I slowed my pace slightly. I wasn't going anywhere unless someone let me out and there were only two people capable of doing that, neither of whom I wanted to speak to.

Bloody bugger it.

Chapter Two

Sean

It took me about three seconds to re-enter the kitchen and work out that Savannah had used my toilet trip to get up to no good. The main clue was the absence of Allie, who I couldn't see anywhere, but the other indications were pretty unmissable: a stool was toppled across the floor, the fruit bowl had been knocked over, and the salt and pepper shakers had cascaded to the ground, spilling their contents across the polished marble.

In short, it looked like someone had had a wrestling match in here, and I could only assume that the contestants had been Allie and Savannah. Seeing as Allie was no longer in the room, and Savannah was looking particularly smug, it seemed like my co-star had been the winner.

'What's happened?'

Taking a slow, leisurely sip of her drink, Savannah raised her eyebrows as if unaware that anything untoward had occurred, and then shrugged, her mouth pouting like a spoilt child. 'Whatever do you mean, *darrrrling*?'

A flash of gold outside the patio doors caught my eye and I felt my stomach drop as I realised it was Allie's blonde hair swirling down the deck steps and into the garden. 'Allie?' But she was already gone. 'Savannah? What the fuck is going on?' I demanded, stepping towards the patio doors and scanning for any sign of her. 'Where's Allie going?'

'Who cares? Now she's outside, you and I can catch up properly.' Savannah moved like a spectre; one minute she was a few feet away, and then the next she was right in front of me and running a blood red fingernail down the centre of my chest.

'How's your day been, sweetie?' My irritation levels had maxed out, and her touch made my skin crawl, so I knocked her hand away with a swipe of my wrist and a frown as I stepped back.

Savannah bit on her bottom lip, a look of mild concern crossing her face as if she suddenly realised that she might have dropped herself in it. The expression was practically gone before I'd even properly seen it, but it confirmed things – she had said something to upset Allie. 'Where. Has. She. Gone?' I repeated, each word ground out between clenched teeth.

'She's just getting some air … I think,' Savannah mumbled, her arrogant confidence wilting under the weight of my glare. The speed with which Allie had been moving was way beyond that of someone just getting some air, so I turned the full force of my anger on to Savannah.

'Stop bullshitting me. What the fuck did you say to her?'

Pouting, she put her glass to one side and ran her eyes down my body and back up again in what I could only assume was supposed to be a heated look. It had totally the opposite effect on me, and actually made me shudder with revulsion.

'I might have hinted that you and I slept together, which let's face it, *darrrrling*, we very nearly did. And we still could …'

What the fuck?

Anger erupted from me before she could even finish her sentence. 'You said what?' I was so furious that spittle shot from my mouth as my hands flew up to clutch at my hair in horror. Holy fucking shit. No wonder Allie had run away like that.

'Set her straight, Savannah. Go and undo your fuck-up right now or you'll need to find a new series to star in.' Savannah drew in a sharp gasp at my threat, but *LA Blue* was based around my character, not hers. I was the real star of the show, and we both knew I could get rid of her in the blink of an eye.

The last trace of fake bravado slipped from her face as she pouted like a petulant kid. 'Fine. Whatever.' As she blustered past me toward the front door, she turned to throw me a disgusted look. 'You're no fun at all any more, Sean.'

'Whatever,' I muttered dismissively as she left the room. But Savannah had it wrong. I had plenty of fun with Allie, more than I'd ever had with any woman before, and it all meant so much more to me because it was genuine, and came without all the bullshit drama that Savannah seemed to need in her gilded existence.

Chapter Three

Allie

The small obstacle of a closed gate didn't stop me from running towards it. I was desperately hoping that perhaps it might be operated by a sensor and magically open once I got closer, or that I'd see an internal button to activate it. That was what I was pinning my hopes on, anyway. Stones were kicking up around my feet on the gravel driveway as I ran, bouncing all over the place, but they didn't disguise the distinct crunch of footsteps behind me.

A brief glance over my shoulder showed a sour-faced Savannah hot on my heels. Damn it. I felt like I'd run miles to get around the house, but she must have taken the route through the hallway. Her puffy fake tits were bouncing with each step as her long legs gained on me, but I continued undeterred.

'For goodness' sake come back here, you're overreacting … just stop for a second and listen!' There was not a chance in hell I was stopping. I was getting out of here, away from all this celebrity bullshit as fast as my boring little British legs could carry me.

But I still needed someone to open the gates for me. Bugger. Seeing as she was close by, that someone may as well be Savannah, so reluctantly I stopped and slowly turned to face her. Maybe if I just told her she could have Sean all to herself she'd let me out straight away. The thought of giving him up pained me so much that I found myself rubbing furiously at my chest, my heart feeling like it was withering away by the second.

I didn't want to lose Sean, of course I didn't, especially not to this silly cow, but keeping him after he'd cheated on me was not a victory in my eyes.

She could have him.

As much as I needed her help to get off the property, I would not be the one to go to her, so I came to a standstill and waited as her spindly legs carried her the last few paces. Holding my ground, I tensed every muscle in my body in an attempt to appear unaffected and composed. Which of course was utter nonsense, because inside I felt like I was dying.

As she drew nearer I saw that Savannah was now in full pout mode, her lips pursed and looking even falser in the bright sunlight. How much of her was actually real? Probably not a great deal any more.

Pulling in a much-needed breath, I swallowed the tears that were threatening to make an appearance and instead concentrated on the anger I felt at my core. Anger was good. It was cathartic and made the possibility of crying reduce marginally. As she stopped before me, my nostrils flared as I tried to hold back the comments bubbling inside of me. I would not lower myself to their level. I was better than that. I was better than this entire fake town and the bullshit that went with it, and as soon as I got out of here I was set on booking a flight home.

'Sean's furious with me …' Savannah started, her eyes darting in the direction of the house, an action I followed. But there was no sign of him, he was obviously hiding away, embarrassed about his indiscretions and upset at being caught out. Would he even feel guilty? Or was it really just sex for him? Easy to get and easy to walk away from? The thought sickened me, because what I felt for him was so, so much more.

'Why? Because he's been lying to me all this time and you accidentally told me your dirty little secret?' I snapped irritably, wishing the gates would open so I could leave and fall apart in private. Because I definitely would be falling apart today, there was no doubt about it – it was just a case of when, not if.

'Look … I …' Huffing a huge breath, she began to toe some gravel with her sandal. 'There is no secret to tell. I was spouting shit in the kitchen. It's me who lied to you, not him.'

A heavy sigh escaped my chest. So she had given away their game and was now attempting to cover her tracks, was she? Folding my arms across my chest I met her gaze and lifted my chin to try and match her height.

'Savannah, you don't have to backtrack. I'm a big girl, if you two slept together, or still sleep together, it's fine. I just won't put up with him lying to me.' It wasn't fine, obviously, it was about as far from fine as my life could possibly get, but I wouldn't let her see that. Giving a simple shrug to indicate I was finished, I watched as Savannah reddened further, her Botoxed mouth puckering like a giant octopus sucker.

'Truthfully, we've never slept together,' she muttered as she worried one of her enormous lips with her teeth.

'I don't need any more lies today, you can have him. Just open the gates so I can leave.' Turning, I realised I had sounded far wearier than I'd wanted to, but I felt myself losing control, so close to a sobbing breakdown I could almost taste my tears.

Reaching out, she grabbed my wrist but I flicked her

bony hand away with a hiss, staring at her as if she'd just burnt me. 'Listen, I'm being serious. We've never had sex. I swear to God.'

Pausing, I ran my gaze over her face as I tried to gauge what was going on. She sounded genuine, and her eyes seemed clouded with apparent regret, but … then why concoct all this bullshit in the first place?

'I wanted us to sleep together, but Sean wouldn't,' she snapped finally, rolling her eyes trying to look like it was his fault. 'He's ridiculously picky about sex these days. I mean, a man that good-looking and famous could have sex with a different woman practically every day if he wanted to.' I flinched at the accuracy of her words. He probably could if he chose to, and from what he'd told me about his younger years, he probably had.

As her voice faded away I watched in mild amusement as a confused look crossed Savannah's eyes. Clearly she was struggling to understand why he wouldn't sleep with her. I supposed if you were as rich, famous, and beautiful as she was, getting a man of your choosing into bed probably wasn't much of a problem.

She wasn't the only one who was confused – my brain was spinning after all these differing stories. Her words did ring true with what Sean had told me about their brief relationship – that they had dated, but never 'fucked' – and he had seemed completely honest when he'd promised me that they'd never slept together … but if this was all made up, where was Sean? And why had Savannah done it in the first place?

Suddenly, Savannah blinked her eyes and turned back to me. 'Apparently I must be flawed, because believe me, I've tried my hardest to get that man into bed. No man ever turns me down,' she added bitterly.

As I stood there trying to process everything, I found that I actually began to believe her, which on one hand was a huge relief because it meant Sean hadn't cheated or lied to me, but on the other hand was concerning because it seemed like I was right about my initial speculation – she still wanted to get Sean back to sleep with him and recover her 'flawless' track record.

'Why did you lie to me? Why tell the truth now?' I asked, suspecting that Savannah wouldn't openly admit she was trying to entice my man into bed.

'I lied, because it was fun to watch your reactions.' My eyebrows shot up at her blunt honesty. 'Don't look so surprised, *darrrling*, I live in Hollywood. I adore a bit of drama, and if I'm the cause of it, so much the better.' I was totally speechless – she was even more of a bitch than I had first thought. 'But unfortunately, Sean doesn't like to play my games,' she sighed. 'He saw you leaving and knew I'd done something. I told him it was just a bit of fun, but he was so furious with me …'

Toying with people's emotions and tearing at their hearts was 'just a bit of fun'? What universe did this woman live in?

'I can't have him staying mad at me. We have to work together, after all.' Savannah glanced towards the house again, and this time I saw Sean standing on the front steps watching us intently, his hands shoved deep into the pockets of his shorts. It looked like he might be scowling, but his expression was difficult to read from this distance.

Turning back to me, she gave me a thorough look over with narrowed eyes, as if she couldn't work out what on earth Sean could ever see in me, before shaking out her hair and sighing. 'I've said what I needed to say.' I noticed Savannah offered no real apology as she flicked her hair over her shoulder and began to strut back towards the house. What a drama queen. I suspected that entire 'apology' had very little to do with making me feel better, and was no doubt just so she could get back in Sean's good books.

'Hey! You didn't let me out!' I called to her rapidly shrinking frame as she made her way back to the house, but Savannah simply ignored my pleas, the direction of her eyes seemingly fixed on Sean as he stared her down.

With nowhere to go, I loitered on the driveway, my emotions in a complete spin, and watched as Sean jogged down the steps towards us. I was still trapped, and now wanted to speak to Sean before leaving, but there was no way I was going back inside with Savannah, so I headed towards the shade of a large tree to my left to escape the heat.

Worried that my legs might give out from the stress of the last ten minutes, I lowered myself down onto the soft grass with a sigh. Bending my knees, I looped my arms around them so I was sitting in a protective ball as I waited for Sean to reach my side.

Watching curiously as Savannah strutted away, I saw Sean pause briefly to talk to her, his face stony and unrelenting, and posture bristling with tension, but as he turned away and caught sight of me, his entire presence seemed to soften, and his eyebrows rose with hope as he strode purposefully in my direction.

Watching him pace towards me it was all too apparent why Savannah was fixated on him. He was so perfectly handsome it almost hurt my eyes to look at him. And virile too, there was something about his swagger that radiated confidence and sexuality. It must surely be obvious to anyone that he would be good in bed. Great in bed.

Gosh, he really was the complete package: handsome, caring, sexy, confident, great between the sheets ... but could I deal with the pomp and prissiness of his career? It was a lot for a normal girl like me to suddenly be confronted with, and this latest episode with Savannah had just reinforced some of my earlier doubts.

Blowing out a breath, I pushed that decision away for now and concentrated on my man. Instead of sitting next to me as I expected, Sean knelt in front of me and gently began to unlink my fingers. Spreading my arms, he edged himself forwards, planting his knees between my thighs so he was wedged pretty much as close as he could get, and then clasped my hands in his.

Leaning forwards, he looked deeply into my eyes and I found myself instantly ensnared by him. Those dark blue pools were so intense that they got me every single time. How could I have doubts about our relationship? I could barely even think when he stared at me like that.

'Allie, I don't know if she cleared things up or not, but I swear to you, Savannah was lying, I never slept with her, not in the past and certainly not now.' His thumbs were massaging small circles on the backs of my hands, making it ridiculously hard to concentrate as heat surged up my arms, but Sean must have taken my pause as concern, because he gave my hands a gentle shake.

'Think about it logically. Why would I bring you here to meet her if I was sleeping with her?' My hands were treated to another shake, firmer this time, and the movement finally broke me from my Sean-induced stupor. As I blinked back to the present, I found Sean tilting his head down so that our faces were just a breath apart. 'Please say you believe me.'

The points he had made were incredibly valid, the

concern in his tone was clear, and as I searched his eyes I could see nothing but sincerity and desperation. He didn't look like a man covering his tracks. He looked like a man in love.

One in love with me.

Which was a pretty fine sight from where I was sitting.

Swallowing hard at the magnitude of my feelings for him, I finally nodded. 'I believe you.'

The sigh of relief that left Sean's body was immense, his dropping shoulders making his entire upper body sag forward until his forehead was resting on my shoulder. I could hear him drawing in several lungfuls of air, as if he had been holding his breath and was only just managing to recover it now, and then finally he looked up at me and grinned so broadly that my head went dizzy for a few moments.

I loved that smile. The corners of his eyes creased, a dimple appeared in his cheek and the blue of his irises seemed to glow with happiness. In the time we'd been together, it seemed that he reserved that particular grin just for me. And it was shining at me on full power right now, making me feel pretty flipping amazing.

Apparently, Sean was rather contented with my reassurance and leant forwards, his lips hovering just millimetres from mine, his breath tickling my lips as he locked our eyes again. 'I thought bringing you here would back up my story …' He shook his head in resignation. 'I knew Savannah could be devious, but I never in a million years though she would act like that. I'm so sorry.'

Then his lips made contact with mine and rational thought was forgotten as his firm, warm mouth began to move slowly against mine.

Chapter Four

Jack

Finally I allowed myself to glance over my shoulder and scan around the studio complex, but as expected, Caitlin was gone. Giving a reluctant nod of acceptance, I quickened my pace to catch up with the group I was with before I got an earful from my director for slacking behind.

This morning had been nightmarishly busy and my head was already aching, but the pleasant shock of seeing Caitlin walk by had perked me up no end. Presumably her sudden appearance meant that Sean had been correct, and she was applying for a job here at the studio.

My heart rate was still slightly accelerated just from the brief glimpse. Shaking my head, I drew in a deep breath and took a moment to simply enjoy the feelings she sparked in me. That girl really did affect me. Regardless of the fact that I barely knew her, my mind, body, and soul seemed to come alive when she was near. I'd never experienced anything like it before, and it was turning out to be seriously addictive.

I'd had pretty decent chemistry with women in the past, but this was different somehow, more visceral. I could barely understand it myself, but I felt an electric thrill whenever she was near.

With her sleek chestnut hair, smattering of freckles, and wide hazel eyes she was incredibly pretty, and her slender body was undeniably appealing, but I was certain that this was more than just lust. She attracted me, aroused me, *and* intrigued me like no one had for a very long time, and that knowledge made me desperate to explore our apparent bond.

I was pretty sure from her reactions in the bar that she felt something for me too, and I'd definitely sensed her curiosity when I'd nearly kissed her, but it had become shadowed by what looked like doubt and fear in her eyes. I'd seen that fear again at the art gallery, and it bugged the hell out of me. What, or who, had caused that to be reflected in her beautiful eyes?

I wanted to get to know her and get to the bottom of her hesitations, but after her request to stay away, I'd figured that playing it cool might be the best way to go, which was why I'd just given her a casual acknowledgement and no more. Not striding across and speaking to her had just about killed me, but I was a patient man, and if Caitlin was to be working here then I was happy to go in for the long game.

My sights were set, and Caitlin Byrne was now firmly on my radar. I just needed to plan my next steps very carefully.

Chapter Five

Cait

I had a job in television. I still couldn't quite believe it. Spinning on the spot, I shielded my eyes from the bright sunshine and gazed up at Dynamic Studio's gateway. A small smile tugged at my lips as pride and excitement welled within me. That job interview couldn't have gone any better. My left eye twitched as I corrected that last thought – it would have been better if my joy hadn't been slightly side-tracked by yet another glimpse of Jack flipping Felton – but pushing that worry aside, I nodded. I'd done well, the job sounded amazing. It was perfect for me.

I couldn't wait to tell Allie, but I knew she had plans to spend the morning with Sean and I wasn't sure if that was at the hotel or out somewhere. Just as I was about to turn on my heel to head back to the hotel, I heard a deep, male voice calling my name somewhere in the distance, and my stomach lurched at the thought that Jack might be following me.

Wincing against the sun, I turned and saw a man in a blue jumpsuit looking at me curiously as he made his way towards me. 'Are you Caitlin Byrne?'

So, not Jack. A relieved breath left my lungs. It was also tinged with a just a small amount of disappointment, but I decided not to let myself dwell on why exactly that might be.

Clearing my throat, I nodded, my body tensing up slightly as I wondered who on earth this guy was. He was tall, clearly strong, and not someone I would usually want to be alone with given the choice, but we were outside in the open, so I guessed it was safe enough.

'Great! I work on site and I just bumped into Jason. He said you're interested in one of the condos opposite.' Glancing down at his blue uniform, I realised it had the Dynamic logo on it, and relaxed slightly more. 'He said to look for a girl with long, brown hair and a pink bag, and here you are!'

Smiling at his jolly demeanour, I glanced down at my bright pink Hello Kitty bag and felt myself blush. It wasn't exactly the most professional bag to take to a job interview, but seeing as I basically lived out of a rucksack, my options were a touch limited.

'I am interested in the apartments, yes.' I still couldn't believe I might actually manage to wangle a cheap, safe apartment as part of this job deal. It would be so refreshing to actually unpack my rucksack and hang up my clothes for a change.

'Apartments? Ha! We call 'em condos but I love your British accent!' He grinned and I found myself blushing, which was stupid because it was hardly my fault that we had different words. 'Anyway, I just wanted to let you know that Tina's over there doing some paperwork and general cleaning if you want to have a look before you head off.' Nodding keenly I followed the direction of his gaze and saw a gated complex on the other side of the road.

'Those over there?' I asked in surprise, because the buildings looked pretty fancy. In fact, they looked like houses and I could have sworn Jason had said they were just flats – or 'condos', according to this guy.

'Yep. Convenient for work, huh?'

Really convenient for work. Door to door I'd probably have about a thirty second commute.

'You head on over and I'll give Tina a call to let her know you're coming.'

Expressing my thanks, I made to cross the road when my phone rang in my handbag. I pulled it out, saw my parents' number, and smiled – obviously my mum had remembered my interview and had stayed up late especially to ring me.

'Hi, Mum!' I greeted, excitement bursting in my voice.

'Hello, love.'

'I got a job, Mum, and it's even better than the temporary one I told you about! They offered me some prop work, similar to the stuff I did in Sydney, so I'm really excited.'

There was a pause down the line, and then I heard Mum clear her throat. 'That's wonderful, darling, congratulations.' Hurrying across the road I stepped onto the pavement and then stopped and narrowed my eyes. I might be away from home, but I spoke to my mum every week, and there was definitely something weird in her tone today. And the nervous throat clearing was odd too, she never usually did that.

'What's the matter. Mum? Are you and Dad OK?'

'We're fine darling, your father says to say hello. He's sitting here having a cup of hot chocolate.' I smiled at that, but then my concern returned as Mum paused again, and then did another strange, throat-clearing cough. 'I was calling because, well, we … we got another postcard this week.'

Every molecule of air seemed to leave my lungs, and my skin, which was warm from the sun, suddenly felt chilled to the core as if I was sitting in an ice bath.

A postcard.

There was no need to ask what she meant or who the postcard was from, because I knew all too well.

My fucked-up ex. Greg.

The vivid dream I'd had last night came rushing back to my mind, swamping my senses until I staggered and had to grab at the nearest fence post to steady myself. God, it was almost like the dream had been a forewarning.

He wouldn't have actually signed his name, of course. He never did, but over the years since I'd left him he'd occasionally send a letter or card to my parents' house. I thought it was his sick way of keeping me from moving on, and unfortunately it worked a treat because here I was four years on and still an emotional wreck at just the thought of him.

Sometimes I wish I hadn't been so stubborn and stopped my therapy when I left to go travelling. Perhaps if I'd persevered with it I wouldn't be quite as screwed up now, but the idea of explaining my past over and over again to a string of different councillors around the world had been so unnerving that I'd chickened out.

Sighing heavily I focused back on my mum's news. The postcards themselves didn't bother me too much, I could even deal with the words he chose to write – always discreet, but with an underlying threat to them – but it was the postmarks that bothered me. The cards came from all around the world, and it made me wonder if he was trying to track me down so he could finish what he started.

A shudder ran through my body and I wrapped my free arm around myself despite the heat of the day.

Plucking up the courage to voice the question I dreaded asking, I drew in a deep breath and gripped the phone in a vice-like hold. 'Where was the card posted from?'

'Australia. It's quite smudged, but we think it says Sydney.'

A stuttered breath slipped from my lungs. Was that just coincidence, or had he worked out that I'd been in Sydney? There was no way to know, which was distinctly unnerving, but at least I was in the US now so he was plenty far enough away, and I didn't feel any immediate threat. As Mum continued to talk, I looked at the houses behind me. I hadn't put down roots anywhere since working in Australia. I'd loved the job at the Opera House so much that I'd stayed for a year. But a postcard from Greg had arrived then too, dropping onto my parents' door mat with the postmark Melbourne. It might have been a completely different city, but that had been way too close for comfort. I'd promptly quit my job, packed my stuff, and moved on, all within twenty-four hours.

'What does it say?'

'It's quite short. It just says, "Dearest Cait, can't wait to catch up with you soon."' Swallowing down the hot bile that rose in my throat, I drew in a deep breath and then released it slowly through my nose. The words didn't mean anything, they didn't. *They couldn't*. He didn't know where I was. They were just his sick way of messing with me.

Turning back to look at the impressive gates of Dynamic, I shook my head defiantly. I refused to let him screw this job up for me. He was thousands of miles away, and I could only assume from the words 'Can't wait to catch up with you soon' that he thought I was still in Oz too. Good. Let his fucked-up mind think that if it kept him away from me.

'Are you OK, darling?' My mum sounded more stressed out by all of this than me, and I felt a further twist of hatred toward Greg. How bloody dare he keep upsetting my parents like this? Fucking coward.

'I'm fine, Mum. Did you take it to the police?'

'I did. Detective Andrews said it's the same as all the others, no fingerprints, no DNA evidence, and not a match for the handwriting sample they have for him.'

That basically meant there was still nothing the police could do to help me. They hadn't been able to serve him with a restraining order because I'd never gone to the police about his abusive behaviour prior to the attack. If there had been some DNA evidence to link him to my assault and then the subsequent letters they would have used that to file charges or apply for a restraining order, but of course there had been neither. Greg had been exceptionally careful, cleaned up after himself and then literally disappeared off the face of the earth.

They couldn't charge him for stalking either, because now they couldn't find him to question him, or link him to the letters. Evil bastard. It was so bloody frustrating for my life to be left hanging in the balance while he gallivanted around the world playing his sick games.

'He's added it to the case file, and as always, he said that if you feel directly threatened or think Greg's watching you then you need to get in touch with him immediately. I get so worried about you, Cait, don't you want to come home for a while?' I didn't say it, but I would be more concerned about my safety if I went home. I'd be like a sitting duck, just waiting for Greg to wander up my parents' front path one day and scare the shit out of me.

'I'm OK. Mum, honestly. Try not to worry. LA is great, and Allie's here now too. In fact, this new job comes with a really safe little house so I'm going to ask her if she wants to live with me for a bit. She's got a boyfriend too, he's really nice and I'm sure he'll be around plenty to keep an eye on all of us.' OK, so this was a bit of an exaggeration, Sean couldn't exactly freely visit at the moment, but I knew it would make my mum feel better to think there was a man around.

'Really?' My mum's voice perked up immediately. 'That sounds good. I'd feel far better knowing you weren't on your own. I haven't seen Allie for ages, tell her I said hi.'

'I will.' Walking to the complex gates, I gave the apartment blocks a more thorough inspection between the bars of the elaborately-wrought iron fence. Every building was neat, clean, and modern and the gardens were well maintained, and just as Jason had said, it was nice and secure. Perfect.

It would be great if the insides were as nice as the exterior, but to be honest, safety was my main concern, especially after today's nasty reminder of Greg, so this place looked to be a goer.

'I've got to go, Mum, but I promise to call soon.' I felt mean ending the call when my mum was obviously a bit upset, but I could see a woman brandishing a clipboard and making a beeline for me, which was presumably Tina coming to let me in for a tour.

'OK, love, take care. Bye.' She sounded reluctant to end the call, bless her, and I made a mental note to ensure that I called or texted a little more than usual in the coming weeks. As I waited for Tina to cross the car park between us I checked out the security again. High fences, security cameras above my head, and number coded gates. Nodding happily, I felt my shoulders slacken with contentment. This could well be the perfect job and the perfect place to make a fresh, Greg-free start to my life.

Chapter Six

Allie

Sean's kiss under the tree had started out soft, apologetic, and full of hope, but as my lips parted and his tongue began to dance gently over mine, the intensity quickly heightened. Working of their own accord, my hands rose to dig in his hair, my desperate fingers causing him to growl against my lips.

'I wish we weren't outside, otherwise I'd be giving you a proper apology right now,' Sean murmured, his hand briefly slipping between my legs and rubbing firmly at the seam of my jeans to show exactly how he would apologise.

Groaning at the hard contact, my pelvis instinctively thrust against his hand in an attempt to grind myself against him in that oh-so perfect spot. Pulling back on a wry chuckle, Sean cupped my face with both palms and smiled at me softly. 'I love you, Allie.'

'I love you too,' I replied without hesitation, although my words sounded distinctly garbled – one small kiss and a brief rub between my legs and I felt like putty in his hands. I really should find it alarming just how easily he could control my body, but I didn't. I loved it.

'I'm so sorry this all happened. Looks like I screwed up again,' he murmured as he moved himself to my side. I felt the loss of his warmth immediately, but Sean flopped back onto the grass and tugged me with him. Arranging my lax body so I was laid in his arms, I threw one leg across his hips as we both stared at the lush, green canopy of leaves above us. Summoning up the energy to speak, I licked my lips and placed a kiss on his chest. 'It's OK. Not many people can say they've seen Savannah Hilton's acting skills first hand, can they?' I joked limply. Sean twisted his head and returned my smile, but it was tight-lipped.

'She's unbelievable. I knew she could be hard-faced but I never thought she'd do something like this. I called her this morning asking if I could bring you over to put your mind at rest and she was as helpful as anything on the phone.'

Hmmm. I'm sure she was, I thought sceptically. It seemed to me that while Sean was an incredibly intelligent man, he was slightly clueless where it came to reading the body language and actions of Savannah. 'If you ask me, she wants you back,' I mumbled quietly, feeling a flush of jealously rush up inside of me and colour my neck.

'Really?' Sean rolled onto his side to look down at me doubtfully, and my heart fluttered at his sudden closeness. 'As far as I'm concerned, that ship has well and truly sailed. I'm pretty sure she just likes to cause a fuss.' As he gazed at me, his blue eyes began darkening with desire, causing the air around us to suddenly feel like it had been sucked away. My lungs were practically paralysed with love and lust for this man, and I struggled to breathe as I watched Sean's gaze move across my face and drift to my lips.

'Assuming this little spectacle hasn't completely put you off me, I wonder if we might resume where we were before our run-in with my less than charming co-star?' His voice was husky and I could have sworn he was moving closer by the second, intent on some outdoor kinkiness. Perhaps he intended to go back to his earlier suggestion of apology sex, which although risky, was a rather tempting prospect. Considering all that had just occurred, I had a lot of pent-up tension that I needed to get rid of, and sex with Sean seemed the perfect outlet.

Regardless of my extensive concerns about Savannah, I threw caution to the wind and nodded mutely, completely unable to speak. Sean smiled at me before brushing his lips ever so gently across mine, causing a small moan to escape from my throat that made him chuckle as he raised his head. 'I am very much looking forward to when this debacle is over and we can be a proper couple.'

'I am too,' I agreed, feeling almost shy all of a sudden, before a giddy laugh escaped from the emotions spinning inside me. 'I can't believe my life is this crazy.'

Leaning in to place another kiss on my lips, he raised a hand and slid it into the hair by my ear, causing my scalp to tingle from the lovely warmth as he pulled me in close for a long, leisurely kiss.

He might have started it, but I was the one to take the action up a notch by teasing the seam of his lips until he gave in with a groan and opened his mouth for me. Over the next few minutes our movements became almost feverish as Sean rolled me over onto my back and covered my body with his as our hands moved over, and under, each other's clothing.

As one of my hands succeeded in pushing his shirt up and running across his chest, so too did Sean's, and he flicked the cup of my bra down with ease and immediately rolled the needy nipple between his thumb and forefinger. I couldn't help but break our kiss to draw in a ragged groan from the delicious contact, my hips going into autopilot and thrusting against him in a futile attempt to get some friction where I needed it the most.

Pulling himself away with a matching groan of frustration, he grinned. 'Mmm. I really wish we were somewhere a little more private so I could apologise properly,' he murmured, giving my nipple one final, hard tweak. I smiled, knowing that however much I reassured him, Sean relied a lot on our physical bond as confirmation that everything was OK between us.

'Unfortunately, we have security cameras out here, and as much as I don't care who sees my arse bouncing in the sunlight, there's not a chance in hell that I'm letting anyone see you naked.' Spluttering at his words, I giggled, my laughter only increasing as I watched him adjust the large bulge in his shorts with an amused glance at it. 'Do you see what you do to me, woman?'

Lowering my right hand, I gave his erection a firm squeeze and licked my lips. 'I do.' We'd had incredible sex in the pool earlier, but I was totally ready to go again, and clearly from the throbbing rod of heated flesh in my hand, so was Sean.

Narrowing his eyes at me, Sean thrust his groin into my palm with a gravely moan, and then, before I'd even realised that we were moving, he had risen to his knees, scooped me into his arms, and was standing.

'Need. You. *Now*,' he muttered heatedly. 'And I happen to know for sure that there aren't any security cameras in the pool house,' he informed me with a wicked grin, before striding from the trees with me giggling in his arms.

Ding, ding, round two!

So, pool sex this morning followed by pool house sex this afternoon ... there was a definite theme for the day emerging. I couldn't say the idea of a little outdoor nookie didn't get me excited though. In fact, I absolutely loved how adventurous I became when I was with Sean. He was a bad influence in the best of ways.

Carrying me as if I weighed nothing, Sean retraced the steps I had taken around the side of the house, then cut hastily across the lawn until I saw the glittering waters of a large swimming pool. It was beautiful: a curved pool with jacuzzi section at one end and water so temptingly blue that I was immediately flooded with memories of our earlier pool tryst. That had certainly been some seriously good skin-slapping, water-splashing fun.

When Sean had mentioned a pool house I'd been expecting some sort of summer house or wooden cabin, but the 'pool house' that we were headed to was so fancy that it looked more like another wing of the villa.

I wasn't given long to admire the view, because Sean burst through the doors, elbowed a switch to close the electronic blinds, and then thrust me up against a wall so hard that the wind was knocked from my lungs.

Holy moly, that was unexpected!

Using my shock to his advantage, Sean wasted no time in grabbing my wrists and pinning them above my head as he growled his desire and lowered his head to nuzzle roughly behind my ear.

Talk about a speedy start. There was barely an opportunity to regain my breath, because the next second his mouth had found mine in a kiss so desperate and hungry that it was all I could do to keep up with him.

I knew exactly what Sean was doing with this dominant display; he was trying to claim me back, reassure himself that we were OK after the Savannah fiasco. What he seemed to have overlooked though, was that he was also mine just as much as I was his, and in this moment, with memories of Savannah's spiteful lies still fresh in my head I wanted to claim him too.

As much as I usually loved his control in the bedroom, today I wanted to reciprocate and feel him beneath my skin – needed to – so I attempted to pull my wrists free, to no avail; Sean's possessive hold on me was just too tight.

Twisting my head to release my mouth from his heated kisses, I managed to make eye contact with him, my gaze clashing with his desire-filled blues. 'Let me touch you, Sean, I need to feel you.' Seeming to sense the reasoning behind my plea, he stared at me for a second before nodding once, and released my hands so we could unite in our desperation to reconnect. My fingers scrabbled in his clothing, craving the feel of skin on skin, and after some fumbling I managed to peel his T-shirt up until it bunched under his arms.

Mumbling a small complaint of protest at having to let me go, Sean raised his hands so I could remove his T-shirt, and then immediately his warm palms descended upon me again, gripping at my waist possessively as he thrust his groin against my stomach.

Suddenly Sean paused, his previously frantic movements stilling as he leant back and gazed at me. His face was flushed, his lips slightly swollen and moist from our desperate kisses, and breath was leaving his mouth in short, hard pants.

'I'm yours, Allie. Just yours, baby. You know that, right?' His tone was low and urgent, and I knew he needed the reassurance just as much as I needed to give it.

'Yes. I know. I love you, Sean.'

'Make me yours. Take the lead,' he urged me, then twisting us around, he sank down onto a sofa so he was lying flat on his back and then pulled me with him until I was straddling his lap. We'd done this position before, of course, but the fact that Sean was offering me the control when he usually craved it for himself showed just how big a deal this was for him. He needed me to show him that I still wanted him.

It was a challenge I wouldn't ever turn down, and after speedily dispensing my clothes, I found myself attacking him with a passion I barely knew I had within me – my teeth found his shoulder, biting and teasing, as my hips undulated urgently on his groin and my fingernails clawed at the button of his shorts.

'Christ, Allie. That's it, baby. Use me.'

Use him? Okey dokey, it would be my pleasure. And his, hopefully. Finally I succeeded in ripping the denim apart and Sean lifted his hips to help me drag his shorts and boxers down his legs.

Chucking the clothing aside, I stopped dead and stared at him. Now, that was a mighty fine sight. Sean Phillips, sprawled naked, his muscled body taut with anticipation, eyes heavy-lidded with desire, and his cock as solid as a rock and bobbing between us frantically.

The sight of him so aroused did nothing to cool my ardour, and as a bead of pre-come escaped from the slit I couldn't help but descend upon his shaft, taking as much of him into my mouth as I could until he bumped against the back of my throat.

'Holy fuck!' His breath escaped him in a hissed curse as I set about sucking on him as if my life depended upon it. He was hard, but got even harder when one of his hands slid into my hair and grasped at the long strands. 'So deep …' he groaned, and I smiled around my mouthful of him, pleased to be causing such an effect. My tongue teased the thick veins on the underside and swirled around the broad top until he gripped my head and attempted to pull me away.

'I want to come inside you, my gorgeous girl. Make it happen, baby.' He might have handed over control to me, but I heard a hint of that low, commanding tone that always sent desire and lust shooting through me.

Crawling up his body, I laid my palms flat on his heaving chest and grinned when I saw Sean's heated face watching my every move with fascination. Letting me lead so fully was fairly rare for us, but from the keen look on Sean's face, he was obviously rather enjoying the change.

Lifting my body, I positioned myself above him, Sean gripping his cock at the base to help line himself up with my opening. The thick head began to enter me, pushing apart my sensitive flesh until I had to pause, my leg muscles quivering with the attempt at holding myself up. As much as I was tempted to just drop down onto him, I was still a bit tender from this morning, so edged him into me a little at a time, absorbing the delicious stretch with a low, drawn-out groan.

'You drive me crazy in the best of ways, baby,' he murmured, his words almost reflecting the exact sentiment I had thought about him earlier. As I neared the end of him, the tightness became exquisite. I felt so full, so owned, and yet somehow so in control. Sean's hands were now flexing repeatedly on my hips, which I suspected was his way of holding himself back from dragging me down onto him. He needn't have bothered, because when I felt another rush of moisture seep between my legs I relaxed my muscles and dropped the final inch so he was embedded in me from root to tip.

'This just keeps getting better,' Sean ground out, his eyes briefly closing before opening again and capturing me with his intense gaze. 'You just keep getting better, Allie.'

Unable to voice a reply I nodded my agreement and began to grind my hips in a circle so I could feel him everywhere inside of me.

And I really do mean everywhere. It was incredible, but suddenly my slow movements weren't enough, and I lifted myself up and dropped rapidly back down, eliciting cries of pleasure from us both.

Sean had wanted me to set the pace, and I would. Repeating the same movement, I slammed my hips down onto him, feeling like a prize rodeo rider as I gyrated and slid up and down his rigid cock until we were both groaning and clutching at each other with needy fingers.

My nails had sunk into him on several occasions already, and as I saw the reddened claw marks across his torso I smiled possessively – my man was going to bear my mark tomorrow, there was no doubt about it.

That thought, combined with the feel of me moving him inside me suddenly triggered me to climax, the pleasure rushing at me so intensely that I think I briefly lost the use of my muscles. My body went lax, a long, drawn-out cry left my lungs, and then I was falling forwards onto him, my trembling body failing and unable to carry on, even though I knew he hadn't found his own release yet.

Strong hands gripped my hips, and suddenly I was turning, finding myself flat on my back and trapped below Sean as he plunged back inside of me again with a bark. 'My turn.' His hips began to draw back, and from the dark look on his face I just knew this was about to be hard.

It was.

Oh my god, it was.

His entire body jacked forward on a plunge that was so hard and so deep that I could barely deal with the intensity of it. Stars spun before my eyes and a yelp flew from my mouth as pleasure lanced through my body, causing me to arch up off the sofa to fully unite us. Ignoring my exhaustion, I clung to his pumping hips and clawed, fingers digging into the firm cheeks of his beautiful arse.

I was pinned below his weight, surrounded by the smell of his clean sweat and the feel of his hot, hard muscles, and I couldn't think of anywhere else I'd rather be. Well, except perhaps pinned below his weight, surrounded by the smell of his clean sweat and the feel of his hot, hard muscles somewhere a million miles away from Savannah Hilton.

As his hips kept up the relentless pace, I writhed below, trying to line up his cock so it would hit just the right spot. I was desperate to orgasm again even though I'd just had a mind-blowing climax minutes earlier that had almost rendered me paralysed. Talk about greedy.

His hips slowed marginally, and I felt him expand even further inside of me, his strokes now hitting perfectly on the g-spot deep inside. *Jackpot.* The contact caused my internal muscles to clench and a growl escaped Sean's throat as he began to climax, his cock throbbing within me, jerking and filling me until my own second orgasm washed over me, gentler than the last one but just as satisfying.

Sean's head fell forwards as his hips continued to work us down from our peak, his sweat-slicked face a twisted mask of passion as it hovered above mine, not once breaking our eye contact.

Finally, he stilled, rolling us over so I was flopped on top of his body. He really did make the best mattress ever. His hot breaths whispered across my temple as he snuggled me into his chest with his cock still buried within me.

'I love you so fucking much, Allie.'

I would never get sick of hearing those words. Feeling drowsy and loved up, I snuggled closer, contentment washing over me and pulling me towards sleep.

Sean

A smile stretched on my lips as I realised that Allie had fallen asleep. Her breathing deepened, and the weight of her body relaxed further until it was almost difficult to work out where I ended and she began. Although seeing as my cock was still buried inside of her, we were technically joined at the hip, a feeling I would never tire of.

It was a stupidly masculine outlook, but the fact that I had worn her out with my sexual antics and was still inside of her made me feel ridiculously proud of myself. So much so that a self-satisfied smirk formed on my face as I cradled her against me.

Whilst Allie was snoozing, I took a moment to indulge my favourite habit – one of several favourites where this woman was concerned – and began trailing a hand over her long hair. God, I loved her hair. Everything about it turned me on: the silky feel of it, the way it trailed through my fingers, the floral scent, the way it wrapped around my wrist when I fucked her from behind … Closing my eyes, I felt my cock begin to thicken slightly inside her tight warmth again. This woman affected me like no other. I only got a semi this time, so it seemed that I had finally managed to wear out my insatiable sex drive. For a while, anyway.

Usually I could snooze after sex too, but today my mind was buzzing. I was going to have serious words with Savannah later, that was for sure. The conniving bitch needed to realise the extent of my seriousness about Allie; no one and nothing would get in the way of my feelings for her, especially not some fake, attention-seeking harlot like her.

A soft, contented whimper left Allie's throat as if she were dreaming, but when she wiggled her hips and gave a hum of pleasure I realised she was waking up. I couldn't resist giving one small upward thrust to remind her that I was still buried deep, and my move immediately caused her to nuzzle into my neck happily and lift her head to flash me a broad grin.

'Hey, you,' I murmured, loving the sleepy, flushed expression on her face.

'Hi. I think you wore me out.' My pride lapped up her words and I returned her smile and dropped a quick kiss on her lips. Slowly easing her onto her back, I set about tracing a finger down her jaw, along the flittering pulse in her neck, and across the top of her breasts until she shuddered. She was so fucking perfect.

Reluctantly, I shifted my hips to pull my length from within her and saw Allie wince slightly as I slid free. Her small flicker of pain immediately caused a frown to tug at my eyebrows. 'Are you OK? Was I too rough?' I loved being rough and hard like that last session had been, but I needed to remember that Allie was far more delicate than me. I'd practically thrown her against a wall, for fuck's sake, what if I had lost control and hurt her?

My girl shook her head and smiled sleepily. 'I'm fine, Sean, I loved every second of it,' she replied huskily, her low, throaty tone setting my mind partially at ease.

As I stared at her I made an on the spot decision. 'I want you to choose a stop word, Allie, just in case I ever get too carried away.' This wasn't something I'd ever done before, but then I'd never been with anyone that made me lose my mind quite like Allie did. She turned me on so much that I literally lost all sense sometimes. It was like some primal need to claim her completely overtook all my actions apart from the urge to get my dick inside her as fast as humanly possible.

'A stop word? Like a safe word?' The hesitation in her tone was clear, but now that I had suggested it, it seemed like the best idea ever, and I found myself nodding keenly.

'I've ... well, I've read about those.' Her voice softened with nerves and I watched as her beautiful eyes narrowed marginally. 'But only ever in connection to bondage or sex that might involve pain. Why would you want that, Sean?'

'I don't want to do anything involving pain, Allie, that's not what this is about. It's actually the complete opposite.' Pausing, I ran a hand through my hair, wondering how I could explain myself without sounding like a complete caveman. 'I just ... well, you know that I sometimes like rough sex ... and I just want to make sure that I never push you too far in the heat of the moment.'

'In which case, a stop word isn't necessary, Sean,' Allie replied immediately. 'I like it rough sometimes too.' I already knew my girl had similar tastes to me, but the way her cheeks flushed with embarrassment still made my cock jerk with excitement. 'Besides, I trust you completely,' she reassured me, giving my arm a rub.

Leaning up on my elbows, I felt my heart clutch a little tighter in my chest. She was just so fucking perfect. 'I know, and truthfully I don't think you'll ever need to use it, but sometimes I ... I lose my head around you, Allie. This would make me feel better, that's all.'

Allie huffed out a cute little sigh and pouted her lips, which just made them look even more kissable than usual. 'It's unnecessary, but it's only a word, I suppose, so if it makes you feel better then fine.' My girl paused, chewing on her lower lip as she pondered a suitable word before finally smiling. 'OK. My word is blizzard.'

Looking at her curiously, I tilted my head, wondering where her peculiar choice had come from. 'We met in a snow storm. I was going to choose snow, but it sounds a bit too similar to no, so blizzard is probably better.'

Now my grin matched hers. What an ideal choice of word. 'Perfect. Blizzard it is. Remember that, my gorgeous girl, and don't be afraid to use it if I ever push you too far.' I had quite a few kinkier things I planned to try with Allie once we were a proper couple, and I couldn't help a satisfied smile curve my lips as I considered them. Oh yes, we were going to have a lot of fun together.

Allie

So I now had a safe word. How bizarre. As Sean sealed the deal with a kiss I briefly wondered if that meant he might be keen on exploring other more imaginative things in the bedroom, but was stopped from considering this further as he climbed lithely from the sofa, giving me a splendid view of his naked perfection.

Groaning, I bit my lip as I watched him walk away. His arse was a frigging work of art. Forget Picasso, da Vinci, or Monet, the entire contents of the Louvre couldn't compare to those two beautifully sculpted butt cheeks.

He disappeared through a door to my left and moments later, returned with a damp wash cloth in his hand, a cheeky smile on his lips, and a twinkle in his eye.

Ah, yes. Sean and his never-ending need to care for me after sex. The first time he'd done this I'd panicked that he'd thought of me as unclean, but that hadn't been the case, of course; he'd felt guilty for being a bit distant with me after we'd had sex, and the caring thing was his way of apologising. As the fond memory flitted through my head a giggle escaped my lips, causing Sean to look at me with a soft smile.

'I love your laugh,' he commented mildly. 'Now open those legs, baby.' Rolling my eyes at his over the top gestures, I didn't bother to try and deny him and simply let my legs flop open. He now had a full-on view of my down below area, and I couldn't care less. Cleaning me attentively with the cloth, I listened to my man humming happily to himself and found myself grinning up at the ceiling.

'Would you like to stay for dinner? I was going to grill some tuna and have it with salsa and salad.' That sounded delicious, but my grin faded and eyebrows shot up at his question. Had he not learnt his lesson from what had happened earlier with Savannah? There was no way on this earth I was going back inside that house with her still there. A shudder ran through me, but this time it had nothing to do with pleasure, and everything to do with the horrific thought of sour-faced Savannah.

I'd probably choke on my food if I had to share a meal with Little Miss Petulant and Pouty, or end up throwing it at her, and neither of those things were particularly high on my to-do list tonight.

Rolling myself to a sitting position, I reached for my clothes on the floor and began to dress. 'I don't think so …' I murmured, my mind filling with images of me lobbing a fistful of salsa into her sickeningly perfect face and watching it drip slowly off her false lips. My own twitched with a small, indulgent smirk. God, that would be so satisfying.

'Three's a crowd, and all that …' My words dropped off as Sean frowned, pulled his shorts back on, and sat beside me, still distractingly bare-chested.

'It's not like you're imagining at all, Allie. I don't ever eat with Savannah. To be honest, we barely see each other. If it weren't for the film company insisting we shared this house I wouldn't choose to spend any time with her. You and I could eat on the deck,' he added in a final attempt to persuade me.

His conviction made my heart feel a little lighter, but I still sighed and shook my head. 'I would love to spend more time with you, Sean, but Cait had her job interview today and I promised to meet up with her to see how she got on. Plus, I got a text from her earlier saying she might move back to the youth hostel for a bit, and I wanted to try and talk her out of it.' If possible, my ego took another boost as I saw the open disappointment flash across Sean's handsome face at my decline of his dinner invitation. He wanted to spend time with me just as much as I did with him, and that realisation made my shoulders feel ten tonnes lighter. It was infinitely reassuring.

'Never mind. I have to be up really early tomorrow, anyway,' he conceded, gently brushing some hair away from my face. He looked and sounded a little frustrated by our continued inability to be together properly, which certainly made two of us.

'So Cait might be moving back to the hostel?' He pulled his T-shirt back on and slid his arm around my shoulders, pulling me firmly against him.

Sighing happily at our entwined position – probably one of my favourite places to be – I gave a little shrug. 'Yeah. I think she feels she should give me and you some privacy so you can come around whenever you get some free time.'

Nodding thoughtfully, Sean suddenly twisted his head down so he could make eye contact and grinned that special smile again. 'So next time I'm over I really can walk around the suite stark naked?' he asked cheekily, to which I merely rolled my eyes and chuckled.

'I seem to recall you did that today, anyway.'

'I did, didn't I? And in the pool …' he added with an endearing wink.

A giggle burst from my throat as memories of our heated pool liaison came to my mind. 'I think you did a whole lot more than just strut around in the pool.'

'You better believe it,' he murmured through a grin, giving my bum a playful squeeze.

After spending a while longer with Sean enjoying the sunshine outside the pool house (chatting, kissing, fondling, and generally making sure that we were definitely OK after the Savannah incident), I reluctantly peeled myself away from his tempting warmth and sat up.

'I need to get back to the hotel. Sorry. Cait should be back and I want to see how she got along. Plus, I promised to take her out for celebratory drinks. Well, hopefully celebratory,' I corrected myself.

'OK. I'll drive you back.' Standing up, Sean held out his hands to assist me, and even though I was perfectly capable of doing it by myself, I took his offer and let him pull me to my feet.

Placing a kiss on the tip of my nose, he sighed. 'Come on then, my gorgeous girl. Let's get you back.' He sounded a little glum, as he often did when we were parting, and after having spent an amazing night and morning together – forgetting about the Savannah blip – I had to say that today, I certainly felt the same melancholy about leaving him.

Chapter Seven

Allie

The drive back to the hotel was quick and eventless, but as Sean pulled into the hotel grounds we found the car park far busier than it had been this morning. In a fit of panic, I yelped and tugged my cap down low again, much to Sean's amusement, and found my heart absolutely racing. Considering it was his job on the line if we got caught, he looked remarkably chilled as he reversed into a parking space. How he stayed so calm and cool I had no idea, because all this stress was seriously taking its toll on me, I'd never been so frigging jumpy in my life. Forget cat on a hot tin roof, I was like hyperactive frog on freshly poured tarmac.

'I doubt anyone has spotted me, but we best not have a goodbye kiss just in case.' I was disappointed, of course, but after two rounds of Sean-loving today I was rather well sated, so instead I nodded my understanding.

Reaching across the gap between us, Sean gave my hand a quick squeeze as we shared a frustrated look.

'It won't be like this forever, babe. Call me tonight when you get in. Or message me,' he reminded me, his face serious and worried as I glanced over, which merely made me roll my eyes.

Nodding, I smiled at his protective ways. I supposed some women might find it a little oppressive, or overbearing, but knowing the backstory of why he worried about me so much, I just saw it as a demonstration of how much he cared. 'Of course. Has there ever been a time I've forgotten, Sean?' I asked, which was supposed to be rhetorical, because I always did it. As soon as I realised just how much he obsessed about my safety it had quickly become our thing, and it was now as much a part of my nightly routine as brushing my teeth.

'When you were angry with me because of the fake engagement,' he muttered, his expression suddenly darkening and reminding me of just how quick his moods could swing. 'You didn't message me properly for two nights. Worse than that, you changed your number so I couldn't even call you.' Slightly surprised by how agitated Sean was suddenly getting, I felt my mouth hang open in surprise. I'd thought this was all behind us, but obviously it was still playing on Sean's mind. 'I got no sleep those nights, Allie,' he murmured grittily, and from the haunted expression on his face, I totally believed him.

Wow. OK, so his fixation with my safety wasn't lessening now that we were in the same city.

'Sorry,' I murmured, unsure what else to say. 'I'm twenty-six, Sean, and I know you worry about me but I can take care of myself.' His blue eyes flashed to mine, looking darker and edgier than before, but just when I thought he was going to challenge me he sighed, flicked off his sunglasses, and ran both his hands over his face as if scrubbing away bad memories.

'I'm sorry. *I'm sorry*. I know you can. I'll try to be less paranoid.' His words were perfect, but the expression on his face wasn't the happiest and I didn't want to get out of the car and leave him looking so miserable without a proper goodbye embrace. Except I couldn't even give him a hug because we were sitting in a crowded car park and weren't supposed to be together.

Bugger it. This situation was so frustrating, I literally couldn't wait for things with Savannah to be sorted out.

Reaching over to squeeze his hand, I stared him right in the eye with a purposeful gaze. 'I love you, Sean, even with your paranoia. I will call tonight before bed, I promise. Any idea when I'll see you next?'

Shaking his head, Sean tried to look perkier by smiling. 'I'm not sure, the next two weeks are pretty jam-packed, but I'll make sure I see you, even if it means sneaking into your hotel room in the middle of the night just to spend an hour with you in my arms.'

A shiver of excitement ran through me at the thought of Sean creeping up on me during the night, and I couldn't help but grin naughtily as my cheeks flushed.

His eyes narrowed. 'Hmmm. You like that idea,' he observed, watching me with a wicked smile twitching at the corners of his lips. 'The thought of an intruder slipping into your room at night turns you on, does it?'

How we had gone from discussing his paranoia to talking about rude sexual fantasies, I had no idea, but we had and it was starting to get me quite hot under the collar. Licking my lips, I nodded slowly and deliberately, which caused Sean's eyes to twinkle with excitement. 'But only if the intruder is you, obviously,' I confirmed hoarsely.

'Of course. That goes without saying,' he agreed smoothly, now looking fully back to his usual calm self. 'In which case, I shall do my upmost to tiptoe in as quietly as possible, pin you to the bed when you are least expecting it, or perhaps even tie you up …' he mused, an idea that made my pulse spike with excitement, '… and then take you however I wish.'

Oh my god.

I was suddenly really hot, my eyes as wide as saucers, mouth feeling as parched as a desert, and so turned on that I was squirming in my seat to try and ease the throbbing between my legs. And I was in the middle of a busy car park. Perfect. The only real sign that Sean was just as affected by all of this was his tone, which was lower and grittier than before, but apart from that he still looked cool as a cucumber.

'I'll leave you with that thought,' he murmured, winking at me before a slightly troubled look crossed his brow. 'And I have a key to the bungalow, so don't get any silly thoughts about leaving the door unlocked for me. Lock it up tight every night, OK?' he demanded while giving me an intense stare.

'Yes, Sir,' I muttered sarcastically around a supressed laugh, trying not to giggle out loud at how quickly he could change from domineering and sexy to a panicky worrier.

With one last squeeze of his hand, I opened the car door and slid out, dropping from the Jeep's high cabin before swivelling to wiggle my fingers in a brief goodbye wave. 'See you soon, and speak to you later.'

Making my way through the lush gardens towards the bungalow, I had to divert my route to avoid the sprinklers currently watering the lawns, but after the intense hours spent with Sean, a wander through the tranquil gardens was actually quite a welcome moment of calm. Pulling off my cap, I shook out my hair, glad to be free from its confines in the warm summer evening. Veering to my right, I took the longer path that zigzagged between beautifully scented rhododendrons. The smell always reminded me of my parents' garden at home.

Finally arriving at the bungalow, I mounted the steps, entered the empty lounge, and following the sound of music I wandered to the garden area and found Cait sprawled on a lounger humming along to Maroon 5. Our small garden was completely surrounded, so since our arrival, Cait had been brave enough to don her bikini most days, and her lovely healthy tan was becoming something to be rather envious of.

'Allie!' Cait beamed. Her cheeks were pink from sunbathing and she looked mightily pleased with herself, which indicated that the job hunt had gone well today. Grabbing a beer from the cooler beside her, she popped the lid and then flapped her spare arm in the direction of the empty sunbed beside her.

'So, you finally managed to peel yourself away from lover boy?' A knowing smirk was twitching on her lips, and in return I nearly laughed – yeah, lover boy *and* his psycho, fake-lipped ex. But that was a story to tell later; now was about Cait's day. 'I was starting to think you weren't going to make it back to join in with my celebrations.'

'Sorry,' I murmured with an apologetic smile. Dropping onto the lounger I sipped my cool beer and raised my eyebrows expectantly. 'Celebrations?' I questioned. 'Does that mean you got the job?'

Suddenly looking incredibly animated, Cait leant forwards, her eyes twinkling in the evening sun. 'I did.' Cait's face reddened further with apparent excitement. 'Actually, I got a full-on upgrade, they offered me a job – a proper job – in the props department for *Dark Blood*, that vampire drama. It comes with a six month contract and everything.'

Giving a small shrug, she sipped her beer casually, as if this wasn't majorly exciting news.

'Oh my god! This is fantastic! Well done, you!' I yelped, almost falling off my lounger in my rush to get up and congratulate her. 'This is *am-az-ing*!'

Smiling modestly, Cait shrugged. 'It is pretty exciting.' Which was about right for Cait, she was always so shy about anything vaguely complimentary, and for once, this trait had nothing to do with her fucked-up ex and everything to do with her sweet, gentle nature – she had always been unassuming, ever since I had known her.

'Yeah. I signed for it straight away ...' She paused, and some of the excitement seemed to fade from her eyes. '... but I'm not sure I should have now,' she murmured, examining her beer bottle with apparent fascination.

'What? Why not?' I squawked, not sure I'd heard her correctly. 'Me and you living it up in LA for the next few months will be amazing!' Cait smiled at my enthusiasm, but I could see hesitation in her eyes and I wondered what on earth it was holding her back. After all, she had no ties in the UK, she'd effectively been a traveller for the past three years, earning cash here and there whenever she could so surely this would be perfect.

'I dunno,' was all the reply she gave. Words so vague that I began to suspect there was more to her hesitation than she was letting on.

'What exactly is the job? The same prop work you did in Oz?'

'Yep, prosthetic accessories, mostly, some stage design work too, I think,' Cait agreed, taking a casual swig of her beer. I narrowed my eyes at her blasé response. She was deliberately trying to stay vague, but I knew Cait well enough that I could see the excited twinkle in her eye. I knew how much she had loved her work in Australia, so if this was similar then it certainly couldn't be the job holding her back. She wanted this job, I could see it in her face. So what was causing her hesitation?

Hmm. If she was feeling defensive then I needed to play it cool. Perhaps if I skirted around the subject for a while I could distract her enough to get her to open up about the cause of her uncertainty.

'I thought you built stage sets in Sydney, but you just said something about prosthetics? What does that involve?'

Chuckling, Cait popped her empty bottle on the floor and lounged back again. 'It's the same silicone material used in prosthetic limbs, but in a prop department we use it in a different way to create masks, or attachments that give a character a different appearance.' It was as if Cait was speaking a foreign language, which I guess if you knew nothing about stage make-up like me, she kind of was. But still, it sounded pretty cool.

'For example, if you want a character to have a vampire bite on their neck, I would create the bite mark from silicone, paint it, and then attach it to the actor's skin with special glue. Then I'd add some make up to smooth down any edges, but's that's not always necessary. It's pretty amazing what we can do with it, really.'

I was impressed. I knew my bestie was arty, but I hadn't quite realised her talent extended to that level. Cait now looked bashful, almost embarrassed by her skills. 'Wow. That sounds seriously technical. You'll get to work with all those dishy vampires too, my god, the lead guy is so hot!'

'Yeah, I guess.' Cait's cheeks flushed red, as was usual when we discussed anything remotely linked to men, relationships, or sex. Deciding to get to the crux of the issue, I sat up, placed my beer down and eyeballed my best friend.

'Come on. Out with it, what's making you hesitant?'

Shifting on her sunbed, I watched as Cait's hand drifted towards her wrist and began to play with the elastic bands. Narrowing my eyes, I began to wonder if her hesitation had anything to do with a certain tall, dark-haired actor that my friend had had several run-ins with recently. Literally. It seemed completely illogical, but something in my gut was screaming at me that it might be the case, so, not pulling any punches, I decided to just come straight out with it.

'Does this have anything to do with Jack Felton?'

Chapter Eight

Cait

'Does this have anything to do with Jack Felton?'

My entire frame stiffened, because while Jack was a bit of an issue (quite a big bit of an issue, if I was being honest), there was also the matter of Mum's phone call that was playing on my mind. Allie didn't know about the letters I received from Greg, nobody did, apart from my parents and the police. I'd never told Allie because even though she was my best friend and I knew I could trust her, I hadn't wanted her to worry about me while I was travelling. Well, we were together again now, hopefully for quite a while, so after rubbing my eyes with the heels of my hands I made the decision to confide in her.

'Actually, there's something I haven't told you.' I paused and cleared my throat in preparation. 'Something about Greg.'

Frowning at my mention of him, Allie looked briefly confused, and then leant in closer.

'He still sends me letters.' Her eyes widened and her mouth popped open to speak, but I beat her to it, wanting to get my bombshell out in the open. 'I found out today that another one arrived this week, so I'm just feeling a bit jittery.'

'Oh my god, Cait ... this is crazy. How does he know where you are?'

'He doesn't.' At least I hoped he didn't. 'They go to my mum's house, some have worldwide postmarks and some are hand delivered. They're basically disguised threats. Postcards saying stuff like "I can't wait until we're together again" and letters …' I had to pause, remembering how upset my mum had been when she'd opened one by mistake. She'd been near hysterical on the phone, '… really graphic letters about what he wants to do to me. Except he makes it sound like a kinky love letter.'

'Fucking hell. Have you told the police and got a restraining order?' Allie looked so mad she was practically frothing at the mouth.

Drawing in a breath through my nose, I nodded. 'We've told the police, but they can't file a restraining order without some solid evidence, and there isn't any. When it first started happening he went in for questioning willingly, but denied everything, and once he was released he just seemed to vanish. Besides, they can't prove the letters are from him. The handwriting isn't a match for a sample that his parents provided, and there isn't any DNA evidence on the paper to implicate him. He was really careful.'

Seems he'd always been careful, because he was really careful to clean up the night he attacked me too. The police said his house was drenched with bleach, which Greg claimed was just from a thorough spring clean, but there wasn't a single scrap of evidence to prove I'd even been there.

Licking my lips, I picked up my phone and absently fiddled with it. 'I know it's him. It's obvious to me, even if it's not to the police.'

Expelling a sharp breath, I shrugged. 'So, basically that's why I never came back to the UK. It's also why I don't do social media and haven't stayed anywhere for very long, just in case he somehow finds me. But I doubt he's really looking for me. I'm sure he has a new woman to order around now. He probably just enjoys playing with me.'

It seemed that with this news I had achieved the impossible – my chatterbox of a best friend appeared totally lost for words. 'Bloody hell. He's even more of a fuckwad than I thought,' she finally murmured after nearly a full minute of silence, making me smile weakly at the unfortunate nickname she always used for him.

Allie

I was completely gobsmacked. Fucking Greg. It was bad enough that he had put her through all sorts of shit in the past, how dare he still be haunting her? If I ever saw him again I swear I would rip him a new neck hole.

Not wanting to alarm Cait with the depth of my anger, I blew out a long breath and tried to lighten the mood a bit. 'Wow, and there was me thinking your hesitation about this new job was because of Jack Felton. Guess I got that totally wrong!' I saw Cait's eyes begin to dart around, looking everywhere but at me, and then the elastic bang pinging began again in earnest, twanging against her skin until I cringed.

'Actually, you were partly right. I saw Jack at the studios,' she suddenly blurted, her voice a scratchy rasp. 'I think he might work there.'

Damn it, I hated it when I was right, but if she was going to turn her back on a job because of the minute risk of seeing Jack Felton, I was going to kill her too.

Shrugging as if that was no big deal, I tried to make her realise how insignificant her worry was. 'So? He's an actor, I bet he has to go around all the big studios. The chances of seeing him very often must be tiny.'

Nodding unconvincingly, she flicked her elastic band so hard that I had to lean over and stop her. 'Hey, stop it.'

'Sorry. But to be honest, Jack scares me more than Greg's threats.'

Seeing my astounded look, because Jack Felton was a

million, billion, gazillion times better for Cait than Greg ever had been, she held up a hand to stop me.

'That came out wrong. What I mean is that Greg is just a vague threat. As scary as it was back when it all happened it's been years and years now, and even though my parents have had postcards here and there, none of us have actually seen Greg. I guess for the sake of my sanity I've had to force the idea of him into a worry in the background …' Cait paused and rubbed at her forehead as if trying to ease her stress. 'Don't get me wrong, he's a serious worry, but … but at the moment, Jack seems to be right in the flipping foreground of my life. He makes me feel …' She huffed out a huge breath and lolled her head to the side to look at me. 'I don't know what exactly, and that's what's so frustrating.' The cloudy worry in her eyes made my chest squeeze at the pain I saw there. 'But he makes me feel something, and it scares the shit out of me.'

Holding back a groan of pain for her, I jumped up and joined her on the lounger, nudging her until she got the hint and made room for me.

'I get what you mean, babes, I really do, but feeling isn't always a bad thing.'

'I know. *I know*. But it is for me, especially when the guy is famous and way out of my league.'

She was going back to that excuse again? Blowing out a dismissive raspberry, I grabbed two more beers and opened them for us. 'Enough of that crap talk, he'd be proud to have you on his arm. You're beautiful and you know it.' Cait met my words with silence and then a heavy sigh so I pulled out my phone and decided to see if I could put her mind at ease. 'He's in *Fire Lab* right?'

'Yeah. Why?' Staying quiet for a second, I did a quick Google search for Dynamic Studios and *Fire Lab* and winced when a list of search results came back. Bugger. It looked like he was based at the same studios. What were the flipping chances?

Desperate to reassure my friend, I pulled up a map and showed it to Cait. 'Do you know which stage you'll be based at?'

Squinting at the map she then pointed to the top right corner. 'Here, number 5. Why?'

'I did a search for *Fire Lab*, and it is filmed at Dynamic, but …' I added my 'but' quickly to cover the sharp inhale of breath Cait had just made. 'But his show is filmed right on the other side of the complex. Look, stage 16, see, all the way down here.' Cait's wide eyes examined the map before she started to chomp on her lower lip.

'Judging from the scale on this map, the complex is massive. The chances of seeing him really are minimal.'

'The site was big,' Cait admitted reluctantly. 'We had to use golf buggies to get around.'

'See?' I nodded my head enthusiastically and decided to use my intimate knowledge of Cait to my advantage. 'Don't turn down a job that's perfect for you just because of a man.' That was a bit sneaky of me, but I knew the one thing Cait hated above all else was feeling weak because of her ex.

Sitting up, I saw her spine straighten defensively and allowed myself a small smile at my victory in this debate.

Pulling in a breath so deep it flared her nostrils, Cait turned to me, her eyes bright and chin set defiantly. 'You're right. It is the perfect job for me.' Nodding firmly, she smiled and finally allowed some enthusiasm to show on her face. 'Actually, I'm pretty excited by it all. You should have seen the facilities, Allie. It was amazing.' I noticed she made no further mention of Jack, but that was fine by me –

we could always raise that topic again at a later date. I would love Cait to take some steps towards dating Jack; he seemed like a complete gent. I got a good vibe from him, but more than that, I liked the fact that he seemed to genuinely like Cait too.

'What are the hours like?'

'Not bad, it varies depending on filming schedule, but to start they're pretty good, lots of morning shoots which means free afternoons so we can still go out.'

'Good. I hope I still get to see plenty of you.' I pouted, glad that Cait had a job and would be staying in LA, but reluctant to give up all the time we were spending together.

'You will, don't worry. Besides, I might have a plan of how we can make sure we see plenty of each other …'

Seeing Cait's face lit with anticipation, I felt my eyebrows rise curiously. 'Come on then, elaborate!' I chuckled impatiently.

'Well, I know you might move in with Sean eventually …' she hesitated, '… but the three weeks at the hotel are almost up, and I was wondering how you felt about me and you living together for a bit?'

She'd barely even finished her sentence before I was standing up and grabbing hold of her and dragging her in for a giddy hug as I whooped joyfully. 'Oh my god! I'd love to!' Once I had put poor Cait down, I made a dismissive noise in my throat and laughed. 'And no more talk about me moving in with Sean, it's *waaay* too early for that.' Not that we even could move in together with all this crazy Savannah engagement stuff hanging over us. I gave an accepting roll of my eyes before grinning at Cait with a near gleeful expression. 'Me and you living together, it'll be just like uni again! We'll have to start looking for a place.'

Cait's face was glowing with excitement. 'Actually, the guy who interviewed me has lined me up with a house, it's a two bed, and cheap because I get an employee discount. I've seen it already, and it's great, but we can view it again this weekend so you can have a look?'

'Yes, that sounds great!' Grinning, I raised my bottle. 'Here's to your new job and our new house together! Cheers!'

Letting out a small chuckle, Cait chinked her bottle against mine and took a healthy swig. 'So, anyway, enough about me … what have you done today?'

It was on the tip of my tongue to start explaining the fiasco that had happened at Sean's house, but I was beaten to speaking by Cait, who suddenly laughed rather sporadically and flashed me a funny look, accompanied by a raised eyebrow.

'Actually, I think I know what you were up to.' She waggled a finger at me, grinning from ear to ear. 'Let me see, bikini bottoms on the bottom of the pool, bikini top flung on the poolside to dry, mighty tighty black boxers chucked carelessly in a heap beside them, and a sopping wet towel …' My cheeks were fast flushing to be the same colour as the red label on our beer bottles as Cait gleefully counted off my mistakes on her fingers.

Shit. Shit. *Shit*. In the rush to leave with Sean after lunch I had completely forgotten about clearing up the things around the pool. Oops.

Rolling my lips between my teeth, I wondered desperately if there was anything I could say to lessen my embarrassment, but with all the evidence so clearly pointing to the fact that I'd had sex in the pool, there really wasn't. Best to take one on the chin, I decided bravely. Holding my hands up in defeat, I smiled sheepishly and nodded slowly.

'Yeah, guilty as charged. Sean and I got a bit intimate in the pool earlier. Sorry. I forgot to tidy up.'

'You had sex in the swimming pool?' Cait yelped, the horror clear in her voice if I hadn't been able to see it in her expression, but I didn't understand her outburst. She had just pointed it all out to me, why was she now looking so shocked?

'Oh my God, that's gross! I thought you'd gone skinny dipping, I didn't think you'd actually had sex in there!'

Oops. Skinny dipping would have been the perfect excuse, why the hell hadn't I thought of that?

'I nearly went for a swim in there this afternoon!' Cait spluttered, the expression on her face still one of marginal revulsion before finally shaking her head and joining me with a chuckle.

'That's what the chlorine is for. It kills everything,' I joked with an embarrassed shrug.

Narrowing her eyes, she glanced at the sopping wet towel. 'And the towel? How did that feature?'

'The towel is my little secret,' I replied sweetly, knowing that as curious as Cait was, she was shy enough that she wouldn't want to know the in-depth details of my intimate liaison with Sean.

'Hmm. Maybe I really should move back to the hostel until the house is ready. That way you two can have the privacy you need.'

'No way. You're staying here until we move into the house. OK?' I stated persuasively.

Cait weighed up my words for a second or two, and then nodded. 'OK, only if you're sure. Oh, and by the way,' she said, turning her grinning face toward me. 'I met your man again at breakfast, so if I'm staying here longer then you need to tell him to start wearing clothes when he visits.'

Her cheeks flushed but I couldn't really hold it against her. After all, Sean was god-like in the body department.

'Yeah, sorry. He stayed over. We went to his house this afternoon too,' I added casually.

'Oh my gosh! What was the house like? Was it nice? I bet it was huge, wasn't it?' Cait asked, but then thwacked her palm to her forehead on a groan. 'What am I thinking? Forget the house, did you meet the fake fiancée? I get the feeling from the media that she's a prize bitch, but I might be wrong,' Cait speculated.

'No, you're spot on. Savannah Hilton is a prize bitch. I did meet her today, and you'll never guess what she did.'

'Oooh. Do tell,' Cait said, suddenly looking rather interested.

Missing out the details of our pool liaison, I set about explaining my afternoon to Cait, but the whole time that I was chatting I couldn't quite shake the sensation that today's incident wouldn't be the last stunt I'd see from Savannah.

That instinct stuck with me all evening, and left me decidedly jittery, so as I curled up in my bed later that night, I grabbed my phone and opened up the internet browser. Searching for Savannah, my lip curled with distaste as a list of results popped up, but thankfully there were no new stories involving her and Sean.

I wondered if, or when, she might try some new ploy 'for fun', so I decided to set up an alert for her name in my search engine that would send me a notification whenever there was a new story involving her. It was a first for me, but if sneaky Savannah, the wicked witch of West Hollywood, was half as cunning as I suspected, then this might allow me to stay at least one step ahead of her.

Chapter Nine

Sean

I finally had a day free, and I wanted to spend it with Allie somewhere there would be no possible interruptions or distractions. Short of going to her place, again, which let's face it, was getting a bit repetitive, I was pretty limited in my options, so it was this predicament that had led me to the gates of my new beach house.

Private, comfortable, and all mine. In short, it was a perfect place to spend the day relaxing with Allie. My director would probably freak if he knew I was bringing her here, but luckily no one in the press seemed to have caught on to the fact that I owned this place yet, and so far on my few visits, journalists hadn't been an issue. For Allie, I was willing to take the risk.

I'd been at the studio first thing today, so to save time I'd asked my driver, David, to pick Allie up and meet me here. As I nodded to Billy on security and waited for the gates to open, I got a restless feeling in my stomach, which I supposed was what some people would describe as butterflies in the tummy. Was Allie already here? I hoped so. I always got these little excited tingles when I knew I would be seeing her, but stupidly they were more pronounced today, because I was actually nervous about whether or not she would like my new place.

Pulling past the gates, I began to wind up the long

driveway until it separated into three and I took the central path to reach my house, hoping I would see the black limo sitting outside.

Rounding the last bend, a broad grin tugged at my lips as I saw David and Allie getting out of the car.

Pulling up beside them, I practically jumped out as the tumbling in my stomach intensified and made me twitchy with excess energy.

David smiled and nodded before sliding back into the limo and leaving Allie and me alone in the warm morning sunshine. She was wearing a sweet, pale yellow sundress that I instantly loved, because not only did she look gorgeous in it, but it showed off her long legs to utter perfection.

'Hey, my gorgeous girl.' I think my excitement and happiness almost quadrupled when Allie practically skipped to my side and promptly threw herself into my arms.

I loved this woman so much.

Pulling her more firmly against me, I hummed my contentment and couldn't resist briefly burying my face in her hair and inhaling her addictive fragrance as one hand got its fix trailing through the long, silky strands.

Allie leant back, her cheeks pink and eyes twinkling before she rolled up on to her tiptoes and placed a kiss on my lips. I'm not sure if it was meant to be a quick 'hello' kiss, but almost as soon as our lips connected she let out a soft moan, clutched a handful of my shirt, and deepened the kiss by pushing her tongue into my mouth.

Fuck. One small moan and a bit of tongue and I was horny as hell and dragging her roughly against me, suddenly intent on finding a fun way to vent my pent-up excitement and nerves.

A seagull squawked loudly just overhead, bringing me vaguely back to the reality of what I was doing on the driveway of my own house. We hadn't even made it inside, for goodness' sake. Pulling back with a wry chuckle, I blinked to clear my lust-filled brain and looked down to see a similarly dazed expression on Allie's face. That was another thing I loved about her – the obvious way she was affected by me just as much as I was by her.

'Wanna look around?' I glanced over my shoulder toward the house and grinned, the newness of it all still so exciting. The house was big, but the compound was bigger still, so there was no feeling of being overlooked by your neighbours. All in all it was pretty amazing, and I felt bloody lucky to own it.

Licking her reddened lips, Allie nodded and linked one hand with mine as she stepped from my embrace.

The house was all on one level so I gave Allie a tour of the four en suite bedrooms, study, and kitchen with an endless supply of modern gadgets, and ended up in the vast lounge/dining area with floor to ceiling windows that overlooked the beach. Allie looked suitably impressed, even though I hadn't really got around to furnishing it a great deal yet – there was a bed, sofa, TV, and appliances in the kitchen, but that was about it. I had a load of gym gear arriving next week for one of the spare rooms, but actually, my lack of effort was secretly deliberate because I was hoping Allie might like to get involved with helping me furnish the place.

Truthfully, if it wasn't for the Savannah issue hanging over us, I would have asked Allie to move in already. I would love to know that I was coming home to her every night. The very idea made my heart speed up a little, but even though I knew Allie loved me too I sensed that it was a bit too early in our relationship for that just yet. Still, if she helped me decorate and furnish the beach house hopefully she'd feel at home enough to want to spend increasing amounts of time here, and then moving in would just be a natural occurrence.

'What do you think?' I asked hesitantly, because although she had made several appreciative noises as we'd walked around, Allie had been unusually quiet.

'It's a really great place, Sean.' Walking to the patio doors, she gazed over the balcony to the sea beyond, her arms wrapping around her body almost defensively and causing my eyes to narrow. 'The view is incredible too.'

Which it was, the three homes within this compound were spread around a pointed spit of land so they all had completely uninterrupted views over the beautiful beaches beyond, but what was with her quiet voice and defensive posture? Concern pulled my brow down into a frown and I immediately walked up behind her and wrapped my arms around her waist. Laying my hands over hers, I pried her clenched fists open and linked our fingers together.

'Why do I think you're going to say 'but'?' I asked softly, trying not to sound defensive, needy, or desperate, but probably managing to sound like all three.

In this position I couldn't see her face, but I did feel the huge sigh that expanded Allie's ribcage and fluttered from her lips in a long, slow breath.

'Allie?' Twisting her in my arms I tipped her chin up so she would meet my gaze and saw her beautiful blue eyes clouded and her lips tightly pursed.

Leaning forward, she rested her forehead on my chest and sighed again. 'It's nothing I haven't said before,' she murmured.

'I don't care. If something is bothering you then tell

me.'

'I'm going to sound like a broken record.' Looking up to meet my gaze, she raised a hand and gently rubbed her thumb across my chin. 'It's just that seeing this place has brought it home to me just how far away our happily ever after seems. I mean, this is your house, but I could only come here because David picked me up. You're my boyfriend but I can't be seen in public with you. It's ridiculous.'

I figured this was always going to be an issue until the Savannah fiasco was sorted. What I didn't think Allie realised was how much it frustrated and affected me too. She wasn't the only one who wanted us to be able to be together properly. I loved her so fucking much and I wanted to scream it from the rooftops.

'I know, baby. But it won't be too much longer. I promise.'

Allie nodded in my arms and gave me a soft, trusting smile that made me desperate to prove to her that she was mine, even if it were just a declaration between the two of us. Sliding open the patio doors, I felt the warm sea breeze around my legs as I guided her onto the balcony and over to the railing.

I wasn't able to publicly announce our relationship yet, but I could do the next best thing. Leaving Allie where she stood, I climbed up onto the balcony rail using one of the upright supports, and raised my arm up and out into the breeze.

'Sean? What are doing? Get down! Don't bloody slip …'

Clearing my throat, I winked at Allie and gave a dramatic sweep of my free arm in her direction. 'This woman here,' I yelled to no one but the beach and sea, 'is the love of my entire life!' Allie's cheeks reddened and her eyes bugged out, but seeing the thrilled grin spread on her lips I continued. 'I love her more than she knows, more than I ever thought possible. I even love her more than she loves chocolate!'

Swinging my arms wildly in the wind, I sobered my expression and stared at her intently. 'And one day I'm going to marry her, right here on this beach, and make her mine forever.'

I might have been hanging from the balcony, but I didn't miss the gasp that flew from Allie's lips at my spontaneous declaration. She might have been shocked, but every single word was true. I did love her, and I would marry her. Preferably sooner, rather than later.

Jumping down from the rail, I immediately dropped to one knee and grabbed her left hand, prompting her already wide eyes to almost burst from their sockets.

'I'm not going to ask you today, because I know the issues with Savannah are still troubling you,' I reassured her, my thumb caressing her ring finger, suddenly desperate to see a band there. 'But you need to be prepared for it, Allie, because one day soon I'm going to be down on one knee asking you to marry me, and I hope with all my heart and soul that you'll say yes.'

We shared an intense stare for several seconds, then Allie gave herself a small shake, licked her lips, and gave a tiny acknowledging nod of her head. I wasn't sure if she was saying yes to the idea of me proposing in the future, or was agreeing to marry me, but I didn't push the subject any further, instead deciding to show her just how much I loved her.

She was mine, and as primal as it sounded, I really needed to bury myself in her body to reassure myself that was still the case.

Springing up from my crouched position, I slid both of my hands into her hair and dragged her forwards onto my waiting lips. I'd planned to give her a deep, gentle kiss, but instead it morphed into a desperate, hungry clash of teeth, tongues, and lips as we both seemed to explode into a lusty mass of clutching hands.

The next moment I was dragging her sundress up over her belly, reluctantly separating our lips for just a second as I pulled the material over her head and threw it onto one of the loungers. The sight of her beautiful breasts met my gaze and I sucked in a breath of surprise. Bra-less? I loved that little sundress even more now.

'What if someone sees us, Sean?' Allie asked, covering her breasts and giving a wary glance out over the sand.

'Private beach,' I muttered, and as soon as the words were out of my mouth, Allie wasted no time in grinning and grabbing the hem of my T-shirt to peel it from my chest before adding it to the growing pile of clothes on the sun bed.

Dropping to my knees, I promptly buried my face in the silk of her panties, causing Allie to groan and sway on her feet as her hands fell to my head and clutched at my hair. Sliding my hands around her gorgeous arse, I gripped a lush cheek in each hand and pulled her snug against my lips as I placed a long kiss there and inhaled deeply. God, she smelt incredible – clean silk, sweet, and with a musky undertone to indicate her arousal.

We'd barely started and she was turned on. I fucking loved that.

Slipping a finger under the lace on either side of her hips, I dragged the panties down her legs, tapping each ankle in turn to get her to step out of them. Leaning back, I let my greedy gaze run over her beautiful body as the sun illuminated it, from the painted tips of her toes to her erect nipples, flushed cheeks, and wild hair that was blowing in the breeze like a golden halo, making her look almost angelic.

It was apt because she was my angel. She'd appeared in my life at a point where I'd started to think I would always be alone. But now there was Allie, and I couldn't ever imagine not having her.

Her delicate fingers buried in my hair again, waking me from my trance and prompting me to get this scene back on track. I placed a hot, open-mouthed kiss just above her sex and then stood up, intent on well and truly worshipping her.

I had an urge to take things further than we had before, so I looked around for something to tie her hands with. A little light bondage had always appealed to me, and I had a feeling my girl might enjoy it too. I came up empty, but I had a sudden idea and slid the belt from my shorts. Quickly fastening it into a small loop, I held it out in front of me. 'Wrists, please.'

Allie raised an eyebrow but followed my instruction without complaint, and once the soft leather was tightened, I turned her to face the view and secured the other end of the belt around the balcony rail, fastening her into a forward facing position.

Dropping to my haunches I took hold of her right ankle, turned her leg outwards slightly, and helped lift her foot onto the mid rail so she was opened up to the sea breeze.

Opened ready for me.

Staying on my knees, I worked myself into the gap between her body and the railings and positioned myself so my head had the most perfect fucking view of her. God, she was perfect. Not to mention trusting. Allie was above me in the open air, one leg turned outwards, exposing herself to me in the most intimate of positions, and she hadn't uttered one word of complaint.

Running my hands reverently up her inner thighs, I watched in fascination as her skin quivered below my touch until a shiver ran through her entire body.

'Oh, Sean.' Glancing up I saw her watching me in aroused fascination, so keeping eye contact I leant forwards and teased her clit briefly with the point of my tongue. Her eyes fluttered shut, mouth parting into a very satisfying 'O' of pleasure as she shifted her hips to bring her core even closer to my lips.

Fucking perfect.

Smiling smugly, I gripped her thighs tighter and really got to work by running my tongue across her throbbing flesh, lapping up her juices as I went and then sucking her clit into my mouth. *Hard.*

Allie bucked against me, yelping and writhing, but I held on tight and continued with my pleasurable torture. Swirling my tongue around her clit several times earned me a groan of contentment so I bit down with just the amount of pressure I knew she loved, and was this time rewarded with a noise that closely resembled a growl. Moving one hand to her core I pressed two fingers against her entrance and hummed in appreciation as her body greedily sucked them in.

Instead of going slow, I thrust right in to the knuckles, pausing briefly so I could watch as I drove my fingers deeply into her again.

Mine. She was mine, and no one would ever touch her like this ever again except for me. That thought might have been proprietary and terrifying for some men, but I wasn't scared of commitment any more, I would love Allie and keep her safe for the rest of my life.

Allie's hips rotated against me, so I happily complied and spread some of her moisture around her opening before giving her more, adding a third finger to the mix and relishing the moan that slid from her mouth. Fuck, she was just so sexy. Her body drove me wild. The three fingers were a tight fit, but as soon as I began to lap at her clit again I felt Allie's muscles gradually relaxing until they suddenly gave a small spasm and I realised just how close she was.

Thrusting with more force, I curled my fingers to hit her g-spot and increased the suction with my mouth so I could literally feel her clit heating and swelling from my attention. I could hear the belt rattling as Allie thrashed against her bindings so I decided to let her have exactly what she wanted.

Taking the little bundle of nerves in between my teeth again I started to rhythmically tug on her clit in time with my thrusts, and after just a few seconds, Allie made a strangled mewl and then exploded into a climax so strong that it briefly stopped the movement of my fingers with her clenching muscles. Gradually working her down from her peak, I licked her juices and slowed my fingers until she had come down from her high and let out a satisfied moan.

Not wasting a second, I edged my way out from my crouched position and practically ripped off my boxers and shorts before positioning myself behind her. Gripping Allie's hips, I adjusted her legs again to make sure her right leg was still spread nice and wide for me, and then pressed the tip off my cock into her welcoming warmth. My hips jerked with the need to be deeper, and she was so wet that I didn't have any of our usual issues with the tight fit and slid in all the way to the root with my first thrust.

Pausing in that deeply joined position, I stopped, groaning out long and low as I lowered my head and kissed her shoulder over and over again in between panted, ragged breaths. My hands reached around her to cup her breasts and I played with her nipples as I soaked up the amazing sensation of being completely buried inside my woman.

'I love you, Sean,' Allie mumbled, her voice rough and sexy, but I was so desperate to come that I could barely even form an answer. Growling loudly, I lowered my hands and gripped her waist so tightly that my fingertips turned white, and pulled out of her before burying myself inside her so hard that we both let out strangled cries of shocked pleasure into the midday air.

'Holy shit. You feel so fucking good, Allie. Was that too hard, baby?'

'It. Was. Perfect,' she murmured, each word punctuated with a roll of her arse so the physical contact between us became as close as possible. Her words were my green light for more, and so widening my stance I began to thrust into her in long, deep strokes, looking down to watch in fascination as my cock disappeared inside her willing body on each movement.

Fuck. That was such an erotic sight.

When I was satisfied that she was building towards release again, I slid a hand around and used two fingers to roll and rub at her swollen clit. Considering she was attached to the rail, Allie was doing a damn good job of writhing against me, and as I sped up my thrusts and rubbed at her clit almost furiously, she bucked and began to come.

Her channel was clenching around my cock, increasing the friction deliciously and making me lose all control as my hips began to jerk back and forth with abandon. As she let out a loud scream I felt my climax explode from the base of my balls and soak her hot insides in a seemingly never-ending series of jerks and twitches.

Mine.

Allie's head collapsed backwards onto my shoulder and I desperately sought her mouth with mine and kissed her slowly and deeply as I gentled my thrusts and brought us down from our climaxes.

My girl had gone lax against me, clearly worn out from her two orgasms, so I supported her weight with one hand and reached around with the other to undo the belt just as her legs gave way and buckled.

Scooping Allie up, I only just managed to get my own wobbly legs to walk us to one of the sun loungers before I sank down onto the soft cover with a relieved sigh. That climax had been so powerful I'd actually thought I might drop Allie for a second there, which certainly wouldn't have been my smoothest ever move.

The lounger wasn't massive, but I managed to manoeuvre us so that we were face to face with our legs entwined and faces just centimetres apart. As we enjoyed our post-coital afterglow, Allie blinked lazily then gazed around. 'It really is a great apartment Sean, I love it. Especially the balcony,' she added cheekily, making me chuckle and lean forward to drop a kiss on the end of her nose.

Pausing in her thoughts, Allie licked her lips as if preparing to say more. 'Actually, talking of apartments … my three weeks at the Beverly Hills Hotel is almost up now.'

Assuming she was bringing this up because she wanted me to extend the booking, I shook my head dismissively and gave a nonchalant shrug. 'No worries, I can extend your stay.'

Allie shifted forward and chewed on her lower lip, which I knew was a sign that she had something to tell me. Why she didn't just come out with it concerned me, and I frowned as I waited for whatever bombshell she was going to drop.

'It's been so generous of you to pay for the hotel, Sean, but I kinda want to be independent again. I feel embarrassed that you pay for me, I'm not with you for your money. Cait's asked me to move in with her, and I've agreed.' Narrowing my eyes, I found my head shaking firmly before I'd even fully digested her words.

'You are not going back to that fucking backpacker's hostel, Allie. Not over my dead body. The place is falling down as it is, not to mention its total disregard for security.' I could feel my eye twitching at just the thought of her going back to that shithole. Closing my eyes for a few seconds to control myself, I re-opened them to find a soft smile playing on her lips. It made me feel more than a little defensive, so I frowned, sat up, and crossed my arms. 'What?'

My girl tried, and failed, to wipe the smirk off her face before she gave a small shrug. 'It's sweet when you get all protective.' Hmm. She'd hit the nail right on the head, and there really was no point trying to deny it. As pathetically pussy-whipped as it made me appear, I *was* protective over her, hugely so, and possessive. It was how I was made. Or perhaps it was how she made me, who knew?

'Anyway, you don't need to get your knickers in a twist, Sean, we're not going back to the hostel. Cait's found a house for us.'

A house … that was certainly better than a hostel, but LA had some dodgy as fuck areas, so I was going to need more details before she had me convinced.

'Whereabouts is it?' I tried to keep my tone cool and casual, but judging by the continued smile trying to break free on her lips, I had obviously failed miserably.

'Right opposite Dynamic. The guy who interviewed her said that employees get a discount on rent too. It's in a complex called Studio City, have you heard of it?'

Now my shoulders really did relax. Not only was that a decent part of town, but Studio City was a relatively new development and I'd heard good things about it. Very good things.

'I have, it's a great complex, and very secure.' Allie gave me another amused smiled, and I realised she was merely humouring me. She would have moved there anyway, even if I'd said no. A small grumble rose in my throat at her independent, stubborn streak. She drove me wild sometimes.

'I haven't seen it yet, but Cait said that while it is small, it's perfectly formed. Really safe too, apparently there's double security, so you go through the main entrance and then have another security gate depending on which sector of the compound your house is in.'

Nodding my head, I tried to recall the layout when I'd visited a friend last year. 'That's right, it's split into boulevards, I think. Some of the actors live there.' I gave another contented nod, feeling relaxed now I knew Allie would be safe, and then a wicked thought sprang to my mind. 'There'll be no sneaking in to see you when you move there. I'd never get past all the guards.' I tried my best attempt at a pout, but my mind was elsewhere. More precisely, I was remembering how I had told Allie that I might sneak into her room one night and surprise her. The very idea made my cock twitch, even though I'd just come.

Could I fit in some intruder role play before she left the

hotel? I'd certainly have to try.

We hadn't discussed what I'd just done to her, but using the belt to secure her had been our first real venture into non-vanilla sex. I knew for sure that I had enjoyed it, and it had certainly seemed that Allie had too, but perhaps it would be best to check. 'Did you enjoy being tied up with the belt?' I asked cautiously.

If possible, her cheeks got even redder and I couldn't help but smile at her shy streak as I moved closer and wrapped an arm around her shoulders.

'You must know I did,' she mumbled softly, one of her hands moving to my thigh and giving it a gentle squeeze. 'I came harder than a point 7 earthquake.'

'So being tied up is something we can try more of?' Bloody hell, just thinking about Allie's soft, lithe body tied up in various positions caused me to get an instant erection as I felt blood rushing to my groin at the X-rated images in my head.

'Yeah … experimentation is fun.'

Fan-bloody-tastic. I had been hoping she'd say that, because now we'd ventured down that path a little I had a few more things I wanted to try with her. Like intruder role play, for a start.

I left Allie lying on the lounger while I disappeared inside to grab something to clean us up. Pausing by the bathroom counter I scowled when I couldn't find any flannels. Damn it. I made a mental note to get some wash cloths for this apartment, and then grabbed a hand towel from the pile instead.

Allie

As I lay there in a state of blissful satiation, a huge grin began to spread on my lips as I thought back over the last hour. I couldn't believe I'd let Sean tie me to the balcony and spread me wide open for all and sundry to see. A delirious giggle gurgled up my throat as I shook my head in amusement. Well, I sort of could believe it. I tended to get lost in a dream-like state whenever Sean was around and just blindly follow his lead, but still, sex outdoors on an exposed balcony like this was a first for me. Private beach or not, it had felt decidedly risqué, but I couldn't deny that I had loved every minute.

The grin on my face sobered slightly as I recalled his earlier emotional declarations. The way he'd dropped down onto one knee had nearly made my eyeballs burst from their sockets in shock. Did he really plan on proposing to me?

What the heck would my reply be?

Sucking my bottom lip into my mouth, I chewed on it as my stomach gave an excited tumble. The idea of being engaged to Sean was incredibly appealing, although we were still so early on in our relationship that I couldn't decide if it was too soon.

Sean had seemed to sense that now wasn't the right time either, so I supposed all I could do was wait and see what happened.

Rolling onto my side, I caught sight of his wallet and keys on the table beside me. They were partially blocking my view of the beautiful beach so I was reaching over to shift them when I spotted a glimpse of a photograph inside that looked like me.

Curiosity got the better of me, and although I knew I shouldn't snoop through his things I couldn't resist, and found my fingers removing not one but two tiny photographs and examining them before a gasp left my lips.

Sean

Walking back to Allie, I found her propped up on her elbow examining something intently. When she realised I was behind her she jumped and looked at me with a small frown between her eyebrows. Her face was still flushed from desire, so the frown looked decidedly out of place and caused me to immediately lower myself behind her in concern.

'Hey, what's up?'

'Where did you take these?' she asked, her voice low and confused as she handed me whatever it was she had been examining. I realised it was just the photographs from my wallet, and relaxed. My eyes scanned the images and a fond smile curled my lips; one showed the two of us looking loved up and flushed in my lounge, and the other was just of Allie. 'I love this one,' I murmured, soaking in the details of the photograph of Allie smiling in my kitchen back in England. These pictures were caught on my security cameras before we'd even got together, and this one in particular represented one of the first times I'd seen her beautiful smile in all its glory.

'But how did you get it?' she asked again, breaking my fond remembrances. 'I recognise that room … but I was alone that night. You weren't there with a camera.'

It was then that I realised my monumental mistake. I'd never told Allie about the security cameras in my house, and how they captured all our movements downstairs. Swallowing hard, I winced. Shit, she didn't know they'd also caught our downstairs sex sessions on tape either. *Double shit.*

Things could be about to get messy.

Blinking rapidly, I tried to think how I could get out of this, but nothing sprang to mind. Beside, we'd said no more secrets between us, so I quickly realised I was going to have to come clean. 'It's from the security footage,' I murmured, and when Allie immediately tensed I snapped my mouth shut, not daring to say any more.

'Security footage? Inside your house?' she murmured, swivelling on the lounger to face me and dragging up her dress from the floor to clutch it across her chest. What the fuck? I hated the fact that she was suddenly trying to cover herself.

'Who else sees that footage?' she demanded, her cheeks turning deep red in a flush that had nothing to do with our earlier love-making. Her words did, however, make sense of her sudden tenseness, and I quickly tried to reassure her.

'No one but me. The cameras were put in by my security team as a precaution, but no one views the footage, I swear.'

'Did they record us … when we … had sex in the lounge, and the kitchen?' My right eye twitched at her cold tone, but seeing as she was spot on the money I couldn't really argue.

'Yeah.'

Allie was silent for a second, her entire frame radiating tension and her eyes infuriatingly blank and unreadable. 'What if your house was broken into? Then your entire security team would get to pick through it for clues, wouldn't they?' Her agitation was visibly growing by the second. 'They could all watch us … us … *fucking* on your kitchen counter, Sean! I can't believe you didn't tell me.'

She was right. Fuck. A brief image of my security crew leering over the images of her popped into my head and my hands clenched at my sides.

The shit had really hit the fan, but even though I could see Allie was furious with me, and understand why, I couldn't think of one useful or consolatory thing to say.

'You've watched it back, haven't you?' she whispered suddenly, her eyes widening.

Busted. Now it was my turn to flush, and I felt my cheeks heating with guilt as I gave a shamed nod. I had watched it back. Multiple times. I'd also pleasured myself to the images, but I wouldn't tell her that.

'Oh my god,' she whispered, clutching the dress even tighter to her body. 'I can't believe you didn't tell me, Sean. This is really screwed up. Are there cameras here too?'

'No.' Wincing, I thought back to the email I'd received yesterday from my security team about the impending camera installation. 'Not yet, anyway. But if it bothers you I'll tell my team to call it off.' Drawing in a breath, I ran a hand tentatively up her thigh, hating the way her leg tensed from my touch.

'I'm so sorry, Allie. At first it didn't even occur to me, the cameras have been there so long that I forget about them. But then I remembered, and I wanted you so badly that I ...' Removing my hand from her leg I ran it through my hair as I remembered just how desperately I'd been trying to deny my attraction to her back then.

'I found myself watching you when you were cooking, or reading in the lounge.' Swallowing so loudly that I saw Allie flash me a look, I finished with my admission. 'And then we finally had sex, and you're so fucking sexy that I ... I just couldn't help watching it back.'

She looked devastated, her hands wringing the thin

fabric barely covering her. 'I've deleted it,' I blurted suddenly, hoping it would make this mess better, but almost immediately realised my lie. I had deleted our kitchen encounter and everything that came before it, but we'd had sex downstairs after that and I'd never got around to clearing the tapes again.

'Well, most of it,' I admitted sheepishly. 'I'll do the rest as soon I get back to the UK, I swear.'

Allie was silent, watching me intently for what seemed like forever, a completely unreadable expression on her face.

'No.' Her head shook, but her gaze wandered off across the balcony towards the sea.

No? What did she mean, no? Suddenly panicking that this was one mistake too far, I quickly sat up to try and plead my case. 'Allie, I swear ...' But she cut me off by turning her crystal clear gaze on me. 'No, don't delete it. I want to watch it.' She paused and ran her tongue slowly and seemingly deliberately along her lower lip.

If we weren't in the middle of an argument then I would have sworn that move was seductive, but we were arguing, so I must have been mistaken. Mustn't I?

'I want us to watch it together.' Her hand dropped the dress so it pooled on her lap, exposing her breasts again, and then her fingers trailed to my groin, giving a gentle fondle as a shy smile curved her lips. 'I want to watch you taking me.'

Ho-ly fuck-a-roo. There was no way I could mistake that, and my eyebrows jumped in surprise as my cock jerked its approval. Jesus, she wanted to watch the tapes of us fucking? The idea was so erotic that I struggled to draw in my next breath and had to flare my nostrils in an attempt at getting enough oxygen to my brain because so much blood was flooding to my groin.

'Am I forgiven?' I managed to murmur, but my intense arousal had caused my voice to turn gravelly and far from its usual confident tone.

'You are. I always knew you were a bit of a perv, this has just proved it.'

Standing up I scooped her into my arms with an agreeing hum. 'Undoubtedly, but I'm your perv. And now I'm going to take you to the shower and do unspeakably naughty things to you to help solidify that theory even further.'

And with that I strode towards the bathroom with Allie giggling in my arms as my mind plotted what I could do to her that would help me live up to my wicked promise.

Chapter Ten

Cait

It was now a week since I'd accepted the job at Dynamic, and I was still mildly in shock. I was now a real, genuine, visa-holding resident of LA … the city of dreams. Which was apt, seeing as it was pretty much my dream job. Not only would I earn a nice little pot of money to boost my flagging bank account, but on top of that I would get to spend more time with Allie in the beautiful LA weather.

Shaking my head in wonderment, a satisfied grin spread across my lips. Yep, all in all, things were pretty great at the moment.

Jason from Dynamic had been in touch this week with my start date (one week from today), a copy of my contract, and a list of social events run by the studios in case I was interested in joining any. He'd even highlighted the runners' club and a sculpture group in the list, and scribbled a note saying that after reading the hobby section of my CV he thought they might appeal. I was quite touched by his effort.

It seemed from the vast array of things listed that the studios' community were a friendly lot, because there was everything on there from fitness clubs and tapestry groups, right through to club nights and meals out.

Acting purely on impulse, I had woken up this morning and decided to make today the day I took the plunge and met some of the people I would be working with. So I was kitted out in my running gear and heading to the studio site where they held the weekly run around the back lots and wooded areas of the compound.

A morning jog was a habit for me now anyway, so combining it with a group of people with similar interests seemed a sensible way to make work friends.

After hopping off the hotel shuttle which stopped just down the road from the studios, I jogged towards the gate and showed them the ID card Jason had provided for me with my contract.

It still felt so surreal to have a job here that I half expected the security guard to laugh and send me packing, but after checking my card and getting me to sign in, he happily waved me through, and even gave me directions to where the running group met.

Rounding the corner of a large warehouse, I got my first glimpse of the runners I would be joining, and blimey, there were far more than I had expected. I'd thought maybe there would be ten or so, but there had to be at least thirty people standing around in running gear, stretching and chatting among themselves.

So many in fact, that I immediately stopped in my tracks and gave the elastic band around my wrist a quick, reassuring ping. I wasn't keen on crowds, especially not when they consisted of entirely new people, and I immediately felt nerves settle in my belly.

Just as I was considering turning for home and doing my usual solitary run, Jason appeared from within the Lycra-clad crowd, waved, and jogged to me, effectively removing any chance of leaving undetected.

'Cait, hi! I'm so glad you came! You can leave any water bottles or bags on these tables if you want.' He pointed to a row of picnic benches already littered with other people's belongings and I quickly left my water bottle and running jumper. Leading me back towards the runners, Jason explained that there were three distances I could choose from – five kilometres, eight kilometres, or a more challenging fifteen through the woods.

'The tracks are all marked with plastic discs on posts or trees, so keep an eye out and you shouldn't get lost. The five kilometre is marked with red, eight is blue, and fifteen is yellow.'

OK. That all sounded pretty straightforward. Jason then introduced me to two girls – Lisa and Mel – who also worked on *Dark Blood*, and I was glad that I'd have a few familiar faces to look out for next week.

Unfortunately, there was one other familiar face within the running crowd too. Someone I was trying desperately not to look at ever since I'd spotted him five minutes ago. Jack Felton. If I'd thought about it I could have guessed he might be here, because I already knew he shared my liking for running but I hadn't really considered the possibility that the actors would come to these social events too.

I was obviously wrong, because as well as Jack I had spotted a few other famous faces, including Christopher Shire, the tall, dark-haired actor who played the lead role in *Dark Blood*. He looked almost as pale and terrifying in real life as he did when fully made up for his role of a vampire, and I found myself quickly looking away from him as nervous tingles ran up my spine.

I'd spotted Jack almost immediately, as if he were somehow magnetic. Maybe he was, at least that might explain why I kept seeing him, thinking about him, and dreaming about him … my cheeks flushed crimson and I closed my eyes for a second and tried to calm my suddenly skittering pulse before giving him another glance. His head was dipped as he stretched out his side, causing his brown hair to flop over his brow, but he still managed to spot me, look briefly surprised, and then give me a casual nod of acknowledgement before turning his attention back to the guys he was warming up with.

I should have been relieved by his lukewarm reaction, but for some ridiculous reason it made me flinch, and my stomach bunched uncomfortably. I couldn't actually be feeling upset by his dismissive behaviour, could I?

Drawing in a long breath, I rolled my eyes at my stupid response and refused to look in his direction again. Unfortunately, knowing he was just a few feet away made it tricky, so I focused on the girls I was with and twisted myself around so my back was toward Jack as I began my own stretches. I supposed I couldn't blame him for his cooler treatment, not after the way I'd practically blanked him when I'd last seen him at the studios.

Luckily, Lisa and Mel were very laid back and really chatty – just my type of people – and their excited talk about working at the studios eventually distracted me from my muddled thoughts.

As the group set off, the three of us decided to run together, but by the time we reached the four kilometre mark, Lisa was starting to struggle, and admitted that she was quite new to running and only just building up to the five kilometre track. So at the next marker where the fifteen kilometre track split off to the right, I bid the two of them goodbye and decided to head off on my own for the challenge of the longer loop.

'Meet back where we set off, there's always some juice and fruit while we stretch off. Good luck with the hill!' Mel called, giving me a wave.

Waving goodbye I followed the yellow marker, but had to laugh as I immediately saw the girls slow to a walk now I was gone. Smiling to myself, I felt quite happy about my new colleagues, and potential friends, and definitely had a spring in my step as I began the ascent up the wooded path.

The path quickly became significantly steeper, but it was far cooler thanks to the shade from the trees. The only problem with this route was that it had now turned thickly forested and I occasionally freaked myself out when running in woods. I say occasionally, but really I mean fairly often. They were inherently beautiful, but I always found something a little sinister in the shadows and dappled shade.

If I allowed my mind to wander, which I often did, I would find myself looking through the trees, squinting until I had convinced myself that I'd seen someone lurking. Of course there was never anyone there, it was just the result of my remaining jumpiness over Greg, which was definitely heightened this week after finding out about his recent postcard.

Shivering slightly, I looked around, but all the other runners had dispersed. Even Jack's yellow vest had disappeared over the next ridge a while ago. Swallowing hard, I picked up my pace, reassuring myself that I was fine.

I was about forty minutes into my run and getting up a nice, comfortable rhythm when I thought I saw a flash of something in the trees to my right. That area was way too densely wooded to be part of the running track. God, that really had looked like something real moving between the thick undergrowth.

Or *someone.*

Had it? Was my overactive imagination playing tricks

on me again? The trees were particularly thick over there so I couldn't see if someone was lurking without stopping to look properly, which I was definitely not about to do.

Chewing my lip, I increased my pace, determined to make the next ridge and hopefully be able to see some of the other runners on the other side. With my defences on high alert, I was now running at full pelt, so when I trod on my own loose shoelace I very nearly went sprawling face first into the gravel. Thankfully, a few long legged strides and some hectic arm flailing later, I'd managed to skid to a halt by a large, gnarly tree and bend to quickly tie my lace.

With my pulse now spiking from the shock of the near fall, not to mention my jumpiness, it was no surprise that I let out a loud, very girly shriek when I stood up and saw someone jogging briskly toward me.

Backtracking a couple of steps, I tried to assess if the man in the distance was a threat or not, and in my over-wrought state it took my panicked brain a couple of seconds to chill out and realise that it was Jack and his hi-vis vest coming toward me.

I was at once both relieved and panicked. Intrinsically, I just knew he wouldn't hurt me. I didn't know how I could be so sure, but I was, but still, meeting him again wasn't exactly ideal considering how much of a response he seemed to cause in me.

The temptation to drop into a commando roll so I could disappear behind a large bush was almost overwhelming, but he had clearly already seen me. I would look utterly ridiculous. Mind you, I usually felt utterly ridiculous around Jack, so it wouldn't be much different from the norm.

This bloody man and his sodding handsomeness had been randomly popping into my thoughts more and more recently, which was not something I was particularly thrilled with. Add into that his rather annoying habit of being everywhere that I was – park, theatre, gallery, studios, and now running club – it was all getting a bit overwhelming.

Jack jogged to my side and stopped before lifting his sunglasses onto the top of his head and wiping the sweat from his unfairly handsome face.

'I noticed you'd fallen back a bit so I thought I'd check you were OK.' His words were rather thoughtful, and thankfully he didn't comment on the way I'd blanked him so rudely last time we'd met. I almost felt myself soften a little, until he added one final sentence. 'Did the hill get the better of you?'

He had said it with a smile, but I found myself rather put out by his implication that I wasn't fit enough to make the hill, and I frowned and crossed my arms as my already heightened defences rose even more, but for altogether different reasons.

'No. My shoelace came undone.' And I nearly fell arse over tit when I accidentally stood on it. But I didn't add that bit. Thank God I hadn't fallen over, otherwise Jack would have come across the ridge and seen me rolling around on the floor for the second time in our brief acquaintance.

His eyebrows rose at my abrupt tone and I had to make a conscious effort to draw in my behaviour. He was only trying to be nice and here I was about to give him a hard time again.

Why on earth did I get so defensive around him? A small niggle at the back of my brain chipped in with the helpful thought that it was because I was trying to deny how much I liked him. I had to swallow hard several times not to panic about it. That was *not* what this was about.

As I looked again at his sweaty face and mud-flecked legs, I sighed. OK, so maybe that was exactly what this was about. The sweat and dirt didn't make a hoot of a difference either, he still looked gorgeous.

'So, first I saw you at the studios last week, and now you're here for the team run, can I assume you've got a job here?'

I nodded stiffly. 'Uh, yeah, well … I got offered one.' I don't know why the partial truth slipped out, but I just wasn't ready for Jack to know that I had agreed to the job in the studio … not yet, anyway. Although my presence here must surely make it pretty bloody obvious and I winced as I watched his eyes narrow. I was such an idiot. Well, I certainly was where this man was concerned.

I bent forwards to re-tie my other lace, using it as an excuse to try and avoid eye contact with him. It was absurd to feel so unbelievably attracted to someone you had only met a few times, but as much as I might want to deny it, I did, and that realisation terrified me.

'Wow. Congratulations. Did you accept it?'

Shit, shit, shit. As I floundered for an answer he magically supplied me with one. 'Or have you not decided yet? I saw you talking to Jason, is he set on persuading you?'

'Uh … yeah, something like that.' What the heck was wrong with me? I never lied, and now that was two in less than a minute.

'What's holding you back?' he enquired casually. Lifting one arm, Jack began stretching off his triceps by bending one arm over his shoulder and pushing down on the elbow. The movement caused me to peer up from my stooped position and check out the way his running top pulled tight across his chest. Really tight. The previously loose cotton was now taut, highlighting each and every muscle – of which there were plenty – and I found that breathing became even more difficult than before.

Something utterly bizarre happened whenever I saw Jack. It was like the air around me thickened, making it harder to draw in breath, and seeming to urge my body to get closer to him as if he could somehow make it all better. I managed to avoid the urge, and joined him in a calf stretch to allow me to stare at the ground, and not his warm brown eyes or mighty fine physique.

Jack finished stretching and rested his hands on his hips, and suddenly I became incredibly aware of the shadow he was casting as he loomed over me. Standing up as quickly as I could, I tried to appear unaffected by his proximity, but there was no denying that I suddenly felt nervous with him this close.

'I … uh … I'm thinking I might just head on with my travelling.' Where that load of rubbish came from I had no idea. Now I'd started telling fibs I couldn't seem to be able to stop, and actually had to snap my teeth shut to prevent more from escaping.

He gave me another narrow-eyed look, as if he somehow knew I was telling a lie, but that was ridiculous. Of course he couldn't know. To fill the tense silence that suddenly hung between us I gave an awkward shrug and kicked at some leaves by my feet.

I knew I couldn't avoid eye contact forever, but as I raised my gaze I found Jack observing me intently with a peculiar look in his brown eyes that I couldn't read. It looked like a combination of curiosity, hope, and challenge, but I just couldn't be sure.

'You should definitely stay,' he stated decisively, and before I had any chance to reply, he closed the small space between the two of us, his body almost caging in around me, before suddenly swooping his head down and pressing his mouth to mine. So that was what the look had meant, it was his *I'm-about-to–kiss-you* expression.

Oh. My. God.

The first thing that hit me was just how soft his lips were, but somehow firm and demanding against mine, and I felt my entire body … melt.

To my complete surprise I didn't tense, or freak out, or panic at all. In fact, it was so confusing for me not to feel repelled by a man's presence in my personal space that for a few seconds I completely forgot to join in with the kiss and simply stood there in shock.

Holy shit. I was blindsided by his unexpected advance, but as I focused on his warm lips pressing keenly against mine and his tongue running along the seam of my mouth, sense gave way to physical instinct and I found myself parting my lips as I surrendered to the moment that had been the focus of my dreams several times since our near kiss in the bar.

My mind was spiralling out of control as Jack gave a small moan and slid his tongue between my lips and into my mouth. He began moving it slowly and carefully as if he were scared I might startle and run away, which I probably should have done, but didn't. Instead I noticed that he tasted fresh and minty, like he'd recently eaten a chewing gum or brushed his teeth.

I greedily soaked up the sensations – his taste, the pressure of his lips, the feel of his tongue – and then, before I knew it I was exploring his mouth with my own tentative licks and flicks. I'd forgotten how amazing it could feel to be kissed. Really kissed. And it was flipping incredible.

Jack Felton is kissing me.

The thought registered through a mixed fog of emotions swirling in my brain. Even with me in my sweaty running gear, Jack Felton, Hollywood star and total heartthrob, was … kissing me. What was still completely shocking was that I was kissing him back, *and* enjoying it. In fact, it felt so bloody good that I couldn't help but reach forward, clutch at his damp T-shirt, and pull him closer.

His response was instant as he gathered me within the circle of his arms and deepened the kiss, sending my mind and body whirling out of control and into a dizzying fluster of hormones.

I may have had some serious issues with men in the past, but even with my hang ups there was no doubt that I was unashamedly enjoying myself. In fact, this was probably the most fantastic moment of my entire life.

But like a moaning old misery guts, my protective conscience began to kick in and loudly argue the negatives of what I was doing. For a few moments my deeply hidden risk-taking side had won out and I had thrown caution to the wind, but now my level-headed, defensive side was caught in a battle of wills, desperately trying to overpower my little devil and make me see sense.

The spiralling thoughts began to make me feel decidedly dizzy. Or perhaps that was just the effect Jack's skilful tongue had upon me, I wasn't sure. What I was fast becoming aware of though, was just how good Jack was at this, and that in turn triggered another thought to root in my brain – this man was way too experienced for me. A man like Jack would never want to deal with me and my baggage.

Bloody bugger it.

I cursed my sensible side, but deep down I knew it was right. Regardless of how much I was enjoying his kiss, I knew I wouldn't be ready for anything more for a very long time. A terrified, practically frigid girlfriend was hardly a tempting proposition for someone like him, was it?

I was torn by these emotions, but knew I couldn't let this continue any longer, so I forced myself to step back, breaking our lips apart by decisively placing my hands on his firm chest and pushing myself away from him with a gasping breath.

The next moment Jack's delicious warmth was completely removed from my personal space as he threw himself away from me with a loud curse.

'Fuck!' His hands shot to his hair and tugged as he stared at me wide-eyed, blinking rapidly and chewing on his lower lip. 'I'm so sorry, Caitlin. I totally forgot myself. Fuck!' He looked wild, repentant, but somehow furious all at the same time and I hastily took a step back in case that anger was directed at me.

'Ouch!' Light-headed from the intensity of our kiss I hadn't realised how close we were standing to a tree, and in my effort to separate myself from Jack I had managed to back straight into it, sharply banging the back of my head on a rough, lumpy branch.

I still hadn't recovered my composure and as a result I felt all floppy and uncoordinated, but before I could even raise my arm to check on my head, Jack reached out a hand and slid it into my hair, gently soothing my pain with soft circles.

'There's no cut. But you might get a bruise,' he murmured quietly.

'I … I can do that …' I stammered, as the effect of his touch began to sizzle through my system again, making my body even more useless than before.

'It was my fault. Let me,' he coaxed softly as his thumb

began rubbing a mesmerising pattern on the back on my head. Oh God. Oh God. Oh God. A full-on meltdown was approaching, I was sure of it. I tensed every muscle in my body in an attempt at maintaining my control, but it was no good. I needed to ground myself, so I plucked at my elastic band. Hard. Hard enough to make both myself and Jack wince.

Marginally more focused, I noted that apart from his outstretched arm, Jack was now being careful to maintain his distance. Irritatingly, his caring response wasn't helping to harden my resolve one little bit, because that kiss had been incredible, and I wanted to experience more of it.

I barely knew him, but no man had ever made me feel as safe and protected as Jack did. Which, given my history, seemed an utterly crazy thought to consider, but it was true. Unfortunately, the counter of that feeling of protection was an immense sensation of vulnerability that came with it and was currently flooding my system. Talk about contradicting emotions.

I didn't let men in, that wasn't something I did.

I was independent, me and my secrets against the world. But yet, Jack almost made me want to try. He made me feel like I could conquer my fears and step beyond my self-enforced barriers one minute, but have my heart crushed like a fragile autumnal leaf the next.

The opposing feelings were confusing me to the point where I felt nauseous, a sensation only furthered by the heat now filling my body, and the light throbbing of the bruise on my head. Was it throbbing because of a forming bruise, or because Jack was touching me?

Bugger it. Here we go again on Cait's roundabout of confusion.

There was no denying one thing though – the heat I

could feel zinging around my body like fireworks and settling low in my belly was definitely lust. Lust and desire for this man standing before me. After years of celibacy it was a relatively alien sensation, but I'd felt it in his presence enough times now to be able to accurately identify it.

Without thinking, I raised a hand to my mouth and gently touched my lips with trembling fingers. They felt tender from his kiss and I instinctively ran my tongue over them, still able to taste him there. Raising my eyes, I saw that Jack had watched this move curiously, but stayed quiet, his eyes intense and seeming to burn holes into me, asking questions I wasn't equipped to deal with.

'I … can't do this, Jack … I'm sorry.' I was well aware that that was twice now I'd used that line and given no further explanation, but I just couldn't. Now that I had some space between us again, my clarity was returning and I felt a sudden need to protect myself and get away from here. If I could have got away with burrowing into the ground and rolling up into the foetal position, I would have.

Jack, however, wasn't giving up so easily. His hand was still gently massaging my head and sending shivers of pleasure through my scalp, and it was obvious from his expression that he had more to say on the matter.

'You feel it too, the connection between us. I could tell from your response,' Jack murmured, his hand still on my scalp and still driving me insane.

Not wanting to admit anything, I lowered my eyes and shook my head, causing Jack to let out a long, frustrated sigh.

'Tell me why you're so skittish, Caitlin, please … is it just me? Or men in general? Someone hurt you, didn't they?'

Shock exploded in my system and my head jerked up. Blinking several times, I stared at him, almost unable to comprehend just how disturbingly accurate his observations were. Was I that obvious? That much of a freak?

The truth stung and caused my defences to shoot back into place, making me lurch my head away from his hand. Frowning, I completely ignored his question and instead blurted out a lame excuse to get away from him.

'I'm sure in your position you're always surrounded by female fans who are more than happy for you to kiss them … or sleep with them, or whatever …' I blushed at my flustered words, '… but I'm not that kind of girl. I won't be another notch on your bedpost.' Where the heck those words had come from I had no idea, and I hastily dropped my gaze, hating my spiteful tongue.

Admittedly, I was also avoiding his gaze for another reason. I was incredibly worried that if I looked at him any longer, my irrational and near desperate desire to kiss him again might overwhelm my good intentions and I'd end up ignoring the consequences and stepping into his arms.

No. *No.* I couldn't do that. I was completely unprepared for a physical relationship, and no matter how tempting Jack might make that prospect seem, I knew I would panic as soon as he tried to take things to the next level. I just wasn't ready for the embarrassment of that yet.

Grimacing at my own weaknesses, I turned to walk away, but Jack stepped with me, effectively trapping me by the large tree, but without actually placing his hands on me.

'Hold on just a minute,' he retorted hotly, his angry tone causing my eyes to fly open. Flinching at the sparking anger in his stare, I tried to take a step back and instantly bumped into the stupid tree again. Damn my bloody clumsiness. My head would be like a bruised plum at this rate.

'Don't turn whatever issues you have with men around on to me, Caitlin,' he growled, losing patience with me. 'I never should have forced that kiss on you, but you don't get to throw wildly untrue accusations at me.' He must have seen the concern in my eyes because Jack flinched slightly and stepped back to give me more space. He might not have been touching me, but I still felt well and truly pinned by his ferocious gaze.

I now had the space to sidestep him and leave, but for some reason I felt strangely compelled to listen to his explanations. 'Firstly, I don't make a habit of kissing fans. In fact, you're the closest thing to a "fan" that I've ever kissed, and I've been acting since I was sixteen.' He paused, stubbornly crossing his arms. 'Secondly, if I sleep with someone it is done with consideration and the utmost discretion, and not to gain another conquest or imaginary notch on my bedpost, as you seem to be implying.' By this point his face was flushing with angry pride, his body was bristling, and his eyes were fierce with pupils like little black bullets.

In short, he looked utterly magnificent but completely terrifying.

I gulped nervously. It seemed that my attempt at pushing him away had well and truly backfired. Unperturbed by my nervous silence, Jack continued with his rant, his arms now opening and flapping expressively as his brows drew together defensively. 'On top of that, I'm immensely proud of the fact that the number of lovers I've had is in single digits, thank you very much. I'm not some serial seducer or sexual predator like you seem to be making me out to be.'

Ignoring Jack's claim about his good behaviour, my entire being had focused in on two of his words.

Sexual predator.

That was what Greg had turned out to be. A shudder ran through my entire body and the intensity very nearly had me collapsing to my knees. That was the trigger I needed to get me out of here, and I held up a hand to interrupt him. If I'd let him go on much more there was quite a chance that his little speech might have won me over, but his accidental reminder of my past had brought me back to reality with a thump like a sumo wrestler taking a tumble.

'I jumped to some wrong conclusions about you, and I apologise, but the fact is … I'm not interested.' I knew my voice was weaker than I wanted as I made the false declaration, but I pushed my shoulders back and sidestepped out of his reach. 'I'm leaving now. Please don't follow me.'

Turning quickly on my heel, I jogged away from Jack and his beautifully seductive eyes before I could change my mind and do something stupid, like fling myself into his arms, consequence be damned.

I knew I'd made the right choice. Continuing that kiss would have led me down a slippery path towards things that I was in no way ready for, but that didn't stop me replaying every glorious detail over and over in my mind as I ran away from him.

Chapter Eleven

Jack

As soon as the pale pink of Caitlin's running top had fully disappeared into the distance, I spun on the spot and swiped at the closest tree in aggravation. A low, frustrated snarl grumbled in my chest as I repeated the smack and then grimaced. The roughness of the bark stabbed at my palm, sending small, shooting pains tingling up my arm, but it was no less than I deserved.

What the hell had I been thinking, pouncing on her like that? For fuck's sake, I was such a bloody idiot.

Panting like I'd run a marathon, I examined the blood on my palm with a scowl and rested my forehead on the tree while I tried to recover my wits. What the hell had happened to my plan of taking it slow?

I knew Caitlin was shy around men, nervous, even. I knew how she shied away from contact, I knew she had told me she didn't date, and I knew I had to tread carefully, but had that stopped me? I'd let my libido and ridiculous fixation with her overrule me for a crazy minute, smashed my lips to hers, and practically dry-humped her like a randy dog.

Closing my eyes, I let out a long groan. Jesus. If she ever spoke to me again it would be a bloody miracle.

I was usually so cool, calm, and collected in every

aspect of my life. I'd even been nicknamed Ice back in my Territorial Army days because of my chilled demeanour. Nothing ruffled or provoked me. Nothing. I had certainly never been wound up enough to punch a tree before, that was for sure. But Caitlin affected me almost beyond my comprehension.

I shook my head and stared upwards through the leafy canopy to the bright blue sky. God, I wanted her so badly. The fact that I'd now had a brief taste of her and felt the way she had responded to me – because I was positive that she had responded and enjoyed that kiss for a few moments – my desire for her was even stronger. She'd clutched at my shirt and pulled me closer, so I knew she wanted me just as much as I wanted her, but she was still holding back.

Blowing out a breath, I ran a hand through my sweaty hair. Interestingly, she'd also lied to me, which gave me further hope that she might be just as affected by me as I was by her. Why else would she tell me she hadn't accepted the Dynamic job when I knew full well from Jason that she'd already said yes?

Caitlin clearly had issues with intimacy, or men, or both, which definitely made me suspect that something had occurred in her past to make her wary. But I would prove that I was trustworthy, and I would pursue her, even if it was just in the name of building a friendship between us. Friends would be better than nothing, and seeing as she utterly fascinated me, I wanted to get to know her more. I needed to. I also wanted to erase the look of timid concern that always seemed to linger in her eyes. The thought that she might genuinely fear me was one I simply couldn't live with. I wanted her to look at me with trust, and if that meant being just friends, then that's what I'd do.

Pulling out my phone from the pocket of my running shorts, I skimmed through the contacts until I found the one I needed. This guy owed me a favour, and I just hoped that he was willing to bend the rules a bit to repay me.

'Ben? Hi, it's Jack. Listen, I need a favour. Can you get me someone's mobile number if I have their full name?'

Chapter Twelve

Sean

'SEAN?'

Wincing as the deep voice bellowed my name, I inadvertently jumped and slopped the coffee I'd been pouring. Grumbling irritably, I looked down at my almost empty mug and the pool of coffee now surrounding it on the counter. For fuck's sake. I was tired after the long day yesterday, had already been on set for six hours today, and now I finally had ten minutes to grab a coffee, my director was yelling my name.

Shaking my head, I mopped up the spillage and reluctantly replaced the coffee pot into the machine. I was in the green room – the room beside the set where the actors and crew could go between shoots to relax and grab some refreshments – but apparently I wasn't going to be allowed my break today.

Mike, one of the sound crew, was with me and cast me a wide-eyed look as Finlay continued screeching for me from somewhere on set. 'Sean? Where the fuck are you?'

Attempting to hide the way he flinched at Finlay's yelling, Mike opened up his sandwich packet and shook his head supportively. 'That does not sound good, dude,' he murmured, before returning to his lunch and book, as if hoping to hide in the pages and avoid the wrath of our director.

No, it didn't sound good, but I couldn't for the life of me think why Finlay was going ballistic. The morning's shoots had run smoothly, and he'd actually seemed in a relatively good mood today – relative to his usual tense, impatient mood, that was. Sighing heavily, I swigged down the coffee that had made it into my mug and headed for the door.

Being famous, and the star of the show, didn't earn me any graces with my director. If Finlay had a bone to pick with me he didn't make any allowances for my fame, and was more than happy to bollock me in front of all and sundry if the mood took him.

Making my way along the short corridor that joined the green room with the set area, I practically ran into Finlay as he strode around the corner and shot a fierce glare in my direction.

'What did I tell you about crap like this?' he roared, thrusting a newspaper at me so hard that it rammed into my chest and knocked me backwards a step.

Recovering my balance, I took the paper and looked to see what he was getting so irate over. On page six were two photographs – admittedly blurry – of Allie and me, followed by a clearer one of me and Savannah, and then the headline, 'Who is Sean Phillip's new mystery woman?'

Regardless of how fuming Finlay was, I couldn't help but smile as I looked again at the picture of Allie and me leaning on a rail, looking decidedly affectionate. It was taken from a distance, far enough away that her face wasn't recognisable, but her blonde hair certainly stood out, making it obvious she wasn't Savannah.

'Wipe that fucking smug grin off your face, Sean, you're on seriously thin ice.'

My smile did fade, not because Finlay had demanded it,

but because I suddenly realised when one of those pictures must have been shot … or more precisely, where. It was obviously from yesterday when we were standing on my balcony. The same balcony that supposedly gave complete seclusion away from prying eyes.

Thank fuck these particular prying eyes hadn't been around an hour or two earlier and seen the seriously hot balcony sex that we had partaken in too. Jeez. Allie would have gone mental if pictures like that had appeared in the papers, and I would probably have been incarcerated for murdering anyone and everyone who dared to look at them.

I would certainly be having words with the apartment supervisor, that was for sure. If I was paying through the nose for complete privacy then I damn well wanted to be getting that complete privacy.

Looking back to Finlay, I saw his anger hadn't dispersed at all. 'We had a deal, Sean. You were supposed to keep her secret until after the season premiere.' His use of 'her' really niggled me and I found myself crossing my arms and matching his frown with one of my own.

'*Her* name is Allie, and we were being careful. I don't know how someone got those pictures, the beach is supposed to be private.'

'It obviously isn't fucking private, is it? What about this one, are you going to try using the same excuse?' The other photograph was from a few days ago, when I'd taken Allie to meet Savannah. It was taken through the window glass of my Jeep, so it was blurry and unfocused. I could make out Allie's cap and blonde hair, but because she had practically slithered down into the footwell, her face wasn't clear. Neither picture gave away her identity, which was a relief, but that clearly wasn't what Finlay was getting himself so wound up about.

As he continued to yell, I dropped my gaze and skimmed through the article. It summarised my 'engagement' with Savannah, and went on to speculate that perhaps there was a rift growing between us because I'd been spotted with the mystery blonde twice in a week. I could see why Finlay was pissed off, but I began to formulate a plan as I finished reading the last line, which said, 'So, is there already trouble in paradise for Sean and Savannah's new engagement? We'll keep you posted on any new developments.'

Braving my director's fearsome glare, I calmly folded the paper and held it out to him, where he snatched it from my hand and tossed it onto a nearby table before crossing his arms.

'Look, Finlay, this could actually be a really good thing.'

Cutting me off, he waved his hands in the air as his eyes boggled further. 'How exactly do you figure that, Sean? Enlighten me.'

Shrugging, I indicated the paper. 'Well, it's getting us, and the show, increased publicity.' I was careful to emphasise my mention of the show, because apparently that was all that Finlay was focusing on at the moment. 'Besides, we had already agreed to tell the public that Savannah and I had broken up eventually, so this will merely support that.'

Seeing his shoulders relax slightly as he processed my words, I decided to capitalise on his silence. 'We should have thought of this earlier, really, because I bet the journos will be going crazy for the story now. Which will bring the show into the spotlight even more than usual.'

Lifting a hand to rub thoughtfully at his chin, Finlay narrowed his eyes and nodded. 'I hadn't thought of it that way … perhaps you're right.' Nodding several times, Finlay then hit me with a firm look. 'Make sure you and Savannah get snapped together this week at some point, I want you both looking tense and irritable as if you're having a lovers' tiff. Play it up for the cameras, Sean, and I'll let your carelessness go this time.'

Look tense? After the stunt Savannah had pulled by telling Allie I had slept with her, looking irritable shouldn't be too difficult. Not that I mentioned that, of course. 'OK, no problem. I'll no doubt be made out in the papers as the cheating bad boy again, but that's fine. As long as I eventually get to have Allie by my side, I don't care.'

Finlay gave my overly romantic comment a marginally derisive look and rolled his eyes before stalking off. He obviously wasn't a fan of romance, which probably explained his four messy divorces in the last ten years.

Just as I turned back in the direction of the green room intent of finally snagging something to eat and drink, Finlay loudly clapped his hands behind me. 'Right, you lot, break's over. Everyone back on set.'

With a long, drawn-out sigh, I spun on my heel and followed his command like a dog going to heel. It looked like it was going to be one of those days.

Chapter Thirteen

Cait

Cutting my run short, I had taken the quickest route back to the main gates, skipped the post-run social, and headed straight back to the hotel. By the time I arrived back I had slipped so deeply into shock that I could barely see straight and ended up walking into reception, instead of heading to the bungalow. Apparently, being kissed by a movie star out of the blue could do that to you.

I came to a standstill when I finally registered the plush carpet beneath my feet and the soft hum of conversation. Huh. Blinking several times, I looked around and realised just how fancy it was here: soft rugs, luxurious sofas, elaborate flower displays and … me. There was a large mirrored wall directly opposite, allowing me to get a full look at the state of myself. Ugh – damp hair, red neck, sweaty running gear, and a pale white face, presumably from my shock.

Oh, and not to forget my muddy trainers. Not exactly five-star attire to match a place as swanky as this. Oops.

I needed some quiet time to recover my shattered composure, but my legs were so shaky that they weren't up to the walk through the tropical hotel grounds just yet. Glancing around, I saw a quiet area to the left of the doors and practically crawled there in relief. Here, there were seemingly hundreds of exotic pot plants, but thankfully, no other guests.

Gosh, I was practically in full meltdown mode. And I mean properly on the verge of a complete brain and body malfunction. To be honest, it was a miracle I was still managing to stand upright.

Once I was immersed in the calmness of my pot planted sanctuary, my brain began to compute all that had occurred, and came up with a lovely, succinct five-word summary – Jack Felton had kissed me.

Ho-ly shit.

I still could not believe that had just happened. Pulling in a full, deep breath for the first time since the run-in with Jack (if being kissed half senseless could be called a run-in …) I wheezed out and clung to the wall behind me as if it were the only thing holding me up. Which at this exact moment, it was.

Jack Felton had kissed me. Really kissed me – with tongues, rushed breaths, pounding heartbeats, wandering hands and … everything. A huge, long sigh fluttered from my lips as they tingled from the memory. I closed my eyes as my tongue hesitantly licked my lips for any remaining traces of Jack, and found my index finger frantically plucking the elastic band on my wrist until it began to sting again.

Raising my arm to examine the damaged, reddened flesh, I bit my lip guiltily. My trauma wasn't helped by the fact that I could still taste him on my mouth. That fresh, minty, almost sweet taste that had engulfed me was back and enflaming my memories until I felt well and truly light-headed. I tried to dredge up a vague remnant of anger at his actions, but I couldn't even manage to get a shred of annoyance. As much as I wanted to deny it, I had enjoyed his kiss.

Really enjoyed it.

What a mess. I seriously needed to get my head on straight before I started work and had to see him again.

I had just about summed up the energy to go and have a shower when I felt my phone vibrate in the pocket of my running shorts. Seeing Allie's name flash up on the screen, I took a deep breath and considered one important question – should I tell her about my kiss with Jack? My amazing, soul shaking, toe-curlingly good kiss with Jack?

'Hi … Allie.' I was breathless again. Crap, just thinking about his kisses winded me.

'Hi, Cait. Wait, you sound all breathless and weird.'

'Yeah? I've … uh … I've been running.'

'You run all the time and you've never sounded this strange afterwards. Are you OK?' Great, so apparently one kiss from Jack had caused me to look awful and sound odd. Awesome. No wonder I'd avoided having a boyfriend. If only that were the only reason for my single status, I thought sourly, briefly recalling Greg again before resolutely shoving his evil face from my mind.

'Um. Kinda. Maybe. Not entirely,' I mumbled, rolling my eyes at how flipping ridiculous I sounded. I needed to get a grip. Actually, I needed to unload these feelings onto Allie and get her opinion, but I'd rather do it in person.

'Right. That makes no sense at all, Cait,' Allie replied in a perplexed tone that was so apparent I could practically see the frown on her face in my mind's eye. 'I was just calling to say I'm running a little late for our shopping trip.' My heart fell. I desperately needed to speak to Allie, like right now. If she cancelled on me my brain would probably explode from the strain. 'I shouldn't be too much longer, back in about twenty minutes, hopefully.'

Feeling my shoulders slump in relief, I actually found

myself nodding, even though she wouldn't be able to see it. 'Twenty minutes is perfect.' The idea of unburdening all of this Jack craziness onto Allie was infinitely reassuring, and after disconnecting the call I rushed on wobbly legs through the grounds to shower and change.

Twenty minutes didn't buy me enough time to get my hair dried after my shower, but at least it was washed clean of sweat by the time I saw Allie jogging up the porch steps. Bursting through the bungalow door, she chucked her bag on the sofa and spun around on the spot. 'Cait! I'm so excited about shopping! Where shall we start …' but her words faded off as soon as she stopped her giddy spinning and clocked me by the bar.

Prowling forwards until she was just in front of me, she propped her hands on her hips and examined me with a narrow-eyed expression that made me feel incredibly self-conscious.

'You're really pale. You look like you've seen a ghost.'

Looking at Allie's expression I knew I must look bad, so I bought myself a last few seconds' reprieve by handing her one of the cups of tea I'd just finished making and wandered to the sofa. Settling beside me, Allie tucked her legs under her so she was basically crossed-legged but facing me, with a curious expression lingering on her face.

Blowing steam from her mug, she took a sip and tilted her head to the side. 'So, missus. You said you'd been running when I spoke to you earlier, but you sounded really weird. What's happened?'

Knowing my friend's innate ability to detect a lie a mile off, I knew I wouldn't be able to get away with anything but the truth, so I steeled myself for a confession. Avoiding her gaze for a second or two longer, I swilled my tea around my mug before finally lifting my head and meeting her inquisitive eyes. Pulling in a deep breath, I slowly released it through my lips with a low whistling noise and then gave her the gossip. 'Jack Felton. I bumped into him again.'

At this news, Allie looked partly surprised, a little bit excited, and a whole lot concerned. 'Ah. Him again. Now it makes sense. Are you OK?'

'Yes,' I replied with a firm nod, which was true, because physically I was fine. It was emotionally I was totally screwed up.

Examining me for a second or two, Allie looked distinctly unconvinced. 'Then why don't you sound OK? Because I've known you for a long time, and believe me, you do not sound OK.'

Flopping back on the sofa, I sucked in a long breath and tried to decide how to word the full version of the story. Seeing how Allie knew the history of why I hadn't dated for so long this was going to be a fairly big bombshell for her.

It was a pretty flipping big bombshell for me.

Staring at the ceiling, I almost laughed hysterically from the craziness of it all. 'Because … because he …' *kissed me and I loved it.* Damn it. I grimaced, finding myself unable to say it out loud. '… Because he's handsome and confident, and it affects me and he knows it, and it's really annoying,' I said, chickening out at the very last minute.

'A little confidence can be attractive though, no?' Allie replied democratically, a statement I chose to ignore, because annoyingly it was true – his calm confidence was attractive. It made me feel safe, even though I barely knew the man. 'I don't really get the egotistical vibe from Jack, confident, yes, but not overtly so. But then I barely know him, so I guess you'd know better than me.'

‘He kissed me,’ I suddenly blurted, losing all control of my tongue. ‘And I kissed him back.’ Apparently my mouth was now running wild. I was so stunned at my own words that I slopped tea over my jeans and cursed under my breath as I frantically tried to rub it off. Once I’d prevented my knee from being scalded, I looked up to find Allie watching me with her jaw hanging open wide enough to catch an entire swarm of flies.

‘Bloody hell, Cait. This is huge.’ That was not the response I had needed, and my heart immediately attempted to leap up my throat and make a break for freedom. Seeing my distress at her excitement, Allie winced and visibly wound her composure in, calming her restless shifting, and neutralising the astounded expression on her face to something that now made her look almost constipated.

My hand was trembling so much that she leant over and gently removed my mug, placed it on the table along with hers, and took my soggy hand supportively.

‘Sorry, I was exaggerating, it’s not huge at all. It’s a, uh … a small, insignificant event. Nothing more than a bump in the road, a mere blip …’

She was flustered, which in turn was making me flustered, and I huffed out a short, grumpy breath, wishing that my usually calm friend could find the composure we both needed. Interrupting her, I gave a pleading look. ‘Allie, you’re not helping.’

‘OK. Sorry.’ A flush reddened her cheeks, but I could see from Allie’s fidgeting that she was just bursting for more information. ‘So was it good?’ My eyebrows jumped towards my hairline. I’d expected support or consolation, but I hadn’t expected that particular question at all.

My mind was screaming, yes, yes, yes! But somehow, I remained silent and calm. Outwardly, at least. Internally, I was a mess of jumbled hormones and combating emotions. Allowing myself a brief flashback to Jack's kiss, I felt my pulse begin to race again as heat crawled up my neck. It had been so much more than 'good'. Amazing didn't cut it, either. In fact, I struggled to think of one adjective which could suitably describe it, one word just wasn't enough. It had been an out of this world, pulse-raising, skin-tingling, wobbly-kneed, bone-meltingly fantastic kiss.

But of course, I didn't actually say that, because I was Cait, the frigid freak, and as a result had this huge wall of deniability and hesitation surrounding me. A heavy sigh escaped my lungs as I wondered if I would ever manage to escape my past.

Somehow, I must have given myself away, because I hadn't even answered Allie when her mouth pursed and she let out a long, low, whistle. 'Wow, that good, huh?' Frowning, I was about to deny her remark when she reached across and tapped my cheek with the cool pad of her index finger as a knowing smile lurked on her lips.

'You're blushing like a ripe tomato. Kinda gives the game away, babe.' Stupid traitorous body. I felt almost dismayed by the uncontrollable reaction I kept having to Jack flipping Felton. I'd done so well avoiding men up to now that suddenly having to deal with this huge quantity of emotion in one go just wasn't fair.

Sighing heavily, I chewed on my bottom lip, and after a long silence I gave Allie an edgy half smile. 'OK, it was good,' I admitted reluctantly. 'But don't go getting your hopes up, I don't plan on following it up or doing anything about it.'

There was a long silence as I watched the hope drain from Allie's face until she shrugged, seeming to shake off her disappointment, and approached the whole subject from a different view point. 'Well, regardless, I need a full account, please, from start to finish. Don't leave out any juicy bits.'

Sighing heavily, I picked up my tea again and took a long sip to moisten my parched throat. Keeping it as brief as possible, I explained how I'd been running, met Jack at the studio, told the lie about having not accepted the job yet, and then been knocked for six when he'd practically leapt upon me and kissed me.

It took an enormous amount of self-control not to relive every fantastic second of the kiss as I spoke about it, but seeing as my body was already feeling rather hot and bothered simply talking about Jack, I didn't think it would be particularly suitable to indulge in further inappropriate fantasies while sitting with Allie.

'Wow. He must have thought that kissing you would convince you to stay here.'

'Hmm,' I agreed in a non-committal hum. I have no idea what he thought kissing me would do, but I'm fairly sure that turning my life upside down hadn't been his exact aim. Or perhaps it had, who knew? That was certainly how it currently felt.

Finishing her tea, Allie placed the cup down and looked at me expectantly. 'So how did you leave things?'

Grimacing with embarrassment, I recalled our argument and began to ping the elastic band on my wrist until Allie leant across and slapped the back of my hand. 'Oi! Enough of that,' she warned me, grabbing my hand so she could examine my wrist. Seeing the firm look on her face, I yanked my hand back, tucked it under my thigh to avoid further temptation, and distracted her by continuing. 'We had a bit of a fight.'

The expression on Allie's face told me that she had not

been expecting me to say that at all. 'He knows about my … problems.' I always hesitated when picking a word to describe my past. Problems, issues, hang-ups, anxieties, fears … none of them exactly sounded great, did they?

'You told him about Greg?' she asked in an astonished whisper, causing me to vigorously shake my head.

'God, no. He asked me why I was so skittish around men, and asked if someone had hurt me in the past, so he's obviously picked up that I have issues.' I felt heat rising to my cheeks. It was so humiliating to think that my freakishness had been that obvious.

Rolling her lips between her teeth, I could see Allie was holding off from saying anything so I sighed and dropped my head. 'It freaked me out. I mean that stuff is really private, so I …' Pulling a hand out from its hiding place, I dragged it through my damp hair to loosen some of the tangles that were forming. 'Well, I might have kind of got a bit defensive and accused him of being a player and leaping on me.'

'What?' I ignored her squawk and finished my recount.

'He got quite annoyed and declared that the number of people he's slept with is still in single figures.'

'Ooohhh … interesting. You'd think that with his job he'd have a higher total,' Allie mused with a nod, but I merely felt my cheeks blushing at the conversation's change in direction. Thinking about Jack in bed with someone was not helping my nerves. In fact, it was making me feel quite uncomfortable, and possibly a little bit jealous.

'Anyway, he told me not to turn my issues with men on to him.' Hanging on my every word, Allie leant forwards in rapt fascination. 'And what did you say?'

My cheeks heated again, but this time it had nothing to

do with remembering Jack's passionate kiss and everything to do with my embarrassment at my childish behaviour. 'I, um … I ran away.' Very mature that had been too, I thought with a wince, well aware that it was by no means the only time I had done it.

'You. Ran. Away,' she stuttered in shock. 'From Jack Felton.'

If humiliation had a precise facial expression, then I must be wearing it by now. 'Yep.' My cheeks were burning and the temptation to start picking at my elastic band again was immense, but I somehow avoided the urge. 'Because apparently, that's the way I roll,' I joked lamely.

Just at that moment, my phone vibrated in my back pocket. Thankful for the well-timed interruption I pulled it out, hoping it might be my mum phoning so I could delay the rest of this embarrassing conversation with Allie.

Frowning, I saw it was a text from a number I didn't recognise. The phone was the one I'd been using since travelling, my family had got it for me as a leaving gift so I'd be able to email them wherever I was. Really, it was more of a security measure than anything, so it was rare that I got calls or messages. Only a handful of people even had the number.

Clicking on the message I skimmed the words, drew in a shocked breath, and practically dropped the phone as if it had suddenly turned to molten lava in my palm.

From: +9012437689
Running away from me AGAIN? ☹
We need to speak, Caitlin. Please call me.

A sad face? Really? Did forty year olds usually make a habit of using emoticons, or was that for my benefit?

Sucking in a breath, I felt a giveaway flush prickle at the back of my neck, because even though I didn't recognise the number, it was pretty flipping obvious who the message was from.

Leaning across, Allie ran the backs of her knuckles over my forehead with a frown. 'You've gone all sweaty,' she observed in a peculiar tone, 'and your hands are shaking again. Who was the message from?' My throat had turned all strange and tight, so I handed my phone over, not entirely trusting myself to speak.

'Oh my god.' Allie joined our gazes with a pointed look. 'He's certainly persistent, isn't he? Are you going to call him?'

My insides tensed at the thought of hearing his deep, rich voice and I rapidly shook my head. 'No.' Pulling the phone back, I decided to play dumb. Pressing reply, I quickly typed my response.

To: +9012437689
I don't know who this is, but this is a private number. Don't use it again.

'That'll never work, Cait,' Allie chided from beside me, and just for once I wished she would keep her helpful comments to herself. Didn't she know I was in denial here?

'How the heck did he get my number?' I mused out loud as I stared at the screen. After years of hoping that Greg couldn't – and wouldn't – track me down, I should probably have been freaking out at just how easily Jack appeared to have traced me. But as I searched my body for signs of an imminent meltdown, I couldn't find any. What did that signify exactly? That I trusted Jack? That I subconsciously knew he didn't mean me harm? Who knew?

Certainly not me, my brain was like a bowl of useless mush at the moment.

Deciding it might be safest to save Jack's number so I didn't accidentally pick up a call from him in the future, I quickly stored it, but no sooner had I put the phone down it vibrated again.

I drew in a breath, flashed Allie a cautious glance, and stared at the phone as it merrily danced its way across the table with each vibration. Allie shifted herself closer to me and after I had sat staring at the phone for several seconds, she gave me a helpful nudge in the ribs with her elbow. 'Ow!' I complained, rubbing my side with one hand and picking up the phone with the other.

From: Jack F
I think you know very well who it is. Or have you run away from many men today? Jack

I couldn't help but snort in surprise. His words were almost teasing and I could feel a peculiar type of excitement welling up inside me … but it was accompanied by a sharp wave of annoyance at my reaction to him.

Leaning over my shoulder to read the message, Allie joined in and smirked at me. 'I think you should joke with him. It's only a text message after all, no real danger in anything coming of it.'

'I don't want to lead him on, it's not fair.' Seeing my hesitation, Allie snatched the phone, her fingers flying over the screen at the speed of light before pressing send and grinning at me proudly. Oh no. She had a sly, smug expression on her face that I didn't like the look of one bit.

'What the hell are you doing?' I yelped, grabbing it back and checking what she had sent as my pulse rocketed in my veins. Didn't she realise this was serious? He was a man, not some inexperienced idiot like me that I could fool around with.

To: Jack F
I've lost count.
Besides, I didn't run away, I jogged.

'I can't believe you sent that.' My stomach was fizzling nervously, flipping and swirling so violently that I felt sick. I'm not sure I was even blinking as I sat on tenterhooks waiting for a response. Seeing as my nerves were now frayed to the point of near panic, it was a good thing I didn't have to wait long. The phone beeped in my hand, and even though I'd been expecting it, I made a little squealing noise, which had Allie's lips twitching in amusement. She was loving this. I however, was hating it.

From: Jack F
I could have caught you.
Easily.

That made me tremble with a mix of suppressed excitement and gut-wrenching fear. Greg had chased me. And he'd caught me. I could still remember the sharp taste of fear on my tongue, the coppery scent of my own blood as it flowed from cuts on my lip and temple, and the utter hopeless I'd felt as he'd dragged me across the rough ground.

Was he still chasing me? Following me as I travelled around the world and waiting for the time to pounce again? Shuddering, I dropped the phone on the table and rested my head in my hands for a second or two before sitting up and pinging the elastic band on my wrist as I felt panic rise up inside of me.

'Hey, it's OK. It's OK,' Allie said, seeming to understand my reaction as she leant in and gave me a firm shake to pull me from my panic.

'He didn't mean it that way, sweetie. He was just joking with you.'

Looking back to the text message, I wondered why the thought of Jack chasing me wasn't nearly as terrifying as it should be after my experiences with Greg. But it wasn't. In fact, the thought of Jack Felton chasing me, catching me, and kissing me again was almost too appealing to handle … especially seeing as my brain was now imagining exactly what he might do to me once he caught me. Not to mention just how much I might enjoy it.

Straightening my posture I nodded at Allie to show I was OK, and even though I knew I should stop this madness, I began to type out another message.

To: Jack F
I did athletics in college, so I can be surprisingly quick when I need to be.
How did you get this number?

Barely a second passed before my phone registered another message. Blimey, he must be sitting staring at his phone waiting for my messages. I couldn't quite decide how I felt about that thought.

From: Jack F
I'm sure you can be, but I think I'm faster.
I knew your surname, and I have a friend at US Mobile who owed me a favour.

Of course he did. A man as rich as Jack Felton probably had 'friends' in all the bloody mobile phone companies across the world, I thought with a sigh, as another message came through before I'd even had a chance to respond to the first. Wondering how he knew my surname, I paused with a frown, suddenly recalling that night at the art gallery where I'd been wearing a name tag. I'd noticed at the time when he'd clocked my surname, not that it really mattered, I suppose.

From: Jack F
Can't we just try being friends?

Raising an eyebrow, I shook my head and tilted the phone so Allie could see it. Instantly I saw hope on her face.

'You could try being friends, Cait. You like him, and you did say you were going to make more effort with getting some male friends.'

'Be friends with Jack after the kiss he's just laid on me?' I stuttered, flabbergasted by her idea. 'That hardly seems sensible, or feasible,' I added. After that kiss I wasn't sure I could trust Jack as far as I could throw him. What was worse though, was that I didn't think I could trust myself around him, either. I was way too affected by him to be just friends, and seeing as I didn't want anything more than friendship it looked like I only had one option.

To: Jack F
I don't think so. In fact, I find your behaviour quite
stalker-like. It's making me uncomfortable.
I meant what I said in the park, I'm not interested.

Allie looked thoroughly dejected when I plonked my phone down on the table, but she gave me a supportive smile anyway, even if it was a bit half-hearted. The trouble was that that last text was only a half-truth. His behaviour was freaking me out slightly – I mean, who goes to their 'friend' at a mobile phone company and breaks every privacy law to get someone's phone number? Is nothing sacred any more? But really, this only freaked me out because thoughts of Greg and his overbearing nature kept floating to the surface of my mind.

Jack finding out my number within half an hour of me leaving was a bit stalker-ish, but because it was him, and not Greg, I also found it quite flattering, and the only reason I was uncomfortable was because I was getting myself hot under the collar imagining Jack chasing me through the woods.

If I were truly honest with myself, my line about not being interested was a complete bag of lies. Jack Felton completely fascinated me. More precisely, the way I responded to him and felt when I was near him fascinated me. It was a freeing sensation that I wasn't used to.

'Shall we go shopping now? I still need to get some clothes for work next week,' I asked, hoping to distract Allie from pursuing the Jack conversation any further. Wandering to the cupboard, I grabbed two chocolate bars and offered Allie one.

As I peeled back the wrapper and took my first bite, I couldn't help but glance at my phone and feel a small stab of disappointment when I saw no new messages. Jack had obviously taken me at my word and decided to leave me alone. Which was probably a good thing, wasn't it? At that moment though, as I recalled our mind-blowing kiss again, it didn’t feel great at all.

Chapter Fourteen

Jack

Ben had come up trumps, and less than twenty minutes after Caitlin had careened away from me, I had her mobile number programmed into my phone. It was some pay-as-you-go travel sim, basically a throwaway, so Ben told me I was lucky that she had registered her name to access the free internet minutes otherwise he wouldn't have been able to trace it at all.

I was still in my sweaty running gear and sitting in my car because Ben's message had come through to me before I'd even had a chance to make it home. So now I was pulled over at the side of the road trying to decide whether to call Caitlin or message her.

Pondering this, I rubbed my chin and sat back with a grimace – judging from the way she had run away from me she wouldn't want to hear from me at all, regardless of what form I chose.

Shit. This girl had seriously got under my skin. If she was going to be working at Dynamic then there was the possibility that I might – just might – manage to build some sort of friendship with her in the future. Who was I kidding? I wanted way more than friendship with the illusive Miss Byrne. If that were to ever be possible then I needed to find a way of gaining her trust.

There was no way she would ever trust me again if she

thought I made a habit of kissing women in the woods, so I needed to make things right, and I needed to do it now.

I drew in a deep breath for confidence and opened up the messaging app on my phone. Having witnessed the way her eyes occasionally flared with fear, I decided that texting was the safest bet, and hopefully she would find it the less intimidating option.

Staring at the screen, I chewed on the inside of my lip as I tried to decide what the hell I should write. *Apologies for my behaviour.* That sounded way too stuffy and formal.

Sorry I pounced on you. But it was an amazing kiss, so I'm not really that sorry. Ugh. No. It was the truth, but perhaps not what Caitlin would want to see.

Blowing out a breath, I wondered why the heck I couldn't dredge up one useful message to send. I was usually a direct kinda guy when it came to women. If I was interested in them I made sure they knew it in a friendly, flirty way, but equally, if they were making advances and weren't my type, I would politely make sure they realised it.

I also didn't pursue women or hassle them, until I'd met Caitlin, of course, but I knew – I just knew – that I had seen attraction in her eyes, and I had definitely felt our potent chemistry and her desire in that incredible kiss. She'd clawed at my T-shirt, for God's sake.

All that considered, my direct approach obviously wasn't the right way to go with Caitlin. I'd already asked her out several times and she'd knocked me back each and every time. Grimacing at that lovely scrape to my ego, I tried again, keeping my message casual, light-hearted, but direct, in the hope that she'd finally give in to her feelings.

To: Caitlin Byrne
Running away from me AGAIN? ☹
We need to speak, Caitlin. Please call me.

Before I pressed send I re-read the message and debated the presence of the sad face. I didn't make a habit of using them, but I did want to keep the message light-hearted in some way. Bugger it, leave it in. Pressing send, I chucked the phone on the passenger seat and restarted the engine, assuming that Caitlin wouldn't reply straight away, if at all.

I'd just put my indicator on to pull out into traffic when my mobile buzzed beside me, startling me and causing me to immediately tuck my car back in and switch off the indicator. I'd either just received a text from one of my contacts with impeccably coincidental timing, or Caitlin had replied to my message practically straight away.

Picking up the phone, I saw a message alert and could barely believe how nervous I was. My stomach was tumbling like I was on a rollercoaster and my fingers felt shaky and useless. Opening up the message I saw her name and my heart rate sky-rocketed even higher.

From: Caitlin Byrne
I don't know who this is, but this is a private number.
Don't use it again.

I re-read her brief text and let out a sigh. That was how she wanted to play things? My ego would have liked to pretend she was playing hard to get, but her message didn't exactly sound playful. Pursing my lips as I considered her request, I almost followed her wish, but then threw caution to the wind and typed out another message, deliberately adding my name this time.

To: Caitlin Byrne
I think you know very well who it is. Or have you run away from many men today? Jack

There was no immediate response this time, and I started to wonder if I should have added another apology to my message. I'd already apologised in the woods, though. Even though my phone still hadn't rung, I was sitting like a complete sap, staring at it as if willing the bloody thing to ring, or beep, or give me any sign of life. Which it finally did.

From: Caitlin Byrne
I've lost count.
Besides, I didn't run away, I jogged.

After her initial message, which had been brusque, to say the least, the lighter, almost jokey tone to this one caught me so off-guard that I actually threw my head back and laughed. It was like a whole different person had written it. Not that I was complaining, jokey was far better than curt and standoffish. A smile pulled at my lips as I read her message again. Hmmm. Perhaps I could get away with joking back a little too.

To: Caitlin Byrne
I could have caught you.
Easily.

The idea of playfully chasing Caitlin made my cock begin to thicken in my shorts. Closing my eyes, I tried to picture the scene and found it all too easy to do: the sun would be shining on us as we laughed and ran, her chestnut hair glinting in the rays as she dodged playfully around trees pretending to evade me, and me watching her gorgeous body as I deliberately trailed behind. When I caught up with her I'd wrap an arm around her waist to pull her flush against me and her hands would fist keenly in my shirt just as they had today. Imagining all this, not to mention the light giggles that she might make as she jumped up and wrapped her legs around me, wasn't helping the tightness in my shorts at all. Damn it.

It was just as well a text arrived to distract me, otherwise I might very well have lost control in my running shorts like a teenager.

From: Caitlin Byrne
I did athletics in college, so I can be surprisingly quick when I need to be.
How did you get this number?

The image of her in a university athletics kit tried to push its way into my mind, but after my earlier wayward thoughts I pushed it away with substantial difficulty and concentrated on re-reading her message. I wondered briefly if Caitlin had any idea that I was literally sitting in my car like an idiot waiting for her replies with almost bated breath.

In the park, she'd seemed jumpy, and it had led me to believe that she might be the type of girl who would like a man to be calm and in control. Someone she could turn to if she needed them, so I hoped to God she didn't know just how desperate I was acting. I'd have to try and come across as marginally more mature from now on. Of course my previous thoughts didn't stop me from acting like a giddy schoolboy and replying almost instantly. So much for being mature and in control.

To: Caitlin Byrne
I'm sure you can be, but I think I'm faster.
I knew your surname, and I have a friend at US Mobile who owed me a favour.

I retained my light, teasing wording, and kept the details about Ben vague. While I realised she was probably still in shock from my kiss in the park, I decided to risk it and send a further text.

To: Caitlin Byrne
Can't we just try being friends?

I wanted more than friendship, but this would be a start. This time, after pressing send I literally did hold my breath. Thankfully the reply came swiftly, but it made my heart sink and an accepting frown settle on my features.

From: Caitlin Byrne
I don't think so. In fact, I find your behaviour quite stalker-like. It's making me uncomfortable.
I meant what I said in the park, I'm not interested.

Fuck. Re-reading her text I let out a heavy sigh. Even I wasn't delirious enough to take that text as jokey or playful in any way. It was blunt and definitely indicated that I'd pushed my luck too far and still drawn a blank.

I had managed to get myself so convinced that she felt the same attraction that it hadn't even occurred to me that Caitlin might find me getting her number 'stalker-like', but

I supposed she wasn't far wrong; I had pushed some serious boundaries, practically demanding that Ben get the number for me and then immediately using it once he'd sent it across. The things this girl was driving me to were insane.

My ego had certainly taken quite a battering at the hands of the enigmatic Miss Byrne, that was for sure. I'd never been knocked back so frequently, or so decisively in my entire life. Perhaps that was why I was so bloody taken with her.

Growling in frustration, I grudgingly decided to do as she'd asked and leave her alone, and chucked my phone on the seat beside me before I could cave and text her again. I was so sure she felt the spark between us, which was why following her wishes was so much harder than it should have been.

If our paths crossed again I would perhaps take it as a sign of fate that I was destined to pursue her, but if they didn't then I supposed it was sensible to just give up now before I embarrassed myself any more.

With all this begging and desperation, I was acting like a reckless kid, not a man nearing forty. Muttering a curse, I shook my head in annoyance. Maybe Caitlin was my version of an early mid-life crisis. Rolling my eyes I shoved my sweat-dampened hair away from my face and drove the rest of the way home in a foul mood.

Chapter Fifteen

Sean

'Come on, let's get this done,' I grumbled, knowing that Savannah and I needed to keep our director happy by going out in public and being spotted together. Personally, I couldn't think of anything I'd rather do less, but Finlay had been flashing me the evil eye all morning, so it seemed easier to do it sooner rather than later.

Turning to see if Savannah was ready, I pulled off my sunglasses to ensure I definitely got recognised. 'We'll grab a quick coffee and let the paparazzi get some pictures. Remember to look pissed off with me, OK?'

'But I'm not angry with you, *darrrling*. I don't see why I should pretend,' Savannah pouted, crossing her arms for effect which just ended up squeezing her tits up and out even further than usual. I suspected that Savannah was hoping to tempt me to check out her cleavage, but I resolutely refused to fall into her trap and glared at her instead.

Raising a hand, I pointed right in her face. 'After all the shit you've put me through with this fucking fake engagement, and then that stupid stunt you pulled with Allie, you owe me.' I was so angry I could feel my cheeks heating with rage. 'Don't even think of playing games with me, or you'll live to regret it.'

Savannah barely even flinched, which only acted to

increase my annoyance as I started stalking towards the gates. 'This is all such a lot of fuss. Dating me would be far easier than her, Sean, you must realise that.'

Spinning on the spot I threw my hands in the air in aggravation. 'But I don't want to date you, Savannah! That's the whole fucking point. When the hell will you get that into your head?' I knew Savannah didn't want that either; she didn't date, she fucked around, but I thought she was pissed off because I had refused to sleep with her. One thing was sure though, even if Savannah didn't play the 'tense, pissed off' card for the journalists, my scrunched up face and mounting fury would certainly make for a good picture.

My words seemed to sink in as Savannah's lips curled contemptuously for a split second before she noticeably deflated and gave an accepting nod. 'Fine.'

Nodding curtly, I reached down and grabbed her hand before practically dragging her towards the studios' exit where there were sure to be a few paparazzi loitering.

'Let's get this freak show on the road.'

Chapter Sixteen

Allie

I was halfway through swimming my thirtieth length of the pool when I came up for a breath and got a glimpse of Cait standing on the poolside. Coming to a stop at the edge, I flicked my goggles up and wiped my eyes as I trod water. Noticing her deep frown I raised my eyebrows curiously. 'What's up?'

'Um … are you done?' She asked, her features still narrowed with apparent concern.

The private pool was tiny, so I usually tried to swim at least sixty lengths just to feel like I'd done a decent distance, but the look on Cait's face made me grab the rail. Dragging myself from the water, I pulled down a towel from the rack and roughly dried myself off. 'I can always have a break. What is it?'

'You might want to see this.' Cait flicked her elastic band once and then held out her phone to me. As I took the mobile I realised it was actually mine, and saw the screen had one new message alert. 'I wasn't snooping, but it flashed up right next to me and I accidentally saw what it said,' Cait blurted. 'I think you might want to read it.'

Unlocking my phone, I brought up the notification and frowned at the words filling the screen.

Savannah Hilton and Sean Phillips spotted having a

reconciliation coffee. Is their love back on track? Click here to read more.

Hmm. Reconciliation? I didn't like the sound of that at all.

'Why did that message come to you?' Cait asked in confusion, and I felt my cheeks heat.

'After the last stunt she pulled I set up an instant alert for Savannah's name so I would get a message every time her name appeared in a new article.'

'Clever. Why is Sean out with her, though? Is this another one of her stunts?'

Luckily, my man had been completely open and up front with me regarding Savannah since our fall-out, so I knew exactly what this message was referring to.

'Nah, this is for the benefit of his director.' I clicked the link and waited while the complete article loaded. 'Apparently there were some blurry shots of Sean and me in the papers last week and his director went nuts. He says they can end the fake engagement soon, but he wants them to hold off until the end of the season. The fact that Sean's been spotted with a mystery blonde put a bit of a spanner in the works, but they decided to use it to their advantage and get some extra publicity by creating the illusion of tension between him and Savannah.'

Scrolling through the article, I saw several pictures of Sean and Savannah sitting over a coffee. Sean's brows were drawn low into a frown and Savannah's lips were puckered so petulantly that she looked like she had swallowed something exceptionally sour. 'The director demanded that they be spotted in public looking strained so people might think there was trouble in paradise. Look.' Turning the phone to Cait I let her scroll through the images.

'Well, they definitely look strained, that's for sure,' she agreed before handing my phone back with a small grimace. 'I don't know how you deal with all this drama Allie, I really don't.'

Neither did I sometimes. But at least Sean had warned me about this, even if I hadn't known that it was going to happen so soon.

'I love him,' I replied simply, a statement that caused Cait to blush, nod, and smile soppily.

'That's not to say I can't make him pay a little,' I added mischievously, opening up my messages and firing off a quick one to Sean.

To: Sean Phillips
I see you and your 'fiancée' are in the papers today. Better get your thinking cap on, because I think you owe me a nice surprise in return. A xx

Smiling as a message instantly popped on to my phone, I opened it up and giggled.

From: Sean Phillips
Deal. I'll put the thinking cap on my pervy head and make it a sexy surprise, so be prepared. Love you. S xx

A pervy sexy surprise from Sean? I couldn't wait, and with that thought in my head I plonked my phone on a sun lounger and jumped back in the pool to finish my swim with a huge grin on my face.

Chapter Seventeen

Allie

I woke with a start, my skin prickling with a bizarre sensation like small, icy pinpricks were dancing across my body. Something was wrong. I could feel it in my gut. Frowning into the darkness, I blinked to clear my sleepy vision and looked around for what had woken me. My heart leapt in my chest and a harsh gasp sucked into my lungs as my eyes settled on what appeared to be a silhouette standing by my patio doors.

Ho-ly fuuuuck. What the hell?

In the blink of an eye I was wide awake, my pulse thundering through my veins as every hair on my body stood up on end and my throat closed with fear. In an uncoordinated attempt at a ninja roll, I threw myself across the bed to switch on my lamp, then flung myself up on the mattress as far away from the glass doors as I could.

Pale lamplight now dimly illuminated my room, but as my eyes adjusted it was obvious that there was no one there.

The room was empty.

A choked breath of relief stuttered from my lungs as I blinked several times and surveyed the room again with my heartbeat raging in my eardrums.

Holy crap balls. That had been really flipping freaky.

Drawing in a gigantic breath, I let it out as a huge sigh and tried to rein in my hammering pulse, noticing that my entire body was covered in a film of cold sweat. Jesus. I was shaken up. That shadow had seemed really frigging real.

Licking my lips, I gingerly slid from the bed and checked the patio doors, but they were still locked. Letting out a small, slightly hysterical giggle, I shook my head and clambered back into the safety of my bed. The sheets were still warm and I wrapped them around myself for comfort as I attempted to reel in my overactive imagination and banish the images of a strange, shadowy figure from my mind.

Clearly my brain had gone haywire tonight, conjuring up phantoms in the dark, although admittedly I did have a pile of clothes thrown over the chair by the window so perhaps it had just been the outline of that that I'd seen.

I'd also been tossing and turning when I'd gone to bed, because I'd been thinking again about Cait's confessions that her scumbag ex had been stalking her via letter. Maybe that was the cause of my horror-like visions. It made me feel sick to my stomach that he was out there somewhere and not rotting in jail like he deserved.

Mind you, it did at least make more sense of why she was struggling so hard to get over him. If he was still haunting her with sick letters and threats, then she was probably struggling to move on completely.

I decided that must be what was causing me to be so jumpy. Settling myself beneath the covers I stretched out my legs in an attempt to calm my rampaging nerves, but even though I knew I was being ridiculous, it was still five minutes before I plucked up the courage to turn the light off again.

Chapter Eighteen

Sean

The carpet smelt of cinnamon, and I couldn't for the life of me imagine why. Every time I dared to take a small, shallow breath that was the scent I got. It was like someone had squished up a cinnamon bun and rubbed the thing across the floor, and the bloody smell was making my nose twitch.

Reducing my inhales to the bare minimum I lay on the floor as still as a statue. That had been such a close call that my heart was still pounding in my chest like a bloody bass drum.

Another shallow breath brought with it more cinnamon and my nose really started to itch. *I must not sneeze.* A loud sneeze would be disastrous, not only giving away my hiding place, but probably scaring the shit out of Allie in the process too.

When Allie had woken up and looked towards the window I'd felt sure she had seen me, and I'd been on the verge of laughing off my failed attempt and crawling into bed with her, but when she'd turned her back to switch on the light, some external force seemed to take over my body, propelling me onto my stomach where I could roll swiftly beneath the bed.

So that's where I was. Flat on my stomach on the thick carpet beneath Allie's bed like some night-time assassin. A night-time assassin who really needed to sneeze. Great.

Nearly getting caught had been my own stupid fault though, because as I'd entered her room earlier I had paused to gaze at her as she slept, wasting precious time that could have been spent putting my plan into action. I couldn't help it, I was seriously addicted to her, and would take any chance I could get to watch my girl unnoticed.

If I had just pounced on her as I'd intended then she wouldn't have woken up and seen me illuminated by the moonlight as I watched her like a love-sick puppy, but here I was, now getting intimately acquainted with the floor like a complete idiot.

My neck was twisted uncomfortably, so I turned to the other side to rest on my cheek and came face to face with a small cardboard carton. Frowning, I shifted my head slightly and then smiled – cinnamon chewing gum. At least twenty packets of the stuff by the looks of it. So that was where the bloody smell was coming from. Shaking my head in amusement, I twitched my nose and settled my head down again to listen for any movements from Allie.

Half of me was tempted to clamber out from my hiding space and just admit my failed attempt at a midnight booty call, but my more determined side had decided that I was seeing this through. Allie had admitted that she quite liked the idea of someone sneaking in and pouncing on her in the middle of the night, and I was determined to make her fantasy a reality. In fact, ever since she'd mentioned it in passing it had taken root in my thoughts and become my fantasy too.

After today's text messages where she'd told me I owed her a 'nice surprise', – something I'd upgraded by promising a 'pervy sexy surprise' – I'd decided this was the perfect opportunity.

The idea of surprising her as she slept and having my

wicked way with her was such a huge turn on for me that even now, as I lay there under her bed barely breathing, my cock was already as hard as granite and digging painfully into the carpeted floor.

I must have really freaked Allie out, because it was at least another five minutes before her light went out again, and then a further fifteen before I heard her breathing deepen and slow with sleep.

Once I was definitely sure that Allie was asleep, I crawled from my hiding space and briefly stretched out my stiff joints before fully turning to face the bed.

Where should I begin?

When Allie had first joked about liking the idea of an intruder sneaking into her room I had salaciously described how I would pin her to the bed or tie her up and take her however I wished. I hadn't actually expected her to look so thrilled by the idea, but thrilled she had been.

A small groan slipped from my lips at the flood of ideas that swept my mind, all deliciously naughty and so arousing that I had to adjust my straining erection as it desperately sought a way free from my trousers.

I wasn't entirely sure how feasible tying her up would be without waking her, but she'd certainly seemed keen on the idea, and after my impromptu use of the belt to fasten her wrists at the beach house I couldn't wait to give it another go.

Hell, the idea of having Allie tied up beneath me was so appealing that I felt my cock give a gigantic lurch of approval. If Allie was up for it, why not try it out?

This night had been in my plans for a while now, it had just been a matter of waiting for my work schedule to ease so I had an evening free. It was also one of the reasons I'd asked her to pick a safe word that day in the pool house, because realistically, tying her up while she slept was more extreme than anything else we'd ever done, so I needed to make sure she was definitely comfortable at all times.

Reaching into one of the side pockets on my combat trousers, I removed two lengths of black silk that I had borrowed from the dressing rooms at work today. I say 'borrowed', but I mean taken. They were sashes from two of the dressing gowns in the make-up area. I'd slip them back in tomorrow, unless they went down really well with Allie, in which case I might just have to keep hold of them until I could purchase a suitable replacement.

Licking my lips, I cautiously approached the bed and smiled. Allie was asleep on her back with her arms thrown above her head. It was the perfect position for me to tie her wrists, and even better, from the glimpse of bare shoulder I could see, it appeared she was naked. Perfect. It was settled. I was tying my girl to the bed.

As I considered her positioning a wicked grin spread across my lips. Instead of using both sashes and tying her wrists to each bedpost, I could tie them together and attach them to the frame above her head. This would be far better, because not only did it mean I only needed to disturb her hands once, but if her wrists were tied together, I'd be able to flip her over onto her stomach, which was a position that presented some rather exciting possibilities.

Pulling on the thin leather gloves I had purchased for this evening, I slid one long sash through the bedframe directly above her hands then carefully tied two loops for her wrists.

Before attempting to move her hands, which would undoubtedly be the trickiest bit, I paused and glanced at the balaclava I had brought with me. Was that a step too far? Would it completely freak her out or just add to the overall excitement and realism? I toyed with the idea for several seconds then pulled it on with a shrug. I was already here and tying her up, I might as well go the whole hog. Besides, I was an actor, using props to enhance a scene was natural for me.

To my surprise I managed to get the sash around Allie's wrists without her even stirring. The knots were tight enough to create the feeling of restraint, but if Allie really tugged I was fairly sure she'd be able to pull herself free.

Carefully kicking off my boots, I stood to the side of the bed and caught sight of my reflection in the mirror; black combat trousers, tight black T-shirt, leather gloves, and a balaclava. I actually looked like an intruder. Which I supposed was exactly what I was. The raging hard-on tenting the front of my trousers was perhaps a little out of place with the burglar visual, but I was so aroused that it couldn't be helped.

I tried to calm the roaring of my heartbeat in my chest, but knowing what I was about to do had me so turned on that my body was barely mine to control; my pulse was wild, my muscles tense with anticipation, and my cock was literally aching.

What to do first?

The sheet. It was definitely in the way. I wanted to see if she really was naked, and I wanted to see now. Holding my breath I gently held the corner of the thin fabric and began to peel it down Allie's sleeping form, exposing her beautiful body inch by teasing inch until my face felt well and truly flushed.

I took a moment to appreciate her in all her glory. Allie was indeed naked. Well, almost, in nothing but some very chaste white cotton knickers. My gaze lingered on the simple underwear and my pulse heated even further. Hmm, it was almost as if she had known I was coming and worn them on purpose, because they looked practically virginal.

As if aware of my gaze, her nipples began to harden, and although I knew it was because they were exposed to the coolness of the room, I couldn't help but grin my approval.

Finally allowing myself to touch her, I ran the pad of a gloved finger gently around one nipple, the nub pebbling and tightening even more under my attentions until it was a tiny pink bullet. Allie gave a soft moan but didn't wake, so I repeated the touch to her other breast, this time being rewarded with a small shift of her hips, as if she were becoming aroused even in her sleep.

My control was pretty much maxed out now. The gloves were a nice prop, but I was desperate to feel her skin, so I dipped my head and took a nipple into my mouth. At first I gave a few gentle licks, savouring the sweet floral taste, but then my control began to fail and I sucked the peak into my mouth, hard, just as she liked it.

Allie jerked below me, her whole body tensing as she woke with a start and arched her body into the contact. A breathy moan left her lips and as I raised my head to watch her pleasure I saw her eyes expand into a terrified expression that twisted her entire face.

I'd been so lost in the moment that I'd briefly forgotten about the balaclava. Oops. That must have scared the shit out of her. It was easy to see the exact second she fully woke up and went into panic mode, because her hands jerked against the restraints and her lungs violently expanded below me.

Fuck, she was about to scream. Aware that Cait was somewhere in the bungalow I moved in a blur of limbs so I was straddling Allie and pinning her down, and clamped a hand over her mouth.

My girl was a fighter, that was for sure, because even without the use of her hands she was bucking wildly, writhing and squirming so violently that she nearly succeeded in flipping me off the bed.

As wrong as it was, I found that her struggling just made my cock even harder, but as I held her down I knew I had to reassure her, let her know it was me, but without directly stopping the scene.

Leaning down close to her ear, I licked at the lobe, which caused her to give a muffled yell of anger against my hand and try to bite down on one of my fingers. Grinning at how feisty she was, I repeated the lick and whispered to her, 'If you want me to stop at any point, just say the safe word. You remember our word, baby?'

Her struggling ceased almost immediately and as I leant my head up to meet her gaze, I found her eyes shadowed with a confused frown as she searched the holes in the balaclava for something recognisable in my eyes.

I saw her features relax marginally and I removed my hand from her mouth.

'S … Sean? It's you?'

I didn't want to answer directly – that felt like it would spoil some of the fun – so I merely persevered with my question. 'What's the safe word, my gorgeous girl?' I lowered one hand and gave a soft tweak to a nipple, causing her to gasp and then flush with colour.

'B … blizzard.' Her body arched upwards towards my touch and I grinned at how keen she was.

'That's my girl,' I praised. 'Do you want to use it, or are we good to continue?'

'I didn't think midnight intruders would have such good manners,' Allie murmured breathily. 'Aren't you just supposed to use me any way you wish?'

Use her any way I wished? Jeez. My balls nearly exploded right there and then.

Well, if that was how she felt about it all, I supposed I better just get on with it. Kneeling up I practically ripped my T-shirt over my head and, leaving the balaclava and gloves on to add some excitement, I descended on her again like a man possessed. Which was exactly what I was.

Allie

This was all so unexpected that it took me a few seconds to get my heart rate back under control. Waking up with a masked man crouched over my body had been the most singularly terrifying thing I had ever experienced, but as soon as I'd realised it was Sean making good on his promise, I felt arousal flooding my body as I relaxed into it.

Although really, I shouldn't be relaxed, should I? If I really wanted to get into the whole role play thing properly then I should probably act like a terrified damsel in distress and at least put up a bit of a fight. At the moment I was limp with relief – where was the fun in that?

Catching Sean off guard, I resumed my violent wriggling, but this time kept quiet so as not to wake Cait. I even managed to half dislodge him from my hips before he looked up at me and I caught sight of a startled look in his eyes. That balaclava was actually rather erotic. Well, not the balaclava as such, but more the fact that it sort of hid his identity. The gloves were sexy too, the soft leather felt so sinful against my skin that I hoped he would dip his hand between my legs soon so I could experience it there too.

'You're going to be a wriggler?' he murmured, re-establishing his mounted position with some difficulty, sitting more of his weight onto my thighs and using his hands to pin my bucking hips to the mattress. 'That's OK, the harder you fight, the harder I get,' he informed me, leaning forward to give a very firm thrust of his very firm groin. And I definitely didn't miss the wiggle of his eyebrows at the edge of the wool before his head dipped to my breast. Oh goodie. Sean was in full teasing mode tonight, and I couldn't have been happier.

This time the bucking of my hips had nothing to do with trying to escape, and everything to do with the deliciously hard suckle he had applied to my nipple. Pleasure soared through my veins, travelling straight from the throbbing tip down to my groin, which was now aching for contact.

As if reading my mind, Sean shifted his position slightly, peeled my knickers off, chucked them carelessly over his shoulder, and slid one gloved hand down from my hip, across my belly, and through the small strip of hair to my clitoris. The teasing bastard then circled it just once – nowhere near enough, in my opinion – and sat back with a smirk, completely removing his touch.

A garbled complaint rose up my throat as I stared at him in shock. He wasn't seriously going to stop, was he?

Chuckling, he proceeded to sink one single leather-clad finger fully inside me. A murmur of pleasure fluttered across my lips because his touch felt so good that I simply couldn't keep quiet. My hands tugged uselessly against the sashes as I wriggled frantically, but remembering that I was restrained only heightened my arousal. 'Oh god …'

'That's not my name, but feel free to call me it for this evening …' Sean mumbled in a gravelly voice, and I could tell from his tone that he was grinning from ear to ear. Arrogant bastard. But what talented fingers my arrogant bastard had. My eyes practically rolled backwards in my skull in appreciation of what he was doing.

A second gloved finger began to press inside me, the slickness of the leather giving a bizarre, but hugely erotic twist to the act. My back arched as he curled the two digits just enough to find my g-spot. Even with his gloves on he managed to zero straight in on it and give it a firm massage with each thrust, and that little bundle of nerves deep inside of me exalted at how skilled Sean was at locating them. It was sheer bliss.

Suddenly his fingers were gone and I was left on the brink of orgasm, empty and whimpering. 'Time for a change,' he whispered beside my ear. 'Over you go.' And gripping my hips, he somehow managed to flip me over with surprising ease so I was flat on my stomach.

Blimey. I had no idea how he had managed that quite so easily, but clearly from the way my face was now squished into the duvet, he had. I wasn't in this new position for long either, because Sean snaked a hand under my hips and pulled me up so I was on my elbows and knees practically presented before him.

Sliding from the bed I heard the sound of his zipper and the soft movement of fabric as he removed his trousers. I couldn't see him, but I hoped he had taken off his boxers too. If he was wearing any, that was, because I'd discovered that Sean quite often went commando when I was around.

The mattress sank as he climbed back onto the bed and I shivered as he ran a gloved hand over my bottom. 'Hmmm. What a perfect sight. Tied up and bowed over for only me to see. You make a very pleasing captive, my gorgeous girl.' In response, I gave a brief, teasing wiggle of my hips, which earned me a sharp spank on my right buttock that caused my eyes to bulge in surprise.

'Oh!' A shocked gasp slipped from my lips, but actually, even though we'd never done anything remotely like punishments before, that had definitely added to my arousal. The feel of the leather had been incredibly erotic, and as bizarre as it was, I almost wanted him to do it again. Hmmm …

This surprising realisation was something Sean had clearly picked up on, because he landed another stinging slap to my other buttock and slid a finger between my legs. I heard a sharp inhalation as he pulled it away and then gently rubbed the excessive moisture on my clit in a series of hard, teasing circles.

'Well, well, you are excitable this evening, aren't you, my little captive? Perhaps you are enjoying being experimental.'

My reply was nothing short of a garbled warble. I was hot, horny, tied up, and *waaay* past speech.

One of Sean's hands gently massaged my warm bum cheek while his other slid from my clit and dipped into my moisture before continuing on around to my other entrance. I tensed slightly at the feel of him massaging at my behind, but I knew from experience that he often did this and no more. Apparently, my man was more than a little obsessed with this other entrance.

Tonight though, instead of just giving it a quick tease, I felt the tip of his moist, gloved finger begin to press against it more firmly, and my body tensed. What he did to me always felt nice, but I wasn't sure I wanted more action around that side. 'Sean ...' My hesitancy must have shown in my voice because he stilled immediately.

'Hush ... trust me, baby. If you don't like it say your safe word.' Hmm ... I wasn't convinced, but I knew with certainty that he would stop if I asked him to, so I gave a small nod of acknowledgement and tried to relax.

'Besides, I'm a heartless robber, remember? I can do whatever I like to you,' he murmured in a low, gravelly tone that sent shimmers of excited pleasure dancing across my skin.

I wondered if that was why he was finally extending our

play to that area, because the role play allowed him more freedom. Whatever the reason, lucid thoughts were pushed from my mind the next second as he splayed a hand on my lower back and began to probe at my back entrance with his gloved thumb. At least I assumed it was his thumb, because it felt thicker than the finger that had gone before.

The sensation was pleasurable but so alien, and as much as I wanted to relax, I found it difficult. Sensing my struggle, Sean reached with his free hand and began to rub at my clitoris with firm, slick circles, and as pleasure radiated out from his touch I felt his thumb sink deeper until it was gently moving in time to his fingers at my clit.

'God, Allie, you are so fucking sexy,' he muttered, before I felt the bed shift and the hot head of his cock press against me. As he pushed forwards he kept up the movement of both his thumb and fingers until suddenly I felt incredibly full and extremely aroused. With his thumb busy round the back, and his shaft now buried to the hilt and bumping against my g-spot, I was literally full to bursting.

'So tight,' he muttered, his voice strained and low. 'I love how receptive your body is for me, baby.' Sean began to move, and with his thumb and cock moving together I was overwhelmed with sensation and knew I wasn't going to last long.

As it was, I only lasted a few minutes, but as soon as the fingers at my clit began to circle again I was a goner, an orgasm rushing up and engulfing me in spasms that seemed to shake my entire body. I was so overwhelmed that a cry escaped my throat and I had to bury my face in the pillow to muffle the sound. Sean grunted his appreciation, his thrusts becoming jerkier as my muscles repeatedly clamped around him until he suddenly gave a long, deep thrust and began to come in several hot, jerking pulses.

Sean was panting hard, but gently removed his thumb and pulled off the gloves, tossing them to the floor along with his balaclava. Reaching up, he untied my wrists, and, leaving his cock buried inside me, he slid a protective arm around my sweaty, trembling body and rolled us both over so we lay spooned on our sides, breathless and sated.

Holy fuck. Talk about a midnight bump and grind.

'You OK, baby?' Sean murmured by my ear. I nodded instinctively, although in truth I was still trying to process all that had just occurred. Did I really let him stick his thumb in there? I winced from embarrassment, but there was no getting away from the fact that I had enjoyed it.

'I'm more than good. That was a hell of a work-out you gave me. Not to mention a shock!'

Sean gave a hot chuckle by my ear that I felt right the way through his body and into mine. 'At first I thought I'd screwed up the surprise when you woke up.'

'So that was you I saw standing by the window?'

'Yep. I dived under the bed as you were turning the bedside lamp on.'

The image of Sean squashed under my bed made me laugh, before my cheeks heated a little. 'You hid under my bed? That's quite pervy.'

'I like to think so,' he agreed, a grin obvious in his tone as he gave me a squeeze. 'I did promise you a pervy, sexy surprise, didn't I? Did this live up to it?'

If possible, my smile got even larger as I looked over my shoulder and placed a quick kiss on his lips. 'Most definitely.'

Nodding rather smugly, he wiggled his eyebrows. 'We'll definitely have to add more pervy, sexy surprises into our future plans. By the way, why have you got a stash of cinnamon chewing gum under your bed?'

I blushed further, and then gave an embarrassed shrug. 'I like it, and you can't get it in the UK.'

'Weirdo. The smell nearly made me sneeze,' Sean chuckled by my ear, and after placing a gentle kiss on the nape of my neck, he eased himself out of me and disappeared into the en suite. Seeing him returning with a damp flannel I rolled my eyes, but didn't complain, and instead merely rolled over on to my back, splayed my legs, and let him do his thing. Sean grinned happily at my compliance, giving me a gentle cleansing and wandering his gloriously naked arse back to the bathroom, humming happily to himself.

Coming back into the room sipping a glass of water, Sean suddenly paused halfway and raised an eyebrow. 'Nice flowers. You have a secret admirer?'

Sean was referring to the gigantic bunch that had arrived for me earlier, but there definitely seemed to be an edge of jealousy in his voice.

It was the middle of the night, he'd just snuck into my room and sexed me silly, and suddenly he was bristling with tension. Not to mention naked. He was most definitely still naked. I nearly burst out laughing, but seeing how concerned Sean suddenly looked, I managed to refrain.

'No, randomly they're from Savannah.' Sean shot me a surprised look and I gave a returning shrug, equally as shocked. 'The card said she was sorry for the scene she made when I came to your house. I've had a few apology texts too.'

'Blimey. Well, I suppose it's a step in the right direction,' Sean conceded before glancing at the clock as I gave a cavernous yawn. Grinning, he approached the bed and offered me his water. 'Come on sleepyhead, let's get some rest.'

He was staying for the rest of the night? This visit just got better and better!

Chapter Nineteen

Cait

The nightmare was suffocating me again. Pulling me under even as I tried to wake up from the terrifying visions of Greg chasing me through the field. It was so vivid I could almost feel the wind rush from my lungs as I fell to the rocky ground, could almost taste the sharp tang of fear on my tongue as the heat of his body began to crowd me as he crawled up my back and rolled me over.

Preparing myself for Greg's angular, fierce features, I tensed and opened my eyes, but instead, I was met with a concerned face and warm, brown eyes.

Wait …

What?

Jack? What was Jack doing in the wheat field? As I tried to take it in, I noticed that he wasn't pinning me to the floor, but instead holding out a hand to me. 'It's OK, Caitlin, you're safe. Take my hand.'

Unsure where he had come from, or where Greg had disappeared to, I didn't hesitate to accept Jack's hand as he gently helped me to sit upright. A flood of warm relief flowed through me from the contact and I managed to pull in a long breath to ease my straining lungs. Talk about perfect timing. He literally couldn't have arrived at a better time.

Beep.

Shaking my head to clear the peculiar noise, I frowned, so confused by this change to my nightmare that I could barely comprehend it. The breeze was still there though, warm on my face, but the horrifying ending didn't seem like it was going to occur, all thanks to Jack's timely arrival.

Beep.

Blinking my heavy eyelids, it took me several seconds to realise that I was in my hotel bedroom. I was in bed, sitting upright, and my right hand was still extended, but there was no Jack, no field, and more importantly, no Greg.

I had been dreaming again, but today's version had been significantly different – I'd had a saviour.

Running a shaky hand over my face, I found my forehead clammy and ice cold, and then realised that my sheets were damp too. I was a mess. My skin was slicked with nervous sweat, hair clinging to my face and back in damp ringlets, and my chest was heaving, but I was safe. Safe and unharmed. This time.

The screen of my mobile phone was glowing on the bedside table, indicating the arrival of a text, which presumably explained the beeping noise that had woken me. It would have to wait, I was too distressed to look at it right now.

Closing my eyes, I tried to breathe deeply to push away the sticky tendrils of the dream that were clinging to me. The breeze was real enough, coming from the cracked open window and billowing the lace curtains in the pale morning rays of the sunrise, but everything else had been part of the nightmare.

Silent tears were already streaming down my face, but suddenly a huge sob broke from my throat and I collapsed my head forward onto my knees as my terror seemed to liquefy into an endless stream of scalding tears. Gasping at the emotional wringer I'd just gone through, I then spent the next five minutes crying out the feelings that had welled up within me until I was a snivelling, snotty mess.

Using the backs of my fingers to swipe at my eyes, I dried my cheeks and picked up my phone with a trembling hand. Unfortunately, my shaking only intensified when I saw a text from the saviour in my nightmare.

From: Jack F
I just wanted to apologise again for my behaviour the other day, I'm appalled with myself and hope you can forgive me. Perhaps I'll see you around the studios in the future. I hope so. Jack

I threw the phone onto the duvet and flopped back with a sigh. How ironic that Jack's text had been the one to interrupt my nightmare just as he had interrupted Greg's attack in my dream. It was surely a coincidence, but what wasn't coincidental was how frequently he was on my mind recently.

It was early, but I slid from the bed, rinsed my face under some cool water, and set off in search of coffee. One thing was for certain – just because Jack had saved the day in my dream and sent me a nice apologetic text didn't mean I was any more inclined to let him in in real life.

I'd shut the door on relationships a long time ago, and for my failing sanity it needed to remain firmly closed, locked, and bolted, no matter how hard Jack tried to break it open.

Chapter Twenty

Allie

Hearing footsteps coming down the corridor from the bedrooms, I turned, assuming it was Sean having finished his shower, but my gaze settled on Cait instead.

'Morning. You're up early.'

Plopping down onto one of the breakfast stools, Cait rubbed her eyes, which looked decidedly red rimmed, and performed a spectacularly wide yawn before nodding.

'Are you OK? Your eyes are red.'

'I'm fine, just couldn't sleep.' Cait murmured drowsily.

My body tightened with embarrassment at her words. Had she heard Sean and me last night? What with the excitement of the burglar role play, I wasn't convinced I had exactly been quiet. Wailing like a banshee or screaming the house down were probably more accurate. Was that why she hadn't slept? Crap. That would be so mortifying.

'Did … um … did I disturb you?'

Cait gave me a sleepy, confused look, shaking her head. 'No. Why would you have disturbed me? You went to bed before me last night.'

Now feeling decidedly flustered, I flapped my hands in reply and busied myself pouring her a coffee to hide my flaming cheeks. 'Oh, no reason, I was just wondering.' Damn it. My voice was way higher than normal and such a bloody giveaway.

As I turned to pass the coffee to Cait, I found her assessing me with a frown, but before she could ask any further questions Sean came strolling in, looking glorious and fresh-faced after his shower. His hair was still damp, and he had a definite 'I got me some sexy time last night' look on his face. Talk about perfect timing. My heart did a little skip in my chest, and I couldn't help the goofy smile that slid to my lips every time I saw him. He was so gorgeous, and all mine.

'Morning, ladies.' He flashed a quick grin at Cait, who now had a knowing smirk on her face and a healthy blush to her cheeks. Looked like I'd been busted. 'Sorry I can't stay for breakfast, I need to get to the studio. I'll call you later, babe.'

Dropping a lingering kiss on my lips, Sean proceeded to slide a hand down my side to give my bum a discreet squeeze and then was gone, leaving behind him a trail of his delicious scent, an embarrassed best friend, and me, practically swooning in his wake.

'So that's the reason you were worried, huh?' Cait enquired lightly as she sipped her coffee with a grin. 'A midnight booty call from Sir Shags-a-Lot?'

A gurgled laugh bubbled up my throat, but my face sobered. 'It wasn't just a booty call,' I clarified, my tone coming out just a touch more defensive than I would have liked. I knew Sean viewed me as far more than just that, but at the moment, it did sometimes feel distinctly like that was exactly the case.

Determined to change the subject, I swivelled the conversation back to Cait. 'So why couldn't you sleep?'

Giving a dismissive shrug, Cait placed her coffee down and gave the elastic band on her wrist a flick, her movement immediately catching my eye. 'I had a bad dream, about … well, you know, about … the fuckwad.' I loved that she didn't use her ex's name any more. As far as I was concerned that was a great step in the right direction. 'And then to top it off I got a nice, early morning text from Jack.'

Oooh. Now that was noteworthy news. 'What did he want?'

'Nothing much, it was just another apology for his behaviour last week.'

My eyebrows rose in amusement at her choice of words. 'His "behaviour"? You mean the fan-bloody-tastic kiss that left you breathless? That "behaviour"?'

'Uhhh, yeah …' Cait was now puce and squirming uncomfortably on her chair, and as much as I was thrilled that Jack wasn't giving up on her, I knew my cautious friend wouldn't appreciate my excitement, so I tried my best to dial it down a few notches and keep our chat casual.

'Well, you're not the only one getting strange texts. Since that incident with Savannah where she told me that she had slept with Sean, I've now received three apology texts, and a bunch of flowers arrived last night from her,' I added, waving my hand in the direction of the beautiful bunch now decorating our kitchen work surface. For some reason, Sean had decided he didn't want *her* flowers in *my* bedroom and had moved them first thing this morning. 'It's totally weird. *She's* totally weird.'

'Maybe she's not as much of a cow as we first thought?' Cait speculated as she examined the flowers and gave an impressed nod. 'Perhaps she really does regret the prank.'

My top lip curled into a sneer as I recalled that horrible day. I wouldn't call professing a sexual relationship with someone else's boyfriend a 'prank', but I knew what Cait meant.

‘Yeah, maybe.’ As nice as the apologies were, I was remaining quietly sceptical where Savannah Hilton was concerned. Sceptical and cautious. Pouring us a top up of our caffeine fix I plucked the card from the flowers and slid it across to Cait so she could read the words.

Sorry again for my silly fun. I hope I’m forgiven. Savannah

‘Silly fun?’ Cait spluttered. ‘Mind you, real flowers and she used the word sorry,’ Cait mused, turning the card in her hand and grinning at me in surprise.

‘I know. I mean, seriously? I didn’t even know the word featured in her vocab.’

Chapter Twenty-One

Cait

After a shower, I made my way back to the kitchen to see if Allie had any plans. I only had a few more days of freedom before I started work, and I planned on making the most of them. Seeing as Sean had left this morning saying he was going to work, I was secretly hoping my bestie might be free to spend the day with me.

As I arrived back, Allie spun towards me with a grin. 'So, to stop you dwelling on last night's bad dream I've decided we need a day out, just the two of us. What do you think?'

She had practically read my mind, and although my plans to be active today weren't just to distract me from the lingering Greg dream, I did want to go out, so I nodded happily.

'Yay! I'm so glad you're free. Pack anything you need and we'll head straight out. Don't forget sun cream, it's a scorcher.'

With a small daypack containing sunglasses, sun cream, a map, and my camera, I made my way to the porch and found Allie waiting for me.

Locking the door, we started off towards the car park, but I couldn't help but catch sight of the pout she was throwing my way and frowned.

‘What’s that look for?’

‘You’ll be starting work soon and I’ll barely get to see you,’ she muttered. Rolling my eyes, I followed her across the car park and linked my arm through hers. ‘Don’t exaggerate. We’ll see each other plenty once we’ve moved in together.’

‘That’s true, I can’t wait! Do you have a date yet?’

‘No, but Jason said he’d chase it up and get someone to call me today. It’s going to be awesome living together in our own place.’ I gave a thumbs up to show my excitement and nodded. ‘So what shall we do today?’ I asked, my voice high and gleeful at not only the prospect of spending the entire day with Allie, but of our imminent move.

‘Well, seeing as we’re basically both residents of LA now …’ This was said with an excited wiggle of her eyebrows and an infectious grin. ‘I thought we should get the final touristy stuff out the way. I looked up the top things to do, so we’re going to tick off a few more of the sights. I know we’ve done some already, but there’s plenty more exciting things to see today.’

Unlinking our arms, Allie reached into the back pocket of her jeans and pulled out a folded piece of paper. Peering over her shoulder, I saw it was a list. ‘So, top of the list was Venice Beach and Hollywood Boulevard, but we’ve done both of those. Next was shopping on Rodeo Drive, but I think that might be a tad over budget, so I figured we’d save that.’

Dodging around a motorbike, we paused by the taxi rank in the hotel car park and waited for one to pull up alongside us. ‘I know how much you love art, so I thought we’d go to the Getty Centre. Art, architecture, beautiful gardens, and not forgetting restaurants for a nice lunch. Plus, some great city views. The gallery is free, but lunch is my treat to say congratulations on the job. How does that sound?'

That sounded like my idea of heaven. 'Wow! Sounds brilliant. What more could we want?'

As a taxi driver waved to indicate he was on his way to us, Allie turned to me with a conspiratorial look. 'Soooo ... you said you were a little worried about the job because of Jack, and the, uh ... letters from Greg. How are you feeling about it all now you've had a little time to think?'

'Honestly? It's perfect. I couldn't have put together a more ideal job description if I'd written the thing myself.'

'So why can I hear a 'but' hanging in the air?' Allie enquired, no doubt knowing full well why. Seeing as Greg appeared to be in Oz at the moment I'd successfully shelved my concerns about him for now. But as much as I hated to admit it – and I really hated to admit it – my thoughts were often revolving around a tall, brown-haired hunk of man who currently resided in LA.

Flushing, a long sigh escaped my lips which caused Allie to flash me a concerned look. 'Same ol' reasons, but I'll get over them, I'm sure,' I answered, my voice wavering just slightly. I'm not sure if my lack of belief showed in my voice, but luckily a cab pulled up at that exact moment and distracted Allie from her inquisition.

The cab ride was a simple twenty minutes drive down Sunset Boulevard, or Sunset Strip as it was known around here. The strip was a feast for the eyes, famed for its huge array of brightly coloured billboards, and believe me, there were a heck of a lot of them. As well as the signs, the streets were lined with boutiques, restaurants, rock clubs, nightclubs ... you name it, it was here.

The cab dropped us at the Getty Centre visitor's entrance, which was at the bottom of a steep slope, and we climbed out into the sun to gaze up at the huge, white buildings perched on the hill top above us. 'Wow. It looks bigger than I expected.' I had assumed it was going to be a regular museum, but this seemed to be an entire estate, and looked incredibly extensive.

Wandering over to the guest information, we had a quick read and discovered we had two choices for getting to the museum complex at the top: walk up the hill, which according to the board would take about twenty minutes, or jump on the small electric tram. Seeing it was already baking hot out, it seemed an easy choice. 'Let's jump on, that way we won't be sweaty while we walk around. If you want some exercise later we can always walk back down the hill.'

The tram had us up the hill in no time, and then it was simply a matter of deciding where we wanted to head for first. With Allie's love of writing and books, and my love of art and history, we had plenty to choose from.

As it was still relatively early, the temperature in the shade was lovely, so we decided to start in the gardens. The Central Garden was amazing, a real sensory treat, as we wound our way around walkways and paths between a fabulous array of beautiful smelling, and looking, plants. Pausing in the shade of some trees, we gazed at a stream in front of us that was tumbling over a small stone waterfall. It was so peaceful here. The only sounds were those of nature: birds singing in the trees, the splashing of the water, and rustling of leaves in the gentle breeze. I felt myself relaxing more and more every second, and decided that now I knew I was staying in LA, I'd have to make sure that this place was a regular visit.

'So, back to our conversation. Greg … and Jack.' All my earlier relaxation evaporated at Allie's cautious inquiry and I turned to face her, leaning back on a pillar and folding my arms as I shook my head.

'Like I said, Greg is just a background issue. And Jack? Honestly? I don't really want to think about him today.' I murmured grumpily.

'I know, but avoiding the issue doesn't make it go away. Let's just brainstorm it, and hopefully you might feel a bit better about everything. Just five minutes and then I promise we won't speak of the six foot of broad-shouldered manliness again all day.'

At her description, I closed my eyes and groaned as his face filled my mind. 'I barely know him, and nothing has happened between us, not really …' I added hastily as a vision of his lips locking with mine popped into my brain and made my core clench. 'And nothing will happen, but the responses he spurs in me are really unnerving. It's like I don't have control over myself when I'm around him.'

'Mmm-hmm, I know what you mean, I'm like that with Sean.' Linking her arm with mine, Allie led me to a bench where we both sat and stretched out our legs. 'The difference is, I love that feeling, it's so freeing,' she added dreamily.

Freeing? Could I ever be like that? So trusting of another person that I totally relaxed my defences?

'After looking up the studios' map and seeing that he films over the other side of the complex, I'm pretty sure you won't see him half as much as you're thinking. I bet you're worrying for nothing.'

Nodding, I gave in to my nerves and began to flick at the elastic band as a soothing distraction, which would have helped me calm down if I hadn't been stopped almost immediately by a sharp slap from Allie. 'Oww! Sorry. He just makes me nervous,' I admitted.

Shifting in her seat, I watched as Allie opened her mouth

and then closed it several times. Obviously she wanted to say something, but was holding back.

'What?' I asked, suspecting that I knew what she was thinking and not liking it one little bit.

'I was just thinking that it's a shame, that's all. I mean, he seems like a really nice guy, you said the kiss was good, and he's obviously keen …'

Her words trailed off, and I dipped my face to stare into my clenched hands. Damn it, I hated it when I was right. Just talking about Jack had caused my heart rate to soar and pound almost painfully in my chest. His kiss had been more than good. It had been spectacular. 'He makes me feel weak … and I hate that,' I finally admitted in a whisper. 'After Greg, I just … I want to be in control, and Jack makes me lose all sense. It's so contradictory, but it's like he scares me *and* attracts me at the same time.'

'I understand that, and I bet it's confusing as hell, but you're stronger than you give yourself credit for, Cait, remember that.' Sliding closer on the bench, Allie slid an arm around my shoulders and gave me a reassuring squeeze, the way only a best friend can, and I tilted my head to rest on her shoulder.

She seemed to sense that nothing she could say would help, so we merely sat in silence. We both came to a quiet agreement not to mention Jack again, and after sitting for a while longer we began to head back towards the galleries.

The walk took us past some stunning sculptures, and after exploring my love of art in the exhibition of European paintings, which to my delight contained a real van Gogh, we moved to the building which housed the Research Institute, where they had a collection of rare manuscripts, photographs, and books which Allie was fascinated by.

'I don't know about you, but I'm starving,' Allie

announced as we declared that the galleries were now done to our satisfaction.

'Me too. What do you fancy, café or restaurant?'

'Let's see if we can get a table in the restaurant, the views are supposed to be stunning.'

Perhaps it was because it was a weekday, but the restaurant was nowhere near as full as we'd expected, and we managed to walk straight in and bag a table right at the edge of the balcony. Allie was right, the outlook was stunning, with a fabulous view over the Santa Monica Mountains in the distance. It really was breathtaking and we both ended up sitting in silence and just gawking for several minutes after arriving.

I had just put my knife and fork down after a delicious warm salad of beetroot, feta cheese, green beans, and asparagus when I saw Allie pause with her fork halfway to her mouth.

'Uh oh,' she murmured, her eyes widening as she suddenly looked very interested in something over my shoulder. I was about to turn and investigate, but Allie reached across and gripped my arm. 'No! Don't turn around. It's, uh, nothing.'

Her words said it was nothing, but her face said entirely the opposite, and I narrowed my eyes on her and shook my head. 'Don't give me that rubbish. I'm turning around in three seconds unless you tell me what it is you've seen. Three, two …'

'OK! All right.' Placing her fork down she leant across the table, her face paling as she looked at me intently. 'You know when I said you wouldn't have to think about Jack Felton again today …?' Even hearing his name made my skin react, and the hairs on my arms stood to attention as if physically seeking him out. 'Well, I might have to retract that statement, because he's just walked in.'

Oh crap. Closing my eyes, I drew in a deep breath and then very calmly let it out through my nose. Opening my eyes, I saw Allie watching me in concern, her eyes occasionally darting across the balcony presumably in Jack's direction.

It was stupid, I knew it was, but I couldn't help but give a tiny glance over my shoulder. And there he was, in all his suited, booted, broad-shouldered gorgeousness. Goddamn that man. Thinking I could just sneak a quick look and then continue with my lunch, I quickly realised that that idea was thrown by the wayside as his gaze skimmed the restaurant and landed straight on me like a homing missile.

There was a flicker of surprise on his face, but those captivating eyes did their usual job of snaring me in so I felt like I couldn't look away. Tilting his head curiously, I watched him nod in my direction, the corners of his lips twitching in a half smile that made a dimple appear in his cheek and caused my stomach to flip-flop wildly. I didn't manage to return his smile, I seemed physically unable, but I did forcibly crank my neck back to stare at my empty plate as I gripped my fork with near lethal force.

It would seem my emotions were in free fall. Again.

I loosened the grip on my fork to ease the ache in my knuckles and registered the urge to look back at him, which began growing in my chest like a nagging itch. Instead, I looked at Allie. 'Is he watching us?' I whispered hoarsely, my voice seeming to have disappeared along with my sanity.

'Um, no, his party is being seated at a table. He's talking to the waiter. Oh, wait … yeah, now he's looking.' It was ridiculous, my conscious, protective side didn't want his attention, but the truth was, I felt a little thrill run through me at the thought of him looking my way. On the occasions I'd met him, he'd made me feel ... well, it was hard to pinpoint. Overwhelmed? Aroused? Terrified? Whatever it was, I felt something, which was certainly a first since Greg.

'Oh shit ...'Allie hissed, completely forgetting the rest of her lunch and dumping down her fork with a loud clatter as her eyes widened like saucers and she stared at me as if I had suddenly grown five heads.

'What?'

'He, um, well, he's either going to the toilets and walking round the entire restaurant to get to them, or he's, um ... coming over here.'

Oh god. Well, given his persistence, I should have expected that. Trying to fortify myself, I sat up straighter and drew in a long, deep breath. However, no amount of oxygen could have prepared me for the close-up view of Jack in a three-piece suit as it arrived by my side ten seconds later.

I could have been attached to an oxygen mask and I would still have felt breathless. Navy trousers, jacket, and waistcoat topped over a light blue shirt and pale grey tie. Quite simply, he looked like perfection wrapped up in high quality, luxury cotton, and I felt my mouth dry up and my confidence falter.

Seeing me sitting stock still and unable to manage even the most basic of actions, Allie jumped in for me. 'Hi, Jack.' Her greeting was far too enthusiastic for my liking, as she practically launched herself from her seat to shake his hand.

'Allie, it's a pleasure to see you again. Bumping into you two seems to be becoming a bit of a habit, doesn't it?' he murmured with a small smile.

Polite and well-mannered as ever. Except for when he'd jumped me in the park and shoved his tongue in my mouth. That hadn't exactly been gentlemanly. Not that I'd complained at first, of course … As memories of me gripping his T-shirt and dragging him closer filled my mind, I swallowed hard and saw Jack swivelling his attention onto me.

Do not look at his lips and the mouth that caused such devastating reactions. *Do not look.* Instead, I was staring at my empty plate, looking like a complete idiot while my mind taunted me by repeatedly replaying the sensations of our shared kiss. Marvellous.

Lifting my head, I met his gaze and blinked several times as his eyes seemed to shoot into me like lasers. Don't look at his lips. It was as if he could see right inside me and peel back all my layers and insecurities. I needed to say something so I didn't look completely ignorant. Anything. But nothing was springing to mind.

'Uh, hi … Jack,' I managed to stutter. It wasn't exactly a genius statement, but it was better than nothing, I suppose.

Not able to hold his gaze without either slapping myself across the forehead in frustration or swooning pathetically, I instead focused my attention on the movement of his hands as he popped open the button on his suit jacket and casually slipped one hand into the pocket of his trousers.

The end result was that I was now staring at Jack's groin. Marvellous. So I had succeeded in not looking at his mouth, but was staring at his crotch instead? That was so much worse than looking at his lips!

Good one, Cait. Really smooth.

Jerking my head up, I saw the corner of his mouth twitch with a supressed smirk and had to swallow hard to try and keep my composure. 'It's, umm, you again.'

‘Yes, me again. It seems almost fated that we are to keep meeting,’ he said mildly, sounding like he was feeling none of the rampaging nerves I currently was.

‘Or perhaps you’re following me,’ I added, suddenly desperately keen to appear as bloody unruffled as he was. ‘I said your behaviour was stalkerish, and look, here you are again,’ I offered, equally as casually and fixing my eyes to his to watch his reaction.

All I got was a thin, tight-lipped smile and a twitch at the corner of his eye to indicate that he disliked my quip. ‘Hmmm. Yes, I got the distinct impression you were unhappy with me last week, Caitlin. Did you get my apology text this morning?’

Unhappy with him?

Unhappy?

Did he have any clue how screwed-up my emotions were now because of that kiss? That stunning, heart-melting, mind-bendingly good kiss ... Turning his attention to Allie, he shook his head as if bemused by something, ‘Did Caitlin tell you that I met her at the studios’ running club and she actually sprinted away from me?’

‘Uh ... she might have mentioned it.’ Allie’s eyes were flicking between mine and Jack’s, but I was so gobsmacked that I merely sat there staring at him in shock. How dare he throw that out there like that? I ran away from him because he had kissed me and it had totally freaked me out, but I couldn’t believe he was really calling me out on that now, when I was sitting with my friend having lunch.

‘I ... I think you know why I ran away, Jack,’ I hissed.

Seemingly ignoring my reply, he huffed out a breath, appeared to roll off some tension in his neck, and continued to chat with Allie as casual as anything, as if my entire sanity wasn’t currently hanging in the balance by a thread.

'So, are you looking for work here, too?'

'No, actually, I'm trying to make it as a writer, so the plan is to crack on with my next book and see how it goes,' Allie explained quickly, her eyes flashing between myself and Jack repeatedly as if she were a spectator at a tennis match.

Looking impressed, Jack nodded. 'Good luck. I've always fancied writing a book myself, but I never get the time.'

'You should go for it. Starting is the trickiest bit.'

'I might just do that.' Turning his attention back to me, I almost flinched under the power of his gaze. 'So, have you managed to persuade Caitlin to accept the studio job, Allie?' The sound of him mentioning my blatant lie did ridiculously silly things to my stomach and I made a desperate grab for my glass to try and distract myself from the guilt churning in my gut.

'Although perhaps persuasion won't be required,' Jack continued before Allie could speak. 'Jason at Dynamic is a running buddy of mine, we're rather good friends. I'm sure he's made Caitlin an offer too good to refuse.'

Oh no. My heart dropped at his words, and the knowing tone to his voice. Busted. If Jack was good friends with Jason then he no doubt already knew I had accepted the job. Bugger. So not only had I lied to him, but I'd now been caught out in that lie. Jeez, this whole situation really couldn't get much more awkward.

Lifting my water to my lips in an attempt at quenching my parched throat, I realised to my horror that my hand had a distinct shake to it, so I ended up swigging half of it down before practically slamming the glass onto the table.

'I'm *sure* she's going to take it,' Allie added conspiratorially, an evil grin flicking at the corners of her lips and giving away the fact that she found my squirming rather amusing.

'I think so too,' Jack nodded, flashing a grin at my traitorous bestie. God, this was the last thing I needed, both of them bloody ganging up on me. As much as she was trying to act supportively, I could see the flash of excitement in Allie's eyes as this all played out, but right now I wanted nothing more than to escape this craziness and allow my normal, sheltered, safe life to resume.

Jack shifted on the spot to broaden his stance and as his jacket moved I got a waft of his minty, slightly sweet scent that served to remind me of how good he had tasted. Really bloody good. Everything about him was so overpowering. Even the way he smelt made me feel dizzy. I made an effort not to breathe in through my nose, but became aware that my mouth was now hanging open and I was practically panting.

Bloody hell, this was insane.

'So are you going to be mute and avoiding me from now on?' he persevered to my horror, now with a teasing half-smile floating around his lips.

Feeling thoroughly flummoxed, I felt my old defences rear to the surface. 'I'm not mute, and I'm not avoiding you. I was just choosing to sit quietly, that's all.' Huffing out an irritable breath I crossed my arms. 'And I barely know you, why would I bother to avoid you?' I sounded decidedly prickly, but was so close to losing my sanity over this man that I didn't care.

'She speaks,' he murmured with a small, soft smile. 'And I think you'll try to avoid me because you feel this thing between us and it scares you.' Totally flabbergasted at his forward claims in front of my best friend – even if they were completely spot on – my eyes shot to his, to see him looking immaculate and calm as anything, as if we were doing nothing more than discussing the weather.

How dare he?

How bloody dare he?

The fact that he had hit the nail right on the head was irrelevant, but my pulse was thundering in my veins so hard that I could feel it trying to burst its way from my chest, and I knew my face had flushed bright red.

Putting on my best glare, I bravely held his stare, and then flailing my arms as if that would help prove my point, I spat out my reply with as much defiance as I could muster. 'There is no *us*, and there is no *thing*.' As much as I wanted them to be true, the words were driven by my fear and felt like salt on my tongue. My fear from Greg. That was what had stopped me seeing it clearly, but there *was* some sort of connection between Jack and me. Even as naïve as I was, I could feel some strange bond that I didn't fully understand, but it continued to draw me to him regardless of my attempts to push it away.

Finally showing some emotion, Jack threw his hands up in the air and then turned to Allie. 'Is she always this stubborn?' he demanded in frustration, to which Allie merely nodded and gave a sad smile. 'Can you see the chemistry between the two of us? Because I feel it so strongly it makes my heart race with possibilities, but for some reason Caitlin just point blank denies it.'

I make his heart race? Wow. Well, that made two of us. For some reason his confession made something in my chest squeeze really tight. And just like him, my heart was definitely racing.

I glared at Allie in a don't-you-dare-utter-a-word kind of way, and watched as she bit down on her lower lip before chewing it furiously. It was clear she was torn; she liked

Jack, and loved the fact that he seemed to like me, but if she jumped in and backed him up now then so help me god she would be in so much trouble.

'I … I … it's not really my place to get involved, Jack. I think I might just, um, go to the toilet.'

As soon as Allie had stumbled away from the table, Jack dropped into a crouch beside me, putting his face just below the level of mine. The jokey look from earlier was gone now, replaced instead by a fiercely purposeful expression.

'All I want is a chance to get to know you, Caitlin,' he stated heatedly. Running a hand through his hair, he left it spiky and messy all over his head, and drew in a long breath. 'I apologise if I upset you in the woods … I seem to lose my mind around you, but I swear that won't happen again.' He lost his mind too? Because that's how I felt all the time when he was near.

'Believe me, I never pursue women like this, and I don't use my fame to get women in bed, I swear. It's *you*, Caitlin. There's something between us, something powerful. Can't you give it a chance? Give me a chance?' He tried to reach out and take my hand, and I was almost tempted to let him just to see if his touch reassured me or freaked me out. But at the last minute I tucked both of my arms down into my lap and linked the fingers tightly. Really tightly. So tightly that they ached.

'Why?' he whispered hoarsely, 'Why are you doing this?' he repeated, sounding defeated.

For a crazy second I toyed with the idea of just telling him the truth. Because my fuck-up of an ex has left me mentally scarred and I'm terrified of ever letting a man get that close to me again. But like a proper coward I used good old-fashioned spitefulness instead.

'Perhaps I'm really just not interested. Is that so hard for your ego to understand?' I whispered. I'd meant to hiss or spit out my reply, but my words were strained and lacked the ferocity I had intended.

I now woke up most mornings having dreamt about him, my subconscious obviously trying to force the issue on me. And when I say most mornings, I actually meant every morning. But to date Jack would mean opening up my past again, dealing with the painful issues that Greg had left me with, and making me the most vulnerable I'd ever allowed.

I couldn't see how I could do that.

Could I do that? For him?

He hadn't replied to my jab, instead Jack just stared at me looking completely dejected. I levelled my gaze on him, trying not to flinch or shake or give any trace of my emotions, and then sighed heavily.

'Allie's coming back. You should go and join your party,' I suggested quietly. To my horror, I could feel tears burning at the backs of my eyes, no doubt from the stress of the situation, but the hot liquid built on the rims of my lower lids with surprising speed. I couldn't let him see me cry, then he'd surely guess that all of my words were complete rubbish. All I had to do was hold it together for a few more seconds, then he'd be gone.

Shaking his head, Jack licked his lips, the brief flick of his tongue immediately drawing my gaze as I broke my rule and looked down at his mouth. Damn it! What would it feel like if he leant up and kissed me right now? Stupidly, this thought made me copy the action and dart my own tongue out to moisten my tingling lips.

I'm fairly sure Jack noticed too, because a tiny flicker of hope seemed to flutter in his eyes as he returned his gaze to mine. As our eyes met he frowned slightly, and I panicked that he would see the tears building in my eyes, so I quickly averted my gaze to the tiled floor.

'I don't believe you when you say you're not interested, Caitlin. I felt it in your kiss, and I can see the emotion in your face right now. You like me too. You feel it,' he murmured, his face twisting and looking just as affected as me.

I couldn't deny it out loud any more. He was right, and my head felt the urge to give just the tiniest nod in response.

Belatedly I became aware that my head was now moving of its own will and I panicked and froze.

Holy crap. Had I actually just nodded?

He'd told me I felt it too, and I had … *nodded* in response? No, *no*, I couldn't have, could I? Oh god, judging from the flaring emotion in Jack's eyes I might well have done. *Shit*. I could barely breathe, let alone accept that I had just given away my true feelings with that seemingly inconsequential little body movement. This was crazy.

Feeling a desperate urge to try and take back what I'd just done I blinked and then swallowed hard. 'Jack, I … I …' But try as I might, I couldn't retract my confession because it was completely true, I *did* like him, and I *did* feel it too, so I ended up sat there stuttering like an idiot.

'It's OK, Caitlin, you're scared, I can see that. But I just don't know what of.' Pulling out a pristine white handkerchief from his suit pocket, he gently laid it across my knee without actually touching me, and gave a small head nod as if acknowledging that I was upset. 'I plan on proving that you don't ever need to be scared of me. Even if it's just as friends, that's OK, but I will prove it to you, Caitlin.'

I didn't know what to do. I was on the verge of a

meltdown and the only thing I could think to do that would make it better was to throw myself at him. For some insane reason, the idea of his arms around me and comforting me seemed like possibly the best idea in the world.

Or perhaps the worst.

My brain was so scrambled I couldn't work out which. My goody two shoes side won out, and I refrained, sitting rigidly frozen in my seat.

Jack closed his eyes for a brief second, drew in a slow breath, and then fixed me with a clear, intent gaze. 'I'm sorry if I've upset you again. I seem to do that a lot,' he murmured, and there was no point denying his words because I was clearly a wreck. 'I'll see you around, Caitlin.' He made those last five words sound like a promise. Or maybe a threat, I couldn't decide which. And with that he stood to his full height, straightened his suit, and with one last, long look, he stalked off to his table.

Chapter Twenty-Two

Jack

I'd promised myself that if my path crossed with Caitlin's again I would take it as a sign of fate and speak to her, so when I'd spotted her in the restaurant I'd barely been able to believe my good fortune. Maybe we really were fated to keep meeting. Or perhaps it was just my lucky day. Mind you, I didn't feel quite so lucky as I walked away after yet another rejection.

I released a deep breath slowly through my nose as I tried desperately not to look over my shoulder to see if she was watching. It literally took all of my fortitude not to glance back, so to distract myself I thought back through our brief encounter to see if there were any positives I could draw from it. Luckily, there were several.

A smile curved on my lips as I recalled her few spunky outbursts – the way she'd practically hissed when I'd brought up the subject of our kiss was particularly noteworthy, because I'm sure I'd seen arousal spark in her eyes for a second or two. Her cheeks had flushed a very appealing pink too, and from the way she had gripped the table I could only assume that she had been enjoying the memories.

Grimacing with embarrassment I swallowed hard as I recalled the way my cock had given a little twitch in response to her watching me. Luckily I'd managed to tamp it down before I got a full on stiffy in the middle of the restaurant, but it was clear that my body seemed to have a mind of its own when she was around.

I hadn't been exaggerating when I'd said I lost my mind around her, because I really did. It was crazy, but she made me think and do things I would never usually do. If, and I knew it was a pretty big if, but *if* Caitlin ever did let her barriers down around me I was going to have to be super careful to stick to my promise not to lose control around her again. With the way she made me feel that would be a bloody difficult task, but even if it stretched my willpower to the extremes of my limits I'd do it.

For her, it would be worth it.

Arriving back at my group, I smiled politely to the occupants of my table – my agent Rick, and Barb, the head of my PR team – and retook my seat. Discussing the moves I wanted to take in my career was literally the last thing on my mind right now, so I was grateful for a few minutes' silence as we all looked at the menus. Well, I pretended to study the menu, but really I was looking over the top of it towards Caitlin. Allie was back, looking tense and concerned, and I definitely didn't miss the way she flashed a few wary glances in my direction.

I'd almost, almost, believed it when Caitlin had said that she wasn't interested. After all, I was only human, and there were only so many knockbacks I could endure, but the tiny nod she'd given me when I'd said she felt it too had almost caused me to yell my joy on the spot.

She *did* like me. And for the first time since meeting her she'd actually admitted it. Not verbally, as I would have liked, but a nod was a start. Something significant had passed between us in that silent moment, and the sudden torrent of emotion that had then flooded her face had nearly done me in. Her expression had been so open and yet so torn, displaying her fear, attraction, and hesitancy so clearly that even a blind man would have been able to sense it and I had wanted to drag her into my arms so desperately.

Watching as she fidgeted nervously at the table, I had to forcibly cross my arms to keep myself from going to her. That wouldn't help matters. With Caitlin, I was going to have to take this a tiny step at a time. She looked upset, and I hated that I was the one to have caused her distress. And even though she didn't look my way again, I couldn't help notice that she still had my handkerchief clutched tightly in her hand, and a small, hopeful smile pulled at my lips.

Chapter Twenty-Three

Cait

Fuck me, that had been seriously flipping intense.

My head was spinning, and my heart was beating so quickly that I was genuinely worried I might pass out. If he hadn't been able to see me, I probably would have collapsed forwards onto the table and burst out crying from the tension, but as it was I squeezed my eyes shut to hold back the tears, clutched his handkerchief in one hand, and gripped the edge of the table with the other.

I needed to curl up in a darkened room for several hours to recover from all this stress.

You like me too. You feel it. Clenching my teeth I ran his words through my head, still unable to believe that I'd actually nodded my confirmation.

Fuckety fuck.

I felt the table cloth pull as Allie silently slid back into her seat opposite. I knew she would be watching me carefully, no doubt with a million things she wanted to say, but I couldn't deal with that here, not with Jack just a few feet away. I could still feel his magnetic presence. I needed to get away. Now.

Opening my eyes, I stared down at her nearly finished plate of pasta. 'Are you finished?' I asked quietly.

'Yes. Are you OK?' The concern was clear in her voice, but I ignored her question.

'Can we go please?' I was still avoiding eye contact, but I was so close to completely falling apart that I didn't dare look up. If I saw even a trace of sympathy on her face, I'd crumble.

'Cait, you're really pale. You're not going to faint, are you?'

Faint? No. Nod my head? Probably. Goddamn it!

Sniffing back my tears, I cleared my throat with considerable difficulty. 'I don't think so, but I don't feel too great.' Wasn't that just an understatement? I felt like I'd been put through an emotional wringer stuck on the spin cycle.

Standing up, I straightened my clothes and ran a trembling hand over my face before gripping Jack's hankie and wringing it in my hands. The cotton was so soft, and as tempting as it was to make a show of throwing it down on the table and leaving it, I found myself taking it with me as I left.

The effort it took not to look in Jack's direction as we walked out was exhausting, but even though I hadn't turned my head his way I knew he was watching me. It was like I could feel his eyes on me, and every hair on my body rose at the attention.

It appeared, that for once, my best friend had been rendered speechless, because we walked out of the restaurant, through the gardens, and towards the tram stop in complete silence. It was only when we were sitting in the carriage for the short ride that Allie spoke again.

'Sooo, that was pretty crazy, huh?' she murmured cautiously.

Blinking long and slow, I raised my gaze to hers for the first time since we'd practically fled from the restaurant. Crazy, intense, emotional, stressful … I could probably list a hundred adjectives to describe that encounter.

'Mmm,' I agreed. 'Can you believe he did that in the middle of a restaurant? Talk about arrogant.'

'It was a bit surprising.' Allie was speaking in that slow, drawn-out way that meant she had more to say but was holding back. I really didn't need any more of her persuasive advice right now, so I gave her a firm look to keep her quiet, but instead of understanding, she shrugged and waved her hands.

'It's just that he didn't seem arrogant to me. He came across as, well, as a little fraught, perhaps, maybe even a tad desperate, but not arrogant. He obviously really likes you.'

'OK, maybe he's not arrogant,' I conceded. 'But he certainly has some air of calm certainty about him that is really frigging unnerving.' Sighing, I ran my hands over my face, realising that I was still holding his handkerchief but still not bothering to dispose of it. 'I don't really want to talk about it any more,' I murmured, but clearly Allie couldn't hold back now she had started.

'I bet he's great in bed.'

'What?' I squeaked, my eyes flying wide as I cast a quick glance around the tram to check that no one was in listening range. Thankfully, we were alone.

'Well, he's mature, and quite intense, and that usually makes for a good lover because they're very focused on you,' Allie explained, making my cheeks flush as red as her Converse trainers.

'Allie, you're really not helping,' I muttered, averting my eyes and staring out of the window to try and distract myself from imagining what it might be like to be the sole focus of Jack's attention while in bed with him. Naked. And quite possibly sweaty. My entire body shivered with delight.

'He was right, you know, the chemistry between you two is really obvious. It's so strong you can almost see it. I really think you should give him a break. Go out with him, Cait.' Here we go again. There was going to be no stopping her now.

I was trying to be patient, but after the run-in with Jack, my nerves were already frayed to tearing point and I was getting close to shouting. 'We went over this at the art gallery, Allie, remember? Me, frigid and inexperienced, and him a world-class player. Not a good mix, and never gonna happen.'

Crossing her arms, she shook her head dismissively. 'It's also wildly untrue. Yes, you are a little inexperienced, but you aren't frigid. You just had a really shitty experience which has made you cautious. And rightly so. And you can believe he's a player if it makes you feel better, but we both know that's not the case. After you told me his number of lovers was in single digits, I did a bit of digging on the internet, and it would seem to be true. The over-all opinion of him is that he's a genuinely nice guy.'

Grudgingly, I could believe that. That night we'd spent in the bar together had been lovely; he'd been sweet, attentive, and friendly. *Genuinely nice*. But taking it to the next level was a whole new issue, and one I was simply too exhausted to even contemplate at the moment.

The tram pulled to a stop and we wandered off in the direction of the line of cabs eagerly awaiting the disembarking passengers. 'If I promise you that I'll consider dating someone, not necessarily Jack, but someone, in the near-ish future, will you please let this subject drop?'

Seeing my weariness Allie caved and linked her arm

with mine. 'I'm sorry. I don't mean to put pressure on you, it's just that I worry about you.'

'But you don't need to, I'm perfectly happy being single. Give me a few more years and you can call me Caitlin Byrne, spinster specialist.'

'That's what worries me,' she said as she pulled open the back door to a taxi and slid in.

Chapter Twenty-Four

Allie

Cait's contact at the studios had come up trumps, because not only was I now standing outside a pretty flashy-looking complex waiting to view the available house with Cait, but if we liked it, we could get the keys today. We could have a place of our own in Los Angeles by the end of the day! How exciting was that?

I have to say, when Cait said she'd meet me by the complex directly opposite the gates to the studio, I'd taken one look at the place and thought she'd got it wrong. These buildings looked way too nice for us to afford, but when I'd checked the name above the gate, Studio City, I'd realised I was in the right place.

The complex looked amazing. Turning away from the buildings, I smiled at just how close to Dynamic Studios this place was – literally just across the road – which would be perfect for Cait's work. I also happened to know that Sean's studios weren't that far away either, so that earned this place a tick in the location box for me, too.

Cait had popped to the studios to get something she'd left there last week on her run, so I was waiting outside on my own itching to get inside and look around.

Fidgeting impatiently, I pulled out my phone and wondered if Sean would be free for a quick chat. We had agreed that if he was on set and not able to talk he would turn his phone off, so I figured it was worth a try.

Pressing call I waited, and was thrilled when it rang and connected almost immediately. 'Hey, my gorgeous girl. This is a nice surprise. How are you?'

'Hey, babe. I'm good, just waiting for Cait. We're viewing the house near her studios. They look quite fancy through the fences.'

'Studio City, right? It is pretty nice in there. When are you moving in?'

'Ha, I've got to see if I like it first! But if we do, the woman said we can get the keys today, so I guess we'd move some stuff in over the weekend.'

'Let me know how you get on.' Sean paused, and I could tell from the tone of his voice that he had something else to say. 'I'm glad you called, actually … I was wondering what you were doing on Monday?'

'Nothing, why?'

'I have a visitor coming, someone I'd really like you to meet,' he said mysteriously.

Well and truly intrigued now, I narrowed my eyes. 'Who?'

'It's a secret.' The smile in his voice was obvious, but I immediately tensed up as memories of the last time Sean took me to meet "someone secret" flooded my mind.

'Nuh-uh, no way. No more secret visits to people Sean. That didn't work out so well for us last time, did it?'

The pause down the line told me that Sean was taking a second or two to fully realise what I was talking about, but as soon as he did I heard a horrified gasp. 'Allie, no. This is completely different. This is something good.'

He'd said the last secret visit would be good too, and now my teeth were fully clenched. I trusted him, but memories of our visit with Savannah were still so fresh that it made me feel fragile to even think about it.

'Fine, fine, I'll tell you.' He paused and I definitely heard a loud swallow down the line. 'I … I want you to meet my mum,' Sean blurted. 'Would you like that, or is it too soon?'

Too soon? Like his almost-but-not-quite-proposal at his beach house? I drew in a deep breath and released it through my nose as I pictured him down on one knee again. Yes, it was perhaps a little early, but things with us had moved fast from the start, so why break tradition now? Besides, the way he sounded so unsure showed his vulnerability, which I supposed made two of us, and my teeth immediately unclenched as I fell a little more in love with him.

'I would love to meet her, Sean. Thank you.'

A relieved breath whistled down the line and Sean chuckled. 'She's flying in on Sunday for work, but we're meeting on Monday for lunch at my new house.'

'OK.' My voice sounded all whispery and shy and I felt my cheeks blushing. Wow. Meeting his mother? Things really were getting serious between us.

What with potentially moving house over the weekend then meeting Sean and his mum, it looked like I was going to have a busy few days ahead.

Cait

I'd left Allie outside the studios while I quickly nipped in to pick up the water bottle and running jumper I'd left there last week. After being kissed half senseless by Jack in the woods, I'd dashed straight out and left them behind at the starting point. Mel had messaged me to say she'd put them in her locker for me, and I'd decided to pop in to grab them.

I was now heading to meet Allie, but the problem was that my over-active imagination had started conjuring up images of Jack all over the place. A brief glimpse of a brown head of hair a few seconds ago had been all it took to set me on to high alert.

What would I say to him next time I saw him? After our intense showdown at the Getty Centre, and my giveaway nod, my mind was running wild. He'd clearly seen through my lies now, so did I front up and tell the complete truth about how I felt, or keep trying to deny my feelings?

As a consequence, I was practically sprinting towards the exit like a lunatic, so it would seem I had moved on from denial to avoidance. I wouldn't deny how I felt any more, but I would avoid discussing it, or seeing him. Seeing as we worked at the same studio complex there were clearly some serious flaws to this plan, but it was the only one I could formulate at the moment so it would have to do.

I could have called for a golf cart to take me back to the entrance or tried to flag one down, but I didn't. I was so paranoid about standing still in case Jack appeared from somewhere that I ran hell for leather until my lungs burnt and my face was streaming with sweat.

Arriving at the studios' gates, I bent forward to rest my hands on my knees, feeling like I'd run a bloody marathon as I desperately tried to drag some air into my lungs.

'Woah! What the heck, Cait? You were running like a pack of zombies were on your tail.'

I felt Allie's hand land on my lower back and the contact somehow grounded me, making me feel slightly calmer as a rueful smile spread on my lips from my stupid overreaction.

Standing up, I took a deep breath, wiped the sheen of sweat from my cheeks, and tried to give Allie a casual smile. I clearly failed, because she plonked both hands on her hips and gave me her best *what-the-fuck?* look.

Groaning, I closed my eyes in embarrassment. I was totally freaking out – again – over a man I barely knew and seriously needed to get a frigging grip. 'Nothing. It's nothing, I'm just being stupid.'

I could see that Allie was suspicious, so I gave her the brightest smile I could manage. Which considering I'd just run faster than Usain bloody Bolt was actually surprisingly difficult. I seriously needed to get a grip on myself. I couldn't go sprinting around like that every day, I'd end up with a flipping hernia.

'We've just got time to eat before our viewing if we're quick,' Allie announced, handing me over one of the delicious-looking chicken wraps we'd bought on our way over earlier.

We ate in silence for several moments until Allie shifted and then nudged me to get my attention. 'So … guess what? I just spoke to Sean and I'm meeting his mum on Monday.'

Swallowing my mouthful, a smile burst to my face at her news. 'Really? Wow, that's a big step.'

'It is.' Nibbling on her sandwich she looked across at me nervously. 'Do you think it's too soon?'

'Nah. Time doesn't matter, it's obvious you guys are perfect for each other.'

Smiling wistfully, Allie nodded and finished her sandwich. 'I'm so excited, Cait. Me and you living together properly, it's going to be great!' Allie's enthusiasm was contagious, and as we began to make our way towards the gates, my earlier panic about Jack melted away. It'd be fine. I'd arrive for work, do my shift, and leave. Thinking about it that simply I realised that the chances of seeing him really were slim to none.

Once we had passed the first security gate, we were met again by Tina, the woman who had showed me around the first time. After briefly introducing herself to Allie, she led us toward the house babbling excitably about the opportunities it presented for us.

Allie

Looking around the rooms, my excitement levels rose and rose until I was bouncing on the spot by the time we met Tina downstairs in the lounge again. As Cait had said, the place was small – although perhaps snug was a nicer adjective – but it was undeniably appealing; spread over three floors it had general living space on the ground floor, and the top two floors contained double bedrooms with small en suites.

Every room was partly furnished too, which was good, because on our miniscule budget we couldn't really afford to splash out on furniture. The ground floor was my favourite part, because it had a lounge/diner that led through to a small well-appointed kitchen, behind which was the jewel of the place … a large deck which spanned the width of the property, providing an outdoor eating area with stunning views of the communal gardens.

I was thrilled with the house, and it was obvious that Cait was relieved by my enthusiasm. 'I'm so glad you like it!' she said with a grin.

'How could I not like it?' Poking my head out to look at the covered deck again, I called, 'It has a deck! I can see us spending many evenings out there with a glass of wine.'

'Me too! I think I actually like the place more than the first time I viewed it.'

Once we signed the contract with Tina and gave the deposit, she winked and handed us a ring containing the keys. 'There's two sets, front and back doors and a window key. Enjoy, ladies!'

Grasping the keys, Cait and I made our way back into the warm afternoon. Clutching at Cait's hands, I bobbed up and down practically bursting with excitement. 'OhmygodIloveit!' I was so excited that all my words rushed together in one long breath, causing Cait to promptly burst out laughing.

'Imagine, we'll be living right opposite the studio so we'll be able to watch all the stars coming and going! How exciting will that be?'

Cait raised an eyebrow, giving me a wry smile. 'You're dating one of the hottest actors on the planet, why the heck would you be bothered about watching other celebrities?'

The excited smile on my face doubled at her words until I probably looked well and truly smug. 'That's true.'

'So, when shall we move in?'

Cait shrugged, 'Well, I start work next week and it would be handy to be in before then.' She paused thoughtfully and jangled the keys. 'Now we have these babies, I reckon we get in as soon as possible'

I had one suitcase, and Cait a single backpack, so 'moving' wouldn't exactly be a taxing task. 'I think tomorrow looks like moving day!' I agreed happily, making a mental note to buy some champagne to toast our new venture.

Chapter Twenty-Five

Sean

It was stupid just how nervous I was as the car containing my mother became visible in the distance. But I was. Really bloody nervous. Nervous to the point where the clamminess of my hands had nothing to do with the humid air and my stomach was flip-flopping all over the place. My parents were based in the UK, in the home counties just west of London, but my mother worked for a large international chain of bookstores and was frequently over in the US and Canada for purchasing and distribution meetings. Regardless of how busy my schedule with work was, I always made time to squeeze in a quick visit, but this would be the first time that our meet-up would be a party of three.

Ramming my hands in my pockets, I tried not to think about the importance of this impending meeting. It would be the first time since Elena that I would be introducing my mum to a girlfriend. I thought about it harder and realised that actually, it was going to be the first time ever introducing my mum to a girl that I truly cared about. I'd dated a string of girls in my teens, none of which had been important enough to warrant meeting my parents, and Mum had met Elena because she'd visited me on set, but even Elena had only been a casual girlfriend.

Bloody hell. I hoped Allie and my mum got on.

The car arrived by the front steps and David climbed out

of the driver's seat, but I held him off with a wave and a smile as I approached the passenger door to open it. David had done a cracking job for me so far this morning, picking Allie up at just gone ten and dropping her here before heading straight back out to Downtown LA where my mother was staying.

So now was crunch time.

'Sean, love, it's so good to see you!' My mum slid from the car and immediately pulled me into a tight hug. Allie was lovely, laid back, and sweet, and much like my mum in a lot of ways, so they would no doubt get on like a house on fire. That's what I was hoping, anyway.

'Hi, Mum. Come on in and see the new place.' I took the small holdall from her hand and guided her up the steps as she 'oohhed' and 'ahhhed' over the wraparound balcony and the glimpse of the sea.

'It looks very fancy, dear.' Which it did, but nowhere near as fancy as some of the other properties the estate agent had showed me. Once they'd realised that it was me, the agents had increased the budget boundaries and taken me to see some absolute mansions, hoping to snag an extra-large commission. But I'd stuck to my four-bed maximum, and was thrilled with the place.

'Yeah, it is pretty nice.' Once we were inside I cleared my throat and dropped my bombshell. 'Actually, there's someone here I'd like you to meet.' I might have ended up telling Allie about today's meeting, but I'd kept my mum in the dark. I wasn't sure if it was just to up the surprise factor or because I'd been too nervous to tell her that I was finally in a relationship, but I guess the time for delaying was up.

As we walked along the corridor, Mum frowned up at me, the curiosity obvious in her clear blue gaze. 'Oh?'

Arriving in the lounge I nodded, left her side, and

quickly strode across to Allie, who was waiting by the couch, looking just as nervous as I felt.

'Mum, this is Allie. Allie, my mum, Sophie.' I watched as my mum's gaze settled on Allie and her eyebrows rose in surprise.

'Hi, Mrs Phillips. It's great to meet you.' Allie's voice wobbled a little but she overcame her nervousness and stepped forward to shake my mum's hand. The greeting looked a bit formal, but I supposed grabbing my mum for a hug was probably a bit premature.

'Hello, Allie, it's nice to meet you too.' Mum smiled hesitantly, obviously trying to work out what was going on, so I decided to make it obvious by sliding my hand down Allie's arm and linking our fingers. The action wasn't missed by my mum's shrewd gaze.

'We're dating. Allie's my girlfriend.' My tone softened and I couldn't help giving her hand a squeeze and flashing my girl a quick wink.

A look of pleasant surprise crossed Mum's face, which was priceless, and did quite a lot to relieve some of my tension.

'Well then, it is *really* lovely to meet you, Allie!' Mum added with a small chuckle. 'I didn't expect this today, that's for sure!' Looking down at her stark suit she smiled, a wry quirk to her dark eyebrows, and looked at me. 'You could have warned me, I look like a monster in this outfit. Can I quickly change?'

'Of course. I'll show you to a guest room.'

'I hate wearing these things but I had an important meeting with the CEO of my company this morning, hence my battle wear,' Mum explained to Allie while giving the lapel of her suit a tug. 'Just give me two minutes, and then we can all relax.'

Walking to the only guest room that had any furniture, I placed Mum's bag on the side and turned to her, expecting an inquisition. Instead, I got a soft smile and a single statement. 'Well, well. This is a turn up for the books. She's very pretty, Sean.'

Pride warmed my cheeks. 'Yeah. She's lovely too, you'll see once you've spent a little while with her.'

'I'm glad you've finally met someone.' Mum was unzipping her small day bag and pulling out a blouse, but I could hear a slight hesitation in her voice. 'You've been careful though, haven't you? I mean, she's not after you for your money, is she?'

I could see why she would have that concern, I was pretty famous, after all, but a laugh burst from my throat and I grinned at my mum and shook my head. 'Definitely not. Allie didn't even recognise me when we met.' A fond smile curved my lips as I recalled the moment on Christmas Eve when she'd been looking through my DVD collection and finally realised. She'd looked horrified, and completely genuine too.

'Apart from the fact that I completely trust her, she's very independent where it comes to money. She insists on paying half the bill when we go out.' On the limited occasions we actually could go out, I thought grimly. 'As well as working hard as a teacher and saving some money, she got some inheritance from her great aunt. Allie might not be rich, but she's definitely not after me for my cash.'

'Sorry if I sound paranoid, but I am your mum, it's my job to worry about these things.'

'I know, Mum. Come here,' I pulled her in for another hug and then stepped back. 'I'll let you change. I thought we could have a BBQ, so meet us out on the deck when you're ready.'

Allie

So far, things weren't going too badly.

When Sean's mum had arrived the first thing I'd noticed were the similarities between them in their dark hair and blue eyes. The second thing that had struck me, was that she'd looked quite severe and unapproachable in her business suit and perfect make-up, and my stomach had tightened up until I'd got cramping, nervous pains.

Sophie had looked so professional and stylish that her appearance was a million miles away from my laid back ways. I'd panicked that she might deem me not good enough for her son, but since her return after changing, her demeanour had noticeably relaxed as had her attire, because she was now dressed in jeans and a pale pink blouse.

The BBQ had been delicious, Sean cooking it all with an easy familiarity that made me think he must actually quite like cooking. There was still so much I didn't know about him, which was at once sad but exciting, because it meant there would be lots of new experiences in our future together once the engagement farce had been sorted out.

Conversation was surprisingly easy. Sophie's blue eyes assessed me whenever she thought I wasn't looking, but I could only assume that she liked what she saw, because as the afternoon wore on it seemed obvious that she was pleased by the presence of me in Sean's life.

We chatted about how different life was out here compared to in the UK, and found that we had lots in common. It turned out that she worked with books too, as a distribution manager, and I excitedly told her I was in the midst of penning my own trilogy of fantasy novels.

'Sean didn't tell me you were a writer! You must send me a copy when you're done, I have some good friends in the industry that might be able to help you out.' I'd had some vague interest from a publisher, but it sounded like having Sophie as a friend could have its advantages.

'I'll grab the white wine and top you ladies up.' Sean stood, dropping a quick kiss on my temple, and headed to the kitchen. His kiss wasn't missed by his mother, who watched his affection with interest and then smiled fondly. It looked very much like an approval, and I felt the last of my tension flow from my body. Phew. Looked like I'd won her over.

'I've never seen him like this before,' she murmured, her clever eyes settling on mine with a weight that I immediately understood – she was worried I might just be having fun and wasn't in this for the long haul. He was loaded, famous, and I was significantly younger, so I could understand her concerns. Smiling happily, I immediately tried to put her mind at ease.

'I'm sure with his money and career you might be a little worried about my intentions toward Sean, but let me just say it straight, I'm …' Pausing, I wondered if I could just declare that I loved him. That might be a touch over the top for the first meeting with his mother, so I dulled it down slightly. 'Well, I'm very serious about your son. I want to be with him. Not the actor, not the money, but *him*.'

Sophie smiled, a soft, affectionate expression that went all the way to her pale blue eyes. 'I can see that. The way you two look at each other takes me right back to how I felt when I first met Richard,' she murmured dreamily.

Leaning forward, she took hold of my hand and nodded.

'Sean has been so withdrawn for years, it's truly wonderful to see him so happy.'

Sean reappeared in the doorway with a bottle in his hand and paused as he took in the hold his mother had on my hand. 'I hope you're not making a move on my girl, Mother,' he remarked playfully, causing both myself and Sophie to chuckle and pull apart.

Excusing myself, I left them alone and nipped to the toilet to freshen up and reapply some sun cream. On my return, I paused just inside the lounge when I heard Sean's mother's voice drift in on the breeze.

'She's perfect, Sean. So sweet! I love her,' Sophie gushed, and I felt my cheeks heat in response. There seemed to be a slightly heavy silence out on the balcony and then Sean spoke again.

'Me too, Mum.'

The gasp from Sophie was loud, and followed by a sniffle that sounded distinctly like crying. 'My boy's in love?'

'Yep, well and truly. She's the one, Mum.' A huge lump of emotion formed in my throat. I knew Sean loved me, but hearing him confess it to his mother was quite monumental. There was now silence on the deck, broken only by muffled noises and sniffles, so I peeked around the corner and saw them in a very touching mother/son embrace.

Deciding to give them a few extra minutes alone together, I snuck back through the apartment to the kitchen. As I filled a jug with ice and cool water, I couldn't help but grin at how well the last few hours had gone.

Sean was happy and relaxed, his mum definitely seemed to like me, and she might be able to help me progress my writing career. All in all, it had been a pretty awesome day.

Chapter Twenty-Six

Cait

I'd been at my job for over a week now, living in the new townhouse for just as long, and I was absolutely loving both. Seeing as Allie and I were both living out of single bags, moving hadn't taken long at all, and although our lack of personal belongings meant the house was still fairly sparse, it was our own little place. The 'new home' look wouldn't last long though, because Allie and I had a shopping spree planned for next Saturday to hit some of the second-hand stores and bargain malls. We'd have the place brightened up and homely in no time.

Work was awesome too. The team at the studio was quite small but very friendly. On my first day I found that Lisa from running club was actually one of the make-up artists and based within the same area as me.

I'd seen Mel around too, but she was a camera assistant, training up to be a full cameraman, so she spent most of her day out on the set. Luckily there was a studio social tomorrow night at the baseball batting cages and we were all going, so I'd get a chance to catch up with her then. I wasn't convinced I'd be any good at hitting a baseball, but getting to know the girls more outside of work would be fun.

My direct manager was Di, the 'Prop Master'. She was in charge of everything to do with the prop department.

Considering she had such a hectic job, she was surprisingly jolly and laid back, and happily spent most of my first day showing me around and making sure I was well settled.

All in all it was going fabulously. Even better, and much to my relief, I'd not seen even a glimpse of Jack Felton either, so I hadn't had to worry about what I would say to him.

My denial might be long gone, but avoidance was still top of my list and working out just fine for me so far. It seemed Allie had been right; the distance between the stages we worked on was enough to ensure we wouldn't cross paths. This was exactly what I had hoped for, but even knowing that this was the best outcome, a tiny, crazy piece of me was almost starting to miss him. Which was so stupid that I really needed someone to slap some sense into me.

Drawing in a harsh breath in an attempt at clearing my head, I stood up to head back into work. Pausing outside the studio door, I turned my head towards the sun for a few last cheeky rays to finish off my coffee break. It warmed my skin, causing a blissful smile to pull at my lips and my body to relax. Today was another fabulous day, with clear, cloudless blue skies as far as I could see. A girl could get used to this type of weather, and luckily, I was that girl.

Stopping just inside the studio doors, I absorbed the buzzing atmosphere with a smile. I loved this job. Everything about it was perfect: the location, the divine weather, my friendly co-workers, and because I was working on a vampire drama, the props I was asked to make were not only challenging, but great fun too. On my very first day I'd had to make a demon hand glove with talons for nails and sharp little fangs on the palm, I mean, how crazy is that? It had turned out fabulously, and the actor I made it for was now taking great pleasure in freaking people out by wearing it off-set and shaking hands with poor unsuspecting victims. There had been more than one shriek of shock thanks to my artistry.

Today's challenge had been a long one. The script involved a rogue vampire going on a feeding rampage, so I had spent the day working with the make-up department moulding and applying vampire bites to several necks. I only had a few more gruesome bite marks to make and apply, and then I was done for the day.

Unfortunately, the pleasurable start to my next shift evaporated seconds later as I walked down the corridor towards the locker room and got a strange, wary sensation in my stomach.

That was odd.

Immediately looking around, I tried to assess what could be setting off my defences, but nothing obvious jumped out at me. I was in the main corridor, so I could see the set ahead of me, the green room to my right, and locker room to my left. The studio had never made me nervous before. Yes, there were always lots of men around, but they had always seemed friendly, and the place was always crowded, so I'd never felt unduly worried. Right now though, my skin was tingling and the hairs on the back of my neck were standing up. What the heck was going on?

Swallowing loudly, I checked my watch and saw that I was going to be late if I dawdled for much longer, so I pulled in a deep breath and was about to take a step forward when a familiar voice caught my ear. A familiar, deep, raspy, exceptionally lovely voice …

Surely it couldn't be …?

With my stomach dropping to my boots, I whipped my head to the right and saw none other than Jack bloody

Felton standing at the coffee counter just inside the door of the green room, chatting amiably with a tall, suited man.

Instantly my body went into alert: muscles stiffening, mouth drying, and heart accelerating until I could feel it banging painfully against the back of my ribs.

Shit, shit, shit. I'd been preparing myself for the possibility of seeing him at some point in the future, but not today, and certainly not in my studio. In fact, what the hell was he doing here? I'd been here since six a.m. and hadn't seen him earlier, that was for sure.

Much to my annoyance, my forehead was now all clammy, and my previously loose clothes suddenly felt distinctly sweaty and tight. How dare he just look so damn casual and put together when I was quickly being reduced to a dithering mess.

The locker room was just to my left so I crept towards its promise of escape, hoping he wouldn't glance my way. I must have looked ridiculous as I did an almost crab-like sideways walk along the corridor wall so I could keep one eye on him and one on my target destination, but luckily he was engrossed in his conversation and didn't see me.

I had definitely seen *him* though, and against all my defences and instincts, there was just one word that spiralled around my mind as I watched him.

Wow. Wow. Wow.

Because wow, he really was such a good-looking man, and wow, did he make a mighty fine sight, and wow, was my avoidance plan totally useless.

His hair was ruffled and unruly today, making him look younger, and his faded grey jeans and black polo shirt accentuated how dark his hair and eyes were. My pathetic gazing wasn't helped by the fact that he was wearing short sleeves, because his tanned, toned forearms did something to my stomach that I just couldn't understand. It felt like it was suddenly twisted into a dozen knots and slithering around inside me.

I couldn't believe he was here. Diving into the locker room, I let out a breath of relief and stashed my bag before staggering through to the toilets to lean on a sink. Giving myself a look in the mirror, I saw my earlier happiness was gone, and in its place a wretchedly confused expression was now haunting my features.

Splashing some cold water on my face I gave the elastic band around my wrist a good ol' ping – just for luck – and then shook my head to dislodge my sinking mood. Allie had often worried that my elastic band pinging had something to do with self-harming, or masochism, but I'd quickly put a stop to her worries by explaining that it stopped me disassociating whenever I thought I was in danger – losing myself to memories was much more dangerous than a slight pain in my wrist. Although, come to think of it, maybe she was right about my masochism, because accepting the six month contract knowing full well that I might bump into Jack was basically the same as self-inflicted torture, wasn't it?

I was such an idiot.

Like a true coward, I hid by the lockers for as long as humanly possible, and only when my watch told me I was seriously pushing it for time did I dare emerge from my hiding place. To my dismay, Jack was still just there, but he was now talking to the director of my show. Bugger. He was pouring himself a fresh cup of coffee too, as if he owned the bloody place.

Crap. Why didn't he just bugger off? Avoiding him was really bloody difficult when he was less than ten feet away from me, that was for sure. There was no other way to get to the set either, so I didn't have any choice but to pass him.

Blowing out a frustrated breath, I tutted at my own stupidity. All this fuss because of a man? I was pathetic. I gave myself a sharp talking to, straightened my back, drew in a breath for confidence, and then decided to just waltz straight past him.

I took two steps and the director shook Jack's hand and turned away. 'Right, five minute call, actors on set, please!' he yelled in a cheerful tone as he chose that exact moment to wander away from Jack.

Well, wasn't that just frigging marvellous? I saw that now Jack was free, his gaze had zeroed straight in on me as he smiled and gave me a tentative wave. Blimey, his eyes really were something else, seeming to drag my gaze to them and ensnare me.

Immediately, my mind filled with images of how gorgeous his eyes had looked when he'd gazed at me with a desire-drenched stare shortly after our knee-buckling kiss. That look had been pretty epic, and was burned into my brain for posterity. As had the feel of his soft lips and exploring tongue … Swallowing loudly, I had to forcibly push the dizzying images away and try to ignore the burning heat that had suddenly settled in my stomach.

My heart rate, which had already been abnormally high, suddenly shot right through the frigging roof and was pounding so fast I was amazed that I hadn't passed out from it.

After our recent encounters, which ranged from highly sexual to completely fraught, I really wasn't sure how to approach this. Should I wave back and stride down the corridor past him? Or should I talk to him? Would he mention my restaurant meltdown and giveaway nod? Or push me on the fact that I had clearly lied to him about both my job and my feelings?

Sighing heavily, I knew in my heart I couldn't just ignore him. That would be rude. Besides, we were both adults, and we'd potentially have to see each other around from time to time, so it would be best to start things off on a polite but distant note. I needed to be friendly, but cool and professional, and above all else, I needed to make sure I didn't lead him on with any more unsolicited nodding incidents.

Decision made, I crossed the space between us and gave a small, tight smile as I arrived at his side.

'Caitlin, hi. Jason mentioned you had accepted the job.' Yet another reminder of my stupid lie. But just when I thought Jack was going to call me out, he just carried on as if it had never happened. 'How are you settling in?'

Polite, casual conversation. OK, that was good. I could do this. There had been no pitying looks or mentions of last week, and his respectful avoidance of it bolstered my courage. 'Good, thanks, the work's great, really exciting.' Talking about work was actually easy, because I genuinely loved it here. Each day had provided a new challenge, and I was already proving to my co-workers that I knew what I was doing, and was good at it too.

Jack offered me the coffee he had just poured from the jug at the machine and even though I'd just had my break, I accepted it gladly, deciding that right now I needed to be as caffeinated and on the ball as possible.

'Thanks.' I took the drink and its promise of caffeine with a polite smile, and immediately took a large swig before my eyes almost burst from my head in shock. Holy moly, that was hot!

I instantly regretted being so hasty, and as my mouth struggled to deal with the scalding liquid, I very nearly spat it out all over Jack.

'Careful … that will be hot,' Jack murmured, trying, and failing, to suppress a humoured smile.

No? *Really?* I was now so flustered that I only just managed to refrain from throwing the bloody coffee all over him in annoyance. Instead, I dug deep down for my inner confidence and settled for reaching past him for the milk, adding a generous dollop to my coffee, and then completing the perfect beverage by adding a small helping of cold water.

I saw Jack raise his eyebrows in surprise. 'Cold water? Is that a regular addition or just because you burnt your tongue?'

My cheeks heated, and my tongue gave a little throb to remind me that I had indeed just scalded it. 'I used to be a teacher, and the breaks were never long enough to make a drink, wait for it to cool, and drink it, so I started to top my tea and coffee off with cold water – I guess the habit has just stuck.'

Looking slightly perplexed – perhaps because he was trying to add this new news to the list of my other oddities – Jack then nodded, and thankfully changed the subject. 'So, how long is your contract?'

Taking a more cautious sip this time, I sighed in appreciation as the delicious coffee slid across my tongue and then answered his question determined not to lie any more. Not about work, anyway. If he asked me if I '*liked him and felt it too*' again I wasn't entirely sure how I'd respond.

'I'm here for six months. This role is similar to something I've done before, so it felt like the perfect opportunity.' As I spoke I had a brief flashback to the unexpected evening I'd spent with Jack at the bar exchanging travelling stories and tales of growing up. Blimey. That felt like so long ago now. So much seemed to have happened between us, which was kind of ironic seeing that nothing had actually changed or developed.

Just as I was wondering if Jack even remembered that night, he seemed to precisely read my thoughts. 'I remember you telling me how much you had loved that job. The Sydney Opera House, right?'

For some reason, the fact that he had not only recollected our conversation, but the exact details of it, made a solid lump form in my throat and a little band develop around my heart. That was sweet. But Jack being sweet was really not something I should be focusing on.

Remaining professional, cool, and calm. That's what I needed to focus on. Clearing my throat, I smiled fondly as I recalled my time in Australia. 'That's right. This is proving just as challenging, which I love.'

I might have been smiling, but this situation really was no good at all. Just being in such close proximity to Jack was sending my much underused hormones into a spinning frenzy, I knew I was still blushing wildly, and my body was quickly slipping away from my own control.

Great, so this technically meant I'd gone from denial, straight through avoidance, and was now at the acceptance stage. Every nerve ending seemed to exulting in this fact and standing to attention while desperately trying to reach out to him, and I had to really keep myself in check not to do exactly that.

'So, is this the set you're based on?' he enquired in a seemingly casual tone, but my more suspicious side couldn't help but wonder if there was more to his interest than he was letting on.

Seeing how frequently we 'bumped' into each other, I

really didn't want him to know, and so a frown instantly settled on my brows. But what plausible reason could I give for avoiding his question? None I could think of.

In the end, I opted to delay myself with the age old tactic of giving a non-decisive 'Ummm …' while Jack merely continued to look at me with those penetrating brown eyes.

What if he suddenly decided to add my stage as a daily visit in his routine? Seeing him every day would kill me. Hmm. Given how quickly he'd managed to obtain my mobile number the other week, he'd probably have no problem finding out which set I was based on. In fact, he probably already did know. Besides, my appearance here already made it pretty obvious, didn't it?

Reluctantly, I gave in and nodded. 'Yes. I'm working on *Dark Blood*.' I was quite pleased that at least my voice now sounded slightly calmer than I felt inside.

'That's the vampire drama, isn't it?'

Intent on keeping the conversation professional, I found myself relaxing at these easier questions. Anything was better than replaying that glorious kiss in my head. Again. 'That's the one. Some of the props are gruesome,' I said, glancing towards the prop area out on set and wishing I could run and hide over there with the fake blood-covered masks and plastic flesh wounds.

Suddenly, my mouth got the better of me and I found myself blurting out the question at the forefront of my mind. 'So, what are you doing here? I thought *Fire Lab* was filmed on the other side of the complex?' I tried desperately to keep the accusation from my voice, but his raised eyebrow showed that I might not have been completely successful in my aim.

I winced at how much I'd just given away … by admitting that I knew where his set was, I'd made it pretty bloody obvious that I'd been checking up on him. This realisation was probably the cause for the tiny hint of pleasure I could see in his expression. Damn, damn, damn.

'Who's stalking who now, Caitlin?' he murmured teasingly, but the soft, affectionate look on his face wasn't nearly as gleeful or smug as I had expected, and actually threw me off balance a bit.

Briefly licking his lips – an action which always seemed to draw my gaze – Jack took pity on me by continuing the conversation, which was just as well, because I was quickly losing the ability to think straight.

'You're right, *Fire Lab* is filmed way over the other side, but I have a weekly meeting with someone over this way and we popped in to grab a coffee.' He gave me a long thoughtful look before cocking his head to one side. 'I have to say, I'm rather glad we did.'

His penetrating gaze never left mine once, and like complete traitors my eyes wouldn't break the sizzling stare now passing between us.

This was definitely acceptance.

I now fully accepted the fact that I was attracted to Jack Felton. Really attracted to him. I just wouldn't declare it out loud. He appealed to me on so many levels that it was difficult to put my finger on why he of all people was the one to gain my attention after four years. He was handsome, obviously, but my attraction to him was more to his confidence and the way he was at ease with himself. It was almost at complete opposites to my character, and it fascinated me.

Practically wrenching my eyes towards the floor, I cleared my throat and shifted awkwardly on my feet. 'I … uh … I really need to go now, I'm already late as it is. Thanks for the coffee. Bye.'

'Goodbye, Caitlin. I'll see you around.' That seemed to be his stock departure phrase, and once again his words sounded like a promise rather than a casual parting, but I didn't dare risk another look at him. Instead, true to tradition, I simply placed my empty cup down and turned and walked away from him.

At least I had said goodbye to him this time, so I supposed I was making progress.

Chapter Twenty-Seven

Cait

Friday night was here, I had survived my first full week at work, and this evening was bringing my first social with my new colleagues. Meeting a big group of people had seemed a bit overwhelming when Mel had pointed out the poster about the social event, so I had invited Allie to come along. Friends were allowed to come, and besides, Sean was filming night shoots so I didn't want to leave her in the new house on her own.

The event was being held at a baseball centre, and I had been clueless about what to expect. As I looked around I decided it basically seemed to be a bit like a bowling alley but for baseball. There were rows and rows of 'cages', (which were actually not metal cages, but enclosures made of thick mesh netting) that contained machines which bowled a baseball for you to hit. The netting, or cage, was purely for the safety of everyone else around you, which given that I'd never even tried to hit a baseball before was probably a very good thing.

As well as the cages, this place had a bar and small café and the studios had hired it all out for the night. I'd thought that seemed a bit of a grand gesture at first, but now I could see just how many employees had turned up, it made sense.

Grabbing a bottle of water each, Allie and I wandered across to join Mel and Lisa in the shade as we waited our turn. I did the introductions, and as expected they all hit it off immediately; with Allie's bubbly personality, Mel's jokes, and Lisa's non-stop chatter, the four of us were giggling away happily within minutes.

'When I imagined this place I thought it would be indoors, like a bowling alley. I never thought we'd be outside,' I remarked, looking across the row of batting cages to the darkening, late afternoon sky.

Mel gave me a fond smile, as if my Britishness amused her no end. 'You can get indoor cages, but this way we can catch some rays as we watch. You guys ever hold a baseball bat before?'

I shook my head just as Allie clutched at my arm and gave me a light shake. 'Yeah, we have. Well, sort of …' Allie grinned at Mel and gave me a cocky wink. 'Cait and I joined an adult rounders team when we were doing our teacher training. We rocked it. It can't be that different.'

My competitive side was excited by the idea of this evening, so I couldn't help joining in with Allie's enthusiasm, even though I suspected that it was going to be vastly different to our rounders days. For starters, the bats were much longer, but more importantly, the machine that fired the balls at you – apparently called a pitching machine – looked way quicker than any bowler I'd ever faced. She'd got one part right though, we *had* rocked the rounders team. Without Allie and me and our top scoring ways the team would have completely flopped.

'I'm just going to the loo,' Allie murmured, before shoving her water bottle into my hand and disappearing.

'So how long do we have to wait?' I asked, impatient for my go, and already trying on the baseball gloves Mel had loaned me for the night.

'It varies, but seeing as the studio has rented the whole

place out I think people will just be doing short sessions and keep swapping to make it more fun.'

Lisa came between Mel and me and slung an arm around our shoulders before rotating us to the left so we were looking at a set of four batting enclosures. 'I gotta say, ladies, I don't mind the wait when we have *that* to look at, you know what I mean?'

Scanning the cages, I just saw various people either hitting or getting ready to bat, so it took me a second to work out what she was talking about. Then, on my second glance I realised that inside the first cage wasn't just anyone – it was Jack, preparing to take his turn.

Oh. That was what Lisa was looking at.

Or should I say who.

For some reason, that realisation caused an irrational flare of possessiveness to flood through me, which was just ridiculous and made me feel rather uncomfortable. He wasn't mine to be possessive over, so I had no idea why I felt that way, and try as I might to shake it off I couldn't seem to dismiss it.

Watching as he tugged a protective helmet over his floppy brown hair, he grinned cockily at the guys standing by his cage – an expression that was so stunning it actually made my stomach feel a bit weird and tense.

This man really had well and truly screwed up my internal workings.

Turning away from us, Jack then swung the bat in practice before cocking it over his shoulder and preparing for the pitching machine to launch the first ball at him.

'You're right, that is a pretty nice sight,' Mel agreed, her voice low and lusty, which only heightened the uncomfortable, slightly irritated feeling swelling inside of me.

'Is he single?' Lisa asked, her head stuck between us as she ogled him. 'Please tell me he's single.'

Swinging the bat as the ball flew towards him, Jack connected with it in near perfection, sending it sailing forwards into the protective nets and prompting a whoop of joy from his spectators. Wow. Both the strike and the man looked pretty phenomenal. The white T-shirt, grey jeans, and black boots he was wearing were a simple enough outfit, but were such a good fit that all his chest and bum muscles were defined through the material as he cocked the bat over his shoulder and prepared for another hit.

Simple, but highly effective.

I was entranced.

There really was no other way to describe it. He looked incredible: toned, athletic, tanned, skilful … the list could go on and on. Not to mention sexy as hell, I couldn't drag my eyes away.

Mel also appeared to be stunned into silence, so I was about to reluctantly say that yes, he was single, when she suddenly found her tongue and beat me to it. 'Yep. But I hear that he's more into guys than gals.'

What?

Those words broke the spell and I swiftly moved my gaze to gawk at Mel. Jack was more into guys? What the heck was she talking about?

'No way! Really?' Lisa sounded as shocked as I was. I couldn't reconcile her words with the Jack I had got to know. He was into guys? He was so masculine, not to mention flirtatious, that it just didn't seem feasible.

'Yep, swings both ways, but his preference is for the guys,' Mel concluded.

'Shame. I'd love see those eyes gazing down at me in the heat of the moment. I swear they must be blue contacts.

I've never seen eyes so pale and intense.'

Blue?

What. The. Heck?

This conversation just got stranger and stranger. Jack's eyes were definitely brown. I knew that with one hundred per cent certainty because I'd stared into them many times in an attempt at memorising the exact colour. They were somewhere between melted milk chocolate and fresh conkers, and a million miles away from being blue.

Trying to work out what was going on, I watched as Jack hit another blinding shot and then turned to the guy in the next cage, laughing. The second man swung rather clumsily, missed the ball completely, and threw his head back in amused frustration.

As I watched the second guy pull off his helmet, I belatedly realised who he was, and suddenly the girls' words started to make sense. Christopher Shire, the actor in *Dark Blood*, voted one of the sexiest men on television last year and a seemingly terrible baseball player. He also had blue eyes. And apparently a preference for men.

They hadn't been talking about Jack at all. I felt a rueful smile pull at my mouth – my fixation with Jack had just led me to think that that was the case. What an idiot.

'Christopher Shire …' Lisa sighed. 'He is literally the man of my dreams.' I nearly laughed out loud at the dreamy quality to her voice, although some of my laughter might have been from relief, because for some reason, the idea of them ogling Christopher was a lot more preferable than them staring at Jack.

'Jack's there too, he looks hot. Not as hot as Chris, though,' Mel giggled. Mel and Lisa were both around my age, and clearly both favoured Christopher, so I was obviously the only one with a thing for a slightly older guy.

Looking at the two of them, I shook my head in bemusement. For me, there really was no comparison, Jack would get my vote every time.

'They're with some of the *Dark Blood* guys. I love that the actors come to these events, it's awesome,' Lisa said, taking a healthy swig on her beer.

Awesome? I nearly blew out a frustrated raspberry at her words. It didn't feel particularly awesome, not seeing as Jack had my emotions so messed up that I felt like I was standing on my hands with my head spinning in circles.

I was attracted to him, and he returned my sentiments, but the newness and strangeness of those feelings made me want to run in the opposite direction. How could he make me feel safe when the thought of getting closer to him terrified me? And tonight's development of my jealous streak was another thing I was unused to dealing with. What a gigantic mess.

Blowing out a long, troubled breath, I forced my eyes away from him and looked back to the girls.

'Yeah, awesome until they turn up to running club and see us dragging ourselves over the finish line like a couple of beached whales,' Lisa muttered. Her comment had me laughing out loud as I remembered just how red her face had gone after running for just five minutes.

'I don't know why you're laughing!' Lisa joked, jabbing a finger at me. 'You can run as well as the guys. It was Mel and me that looked like the most unfit women in LA!'

'Hey, I stuck with you, I could have gone quicker!' Mel complained amiably.

'True. OK, the single most unfit woman in LA and her loyal friend.'

Our loud laughter was drawing glances from some of the other crew, and I saw Jack and his friends looking our way.

I couldn't look away no matter how I tried, and a second later his eyes met mine and a small smile pulled at his lips as he left the cage and handed his bat across to the next person. His hair was ruffled from the helmet, and one sleeve of his T-shirt had rolled right up from his exertion, filling me with the peculiar urge to walk across and sort it out for him.

Even looking dishevelled he still looked lovely, and I couldn't help responding to his smile with a small one of my own.

'Check you out,' Allie suddenly whispered next to my ear, making me jump and clutch at my chest. A blush crept up my cheeks as I turned to her, wondering how long she had been back from the toilet. The knowing grin on her face spoke volumes. 'I saw you smiling. You didn't baulk, you didn't run away, you didn't blank him, and you didn't freak out. See? It's not so hard to be friendly with him, is it?'

I was about to say that smiling at him was far easier when we had a huge distance between us, but my cheeks heated at her reminder of the awful things I'd done to Jack since meeting him.

Given my appalling behaviour I was amazed that he still even wanted to smile at me. Shaking my head ruefully, I gave an embarrassed shrug before accepting a baseball bat that Mel was shoving into my hands.

'Come on, let's see the rounders champ in action.'

'Just remember, this is my first time. Besides, I was more of a bowler than a batter, so if I'm terrible then that's why,' I muttered, feeling excited but slightly panicked at the prospect of the solid baseballs that would soon be flying at me.

'Yeah, yeah, enough of the excuses, sport. Get yourself in there and show us how it's done.'

Jack

I loved the batting cages. I could still vividly remember the first time my mum took me to one during one of our childhood trips to the US to see her family. My uncle taught me how to hold the bat, when to swing, and how to get the best from the hit, and I still recall his tips whenever I pick up a bat. I'd never played baseball at school because I grew up in the UK, but I was good enough that I could mix it up with my American cousins whenever we were over here.

There was something incredibly satisfying about getting the perfect contact with the ball and watching it sail into the nets. Not to mention the adrenaline rush I got from slogging out a good hit or two. The power of the contact as it transferred down the bat and rushed up your arm was like a bolt of lightning sent straight from the skies. It was incredible, and after my few hits tonight I realised how much I'd missed it.

I was getting quite an adrenaline rush now though, and it had nothing to do with hitting a ball, and everything to do with the excited giggles coming from the sweet British girl currently lining up to take her first ever swing at a baseball.

I let out a long, low breath. Caitlin was so bloody lovely that I was having a seriously hard time keeping myself at a distance as I observed her with her friends.

Watching as she tightened her gloves and chatted openly to a red-headed girl I vaguely recognised from running club – Mel, I think – I realised that this was the most relaxed and open I'd ever seen Caitlin. Her eyes were sparkling, her body relaxed, face lit with excitement, and her eyes twinkling with happiness.

She really was gorgeous, a true definition of a natural beauty, and the sight of her looking so carefree was doing absolutely nothing to cool my attraction towards her. Taking another controlled breath, I took a swig from my bottle of water as I continued to watch her.

Caitlin had even smiled at me earlier, a small, cautious one, but she'd made direct eye contact and the smile had been long enough and real enough that I'd committed it to memory. Just like her nod, that was stowed away in my memory banks too. Surely a smile was a positive sign that we were moving in the right direction? Hopefully she was finally beginning to relax around me.

I stood up a little straighter as I realised that Caitlin was nearly ready to take her first swing. The red-head left the cage and pulled the gate shut and I watched as Caitlin pulled a helmet on over her beautiful tresses, rolled off her neck, and slung the bat over her shoulder ready to face the pitch.

The heavy clunk of the ball machine sounded in the air and Caitlin swung, and missed, her whole body swirling from the effort. Her friends giggled, but instead of laughing it off in embarrassment, I watched her weigh the bat more carefully in her hand, her eyebrows pulling together in concentration as she assessed what she'd done wrong and then retook her stance. I grinned, immediately recognising her competitive spirit because I had plenty of it myself. She obviously wanted to do well, and that thrilled me. I'd suspected she had spunk, but I loved seeing this new side to her.

Pitch and swing. This time she clipped the ball, but not quite enough to send it moving forwards. For a beginner, her technique actually looked pretty good. My uncle would no doubt approve.

Mel called some advice through the nets, and giving a nod of understanding Caitlin adjusted her stance slightly and stared straight ahead, waiting for the next bowl. I couldn't help smirking at just how seriously she was taking this.

This time, when the ball sailed out from the pitching machine, Caitlin prepared herself and using the torque in her body, rotated at the perfect moment and pulled the bat through to perform an almost flawless strike. The girls by her cage let out yelps of excitement and I even found myself expressing a cheer and clapping, which I noticed drew curious glances from a few of my colleagues. I didn't care; I was single, Caitlin was single, and I had made my interest in her more than clear. If people drew the same conclusion then so be it.

After ten pitches, Caitlin switched off the machine and was about the leave the cage when Mel ushered her back inside. Taking on the role of tutor, she then proceeded to stand behind Caitlin and wrap her arms around her as she guided her on the exact body positioning needed for the perfect swing. My eyes narrowed slightly as I saw Caitlin tense a little, but she didn't actively flinch away from the body contact, further enhancing my belief that it was purely men she feared close proximity to.

To say I was jealous of Mel's close contact with Caitlin would be a huge understatement. I wanted it to be me holding her close and helping her learn new things, but more than that, I wanted it to be me causing her eyes to light and sparkle with happiness.

Seeing Allie in the small group supporting Caitlin, I decided to take my opportunity to move closer. She was dating my best friend, so it was only normal for me to go and speak to her. That's what I used as my excuse, anyway.

'Allie, hi. How are you?'

Allie turned to me with a broad smile, which quickly turned to a knowing grin. She seemed like a shrewd girl, and obviously recognised why I was speaking to her, but she still greeted me enthusiastically, which made me think that while I had significant work to do on persuading Caitlin of my good intentions, it seemed I had her friend convinced.

'Jack, hi! I'm great, thank you, how are you?'

'Very well, thank you. I'm enjoying being back at the cages, actually. I felt a bit rusty, but I'd forgotten how much I enjoy it.'

'You didn't look rusty to us,' Allie replied cheerfully, and I immediately wondered if her use of 'us' was just generic or if she had specifically meant herself and Caitlin? Had Caitlin watched me? Had she been impressed? The idea made my heart rate pick up slightly before I shoved my hands in my pockets, suddenly feeling really stupid. I felt like I was back at school trying to show off to the girl I fancied. It was pathetic how desperate I was to get closer to her.

'Have you had a go yet?' I asked, desperately trying to act and sound my age, and not like a hormonal teenager.

'Yeah, I was rubbish,' Allie grimaced, 'I thought that because I was good at rounders I'd be just as good at this, but it turns out you can't use a baseball bat one handed like I'd thought. Cait's taking to it much better than me.'

Her words gave me the perfect excuse to look at Caitlin just in time to see her hit another almost perfect shot. She was rather good, and it really was stupid how proud that made me feel. I knew I had absolutely no right to feel that way about her – she wasn't mine to feel proud of. She barely tolerated me most of the time, but I just couldn't help it.

Caitlin handed the bat to another girl and began to take off her protective gear to leave the cage but my attention was drawn back to Allie as she spoke again. 'Have you seen Cait much since she's been working at the studio?'

Turning back, I tried to work out how much she knew. Obviously after my little outburst at the Getty Centre she knew I was interested in Caitlin, but had they talked about me? Did Caitlin express a curiosity about me too? Had she even told Allie about our 'accidental' meeting yesterday? Truthfully, it wasn't accidental at all; I'd been dying to go to her set ever since she had started, and had finally caved on Thursday and made up a reason to go over there.

Seeing as I was committed to pursuing Caitlin, even if it just ended in friendship, I decided I had nothing to hide from her best friend. 'A little. I think she's still pretty wary of me, but my intentions are genuine, Allie, I promise you.'

Allie's face softened, concern and affection for her friend obvious in her expression as she nodded. 'I know. I can see that, Jack. I think Cait can too, but she's scared.'

Scared of what? That was the question on the tip of my tongue, but I knew it wasn't fair to ask Allie for personal information on her friend, so I held back and gave an accepting nod instead.

Licking her lips, Allie narrowed her eyes as if considering sharing something with me, and I found myself holding my breath in anticipation. As several seconds ticked by, my eyebrows rose in curiosity. I was desperate to know what she was going to say but determined not to push her.

'She doesn't date. I know she's told you this, and I can't

promise she'll ever change her mind on that, but …' Allie looked uncomfortable, glancing across to where Caitlin was standing and back to me furtively. Waving her hands around as if she was struggling for the right words, I found myself almost on the verge of exploding from expectation. 'I don't know, but she's definitely different when she talks about you, Jack.'

She was different when she spoke about me? I could only assume Allie meant that in a good way, and she could have no idea how much those few words meant to me. Maybe I would have a chance for more with Caitlin after all.

'Don't write her off yet, OK?' Allie finished softly, hope clear in the soft tone of her voice.

Write her off? The very thought made my teeth clench. *Never*. 'I won't,' I promised gruffly, just as Caitlin joined the group of girls and exchanged several congratulatory high fives on her stellar performance. Her eyes flashed towards where Allie and I were talking and I saw curiosity in her expression, accompanied by a mild flush to her cheeks before her eyes flicked between Allie and me one more time and then looked away.

I would pay millions to know the cause of that blush. Was it because she was embarrassed by all the attention she was getting, or because she'd seen me? I knew that was an egotistical thought, but every time I saw Caitlin I felt warm and my heart sped up, so it was possible that she had a similar response. God, I hoped that was the case.

Over the next twenty or so minutes the people standing with us wandered off to get some food or take their turn in the batting cages and I was finally left with just Caitlin. This was exactly where I wanted to be, so I didn't complain one little bit. I was finally alone with her again, close enough to smell her light, sweet scent and watch her tentative response to me as she realised we were alone.

She might be feigning indifference, but I'd caught her watching me on several occasions tonight, her cheeks pink with a blush and her eyes wide with curiosity. Small steps and signs, but I soaked them up nonetheless.

Suddenly there was an almighty crash behind us which had me jumping on the spot as my head flew around to see a large stack of metal chairs from the drink stand toppling over and noisily scattering everywhere.

Jeez, that had been loud, but I was suddenly completely distracted from the source of the noise when I felt two soft, warm hands gripping my right arm in a hold tight enough to make me wince.

Caitlin was tucked in by my side, closer to me than she had ever been before, as her hands held on to my arm in a death grip. Her hazel eyes were wide like saucers as she stared past me to the scattered chairs. The loud noise had made my pulse spike, but the continued thumping of my heart was now down to one simple thing – Caitlin. The girl who fascinated me more than any other was touching me.

Staring down at our joined hands, I blinked several times in disbelief. This girl who hated physical contact with men was voluntarily holding on to me for dear life, and I could barely comprehend how good it felt. One of her hands was locked around mine, and the other wrapped around my wrist. I was so thrilled that she was turning to me for support that I barely knew what to say or do.

Giving her hand just a tiny squeeze of reassurance, I cleared my throat. 'That was pretty loud, huh? It even made me jump,' I murmured, immediately wincing at how lame that had sounded. Bloody hell, all she was doing was touching my arm and it had me completely messed up and unable to act normally.

Suddenly, Caitlin's shocked eyes widened even further as she cast a stunned glance down at where she was clinging to me. A spluttered, choked noise escaped her throat as she seemed to realise what she was doing, and then she practically threw my arm down and jumped away from me as if I were the devil himself.

'I … I …' Caitlin seemed to be floundering now, completely lost for words and just as surprised about her sudden use of physical contact as I was.

Quickly gathering my wits before this all got out of hand and freaked her out, I held up my hands in a calming gesture and nodded. 'Hey, it's OK,' I murmured softly, but she blinked rapidly three times, frowned, and gave her hands a shake, looking decidedly like she wanted to wipe them on her jeans to clear away the feel of me. Charming, and not exactly the reaction I had been hoping for.

I tried not to be offended by her response, but it was difficult. She seemed to want to clear the evidence of my touch from her hands, whereas my arm was still tingling with awareness from her grip and craving more. Did she not feel that way too?

'It's normal to turn to other people for comfort, Caitlin, especially if something makes you jump like that,' I added, hoping to reassure her, but instead of looking comforted, she rammed her hands into the pockets of her jeans and averted her eyes, her expression still troubled. She seemed to have reverted back to her old shuttered self, which was incredibly frustrating after the progress I thought we'd been making.

Caitlin turned her face toward me and I saw the familiar frown that was settled on her brows. 'Not for me it isn't,' she muttered quietly. God, this woman even looked sexy when she was pissed off. But there was a slight catch in her voice that indicated a vulnerability below the surface that made my chest compress with emotion. A vulnerability that I desperately wanted to help her ease if only she would let me in.

Caitlin removed her hands from her pockets and rubbed them together in apparent agitation. Was she still trying to remove the feel of me from her skin? That was an idea I didn't like at all. Suddenly, a more pleasing thought occurred to me. Perhaps she was reacting like this because she *could* still feel our connection. Her hands might be tingling just like my arm was. Nodding, I decided this was much more preferable than her wanting to rub her hands clean of me. She felt the electricity too, and it scared her.

'Are you seriously telling me you never go to Allie to talk something through when you need some advice? You never get a hug from her to make you feel better?' I saw the weakening of her expression and immediately knew that I was on to something. 'It's what friends do for each other,' I pointed out casually.

'But we're not friends, Jack,' she replied, almost as if on autopilot, her weak tone not supporting the words at all.

'Yeah, we are. We chat at work, we see each other at social events, that's what friends do.'

Caitlin finally lifted her gaze from the floor and met mine as if she were considering my words carefully. Biting her lower lip, she finally gave a small shrug. 'OK. Fine. Friends.' Giving a nervous scratch to the back of her neck she flushed, and finally allowed a small smile to escape again. 'But don't think that means I'm going to be grabbing on to you from now on. That was a one-time mistake.'

A smile stretched my lips at her playful and defiant reply, loving how she had so quickly recovered herself.

'Noted.' I didn't want to push her too much, so I decided to give her some space, but as I turned to walk away I couldn't resist one last little joke, so I wiggled my fingers at her with a cheeky smile. 'But just so you know, these are here for you to grab on to anytime.'

I saw her stutter in shock and then open her mouth, no doubt about to fire a snarky reply back to me, so I grinned, waved, and made a hasty exit.

Chapter Twenty-Eight

Allie

The studio social event moved to a funky, relaxed bar in Beverly Hills called the Bunker Hill Bar and Grill. The place was rammed to the rafters, mostly with faces I recognised from the batting cages, so it seemed we were pretty much dominating the small bar. Luckily, even with the busy night we'd still managed to get an almost continuous supply of beer to our table, and some amazing Buffalo wings and nachos to soak up some of the alcohol.

Mel and Lisa wandered toward the bar to get us another refill, so I took the opportunity of finally being alone with Cait again to dig for any gossip.

'I saw you talking to Jack at the batting cages,' I murmured softly, watching Cait's reaction carefully. As expected, I immediately saw a guarded expression settle on her features, as it always did when the conversation turned towards men. Or in more recent weeks, Jack Felton in particular.

Her eyes flicked warily to mine, and then focused on the glass in her hand. 'Yeah? I could say the same about you,' she replied, the beer bravery obviously making her deliberately difficult.

'I was, yes, were you jealous?' I teased, giving her a nudge in the ribs to try and get her to lighten up.

'No!' The horrified look on her face indicated her lie, and I couldn't help but persist with my mischievous banter.

'Are you sure? You certainly looked jealous when you thought Mel and Lisa were checking him out at the batting cages.' Cait gasped and her cheeks suddenly flushed a deep beetroot colour as she rapidly turned her eyes away from me and began to fiddle with a beer mat on the table.

'I don't know what you're talking about,' she muttered, suddenly looking exceptionally interested in the grain of the wooden table. Fiddling fingers, pink cheeks, low voice, and a massive avoidance of eye contact – yep, Cait had certainly triggered my bullshit detector, so I grinned and nudged her again.

'Yeah, you do. I got back from the toilet when Lisa was going on about one of the guys being the man of her dreams, and you got all tense because you thought she was talking about Jack.'

After a second, Cait's eyes flicked briefly to mine before she slumped forwards on the table and buried her head in her hands with a long groan. 'God. Was I that obvious?' she asked in a muffled voice from underneath thick masses of hair.

'A little, but only to me because I know you so well.' Seeing as Cait was drunk and actually seemed to be openly admitting her feelings for Jack, I decided to press on. 'He's a nice guy, Cait.'

'You've already said that before,' she complained, still hiding her face.

'I know, but you don't seem to accept it. *Gen-u-ine-ly nice.*' I broke it up this time into sounds so she might finally let it sink in.

Another groan came from her and she turned her head sideways and pushed the hair from her face. Her eyes were a little unfocused from the alcohol, but the pinched, tight line of her lips still showed her hesitation. 'I know he is. He's a complete gentleman and I like him, I really do. But I'm afraid to let anyone in again.'

Hallelujah! We had a breakthrough!

'I get why you might be scared of jumping into a relationship, but how about friendship first? That's not so confusing, is it? Can you give that a chance?'

Pushing up from the table, Cait brushed her long hair back over her shoulders and puffed out a breath through her nose. 'We agreed tonight that we're friends now,' she confessed, her words thrilling me no end. 'I guess I'll just have to toughen up and see where it goes.'

Blinking slowly, Cait turned to me and raised her bottle. 'Now, I think it's time to get properly drunk to celebrate how rubbish you were at baseball.'

I wasn't convinced it would take much more to get Cait 'properly drunk', but that was obviously her way of saying she'd had enough talk of Jack for one night, and I was happy to give in and leave the topic there.

Progress had been made, albeit small, but it was progress nonetheless. Besides, she had one thing right – I had been showing off like crazy at the batting cages and then turned out to be really terrible. Giving my bestie a wink and an agreeing nod we went to join Lisa and Mel at the bar where they had just snagged the attention of a barman.

Jack

Even though the bar was quite full, it wasn't hard to find Caitlin and Allie, not because they were dressed flamboyantly or dancing crazily, but because I'd been watching them on and off ever since I'd arrived. Well, I'd been watching Caitlin, anyway. Both girls seemed quite tipsy, leaning on each other, sharing conspiratorial whispers, and laughing with their friends. Caitlin looked completely relaxed and at ease, although on the two occasions that some guys had approached them she had tensed up and politely knocked them back.

Just as well, really. I'm not sure how I would have coped watching her flirt with someone else when I wanted her as badly as I did.

They seemed to have had a great night, as had I, although I'd deliberately kept my distance from Caitlin all evening. I'd thought that by giving her space after our 'we're now friends' declaration, I'd prove to her that I wouldn't try to push things too quickly. Hopefully, it had worked, because staying away from her when I knew she was just across the room had pretty much killed me.

It was getting late. Their friends had already left and I could tell from the way they had their arms linked and were both staggering a bit that perhaps they would be leaving soon too.

Which meant it was time for me to make my next move.

Sliding through the crowd, I reached their sides and nodded a greeting as I smiled at them both. 'Evening.

Seeing as I haven't been drinking, I was wondering if I could offer you two lovely ladies a lift home?'

Allie was first to respond, grinning and nodding enthusiastically, but as my focus drifted to Caitlin, I found that her usually guarded expression seemed to be absent. Perhaps it was the alcohol loosening her defences, or maybe our new friendship status, but whatever the reason, she was definitely gazing at me with an openly curious expression that morphed into a tiny, shy smile which sent my pulse rocketing, and had my cock instantly twitching in my trousers.

Fuck. I was getting a stiffy just because she smiled at me? What the hell did this girl do to me? I was nearly forty, but she had me responding like a teenager barely out of puberty.

Shoving my hands in my pockets to disguise the semi I was now sporting, I smiled back and watched with pleasure as her cheeks flushed and she began to fidget with her jacket. That smile, though. It was gone in the blink of an eye, replaced by a slightly less telling expression, but that had been the sweetest, most sexy sight I had ever seen in my entire life.

If I could be the man to make her smile like that every day then I would feel like the king of the world.

'That would be awesome, thank you, Jack. We're both a bit tipsy,' Allie confirmed, and I actually found it difficult to drag my eyes away from Caitlin so I could politely reply to her friend.

'I would have been too, but I have a long day on set tomorrow so decided not to risk a hangover.'

'Ugh. Yeah, my head is spinning. I think there will be some sore heads at our place tomorrow,' Allie joked with a slur as we began to head towards the exit. On our way out, I passed the bar and grabbed two bottles of water and signalled to Flynn in the corner that we were leaving.

After catching up with me, Flynn stepped in close to my side and leant in near my ear as we cut across the car park. 'You're upping your quest from one woman to two? They both gonna knock you back?' he joked, but I was still on such a high from Caitlin's smile that I didn't even bother to respond to his ribbing. Flynn offered to drive, but I decided I rather liked the idea of being the one to chauffer them home, so with me driving, Flynn as passenger, and the two girls giggling drunkenly in the back seats, we were ready to set off.

Swivelling in my seat, I offered the two water bottles to them and watched as Caitlin tentatively leant forwards to take them from me. Our fingers briefly brushed, and her eyes jumped to lock with mine for just a second as she murmured a soft 'Thank you'. They were the first words she'd uttered to me since I'd offered them a lift, but that was fine – she could be as quiet as she liked as long as she kept giving me those little looks and smiles.

Once we got to the compound I'd planned to stay in the car so as not to make Caitlin feel uncomfortable, but both girls practically fell from the vehicle in a giggling, drunken heap, so I told Flynn to stay in the car while I saw them inside.

'Thanks so much for the lift, Jack. You should start a celebrity cab service, you'd make a fortune,' Allie joked, causing Caitlin to giggle so infectiously that I couldn't help but chuckle. 'God, I really need the loo,' Allie suddenly announced as soon as we were inside the front door, before she charged off towards the stairs, dragging a staggering Caitlin behind her as they both swayed.

'Goodnight, ladies.' I was about to turn and leave them

to it when I watched Caitlin manage two steps and come to rest against the wall, giggling.

'Come on Cait, I'm bursting for the toilet!' Allie was practically hopping back and forth on the spot, so I lingered for a moment then decided to offer my help. I wasn't sure Caitlin would want my offer of assistance, but I could try.

'You go on ahead, Allie, I'll help Caitlin.' Seeing Caitlin flash me a bleary-eyed, slightly wary glance I nodded and softened my voice. 'It's OK, Caitlin, I'll just follow you up the stairs to make sure you don't fall, I won't touch you, I promise.'

She observed me through her drink dilated pupils for a second and after giving me a wobbly nod of acceptance, she began climbing the stairs again as Allie dashed off ahead.

A satisfied smile curved my lips, but I couldn't help but roll my eyes at the way this girl and her silent nods already had me wrapped around her little finger.

Watching her drunken struggle over the next five minutes was like utter torture because all I wanted to do was scoop her up in my arms and carry her to her room, but I didn't dare touch her for fear of ruining what seemed to be developing.

Eventually, she made it to the top step and I followed Caitlin into the first room on the left, careful to keep my distance, and then watched as she lurched forwards and immediately sank down on the side of the bed with a grateful sigh. I had experienced that same drunken relief to be home many a night in my time, that was for sure.

'Thank you,' she murmured, before flopping backwards and giggling at the ceiling. 'You're such a gentleman.' Her mumbled words had me smiling like a complete idiot.

Still smiling fondly, I gave her one last look before leaving. 'Good night, Caitlin.'

'G'night, Jack.' As I was turning, I heard her sigh behind me and speak again, this time her voice slightly less slurred. 'You make me feel really safe.' Those words caused me to freeze and turn back to see if she was actually addressing me or just mumbling drunkenly. Her eyes were closed, so I guessed the latter, but couldn't help but feel elated. I made her feel safe, and that knowledge had my chest swelling with pride.

'I'm glad we're friends now. I like you, Jack.' Wow. My eyebrows rose so suddenly that they practically jumped from my head. The confessions were just flowing out of her now. I knew I should probably leave her to sleep, but this was so incredible that I remained glued to the spot just in case she chose to share any more drunken insights with me.

One of her hands rose up and then flopped onto her face to rub at her cheeks before clumsily trying to brush the hair from her eyes. She failed, and her hair still half covered her face, but she gave up and dropped the arm to the bed in defeat. Her uncoordinated attempts made me itch to help her, but I didn't. My heart was still pounding from her confessions, the last thing I wanted to do was wake her up fully and break the spell.

'Like *yooou*,' she murmured. '*Waaay* more than I should,' she added in a slurred voice so quiet that I wondered if I'd conjured the words up in my imagination.

She liked me, way more than she should? My pulse was now rocketing in my veins and thumping so loudly in my ears that it felt like half the compound would be able to hear it. Licking my dry lips, I blinked several times as I ran her words through my mind again. They had been garbled, but they were the exact emotions I had dreamed of hearing her say to me.

I'd rather Caitlin had said them when she wasn't

plastered off her face, but still, she'd said them. Wasn't it generally believed that people were at their most honest when they'd had a few drinks?

'Just wish I wasn't sooo screwed up. So much baggage,' she murmured next with a hiccup, a frown creasing her eyebrows and mine. She was intoxicated, so I wouldn't attempt to follow this up now, but there was no doubt in my mind that I would prove to her that she wasn't screwed up, and that I wanted her regardless of whatever baggage she carried around. Everyone had some baggage, and I was ready and willing to take on some of hers to lighten her load.

Pulling in a deep breath to calm myself I looked at her again and frowned. I couldn't leave her like that. She was half on the bed and half off of it. Her feet were on the floor, but back and shoulders on the bed, and I knew that if I left her like that then she would either fall off in her sleep or wake up with a seriously bad back.

Her position on the foot end of the bed was awkward, because I couldn't lay her down with her head on the pillows unless I shifted her entire body. I didn't want her to wake up and find me pawing her, so I opted for simply lifting her feet up and placing them on the bed.

Stepping forward, I gently circled her ankles, one in each of my hands, the feel of her warmth beneath my fingers causing a strained groan to rise up my throat as I shifted her legs as slowly and carefully as I could.

Caitlin was now fully on the bed, her feet by the pillows, and her head at the foot of the bed, but at least she would be more comfortable.

Picking up her pillow, I was about to see if I could somehow get it under her head when something underneath it caught my eye. A small square of white cotton. Blinking hard, I clutched the pillow in my hands as I stared at the white square laying on her bed. If I wasn't mistaken that was the handkerchief I had given her at the Getty Centre.

My handkerchief was under *her* pillow.

The fact that she had not only kept it, but chosen to keep it under her pillow nearly winded me with emotion and I let out a strangled breath as I looked at her peaceful face.

It couldn't have got there by mistake, so surely if she'd kept the hankie under her pillow it meant she had wanted to keep a part of me close by? '*Caitlin*,' I whispered, my voice hoarse from the implications of her simple action.

I had a feeling that Caitlin would be mortified if she knew I'd seen it, so I placed the pillow back on top of it to keep her secret safe. She'd have to sleep without a pillow, but she was so drunk I didn't think she'd even notice.

Knowing I had already been in her room for way too long *and* broken my promise not to touch her, I felt a little bad for lingering, but I felt like tonight had been so monumental for us that I could hardly bring myself to leave.

Hopefully, Caitlin was so drunk that she wouldn't remember my trespassing in the morning. Although having said that, there were certain things about the last few minutes I did want her to remember – like her declarations of liking me.

More than she should.

Smiling again, I couldn't help but step closer to her and gently finish the job she had started by carefully brushing the hair back from her face properly. My touch prompted her to sigh and then roll onto her side so she was facing me, but her eyes remained closed in relaxation.

'For the record, I like you too.' I whispered the words, but it still felt good to actually say them out loud to her.

Grinning, I decided to add on her extra phrase as well, because regardless of how clumsy it was, it was true for me too. 'Waaaay more than I should.'

Dropping into a crouch beside her, I was now level with her face, and just a small gap separated us. If I rolled forward on my feet I could easily kiss her, but I wouldn't break her confidence like that.

The next time I kissed Caitlin Byrne would be when she was awake, sober, and wanting me to.

Caitlin shifted slightly, and for a second I panicked that she was waking up and would see me this close and freak out, but then she murmured quietly and curled further into a ball. 'You know what else I really like?' she mumbled with a smile that was so addictive I found myself mirroring it.

'No, what's that?'

'Bacon.'

A sporadic laugh flew from my mouth as I stood up and pulled as much of the duvet around her as I could. I had been hoping for more heartfelt words, but no, she was dreaming about bacon. Perhaps it was time I left her to sleep.

'Bacon, huh?'

'Yep. I would totally love you forever if you could get me a bacon sandwich. Mmmm. Bacon …'

Love me forever? My eyebrows rose in amusement, but all joking aside that was a prospect so appealing that I was almost tempted to go and hunt down some bacon right that second. Or perhaps I could just get Flynn to drive out to an all-night store and buy some, but then, hearing a small snore escape Caitlin's throat, I realised she had finally fallen properly asleep.

Shaking my head, I watched her for a few more seconds as her eyelids fluttered. She was so hammered I doubted that she would remember any of this in the morning, but the majority of the evening was certainly engrained into my mind for eternity. Her smiles, laughs, drunken confessions, hidden handkerchiefs … tonight had been amazing. Not to mention when she'd grabbed me earlier at the batting cage. A groan rose in my throat as I remembered how soft her skin had felt and I had to force myself to back towards the door and leave her alone.

Jogging downstairs to the kitchen, I filled two large glasses with ice water, and then dug around looking for some painkillers. Ibuprofen usually worked best if I had a hangover, but all I could find were paracetamol, so they'd have to do.

Carrying my collection back upstairs I placed one of the glasses beside Caitlin's bed along with two tablets and then turned to leave the room after giving her sweet, sleep-relaxed face one last look.

'Is she OK?' Turning at the door, I found Allie staggering around the corridor and coming to check on us.

'Yep, drunk, half-asleep and talking about bacon,' I said with an affectionate chuckle.

'Ah yes, Cait's favourite hangover cure is a bacon sandwich.' Allie half leant and half flopped onto the wall beside me, clearly feeling the effects of the drinks too, although perhaps not quite to the extent that Caitlin was. 'She'll be disappointed, because there's none in the fridge. In fact, there's not much in the fridge at all.' Making a mental note of Caitlin's preference for bacon, I held out the second glass of iced water and the box of paracetamol. 'Here, these are for you.'

Allie looked surprised by my gesture and took both gratefully, immediately taking a long drink from the glass and licking her lips in appreciation.

‘Thank you so much. Cait’s right when she says you’re a gentleman,’ Allie murmured, giving me a surprisingly intense look considering her drunken state. ‘Good night, Jack. If you pull the front door shut behind you it’ll automatically lock.’

Allie turned away, and made her way back upstairs but I paused in the corridor for a second as I wondered whether she had been standing at the door earlier and heard Cait call me a gentleman, or if it was something she had said at another point when sober.

Whichever it was, I definitely left their house with a spring in my step and a decidedly positive feeling about the future buzzing in my system.

Chapter Twenty-Nine

Cait

Opening my eyes, I immediately felt like the daylight seeping between my lashes was trying to sear my eyeballs. Cursing, I squeezed them shut again and groaned loudly. Jeez. I felt like utter crap. Tentatively lifting a hand, I rubbed it over my face and tried to assess the state of my body. My head felt like I had an out of tune bongo band playing in my temples, my throat was sore, and my feet hurt like hell.

In other circumstances I would think that I was sick, or coming down with something, but the sour taste of stale booze on my tongue gave me an unpleasant reminder of the vast quantities of alcohol I had consumed, which was no doubt the cause of my current state. Well, not my sore feet, they were no doubt a result of the heels I'd changed into to go to the bar last night.

Clearing my throat, I tried to lick my lips, but my tongue was so dry that I failed horribly and ended up opening and closing my mouth pathetically instead. Ugh. My tongue was like a slab of sand-encrusted carpet sitting within the Sahara desert of my mouth. Rolling over to get a drink, I tentatively peeled my eyes open and frowned. Instead of seeing my bedside table, I was staring out at my bedroom, because I seemed to be upside down on my bed. Huh. Weird.

Gingerly sitting up, I pushed my hair from my face as my bleary eyes settled on a large glass on my bedside table. Water. Thank God. My tongue tried to salivate at the thought of the cool liquid refreshing my parched mouth, and I lurched along the mattress and reached for it desperately.

Gulping down half the glass in one go, I sighed my appreciation and then saw two small tablets sitting beside it. Paracetamol. Perfect. Allie had obviously taken care of me last night and left these for me. Popping the tablets in my mouth, I swallowed, and as I gazed around in a hungover fog, I had a sudden recollection of Jack Felton being in my room.

Almost choking on the tablets, I forced them down and then frowned at the blurring images in my mind. I could picture him standing in front of my wardrobe so clearly. Had he been here? I couldn't for the life of me imagine why he would have been. I wouldn't have knowingly invited a man in … but then again, I did have some serious blanks in last night's events.

I gave my wardrobe another scrutinising look and felt my heart leap with worry as I turned and quickly picked up my pillow. Jack's hankie was still hidden, safe and sound and folded neatly. Phew. I don't know why I still had it there, but for some reason I'd felt a weird urge to keep it close since he'd given it to me.

Dismissing my blurry visions of him as a trick of my fuzzy post-drink brain, I shrugged off the strange sensation and looked down at my rumpled state. A small smile pulled at the corners of my lips when I realised that I was still in last night's clothes. At least if I was still fully dressed it would seem I hadn't been up to anything too crazy.

Did sleeping in your clothes mean you'd had an

awesome night, or a really dreadful one? I couldn't decide, but it'd been a long while since I'd fallen into bed fully dressed and upside down, that was for sure.

I thought I'd had a good time last night. I *thought*, but I couldn't quite remember.

Squinting, I thought back over yesterday's events and tried to piece together what I could recall. I hadn't started drinking until the bar, so the afternoon at the batting cages was pretty clear. It had been great fun, and I'd actually been quite good in the end. Mel and Lisa had hit it off with Allie straight away, and between us we'd made quite a fun-loving little group.

Yep, all in all the batting cages had been great. I'd even dealt well with seeing Jack again. Apart from my one slip up when I'd grabbed him in a panic, of course. Grimacing, I shook my head, then groaned and clutched at my skull as my brain pounded out a painful reminder of my hangover.

Keeping my head still, I gave the elastic band at my wrist a flick in agitation. I still couldn't believe I'd grabbed him. Me. Caitlin Byrne, spinster specialist and the girl who avoided contact with men at all costs had actually made the first move.

Jeez. My cheeks heated as I thought about it. The chairs falling behind me had been so bloody loud that my heart had tried to burst from my chest in shock, and a second later I'd almost passed out when I'd looked down and seen my hands wrapped around Jack's. A wry chuckle escaped my throat as I recalled just how shocked he'd also looked, but he couldn't have been half as stunned by the forward gesture as I had been.

I still was. Apparently after years of being completely independent from men, my subconscious was seeing him as the one man I could turn to for physical support, which was certainly an interesting, if somewhat shocking, development for me.

I remembered that we'd officially agreed that we were friends. Me and Jack Felton. Friends. Mates. Buddies. I had to roll my eyes, and then wondered if the title would change much between us. I supposed not, but it still felt like a pretty major step.

Even in my hungover state, my heart sped up a little bit as I continued to think about Jack, and annoyingly I found an accompanying smile curving my lips. Bloody man. Sighing heavily, I rubbed at my temples and wondered if he had any idea just how badly he'd thrown my life, and emotions, into complete turmoil.

As much as those thoughts were playing on my mind, my stomach suddenly gave a huge growl, alerting me to the fact that I was ravenously hungry. I rarely got rip-roaringly drunk these days, but on the occasions that I did have a few drinks, I always found that a good breakfast the following morning would send any lingering hangover packing. I really hoped that would be the case today, because my head was pounding.

Another grumble from my tummy had me cautiously standing up, peeling off last night's clothes, dragging on my dressing gown, and stumbling in the direction of the hall. I needed coffee and food, and I needed them pronto. Preferably bacon.

Unfortunately, once I was downstairs, one quick glance in the fridge showed no exciting goodies at all, meaning that there would be no bacon sarnies for me. But we did at least have coffee and milk, so I immediately set to work getting a pot going.

Just as I picked up the jug in preparation to pour myself a mug, there was a knock at the front door. It was so unexpected that it startled me into spilling some of the coffee before I placed the jug down and traipsed in the direction of the door warily.

We hadn't exactly lived here long, and I didn't think that anyone had the address, apart from Sean, and seeing as he'd been filming night shoots, he would no doubt be in bed by now.

Checking the peep hole, which I always did, I almost leapt back in surprise when I saw Jack on the step. What the heck? Not only was I questioning why he was here, but more importantly, how was he here? I'd never told him where I lived, so appearing on the doorstep was slightly unnerving. Especially seeing as I was decidedly under par this morning and definitely not prepared to deal with him and his hormone-stirring presence.

Wanting to run and hide but feeling too guilty to ignore him, I tried my best to disregard my pounding head and look relaxed and calm as I pulled open the door. Unfortunately, the bright sunlight was just too much for my poor eyeballs, and as it hit my retinas I ended up groaning and covering my face with my hands instead of being calm and relaxed. This really was just the perfect start to the day. Not.

'Good morning, Caitlin.' Wincing as I dropped my hands, I squinted up at Jack and saw he looked fresh as a frigging daisy, and just as hot as ever in a pair of reflective sunglasses, navy T-shirt, and the same grey jeans he'd had on last night. They were obviously his choice pair, and I had to say they featured fairly high on my favourites list too, because boy, did they fit him perfectly in all the right places.

Glancing down at myself, I grimaced. No fresh as a daisy looks here; I was wrapped in a dressing gown, drowsy, dishevelled, and probably coated in the smeared remains of last night's make-up. Awesome.

'Morning,' I mumbled, not able to add the 'good', because as far as I was concerned the morning was pretty abysmal. Not only was I lumbered with the most monstrous hangover known to man, but I had to deal with Jack too, the one man who took my carefully built defences and seemed to brush them aside with ease, leaving me open, vulnerable, and completely flummoxed about what the heck it was I was feeling.

'I have to get to the studio, so I can't stop long, but I brought you both some breakfast.' He lifted his arm to waggle a brown paper bag, and then when I stepped back and wafted a hand to indicate that he should come in he happily wandered past me into the lounge and straight towards the kitchen.

Huh? His mere presence here was confusing, but now he knew the layout of my place, and had brought food too? In what universe did Jack Felton deliver food to my door? In what world did he deliver food to anyone's door? Surely being a movie star it should be him demanding deliveries and then sitting back to be waited upon.

Following him through to the kitchen, I found Jack unpacking the paper sack onto the table and couldn't help but stare at the oddly domestic scene for a few seconds. He was absorbed in his task of pulling out various tubs and packages and humming quietly to himself as he did so.

Humming?

Jack Felton was humming in my kitchen, while preparing my breakfast? God, this was weird.

'How do you know where I live?' My tone was more curious than accusatory, but Jack still paused and looked at me with a small smile and a raised eyebrow. 'Got a few blanks, eh?'

I nodded, my aching brain begging me not to repeat the action, but as I spotted some chocolate croissants on the table, my stomach gave an almighty growl and I found my mouth salivating.

Presented with the food, I suddenly wasn't quite as bothered by my headache or the answer to my question, but Jack seemed intent on giving it anyway. 'I dropped you and Allie home last night. You mentioned a craving for bacon, but Allie said there wasn't much food in the house so I figured you might like a breakfast delivery.'

Wow. How thoughtful. Not to mention slightly embarrassing that I had apparently been drunkenly rambling on about bacon. Oops.

'Turns out you're quite the chatterbox when you're drunk,' he murmured, his words making my stomach drop. Oh god. What had I said last night?

'Uh … really? What else did I say?' Please don't tell me I'd said how gorgeous I thought he was. Please not that. Anything but that.

'Just bits and pieces. Nothing to panic over.'

Hmm. There was a twinkle in his eye that said otherwise, but I wasn't going to pursue it if it meant I would embarrass myself even further. Changing the subject, I eyed the bag of food hopefully. 'I think I might love you forever if you've bought me bacon,' I mumbled, as my eyes scanned the table trying to work out if he had a packet hidden away somewhere.

Suddenly, I brought myself up short. Oh god. Had I just said the 'L' word to Jack Felton? Why had I chosen that word? I could have said I'd be forever grateful or hugely appreciative, but no, I'd said I'd love him forever.

Thankfully, Jack seemed to overlook my slip and merely

smiled at me, pulling out a bowl of fruit salad. 'That's one of the things you said last night,' he murmured, his voice dropping slightly and causing me to lift my eyes from the food to look at his face.

There was a strange, soft look to his expression that made my stomach clench and heart leap as our eyes locked and held, but before I could make any more of it, we were interrupted by Allie practically falling into the kitchen and clutching her head in both hands.

'I am hungover as fuck! Please tell me we have coffee. Oh! Jack ...' Allie's cheeks flushed beetroot red, presumably over her hilariously filthy mouth this morning. 'Hi, sorry, I didn't expect to see you here.' She might have been talking to Jack, but Allie was now staring straight at me, clearly wondering where the heck Jack the breakfast bringer had appeared from.

I gave a shrug, then Jack jumped in.

'Morning, Allie. I was passing on my way to the studios and seeing as you said there was no food in the house last night I decided to bring you girls some breakfast.'

'Wow. Wow... thank you. That's amazing.' Allie's gaze bounced between Jack and me curiously before landing on the coffee pot on the side. 'Coffee ... thank God ...'

'Wait, drink this first.' Jack dug into the paper bag and produced two small bottles containing a pale white liquid, one of which he handed to Allie. 'You too, Caitlin,' he said, passing me an identical bottle. 'It's coconut water, great for hangovers because it's rich in potassium and magnesium, which help the body to hydrate.' Our fingers brushed as I accepted the bottle and as I felt a heated tingle rushing up my arm, I was instantly reminded of how good it had felt to cling on to Jack yesterday. I couldn't be entirely sure, but from the way our eyes joined again for a heated second or too, I'm pretty sure he felt it too.

Feeling decidedly hot under the collar I looked away from him and popped the cap on the bottle before taking a tentative sip, allowing a tiny amount to slip over my tongue. To my pleasant surprise it tasted great: icy cold, sweet, and so refreshing that I proceeded to down the entire bottle in one go. Licking my lips, I smiled and placed the bottle down. 'Tasty. Thanks.'

Jack gave me a sweet smile and looked to blush a little. 'You're welcome. Now have this.' He handed me a paper-wrapped package which I began to open, and paused as my nose latched onto the smell of bacon and sent my saliva glands into overdrive.

Oh my god. He really had brought me bacon? My eyes jerked back to Jack, where I found him with that same weird, soft expression on his face as he watched me carefully.

'Ask and you shall receive,' he murmured with a wink. 'Let's hope you keep your end of the deal someday,' he added, causing my brain to completely flip out. 'Well, enjoy, ladies. I'm afraid I've got to go.'

With that, Jack was gone, leaving Allie and me with just a hint of his scent in the air and the vast quantities of food on the table to show he really had been here. What a completely bizarre way to start the day.

'What did he mean when he said "let's hope you keep your end of the deal"?' Allie asked as she slumped into a seat and began to shove a chocolate croissant into her mouth. Following her to the table, I bit into my bacon sandwich, hummed my appreciation, and then swallowed before meeting her curious gaze. Gosh, this was embarrassing.

'Uh … apparently when I was drunk last night I, uh… I

said I would love him forever if he bought me bacon.'

The croissant fell from her hands onto the table in a shower of flaky crumbs as Allie gaped at me. 'I didn't mean it literally, I was drunk,' I added quickly, deciding to leave out the fact that I had also said it this morning sober. Well, sober-ish. 'Anyway, he was just joking around,' I murmured, hoping to convince both myself and Allie.

'Hmmm.' Allie picked up her croissant and took another bite, looking at me thoughtfully. 'He could certainly teach Sean a thing or two about how to treat his woman, that's for sure. Lifts home, breakfast deliveries, special hangover-curing drinks … I could get used to this kind of service!'

'I'm not his woman,' I corrected quickly, but looking at the table I gave in with a smile. 'But yeah, this is all really thoughtful.' A really thoughtful gesture by my bacon-bringing, handsome as sin new 'friend'. Hmm. I certainly had a lot to process.

'Do you remember much of last night?' Allie asked curiously.

Peeling off a crispy bit of bacon, I popped it in my mouth, savoured the deliciously salty taste, and licked my fingers clean. 'Not really. Jack said he brought us home, and I certainly don't remember that.'

'He did. Helped you up the stairs and got us glasses of water and some paracetamol.' The drink and tablets had been from Jack? His list of gallant deeds just went on and on, didn't it?

I recalled the strange half visions I'd had of Jack standing by my wardrobe. 'He was in my room?' I squeaked, not entirely sure how I felt about that.

'Yeah, but not for long. I had to run to the toilet so he helped you, that's all. He promised not to touch you, and he stuck to it.'

'He actually promised that?' I whispered, my voice suddenly feeling quite tight for a reason I couldn't quite place.

'Yep. I told you he was a genuinely nice guy. He is a total gentleman, Cait. It was really rather sweet.'

Sweet. And genuinely nice.

Damn it, I really wished I hadn't been so drunk so I could remember what he'd said. As I considered that, a more alarming thought entered my brain. 'Did I say anything embarrassing?'

Allie giggled, then took a sip of her coffee and sighed happily. 'Nothing much, just that you think he's totally hot.'

The final bite of my sandwich went sailing across the room as I choked on it and spluttered loudly. 'I told him that?' I screeched, all thoughts of food gone, along with the lingering remnants of my hangover as panic flooded my brain thick and fast.

Swallowing another sip of her drink, Allie eyed me innocently over the top of her mug, and finally gave in and laughed. 'Nah, of course not. But the look on your face is priceless.'

Holy shit, I'd believed her, and now my pulse was racing and my head was banging again. 'Jeez, Allie, don't do stuff like that.' I felt my heart hammering below my breastbone like a freight train.

Grinning at me cheekily, she wiggled her eyebrows and shrugged. 'You could have said it, it's obviously true.'

I was about to resort to my custom denial, but seeing her sceptical look I instead gave in with a groan. 'Yeah, yeah, he's good looking, and kind and 'genuinely nice' and all sorts of appealing. I'm celibate, not blind,' I added snappily, before picking absently at some crumbs on the table. 'But seeing as we've only just established a friends thing, I don't exactly want to go blabbing how attractive I find him, do I?'

'I guess not …'

Allie's tone made it obvious that she wanted to say more so I pulled in a deep breath and raised my eyebrows. 'What?'

'Nothing, really. I'm just really glad that you're giving this friendship a chance. I'm really proud of you.'

Proud of me for being friends with a man. It was embarrassing. That was something most women took for granted and did naturally without any fuss. But I guess for me, with all my baggage, it *was* a big deal and something to be proud of, so instead of saying anything, I just nodded and gladly accepted the hug Allie pulled me into.

Chapter Thirty

Allie

It had been four days since I'd gone with Cait to the batting cages, which meant four days since she had agreed to be friends with Jack. It also translated to four long, hard days of me desperately wanting to push her on the subject but knowing I needed to refrain so she didn't freak out about it.

I had, however, decided that today was the day to broach the subject again and see if she had spoken to him since the weekend. Gossip was practically my middle name, and if this had been a different friend we were talking about, then I would have been all over them like a rash the very next day. But this wasn't just any girl, this was Cait, my best friend and someone so hesitant about relationships that I knew what a big deal it was for her to even be moving forward with a friendship with a man, let alone anything more.

It was a little past ten in the morning, and we were heading out onto the deck to lounge over a second pot of coffee, which seemed the perfect opportunity to corner my bestie on the topic of Mr Hot-to-Trot Jack Felton.

Before we'd even got outside though, my phone started to ring on the kitchen table. Turning back for it, I saw Savannah's number flashing up and sighed. God, this woman was persistent. I'd accepted her apology, even though I didn't truly believe that she was actually sorry, but she suddenly seemed to want to be my best bloody buddy.

Cait held the coffee pot up and waggled it in my direction so I nodded and gave her a thumbs up to indicate I would like another cup. That would probably be my third for the day, no wonder I was feeling so alert.

Answering the call, I lifted the phone warily to my ear. 'Hello?'

'Allie, *darrrrling*. How are you?' I winced and rolled my eyes, still hating the way she rolled her rrrr's.

'Fine, thanks, Savannah. And you?' I disliked being this friendly with her, but I didn't see that I had any other option. Sean had to work with her, and if I wanted to be able to see him when she was around then being polite was the best course.

Savannah began droning on about her morning and there didn't seem to be any stopping her, so it seemed easier to just join Cait outside, sit back on the wicker sofa, sip my coffee, and let her get on with it. Finally, Savannah paused for breath.

'You're very quiet, *darrrrrling*.' That's because you won't shut up, I thought, rolling my eyes at her over the top tone as I kicked my legs up onto a footstool.

'Are you still terribly angry with me for my little prank?' My eyes widened. Telling someone you had slept with their boyfriend – no, not slept with, 'fucked'– was not just a little prank, it was downright deceitful. But I kept quiet. Savannah was exhausting and I couldn't even be bothered to try and compete.

'What more can I say? I'm an actress, sometimes I get off on using my talents to wind people up. It was wrong of me, I know that. Please, Allie, say you've forgiven me? If you're dating Sean and I'm working with him, you and I need to get along.'

Reluctantly, I had to agree. If Sean and I worked out, which I was determined that we would, then I would have to see Savannah for the next few years whenever they were filming.

Stubbornly, I stayed silent though, not wanting to have to agree with her about anything. 'Look, the reason I was calling was to ask you if you wanted to come to the set today. You and I could grab a coffee and start over. Please?'

My eyes narrowed. Coffee with Savannah? I couldn't think of anything I'd like less. Poking my own eyes out with the coffee scoop would probably be more enjoyable. 'Sean said you like writing, so I was thinking I could introduce you to some of the scriptwriters.'

Hmmm, I'd always fancied moving across to screenplays, or scriptwriting, so that offer did sound pretty tempting, but hearing my continued silence, she persevered. 'He mentioned that he was disappointed that you can't come down to watch him in action because you have to stay secret, but if I sign you in as my friend no one will suspect anything. What do you say? He'd be so thrilled if you got to see him acting, I just know it.'

Watching Sean act *was* high up on my list of fantasies, so was a temptation too great to turn down. I'd have to delay my chat with Cait, but that could always wait until tonight. Weighing it all up, I shrugged. Savannah had been pretty persistent with her apology texts and flowers, so perhaps she really was trying to extend the olive branch. In the end, the offer of seeing Sean on set was just too much to resist.

'OK, sounds good.'

'Yay! Oh thank you, Allie, we'll have such fun.' Resting a hand on my hip, I gave an ironic smile. I very much doubted we'd have 'such fun' but it would be an interesting way to spend the day.

Savannah seemed flustered and rushed when I arrived at the set an hour later. She plonked me in a corner and disappeared almost immediately to prepare for filming, promising that we would get a coffee together afterwards. That was fine by me, I'd much rather sit on my own and watch Sean in action than make small talk with a woman I didn't particularly like.

Pulling out my phone, I was about to send Sean a text telling him I was here when I paused. Would that put him off his game? If he knew I was somewhere behind the scenes, it might well make him nervous. I knew it would affect me if things were the other way around, so I switched my phone off and stashed it back in my bag instead.

Tucking my stool back into the corner so I could lean on the wall, I relaxed back and absorbed the action going on around me. Filming hadn't started yet and I couldn't see Sean or Savannah anywhere, but the studio was busy with people rushing to and fro, cameras being shifted along tracks, and a general feeling of anticipation hung in the air.

I'd done a behind the scenes tour of a local television studio in the UK with my class when I was a teacher, but this was different. It was live and real, and the excitement was tangible and thrilling to the point where the hairs on my arms were standing up in expectation.

I felt a subtle shift in the air around me and I got a familiar warm sensation on my skin. *Sean*. The reaction in my body told me he was somewhere nearby, but it was still a second or so until I could locate where he was.

As my eyes searched the space I suddenly saw him across the stage talking to another man, their eyes intently focused on a clipboard before them. As was always the case, my heart gave a little kick of joy at the sight of Sean and I felt a familiar tightening of desire in my belly. Dressed in navy trousers, a matching polo shirt with a police logo on the chest, and chunky boots, he was already in his uniform for the show, and boy, did he look hot.

Really flipping hot. And all mine.

A smirk curled my lips as I secretly ogled him, absorbing every little detail into my memory banks. Yep, that outfit was gorgeous. And so was my man. He could arrest me any day of the week. In fact, seeing as our recent midnight intruder role play had gone so well, maybe I'd ask him to bring that outfit home so we could play an X-rated version of cops and robbers.

It felt strange watching him. Illicit and oddly arousing, especially because nobody else in the room was aware that we were together. Apart from Savannah, of course, but I dismissed that thought with a grunt – I was attempting not to think about her at all.

Yeah, this secret relationship with Sean was actually quite exhilarating when I thought about it. The sensation of illegality added an exciting edge to it. There was nothing quite like an element of sneaking something forbidden to ramp up the lust levels, that was for sure.

Suddenly, things got going. A director called the actors to the set and I watched as the lighting subtly altered and cameras turned on. As Sean, Savannah, and two other men took their positions on the set, a hush of anticipation fell over the room, and then somebody snapped a black and white clapper board which said scene 5, take 1. Huh, I'd thought those things were just a joke.

Sean had such stage presence that he dominated the scene with ease. Even when he wasn't the one speaking I found my eyes were glued to him. Mind you, I supposed I might have been just a tiny bit biased. I was so engrossed in the action that I found myself often holding my breath and having to quickly suck in a gasp of air when the tension on set eased.

Obviously, I hadn't seen what had led up to this scene, so I wasn't entirely sure what was going on, but the actors seemed to be involved in an argument about some evidence which had been lost, and to my glee, the focus of their ire was Savannah. Ha! Sean got to yell at her, and best of all, I could watch. It was ridiculous quite how much that pleased me, even though it was fake.

The two other detectives shouted one final curse and then stormed off the stage, leaving just Sean and Savannah on the stage. Sean was bristling with annoyance, pacing back and forth like a prowling tiger, and gosh, did he act it well. He really did look furious, so much so in fact that it had made the hairs on my arms stand on end. Mind you, so did Savannah. I might not be her number one fan, but it was clear she was a very good actress.

Stalking towards her, the argument continued until suddenly, to my utter horror, the two of them came together in a clashing of lips and limbs as their argumentative anger turned to a sudden explosion of heated lust.

Oh. My. God.

They were kissing the hell out of each other and it was like all of my nightmares coming true. Their hands were all over each other, her red, glossy nails digging into his shoulders as moans of pleasure left her lips.

The worst thing was they actually looked good together. There was obvious chemistry between them, plus, they were both stunningly good-looking, tanned, and perfectly preened. Ugh. She was literally everything I wasn't.

Annoyingly, Sean seemed just as into it as she was, but was apparently using his character's anger to drive his lust, as he regularly cursed or muttered heated things to her that I couldn't hear. Or perhaps I was just blocking them out, who knew?

Suddenly, I was reminded of the night Sean and I had argued at the art gallery and then made up over a round of spectacular angry sex. When I arrived back at the hotel that night I'd found Sean in my bed, furious and horny and hell bent on sexing me silly until I apologised. The more I watched, the more I realised that this scene was just like that night. Angry, hot, lusty sex, and I was suddenly so filled with jealousy that I very nearly launched myself from my seat to attack Savannah. Or perhaps Sean. I couldn't decide who most deserved a slap.

Breathe. *Breathe.*

This is just his job. It's fake. *It. Is. Fake.*

But no matter how many times I repeated those three words, nothing could distract me from the very real evidence in front of me that said otherwise. Sean and Savannah were still almost violently lip-locked and her fingers were now attempting to pull his shirt from his trousers. Clinging to the edge of my chair to stop myself moving, I swallowed down the hot bile that rose up my throat and only just managed to hold back from throwing up there and then.

I felt trapped and utterly helpless. I'd been told I couldn't leave the stage during live filming, and that I had to stay still and quiet until someone shouted 'cut', but literally all I wanted to do was run away. Far, far away from this claustrophobic room.

Sucking in several breaths, I tried to calm myself before I did something stupid like wail out my misery and cause everyone to turn and look at me, but it was difficult. So fucking difficult. Jesus. I thought I would actually puke if they carried on for much longer. Or faint. Although, actually, being unconscious was far more preferable to having to sit here and witness all of this.

Suddenly, I heard the word I had been praying for. 'Cut.'

Immediately, I watched as Savannah leant back from Sean marginally, her eyes seeking mine instantly as she flashed me a devious smirk and proceeded to trail her fingers down his arms until they rested on his arse.

As I sat in shock watching her it suddenly all became clear.

The fucking bitch had done this on purpose! Her phone calls, flowers, and text messages had been to lull me into a false sense of security so she could lure me down here today. She must have been planning this for ages, the fucking bitch. She must have learnt that they were filming this scene today and she'd wanted me to witness it so she'd invited me under the pretence of an apology. She'd never had any intention of making up with me. She just wanted to rub this in my face.

And boy had she succeeded. Even if Sean wasn't sleeping with Savannah, she had made it perfectly clear that she would still regularly get to kiss him and put her skinny hands all over him.

My head was in such a mess, I couldn't process which emotion to feel first, jealousy was ripping my chest apart, anger surging through me towards Savannah and her childish trickery, betrayal at Sean for not telling me he was going to be doing this, and irritation at myself for not realising that kissing her would be part of his bloody annoying job. Ugh, it was enough to make me dizzy.

Savannah briefly rested her chin on Sean's shoulder, her eyes linked with mine while her hands continued to grip him purposefully. The fact that he shoved her off a second later didn't matter to me; Savannah's intent was clear in her stare – 'I don't lose.'

Rather abruptly, my complete normalness hit me like a sucker punch as I stared at Savannah and watched her strut away, her hips swaying seductively. How could I compete with that? Apart from her puffy lips, Savannah definitely fell in the category of 'sex on legs' and could surely bag any man she wanted … but could she bag Sean again? More to the point, did I want to be the poor sap stuck in the middle while she tried?

I was standing in a fairly quiet spot now, the crew had moved away for a break and Sean turned, spotted me, did a double take, and then a broad grin split on his face as he walked my way. 'Well, I certainly didn't expect to see you today. What a nice surprise,' he said, grabbing a bottle of water.

I was still stunned from the depths that Savannah had sunk to and watched him frown as he got closer and took in my pale-faced expression. 'What's up, my gorgeous girl?' he asked, and I noticed bitterly how he was careful to lower his voice so those nearby didn't hear his affectionate term.

I finally found my voice, albeit falteringly. 'I … uh, that was horrible, watching you … kiss her and grab her … I feel sick.' To my amazement, my words seemed to fall completely on deaf ears. Sean just shrugged it off and swigged his water, seemingly oblivious of how it might be from the other side of the camera, and clearly didn't understand my annoyance at all, which only served to wind me up further.

'It's my job, it doesn't mean anything,' he said

dismissively with a casual shrug and a playful grin, but his attempt to lighten the mood merely acted to rub me the wrong way and I felt my eyes flare indignantly.

'Don't you dare laugh at me! It's not a matter of comedy, I'm serious, Sean.' I ran a hand through my hair in agitation, hating how much I was trembling, and shook my head. 'I think I was right at the beginning, I'm not sure I can deal with all this.' Staring at the ground, I fidgeted nervously, unable to clear the image of him and Savannah from my mind as it burrowed into my brain like a poisonous worm.

'All what?' Sean said, exasperated by the drama that was appearing from nowhere.

'It was like watching you cheat on me.' My gaze drifted across his face and I saw his expression change as my concerns finally seemed to hit home. 'It made me feel physically sick. I hated it ... I can't believe you have to kiss her like that.'

'You must have known that kissing was involved in the show though,' Sean pointed out in an increasingly panicked tone.

'No!' Huffing out a sharp breath, I shook my head. 'I told you I'd never seen the series, Sean. I thought you were in a police drama, not some steamy X-rated show.' How I wished I *had* seen *LA Blue* now, at least I would have been a bit more prepared. God, I felt so naïve it was untrue. Not to mention let down. He should have told me.

'Do you have to do that often? Kiss her? Touch her?'

Swallowing hard, Sean shoved his hands in his pockets then nodded slowly and in response my eyes squeezed shut at the flurry of images invading my brain. So when he came to see me straight from filming and kissed me, there was a high chance he'd recently been kissing her? 'Fuck, Sean. I feel really betrayed. This is nuts. You should have told me.'

'I see that now. I'm so sorry …'

Sorry wasn't going to erase the images from my head. 'I'm not sure I'm cut out to date a famous person,' I murmured. 'This is your job, I get that, and maybe you didn't realise how much it would upset me, but it really has. The differences between us are just so clear now …' I finished in a whisper.

'Sean, we need you back on set now,' someone called from behind him, but Sean ignored him, his gaze locked on mine now.

'Just give me five minutes,' Sean tossed back over his shoulder without even giving the director a glance. Having finally registered my distressed expression it seemed I well and truly had his attention now.

'Look, you're needed back on set and I need a little time to have a think, Sean. I'll speak to you later,' I mumbled as I turned for the exit and started to leave without even glancing at him.

'Sean, now, please?' This time a man I recognised was calling for Sean, Finlay James, the director and all-round Hollywood hotshot, obviously agitated by Sean's continuing absence.

I was nearly at the exit, but behind me I heard Sean yelling, 'I said I need five minutes. You'll have to wait.' The next second my ears filled with the distinct sound of shoes hitting the concrete floor at a fast pace.

He was coming after me.

Chapter Thirty-One

Allie

With tears now burning at the back of my eyes, I reached out and hastily shoved down on the exit door bar. I could hear Sean calling after me, but had no intention of stopping, not with Savannah around to watch my misery and soak it up like a sick, pity-loving sponge.

Making my break for freedom, the studio door swung open under my hand but I staggered backwards as the bright midday sun hit my eyes like the scorch of a laser, temporarily blinding me.

'Bloody hell!' I exclaimed, clutching at my eyes. Desperately shielding them, I trudged on sightlessly, determined not to give Sean chance to catch up.

Unfortunately, years of working on television sets seemed to have trained Sean in the art of successfully leaving a dark studio without causing permanent eye damage, because I caught a glimpse of him as he came charging through the door with his hand already raised to shield his eyes. With five large strides he was level with me and caught hold of my hand.

'Allie, wait, please,' he begged.

'Sean, please …' I wasn't entirely sure what I was pleading for as I rubbed my eyes with my free hand, trying to simultaneously regain my sight and wipe away the spilling tears. At my plea, Sean's hand dropped and when I could finally see through the sun blindness I watched as his shoulders slumped in defeat. 'At least let's talk about this,' he begged.

'We will talk, Sean, but later, somewhere private. If you want to talk to anyone right now, I suggest you have a word with your jealous ex and tell her to sort herself out,' I muttered, crossing my arms and trying to calm my thundering pulse.

'What? Who?'

I hissed her name like a curse. 'Savannah.'

'Savannah? What on earth are you talking about?' he said with a further frown.

'She phoned me this morning, all nice and friendly and persuaded me to come to the set and watch you filming. She said you desperately wanted me here to watch what you do.' I paused to drag in a breath and run a swipe of my knuckles across my wet cheeks. 'But do you know what? She knew you were doing a kissing scene and she knew it would drive me bonkers. I bet she was secretly hoping it would bring me to my senses so I'd finish with you so she could make her move again.' I huffed out an agitated breath and slammed my hands on my hips. 'I told you she wasn't over you, Sean.'

'Savannah did that?' he whispered, anger bubbling just below the surface of his voice, and I jerkily nodded my response.

Then, right on cue, the studio door flew open again and the subject of our conversation appeared in the sunlight. My eyes narrowed as I watched her overly seductive walk coming toward us. Savannah fucking Hilton. I hated her more than I could ever have thought possible.

'Sean, *darrrrling*, we need you back inside to carry on

our love scene,' she purred, acting as if butter wouldn't melt. Her gaze slid across to me and she put on a very decent impression of mock concern. 'Allie, you look upset, whatever is the matter? Aren't you enjoying the filming?'

In reply, I spluttered. Yep, spluttered. I was so shocked by the lengths she would go to that I was struck speechless.

'Savannah, what the fuck have you been playing at this time?' Sean growled, crossing his arms and turning a glare on his co-star.

'Me? I haven't done anything. I just thought Allie might enjoy coming down to watch us filming together. I didn't know we'd be kissing. We're so good together on set, don't you think?'

Thankfully I was saved from answering her ridiculous question by Sean's erupting anger. 'Enough, Savannah. We've had the scripts for weeks. Apologise to Allie right now, then stay the fuck away from her.'

In the blink of an eye, her mock concern was gone and replaced with a look that could only be described as bitter hatred. Her previous prettiness vanished, contorting into ugly bared teeth and squinty eyes as she flung her hair back and sniffed disdainfully.

'I'm not apologising for anything,' she replied with a scoff. 'It's not my fault if she's jealous about what a great couple you and I make.' As she finished speaking Savannah slid one arm around Sean's back and rubbed the other lovingly across his chest in a gesture far too intimate for mere friends.

Sean was tutting his annoyance and pushing her away, but something inside me snapped. Perhaps it was finally my sanity giving way, I wasn't sure, but her overly familiar gesture was the final trigger I needed to launch myself forwards with a shriek.

'Get your fucking hands off him!' I had lost all dignity, but I didn't care, and before I had even processed what I was doing, I found my right hand rearing back and then delivering a heavy slap across her perfect, cosmetically-enhanced face. Fuck me that had been incredibly hard.

Not to mention incredibly satisfying.

Savannah's head snapped sideways, causing her to stagger away from Sean on her high heels, clutching at her cheek and letting out a high, whiny sob like a dog that had been accidentally kicked.

Sucking in a long, shocked breath, I glanced down at my stinging palm to find it almost as red as Savannah's glowing cheek and the sight caused reality to slowly sink back in. I'd hit her. *Oops*. I'd never been prone to violence before, but Savannah had brought out my inner fighter.

'You see what she's like? We shared one kiss on set and she's gone insane!' Savannah screeched. 'I told you a relationship with a normal person was crazy, you need someone who understands the business, Sean, you need …' but Sean cut her off with a glower that was so terrifying that even I took a step back.

'Stop telling me what I need, and leave us the hell alone. Allie's not the crazy one here.'

That statement had Savannah floundering. From the crestfallen look on her face – her recently slapped and still glowing face – I genuinely think that she had expected him to agree with her and fall into her arms. Was she delusional?

'Fine. I'll fucking sue her for attacking me.' The words were barely out of Savannah's puckered little mouth when Sean grabbed her wrist and dragged her to within an inch of his face. He looked murderous, and as I watched Savannah squirming and flinching, I almost felt sorry for her. Pah!

Who was I kidding? I didn't feel sorry for her at all.

'You will not sue anyone. You know very well that all of this is your fault. Get some dignity, Savannah. I'm with Allie. *I choose her*. Now go inside, get your make-up touched up, and leave us alone.'

He chooses me.

Even in the midst of all this fucked-up-ness, those words made my heart constrict with so much love that it was almost painful enough to make me double over and clutch at my chest.

Savannah hesitated for one second, her eyes darting between me and Sean one last time before she blinked, nodded once, and turned on her heel to wobble away. Her step was far less sure now, the sultry sway absent from her hips as she struggled with her balance. Maybe my slap had knocked some sense into her.

Once Savannah was back inside, Sean turned to me, his eyes blazing and intent as he focused on me again. 'Fucking hell, what a mess. I have to say though, seeing you get possessive over me was really hot.' Sean moved quickly, capturing my head with one hand and swooping his lips towards mine. Lips I usually craved, but lips that had recently been locked with Savannah's, and that grisly image was enough to cause me to freak out for the second time in just a few minutes.

'Get off me!' My hands were flapping uselessly at his chest and my voice was high-pitched and squeaky as panic well and truly set in. 'Don't you dare kiss me when you've just had your tongue down her throat!'

Sean stepped back instantly, his hands rising in a conciliatory gesture and a look of utter shock on his face before he subconsciously wiped his mouth with the back of one hand. I couldn't see any lingering evidence of their kiss, but it was the thought of it that shook me up.

'Jesus, Allie, it's not like that at all. It was a stage kiss, we didn't even use tongues.' His left eye flinched slightly, and his shoulders slumped as he swallowed so hard that I heard it. 'Well, I didn't …'

So as well as fondling his arse, stroking his arms, and sucking on his lips Savannah had thrust her tongue into my man's mouth. Ugh. That was too much information, and I wished I had slapped her harder. Far, far, harder.

'I can't believe I didn't realise her intentions sooner. You kept telling me to watch out for her but I just didn't see it.' He suddenly looked broken, and the temptation to console him nearly overwhelmed me.

Shaking his head, Sean approached me again, stopping just inches away, but he made no attempt to touch me this time. 'Look, Allie, I'm sorry I wasn't more understanding. I've never considered what it must be like from your side of things. But you have to believe me, what happens out there,' he indicated to the film set behind us with a jerk of his thumb, 'is just work. It means nothing, it's just my job.'

I knew this, I did, but it wasn't just a job for Savannah. It was a challenge, and I didn't seem to be able to separate it. In my mind, all I could see was a continual replay of his passionate and fiery embrace with Savannah, their lips locked and hands clawing at each other's bodies, and the victorious smirk that had crossed her face after she'd shoved her tongue in his mouth.

'I know,' I answered croakily. 'But I keep seeing you and her together …' I decided to just be completely honest with him. 'I feel like I'm dying inside.' That caused his expression to slip into a mask of agony before he spun and seemed to scrub at his face with his hands.

'If it were the other way around, how would you feel?' I

asked softly, thinking his answer might help me to justify how I felt inside, and help him understand what I was going through.

Swinging back around to face me, Sean's eyes were wide and intent. 'If I had to watch someone else kiss you?' His hands clenched at his sides and I heard his teeth squeak as he ground them together. 'I'd kill him.' Blowing out a long breath, he rubbed at his eyes and dropped his arm limply to his side. 'And I'd probably hope that you'd quit your job.'

We both stood in silence before Sean nodded with determination. 'I'll do it. I'll quit. That will solve all our problems.' Although I had to say the idea did hold some temptation for me because he would no longer have to see Savannah, I couldn't live with myself if I let him do something so monumentally impulsive.

'No, wait.' I sighed heavily. 'You can't quit, Sean. It might seem like the best solution now, but what about in a year's time? Or two, or ten, when you miss it? You might start to resent me for it, and that would be the end of us. Think about it seriously for a second or two. You love your job, don't you?'

Sean linked his hands at the back of his neck as he ran my words through his head. 'I do,' he agreed. 'But I don't see any other solution. There's still weeks left until the premiere of the new season when Finlay says I can go to the press. *Weeks*.' The implications made me feel sick to my core – weeks of him being with Savannah, weeks of that bitch thinking she'd won, weeks of misery.

'I hate that I'm the one hurting you,' he murmured, his haunted expression an exact reflection of how I felt inside.

Lifting a hand, he held it out to me, obviously hoping that I would accept it. Instead, I shook my head rapidly, not sure how we should, or could, progress from here. Unfortunately I could only see one possible solution. 'I need to think really hard about all of this. Dating you … someone famous … I told you at the start that I thought it was a crazy idea.' I knew my words weren't the ones he wanted to hear, but they were the best I could offer without giving up my own needs and sanity too.

'Fuck!' Sean threw both of his hands up into his hair, gripping it as if he desperately needed something to hold on to. 'I hate that my lifestyle is making you feel like this, Allie, but please don't run from me. You promised you wouldn't, but you keep running.'

My shoulders slumped at the truth in his words. I did keep running, but I think I'd had some pretty valid reasons: finding out my boyfriend was engaged to his co-star, then being told they still fucked, and now, witnessing how determined she was to win, not to mention how much chemistry they had, and how perfect they looked together. I felt well and truly like a dowdy spare part.

I was shredded. This was just all too much. I'd had emotional spats with past boyfriends, but nothing could have prepared me for how much this hurt. 'It's just too painful. I … I don't think I can do it any more,' I whispered finally.

There was a second of stunned silence, and it hung between us like a thick, clogging fog. 'What are you saying? Are you … are you breaking up with me?' he asked, his voice a barely audible whisper.

When he said it like that, it sounded so horrifically permanent and I started to feel panic rise in my veins.

Was I breaking it off with him?

Resolutely holding my composure, just, I rolled my lips between my teeth and considered the alternative – a relationship with Sean *and* Savannah, his so-called fiancée and a woman who had it in for me big time. It wouldn't stop. She wouldn't stop.

'I …' I couldn't vocalise it, no matter how hard I tried the words wouldn't quite come. 'Maybe. For now. I just need some space to think.'

There was complete silence as Sean stared at me open-mouthed, and then nodded, looking completely defeated. 'Maybe this is for the best. I just keep hurting you, and I hate that.'

My heart just about exploded in my chest and I sucked in a wheezy breath as Sean's eyes flickered shut and clenched. 'I fuck everything up,' he murmured, his shoulders sinking. It was highly possible that he was tempted to kill Savannah for ruining things. It would certainly clear the way if Savannah was out of the picture. But she wasn't, and seeing as he worked with her, she never would be completely gone, would she?

'I knew this would happen. I can never manage to take care of the people I care for most. I'm such a fuck-up.' He choked on the words, his voice hitched and breathless as if he was on the verge of tears, and judging from his glassy eyes, he was.

My heart clenched. He wasn't fucked-up, he just had a strange, possessive perspective on things. One of them being me. And as for not being able to take care of me? He could do it perfectly when we were together just the two of us, it was just out here in the big wide world where our weaknesses had been exposed.

We'd had such an amazing time together in the UK, but here, these past few weeks? Yeah, there had been some highs, but there had been some tough, tough times too. Hollywood put a whole different slant on our relationship, and I wasn't sure I was strong enough to survive it.

Suddenly, Sean became agitated and started to fidget, chewing on his lip and scrubbing at his scalp with his fingertips. 'Fuck! What the hell am I saying? I can't lose you, Allie. I can't. There's got to be another way.' Pacing three strides, he spun back to face me. 'When I asked if you were breaking up with me you said "Maybe, for now." So how about we just have a break until the season premiere? Until this shit with Savannah is sorted?'

A break.

I didn't want to lose him, but I didn't want to lose myself either. Perhaps a break could work? But even without Savannah on the scene there would always be women ogling him, thinking that because he put himself in the public eye that they had some claim to him. From today's little display it was clear that jealousy and me were not a good mix. I could still feel its lingering remnants swirling bitterly in my stomach.

What it all came down to was simple – could I really deal with this? Was I just too normal to cope with dating a TV star? Or too possessive and protective? Could I handle the horrendous jealousy attached to being involved with someone like Sean?

'Please, Allie. What we have is too special to give up on. You see me out there acting for all and sundry to watch, but you have to believe me when I say that I am unconditionally one-hundred per cent yours,' after this statement he paused, blushing, and gave a self-conscious shrug.

I had to admit that even I was a little blown away by his last remark.

One-hundred per cent was a lot. It was everything.

Blimey. Gazing up at Sean's hopeful face, I felt rather

shell-shocked, but Sean remained silent, allowing me to form my own conclusions. Unfortunately, decisions weren't presenting themselves readily to me and as a result my mind was reeling. The best response I could give was a tight-lipped stare and a hopeless shrug.

'I totally understand why you need space until I go to the press, I do. It would kill me too. If things were reversed I'd need to distance myself from it as well. But what do you say? Can we call it a temporary break, and not an actual break-up?'

'Honestly?' I questioned weakly. 'I don't know.'

My mind was clearing marginally now and as I looked at Sean's crestfallen face, I knew that I needed space and time to process everything. 'I need some time. I promise I'll call when I've had some space to think.'

Any further words I may have said were stopped as Finlay James appeared from the studio door with a face like thunder. Apparently he wasn't used to being ignored and wasn't going to stand for it one second longer.

'Please don't call me, Sean … I'll be in touch when I'm ready,' I whispered weakly, feeling like a complete cow, but knowing that if he called me later when I was alone and sad and vulnerable that I would probably crumble.

'*Sean* …' Finlay's voice was menacingly low and didn't need any more words to make his point clear – he was mad, and not prepared to wait a millisecond longer.

Sean hesitated, looking desperately at me before cursing loudly and throwing his hands into the air in defeat. 'Fine, OK … no pressure. I won't call,' he murmured, but even though he was agreeing to my request, all I could do was look at him despairingly before turning on my heel and walking away.

Hot tears began to stream down my cheeks almost as

soon as I turned away from him, but I was stopped from sobbing by the sound of an almighty crash behind me, and a loud wail.

Spinning in panic, I looked back to see Sean flailing his arms in apparent distress, one hand smashing into a wooden studio sign in the process before he collapsed to his knees and thrust his hands into his hair.

The misery pouring from him was palpable, and incredibly shocking, and I stood frozen to the spot as he suddenly ceased his howling and turned his eyes towards me. From the way he had just been acting I had maybe expected to see anger on his face, but as soon as he registered that I had stopped in my tracks, his face softened, crumpled, into a look of complete defeat and distress that was enough to choke me up.

Blinking twice, he then nodded at me with sad acceptance, got wearily to his feet and turned away, shaking out his bleeding hand and stalking towards Finlay.

Oh God. What had we done? And more importantly, what the hell was I going to do?

Chapter Thirty-Two

Sean

Stalking back inside the studio, I stopped by the side of the stage to catch my breath. As I sucked in several deep gulps I belatedly realised that the entire room had fallen silent. I saw every pair of eyes focused on me, mostly looking wide and alarmed, and casting curious glances at my hand.

Dropping my gaze I realised why I was drawing so many looks – my right hand had a large crimson gouge in it from where I had accidentally hit the sign and it was dripping blood all over the floor. Belatedly, I began to feel the throbbing of pain in it and winced before tentatively giving my sore fingers a wiggle. Fuck. From the deep ache I guessed I'd broken at least one bone if not more.

Glancing to my right, I caught a glimpse of my reflection in a mirror and grimaced. As well as the bloodied hand I looked a complete state. My face was ashen, my hair a dishevelled mess, and my clothes splattered with dark blobs of my own blood.

Allie was gone.

The realisation hit me so hard that my legs gave way and I sank into a crouched position. She'd left me. Fuck. I wasn't sure I could deal with this. Especially not now, surrounded by a room full of gawking people.

'For fuck's sake.' Finlay was cursing loudly in the uptight way that only an impatient director could when he'd just seen his lead star have a breakdown on set. 'Clear out. Everyone take the rest of the day off.' His smartly-clad feet entered my downcast vision as I heard people begin to move around, but I didn't look up. I couldn't. 'What the fuck, Sean?'

I couldn't speak. All I could focus on was Allie's broken expression as she'd walked away. I'd done that to her. Fucking fuck. The one person I'd wanted to pull close and hold on to and I'd pushed her away. I was such an idiot.

A second later, Finlay's shoes were joined by another set of feet, these ones dressed in strappy red sandals and attached to thin, tanned ankles.

'Sean, *darrrrrling*, you're bleeding … can I help?' Hearing Savannah's sickly tones had me thrusting to my feet like a rocket and glaring at her.

Allie hadn't left because of me. This wasn't my fault. The pain that Allie and I felt was Savannah's doing, and that was something I was determined to deal with right away.

'Don't even fucking speak to me,' I snarled, causing her to recoil away from me. Her cheek was still reddened from Allie's slap, which I gained a small amount of pleasure from, but I was so furious with her that I could barely contain myself.

Turning to Finlay, I shook my head defiantly as my face pulled into a grimace of determination. 'This farce ends now, Finlay. Arrange a press conference so I can come clean to the public about our engagement.'

'Sean, the end of the season is just a few weeks away, let's leave it until then …' Any other words he was about to say got cut off by the manic roar that spiralled up my throat and echoed from the walls.

'No! No more lies! Arrange the press conference, and

make it soon, or I'll do it myself.'

'OK, OK … It'll take a week. I need to make sure the right people are there.' I saw a flinch of remorse on Finlay's face, which was fairly amazing seeing as he was usually so hard-nosed and closed off. Savannah reacted too, a brief look of undisguised joy crossing her face at my distress and making me want to hit her. But I didn't, I would never hit a woman. I'd have to cherish the memory of Allie slapping her instead. I did, however, know one way I could hurt her.

'And she,' I jabbed a finger in Savannah's direction, 'needs to leave the show, or I will.'

Finlay and Savannah drew in shocked gasps, Savannah being the first to regain her composure and speak. 'Sean, don't overreact …'

I didn't even give Savannah the satisfaction of looking in her direction, instead choosing to speak as if she wasn't in the room. 'I'll finish filming this season with her, but I refuse to speak to her again. I mean it. She goes, or I do. It's your choice, Finlay. Call me when the press conference is arranged. I'm taking a few days off.'

And with that I turned on my heel and stalked out of the studio, wondering how my life had ever got so crazy. Allie, she was the reason, and I loved how crazy my life was with her in it. I just hoped, with everything I had in me, that I'd be able to get her back.

Chapter Thirty-Three

Sean

Later that evening, after stewing in my own depressing thoughts for far too long, I gave in and called Jack. As a man I was not quite as keen as women are to share my feelings with gossipy chats, but if I didn't talk to someone soon I was going to explode. Or have a meltdown. And I wasn't sure which would be worse right now.

Much to my annoyance, the call went through to voicemail, so I ended it and stood in the middle of my bedroom wondering what else I could do to keep my mind active and stop me heading straight to Allie's house.

Of course I'd already been over there once tonight. It had been instinctive, some sort of magnetic autopilot that had led me to drive there on my way home from the studio. I'd intended to go to her and beg her to take me back, but in the end I somehow managed to obey her wish for time and space.

I had however taken up my old stalker habits and loitered in the car park so I could watch her through the windows for a while. Thank goodness I was registered on her guest list at the front gates or I might have ended up attempting to scale the goddamn fence in an attempt to be closer to her.

Yep, stalker Sean was well and truly back on duty. I wasn't proud of my actions, but I'd desperately needed to be near her, even if it was in the form of a twisted observer.

Secretly I'd been hoping she would look out the window, see me, and invite me in, but she hadn't. Instead, Allie had wandered aimlessly around the lounge for a while, wiping at her face every now and then as if she were still crying. Eventually she'd made herself a drink and sat on the sofa, but the drink had been forgotten and left to go cold as she simply sat there like a statue and stared at the floor.

It had given me a small flicker of hope to see her looking just as shattered as I felt. Not that I wanted her to hurt, of course, but seeing her so torn up made me believe that she felt as strongly about me as I did for her, and would eventually be willing to take me back.

I'd left shortly after that and headed back to the house to hole up in my room, which was where I was now, fidgety and clueless about what I should do next.

Without the distraction of Jack to talk to, I started to think about going back to see Allie again, but then I'd just be failing her by not abiding by her wishes. Fuck. This was torture. I ran my hands through my hair and gripped the back of my neck as I wondered what to do. It was nearly ten o'clock, so technically I could go to bed, but with my mind this active there was no way I would be able to sleep.

Besides, I didn't even have to be up early tomorrow. After I'd seen the studios' nurse to get my hand bandaged she'd told me I'd broken two knuckles and that I needed to take at least three days off to allow my wounds to begin their healing.

I suddenly desperately wished my sister was here and not in Ireland thousands of miles away. We lived on separate continents for much of the year, but we were close and she was a great listener. Evie and I had never really discussed my dating issues, but I had a sneaking suspicion she would definitely know exactly what I should do to win Allie back. Pursing my lips, I quickly calculated the time difference. It was nine forty here, which meant it would be five forty in the morning for her, and after a brief deliberation I decided that she probably would be awake.

Evie was an artist, and a good one too, her work consisting of mostly photographs and oil paintings of the stunning Irish landscapes. I also happened to know that early morning was her favourite time of day, because she said the light was at its most magical as the sun was rising.

I grabbed my phone and scrolled through my contacts until I found her number and pressed call before I could change my mind.

Evie answered on practically the first ring, her voice cheery and chipper, even with the early hour. 'Hey, big bro! It's not often I get a call from the famous one on a weekday, to what do I owe this pleasure?' I winced at the nickname. Not 'big bro', I actually quite liked that term, but 'The Famous One' was her favourite way to wind me up, and so knowing I didn't like it, she obviously used it all the time.

'Hi, E. I just wanted a chat with my favourite sister, that's all.' I felt stupid calling my baby sister for advice on women. I never did this type of thing. Mind you, that was because, until Allie, I'd never really dated.

'I'm your only sister, Sean, and you never just want a chat. What's up?' Chewing on my lip I pondered if I could just dive right in and ask her. Was it weird to go to Evie for advice on my love life? She was eleven years my junior, for goodness' sakes, it should probably be me offering her advice. Although thinking about it, Evie and Allie were about the same age, so perhaps she was exactly the person I should be talking to.

'I, uh, I was hoping for some advice.' Clearing my throat several times I finally spat out my final words. 'About a girl.'

'A girl? Oooh, this sounds juicy. Hang on, let me just wash my hands and then I can give you my full attention. Mum mentioned you had a girlfriend, but I thought she was winding me up. I mean, you *never* have a girlfriend.' My sister gave a snort of laughter.

My cheeks felt like they were flaming from embarrassment, but I definitely felt better talking to Evie than just sitting in my room on my own. 'Yeah, yeah. Are you painting?'

'Yep. As always.' I could hear running water in the background and then the rustle of a towel before Evie spoke again. 'OK, I'm all ears. So come on, tell me all about it. Who's this girl? Please tell me it's not that dog of a woman you work with?' Despite my low spirits I couldn't help the smile that slipped to my lips at my sister's eager enthusiasm to insult Savannah.

My parents had supported the fake engagement idea when I'd told them, both agreeing that the extra money was too much to turn down, especially seeing as I was single and had been for practically forever. But my sister had hated the idea, because quite simply, she hated Savannah. They'd met a few times over the years during Evie's visits, and the dislike had been instantaneous. Evie's gentle, almost hippy-like disposition had clashed with Savannah's greed and extroverted ways.

I had a feeling she'd like Allie if they ever got the chance to meet. That thought had me swallowing down a huge lump that formed in my throat.

'God no, of course not. She's called Allie, and I've been

seeing her since Christmas.'

There was a splutter down the line. 'And I'm only hearing about her now?'

'Yeah, sorry, but with my filming schedule we haven't spent that much time together so things are still pretty new.'

'Hmm. OK, I'll let you off. But still, my bachelor brother is actually dating a woman? A real flesh and blood woman? This is huge news!'

My heart sank as I realised I needed to correct her. 'Well, technically we kind of broke up, but I want her back.' I wanted her back so badly that it hurt. Swallowing hard, I tried to clear that stupid lump of emotion that had formed in my throat, making my voice all reedy and thin. 'That's what I need your advice on.'

'Wow … OK. I'll do my best, but maybe you should fill me in on some background first.'

So I did. I told Evie everything about my time with Allie, right from our days being snowbound in England, through to the disaster of her arrival in LA when she'd learnt about the fake engagement, to a recount of today's debacle, with Savannah trying to make some sort of deranged play for me.

'Jesus, that woman is a bitch!' Evie exclaimed heatedly. 'I can't believe Allie slapped Savannah though, I would have paid to see that! I think I love your girlfriend already.'

Evie's laughter was cut short when I let out a heavy sigh, because at the moment Allie wasn't my girlfriend, was she? We were on a break.

'Sorry, I got side-tracked,' Evie murmured, but I could still imagine the glee she felt about Savannah finally getting her comeuppance.

'So let me see if I've got this right. As it stands now, you and Allie are on a break, you've demanded that

Savannah be removed from *LA Blue*, and there's going to be a press conference soon to announce that you aren't engaged to her?'

'Yep.'

'But you want Allie back, right?'

'More than anything.' There was a sniff down the line, probably my sister getting a little emotional, and then she cleared her throat and got back to business.

'Well, so far I think you've done all the right things. It would have been better to have the press conference a while ago when you knew you were serious about Allie, but hey, we live and learn.' Shaking my head at my sister's never-ending positivity, I lowered myself to the edge of the bed.

'And do you think Allie loves you?' Evie asked softly, her tone more carefully controlled this time.

'Yes. She says she does, anyway. I think it's just all this shit with Savannah that has her freaked.'

'Hmm,' I could almost see my sister nodding down the phone as she thought it through. 'I think you should give her a few days' space, like she asked for, and use that time to stay the heck away from Savannah. Hopefully by then the press conference will be organised and you can clear up the rumours about the engagement, which will allow you to date Allie properly. Being with you officially should make things more concrete for her.'

Pulling in a breath through my nose, I nodded, hoping with every fibre of my being that Allie would give me that chance.

'Dating a celeb would be hard enough in the first place, but hiding your relationship must have been really tough for Allie. I think once you two can be a real couple, it'll be easier for her. From what you've told me it sounds like she's really into you, so I'm sure she'll give you a second chance.'

Since Allie and I had sort of spilt up when she'd first heard about the fake engagement, this would technically by my third chance, but I didn't bother to point that out to Evie.

'OK. Thanks, E.'

'No problemo. Once you get your arse in gear and sort things out with this girl, I want to come for a visit and meet her. Any woman who has slapped Savannah Hilton will be a lifelong friend of mine.' I gave a dry snort of laughter and nodded.

'You're welcome here anytime, you know that. I'd love to see you. I tell you what, I'll transfer some money to you and you can book flights for a convenient time.'

'The famous one is paying for my flights too?' she teased, knowing that I always happily paid for her to fly out and see me. 'Awesome! In that case, I'm definitely coming out to visit. Once I finish this commission I'll have a bit of spare time so I'll arrange someone to look after the cats and text you the dates I've picked.'

'One last thing,' Evie said, her tone suddenly more serious. 'Where are you staying?'

Looking around the room miserably I sighed heavily. 'I'm at the house the studios put me in. Why?'

'You're seriously still in the house you share with Savannah? Jeez, Sean, get your bags packed and get the hell out of there! How do you think that will look to Allie if she decides to check up on you?'

Shit. I hadn't even thought of that. Fuck. Fuck. *Fuck.* Immediately I stood up and began pacing back and forth across the room as I briefly catalogued everything I'd need to take with me.

'You're right, E, I need to get outta here.' Thank god I

had my apartment to fall back on. It would be a bloody relief to get out of this stifling house and finally move into the beachfront place. In fact, as I thought about it now, I couldn't believe I hadn't put my foot down earlier and moved there weeks ago.

When the hell had I become such a pushover?

Nodding my head, I gingerly swapped the phone to my busted hand and used my good hand to yank open the door to my walk-in wardrobe where I kept my suitcase and the holdall for my gym gear. As soon as I ended this call I was going to pack up and move, which was a plan that had dual positives: firstly it would get me away from Savannah, but also, it would give me something to occupy my time and stop me running to Allie.

'Evie, as always you've been amazing, thank you so much.'

'No worries. I'm just glad you felt you could call me. I'm here anytime you wanna chat. I know we're far apart, but you know I love you, right?'

Pausing in my scrambled start to my packing, I closed my eyes for a second as I felt my chest swell with affection. 'Yeah, course I do. I love you too, E.'

'Cool. Well, enough of that sentimental crap, go pack your things and get the hell outta Dodge. Call me in the next few days with an update, yeah?'

'Will do.' Hopefully I'd have some good news by then and I could call my sister on Skype with Allie firmly tucked by my side. Please let that be the case. If Allie did take me back, then it was about time they met, even if it was only over a video call.

Finishing the call, I began to pack my stuff. The task was slowed by my dodgy hand, but I continued regardless, opening drawers left, right, and centre and shoving the contents into my cases without even bothering to fold them. I could kill some time in the new place hanging them up, but right now I was set on leaving and wanted to get out as speedily as I could.

Looping the empty holdall over my shoulder I picked up my case and left my room to head downstairs. Dumping it by the front door I drew in a relieved breath that there was no sign of Savannah, and took the empty bag and descended the second set of steps that led to the gym so I could grab the things that belonged to me.

Unfortunately, as I rounded the corner I practically ran headfirst into the woman herself. Fuck. I'd been hoping not to see her. Mind you, it didn't matter if she was here or not; I wasn't planning on communicating with her in any way, shape, or form.

'Sean! Thank goodness! I was wondering where you were.' Her voice was syrupy sweet and so flirtatious that I wanted to gag. I didn't, instead choosing to blatantly ignore her. 'Are you heading to the gym? I'll join you.'

I sidestepped across the corridor and continued on my way, irritated when Savannah and her cloyingly musky perfume followed me.

'Look, Sean, about today … I know it was probably a bit of a shock, but it's for the best.' Even though I was snubbing every word that came from her puffy Botoxed mouth, Savannah just didn't seem able to stop herself. 'I mean, she was just so, so normal. You'd be far better off with someone like me, wouldn't you?'

Ignore. Ignore, *Ignore*. I could hear her, but by focusing on images of Allie in my mind I found it surprisingly easy to block Savannah out so all I heard was a mildly irritating squeak. It was like a fly trapped in a bottle. Whine, whine, whine. I should have trained myself to block her like this years ago.

I tugged my iPod deck from the wall and wrapped the wire up before tucking it in the end pocket of my holdall and scanning the room for my other items.

'Sean?' Even I noticed when Savannah's voice lost its sultry edge and took on a high, wobbly, panicked sound. Good, she fucking deserved it.

Making my way to the kit area, I grabbed my sparring gloves, the heavy gloves I used on the punch bag, the focus mitts, stopwatch, and my skipping rope, stowing them all in the holdall and lifting it to my shoulder. The dumbbells and weights bar were mine too, but with my busted hand and Savannah hanging around me like a pesky fly I decided to get them on a different day.

Turning towards the door, I strode back along the corridor and up the stairs two at a time, aware of Savannah practically tripping over her feet in an effort to keep up with me.

'Sean? Stop it now, you're being silly.'

Dragging the front door open, I lugged my case outside, shaking off Savannah with a low snarl when she attempted to grab my arm and stop me.

'Where are you going? Sean? *Sean?*' Savannah was so high-pitched that I actually winced as she continued to wail as I threw my cases in the back of the Jeep and jumped into the driver's seat.

'All right, all right, I'm sorry, OK? I'm sorry. I went too far and it was stupid. Don't leave like this, Sean. I'm sorry!'

Well, what do you know? Savannah did know the meaning of sorry. I thought that was genuinely the first time I'd ever heard her say it in a tone that was even vaguely sincere. It was too late, by a very long shot, but interesting nonetheless.

Flicking the key in the ignition, my trusty Jeep started immediately, so with a rev of the engine I roared off down the driveway leaving a trail of bouncing gravel in my wake and Savannah's figure throwing her arms into the air in frustration. That sight filled me with twisted contentment and bought a smile to my face for the first time in several hours.

So, that was it. I'd left the house and I'd left Savannah, and was now headed to the peace of my beachside house. After the craziness of today that sounded like utter heaven. Plus, I'd really upset and pissed off Savannah, which was always an added bonus.

Yeah, all things considered, that had gone pretty damn well, even if the rest of my life seemed to be sliding down the shitter.

Chapter Thirty-Four

Cait

The excitement of the new house still hadn't worn off, and when I woke up and realised it was Saturday, which as well as being my day off was my planned shopping day with Allie, I practically bounced out of bed with excitement. We weren't planning on buying anything particularly extravagant, just bits and pieces for the house, but seeing as I hadn't actually put down roots anywhere for nearly four years, this was a pretty big deal, and I was really giddy about it.

Skipping down the stairs, I found Allie already on the sofa and grinned across at her. 'Morning!' To my surprise, Allie didn't reply or even move. Huh. It seemed like she hadn't even heard me.

I leant over so I was in her field of vision, but she looked totally spaced out. It was still early, so maybe she was just tired. Waving a hand in front her face, I tried again. 'Allie? Babe? You in there?' Finally I got a reaction as Allie blinked twice and her blue eyes dilated and focused on me. Her eyes that I noticed were puffy and red-rimmed. Had she been crying?

'Oh, hi, Cait. Sorry, I was miles away.' A million miles away from the look of it. Allie had been distant for a few days now, but every time I'd questioned her on it she'd just blamed it on being in 'writing mode'. I knew from experience that when Allie was deep in her writing she often withdrew a bit, so while I'd accepted her excuse up to now, her red-rimmed eyes were definitely causing me concern.

'Hey, are you OK?' I perched on the arm of the sofa, worry pushing away my previously happy feelings as it settled in my stomach like a lead weight. What on earth was wrong with her?

Blinking again, Allie suddenly jerked forwards as if she'd finally become alert again, almost spilling the drink in her hands in the process. 'What? Oh, yeah, I'm fine.' Taking the cup from her before she spilt it, I frowned when I found it was stone cold. How long had she been sitting here?

'Are you sure? It looks like you've been crying,' I asked softly.

Allie raised a hand to rub distractedly at her eyes, but seemed to shake herself slightly and gave me a small smile. 'That must be from the chlorine, I had a swim when I woke up earlier.'

Giving my bestie a narrow-eyed look, I tried to work out if she was telling the truth or not. I had a pretty good built-in lie detector – not as good as Allie's bullshit meter, but not bad – and right now there was a warning klaxon blaring inside my head. But why would she say she was fine if she wasn't?

'You still up for shopping later?' I asked cautiously, but Allie seemed more alert now and nodded.

'Yeah, it'll be good fun. I'm going to go for a run first, though.'

'Running as well as swimming?' I asked. I was a bit of a fitness freak, but even to me that seemed a bit excessive for a weekend.

'Yeah, I didn't swim much. I won't be too long, I promise.' And with that, Allie jumped up and headed off to change, leaving me wondering what could be the cause of her slightly odd mood.

About an hour later I was showered, dressed, and midway through sorting out my washing pile when there was a loud knocking from the other room. Allie had disappeared out for her run and hadn't returned, so chucking down the clothes I had been folding I wandered from my room.

Who could be here knocking? Unless Allie had forgotten her key. No one else knew we lived here. Except Jack. Jack knew where we lived ... Oh God, what if it was him again? I still hadn't decided how to progress with him yet.

But when I checked the peep-hole, it wasn't Allie, or even Jack, but Sean, pacing back and forth across the porch. He was disguised, sort of, in a baseball cap and shades, and his hand bore some padded plasters, but even with the distorted glass of the peep-hole there was no mistaking his profile.

As I stepped out to join him on the porch, Sean seemed to register my appearance, stopped his pacing, removing his glasses, and giving me a brief nod accompanied by a mightily penetrating look.

I'd never been quite this close to Sean before, and those were certainly some big blues he was rocking. I swallowed hard and blinked back. No wonder Allie always went on about how his 'intense looks' made her melt. Except I wasn't melting, I was practically quaking in my flip-flops.

'Cait, hi. Is Allie here?'

Allie was right about him getting into your personal space too, because Sean was leaning right over me to the point that I had to crane my neck up to meet his gaze. How unnerving. Taking a small step back, I tried to loosen off my suddenly tense muscles and instead smiled at how bizarre my life now was – meetings with celebrities were run of the mill occurrences for me nowadays.

Remembering his question, I shook my head, about to inform him that she was out running, when I noticed how dreadful Sean looked. He was pale, a little dishevelled-looking – although that could have been part of his disguise, I supposed – with a thick chin of stubble and some seriously dark bags under his eyes.

'She's out running.' His appearance and the way his eyes were darting around put me on edge and I instinctively found myself reaching for my phone, assuming that something was wrong. 'Hang on, she always takes her phone with her, let me call her.'

Sean threw his hands up, pushing his baseball cap backwards as he clutched his fingers in his hair. 'Fuck! No, don't call her!' Spinning on the spot, he stared at the parking lot for a second before looking back at me with almost wild eyes. 'I shouldn't be here. I'll go.'

What the heck? I raised my eyebrows. He looked so dazed that I didn't think it would be a good idea to let him go.

'Wanna come in?' Tipping my head in the direction of the lounge in way of invitation, I was quite surprised when Sean nodded and stepped inside with very minimal resistance.

Closing the door, I stepped away to keep a good distance between us as I observed him with concern. I didn't know Sean well, but it was obvious he was in turmoil over something, and after staying silent for several seconds he seemed to wince as he looked back at me. 'I'm … I … I'm not supposed to contact her,' he admitted through gritted teeth as he raised a hand and rubbed viciously at the back of his neck.

Not supposed to contact her? What was he talking about? As far as I knew things were going fine between the two of them. Sean's fake engagement to Savannah was an issue, but they had been meeting in secret and it had all seemed to be going OK.

'What do you mean?'

At my confused tone, Sean looked up, his eyes wide with shock as his mouth dropped open. 'She hasn't told you?' he asked in surprise, his eyes widening. Told me what? Suddenly expelling a frustrated noise quite similar to a growl, Sean shook his head dejectedly and spun on the spot before collapsing onto one of the armchairs.

I, however, was frozen to the spot by his peculiar behaviour. I felt like I'd fallen into some weird parallel universe. What the heck was going on?

'I'm even fucking this up.' Tipping his head back, he stared at the ceiling, 'I'm fucking everything up,' he muttered. Dropping his head back down, Sean met my gaze and I saw his eyes were glassy as if he were on the verge of tears.

Blimey. Seeing such a big guy have such an emotional collapse was really frigging unnerving. 'Allie split up with me. Well, we're on a break, but I don't know if she'll take me back.' My eyes boggled at his words, but before I could ask the questions swirling in my mind – most predominantly, *when the hell did this happen*, and *why in the name of all things holy would she do that* – he continued. 'Told me she needed space.'

She hadn't said a thing about this to me, but the news certainly made sense of her strange mood. I thought all their issues about the fake engagement were behind them, so this made no sense whatsoever and my poor brain was whirling as it tried to keep up.

'Why did she split up with you?' I asked in astonishment, almost unable to believe that this was happening. Allie was crazy about Sean, like loop-the-loop, head-over-heels-in-love kind of crazy. And let's face it, he was undeniably gorgeous and lovely, so all in all a pretty good catch – what could have prompted this?

Shaking his head, Sean blew out a long breath and lowered his elbows onto his knees so he was leaning forward, his eyes now diverted away from mine.

'Savannah.' He practically spat the name from his mouth, his lips twisting with disgust. 'She invited Allie to the studio to watch us filming last Wednesday.' I nodded, recalling the morning Allie had got her call and headed off, excited about watching Sean in action.

Sean ran his bandaged hand over his face before continuing, 'I had no idea Savannah had called her, I didn't even know Allie was there until after the shoot was finished.' Ruffling his hair he chewed his lower lip before sighing heavily and continuing.

'Anyway, it was a day where Savannah and I had to film a kissing scene. Savannah went over the top, hands all over me, trying to force the kiss to be more than a stage kiss, all for the benefit of Allie, who was watching in the wings.'

Oh shit. Wincing, I tried to imagine how that would have felt. It must have been horrific. I couldn't believe she hadn't told me. Mind you, it made sense of her quieter behaviour these last few days, not to mention how zoned out she'd seemed this morning.

'That must have been pretty horrible, but why would that make her break up with you?'

Closing his eyes, Sean seemed to be reliving their last conversation, his eyelids fluttering as his mouth twisted into a grimace. 'She said she couldn't deal with the jealousy. That dating someone famous was harder than she'd thought it would be.' Running a hand up and down his leg in agitation, Sean finally made eye contact with me again. 'Worse than that though, she … she said I'd betrayed her by kissing Savannah and not telling her.' Sean rolled his neck with an audible click and then grimaced. 'She's right, but I never meant to. I just didn't even think she'd see it that way.

'Then she asked me to stay away while she had some time to think.' Letting out a humourless laugh, Sean shook his head. 'And here I am, messing up already because you'll tell her I was here and she'll be even more pissed off with me.'

I was silent for several seconds as I tried to absorb all that he'd said. This was insane. He was clearly crazy about her and she was running away? A small niggle at the back of my mind whispered that that was exactly what I was doing with Jack, running, running, running, as fast as my little legs could carry me, but I pushed it aside – it was a totally different situation.

Focusing back on Sean's slumped shoulders, I pursed my lips and decided to help him. 'Will it help if I conveniently forget your visit?' I asked softly.

Sean's head snapped up, his eyes laser sharp and focused. 'You'd do that?'

I shrugged and leant against the wall. 'I'm kind of rooting for the two of you,' I explained with a fond smile. 'I've never seen Allie like this about a man before, there's obviously something special between you.'

Shooting up from his chair, Sean was suddenly right in

front of me again. 'There is, Cait,' he nodded vigorously. 'I love her so much. Fuck. I've never felt anything like it. I don't think I could function if she left me.' Crikey, talk about emotional. I really felt for the guy; he looked like someone had ripped out his heart, stamped on it, and chucked it in a food processor.

'I'm going to sort out the issues with Savannah. I've forced the director to contact the show's PR team and asked them to arrange a press conference so I can clear up the lies once and for all. I'll prove to Allie that I'm serious about her, and only her.'

I nodded. I couldn't say anything else because Sean's open, raw honesty was making me quite emotional and I didn't trust myself to speak just yet.

How would it feel to be that crazy in love with someone? If I kept up my protective walls I'd never get the chance to find out. Swallowing hard, I frowned. It was a thought that didn't sit very well in my stomach.

'How is she?' he asked, his head tilting, lip back between his teeth as he chewed on it anxiously.

'Pretty miserable,' I said, annoyed with myself for not realising that there was more to Allie's glumness over the last few days.

Turning away from me, Sean looked around the lounge before striding over to the dining table and ripping off the corner of a notepad. Grabbing a pen, he scrawled on the paper and strode back over to me. 'This is my number. Will you call me if Allie needs me? Or maybe just text me each day to let me know she's OK?'

Holding up my hands, I shook my head. 'Uh-uh. I'm willing to keep quiet about today's visit, but don't ask me to spy on my best friend for you. That's too much.'

His hand dropped dejectedly to his side, before he

screwed up the paper and threw it on the floor. 'You're right, I'm sorry. I'm such a mess. I hate being the cause of her sadness, and not knowing if she's all right is killing me. We'd been apart for so long and now she's finally in LA and this happens. I just don't know how to handle it.'

Seeing how tortured Sean was, I relented marginally and bent to retrieve the scrunched-up ball of paper. 'I tell you what. I'll save this in my phone, just in case of an emergency,' I said, retrieving my phone and adding his number. I saved it as 'Phillip' just in case Allie happened to see it. 'But don't expect daily updates, Sean.'

'No, that's OK. Thank you, Cait. Thank you.' He did look less stressed, so perhaps I had helped. Now all I needed to do was discreetly persuade my stubborn best friend just how much this man clearly loved and needed her.

Chapter Thirty-Five

Allie

When I got back from my run, Cait was nowhere to be seen, which was probably just as well because if she'd seen the state of me – bright red, staggering, and utterly exhausted – she'd definitely start to question why I'd been running so much over the past few days.

And running I had been. I'd literally jogged until my legs failed me and I'd felt sick, just in an attempt to take my mind off Sean. It had worked to some extent, because I'd fallen into shattered, dreamless sleeps the last three nights without fail, but there was only so long I could keep this up without doing myself an injury.

Dragging myself to the sink, I clung to the counter and hung my head as I tried to recover my breathing. Jeez, I must have covered fifteen miles today. I loved my runs, but that was a distance record even for me. I'd only turned for home because the charge in my iPod had died, and instead of the distracting beats of The Foo Fighters filling my head, thoughts of Sean had begun to swamp my mind. Again.

Filling a glass with water, I took a greedy swig, which I almost immediately brought back up again. *Ugh.* I had definitely overdone it today. Opening one of the drawers, I pulled out a straw and took a more cautious sip, which thankfully stayed down, and turned to make my way back to my bedroom.

Unfortunately, I found the previously empty room now contained Cait, who was standing with a towel wrapped around her head and an odd look on her face.

'Hey. Been for a swim?' I asked, hoping that she hadn't just witnessed my staggering and near vomiting episode.

'No, just a shower. How are you feeling?'

How was I feeling? Desolate, desperate, and depressed. Swallowing some more water, I tried to give a casual shrug that didn't give away my wretched state. 'I'm fine. Why?'

Cait moved closer and leant back on the counter, appearing casual, until she opened her mouth and spoke again. 'You're not fine. You're a mess. I saw you staggering, and we've been friends long enough for me to know that you only run yourself into the ground when something bad has happened.'

'I ran a bit too far, that's all.' My lies weren't even convincing me, so goodness only knows what Cait was making of all this.

'Does all this running have anything to do with Sean? Because he just stopped by and we had a very enlightening chat. I promised I wouldn't tell you, but seeing as you look just as awful as he did, I can't keep it a secret.'

Sean just stopped by? At those four small, seemingly insignificant words my legs buckled and the glass in my hand almost slipped through my fingers. Oh god. I'd been hoping I could have had a quick chat and made a break for my room, but no, no, no. My secret had been discovered.

'You split up with him on Wednesday?' she asked softly, taking the glass from my trembling fingers before I dropped the bloody thing. 'Why didn't you tell me?' As much as I loved Cait – and I really did, she was completely and utterly the greatest friend a girl could ever ask for – I had been avoiding her since my split from Sean, because, quite simply, I didn't know how to even begin talking about it.

Giving a small shrug, I lifted a hand and chewed on a fingernail until Cait gently tugged my hand away and held it between the warmth of her two palms.

'I don't know ...' A huge sigh, heavy with emotion, slipped from my lips. '... I suppose I thought that talking about it would make it all more real.'

'Oh Allie, hun.' There was a catch in Cait's voice as she pulled me into a tight hug. 'You wanna talk about it now?'

Did I? It was hard enough to even think about the fact that Sean and I were on a break, let alone vocalise those feelings. Deciding that actually, talking it through might help me decide what to do next, I pulled back from her and gave a hesitant nod. 'OK, but I'm all sweaty from my run, so let me take a quick shower first.'

When I reappeared in the lounge fifteen minutes later, Cait was waiting on the sofa, the table laden with goodies: my glass of water, a bowl of fruit salad, a box of tissues, and a full coffee pot, milk, and two mugs.

Apparently we were settling in for the duration.

I accepted a small bowl of the fruit salad, even though I had no appetite whatsoever, and looked at Cait. 'You said Sean was here, but you didn't tell me what he said.'

Levelling me with a sober gaze, Cait shook her head. 'No, I didn't. I wasn't sure you were ready for that.'

'I probably wasn't,' I admitted, 'but the shower has cleared my head a bit. How was he?'

'Honestly?'

I nodded and she grimaced. 'He was distraught.'

Distraught? God. Now I felt guilty as hell in addition to wretched.

'He was all scruffy and unshaven. To be honest, he

looked like shit. From the bags under his eyes I'd say he's not slept since Wednesday.'

Wincing, I held up a hand to stop her. There was only so much honesty I could take.

'Sorry. But there is light at the end of the tunnel. Sean said he'd demanded that the press conference be arranged so that he can clear things up with the public.'

My eyebrows rose and I found my heartbeat accelerating at that news. 'OK … that sounds promising,' I agreed with a nod.

'So what are you going to do?' Cait asked, her face tight with worry.

Shrugging, I pushed a piece of pineapple around the bowl with absolutely no intention of eating it.

'I guess I'll just have to wait and see if he comes through on his promise to sort things out. There's not much else I can do, is there? I won't date him if he's pretending to be with her every day. It would kill me.'

And that was the depressing but accurate summary of my situation. I was in love with a man I couldn't be with without losing a part of myself.

Chapter Thirty-Six

Allie

I'd now had a full week to stew on my problems with Sean, and as much as I wanted to just ignore the Savannah issues and say that everything between us was rosy, it wasn't and I couldn't. If I stayed with him and had to see that scheming bitch pawing all over him every day then I just knew it would eventually sour my feelings for him, and drive an irreparable wedge between us.

All hope wasn't lost though; I was determined to try for a future with Sean, and after many near sleepless nights I had finally decided to go with his idea of us being on a temporary 'break'. I had my own stipulations to add to it, though.

My idea was relatively simple – until Sean had arranged the press conference and set the world straight about Savannah, we would basically be separated as he had suggested, but I *would* stay in LA, so that as soon as he was completely free to date me properly, we could try again. If he still wanted to.

My main condition was a tricky one though, during our break I would insist on no contact between us. At all. No calls, meetings, or even our nightly text messages. Nada. It seemed fairly drastic, but I just couldn't deal with seeing him with her, or even knowing that he'd spent the day working with Savannah.

Now I just needed to see what he thought of the idea, but the idea of calling him and hearing his sexy as sin voice after seven days of abstinence was causing me to bite nervously on my lip and stare at the phone in my hand.

As if sensing my stare, the phone suddenly chirped to indicate a text, and nearly made me jump out of my skin with shock. Pulling in a breath, I gathered my wits, and then frowned as I saw the last name I had expected, or wanted to see – Savannah Hilton. Or more accurately, 'Fish Lips' as she was now saved in my phone.

The idea of immediately deleting it crossed my mind, but curiosity got the better of me and I opened the text.

From: Fish Lips
I'm sure I am the last person you want to hear from, but I need to know if you've seen Sean? He disappeared after your break-up to go to his beach house and no one has seen him since. He's not turned up to work and he's not answering his phone. The director is going mental. Please let me know if he's with you. Savannah

I was momentarily surprised by her use of the word 'please'. Never in a million years had I expected her to be quite so polite, but my frown significantly deepened as I re-read it. Sean was missing? And had been for a week? Thinking about how upset he'd looked when I'd walked away, I felt my throat tighten and my stomach do some strange flip that made me feel instantly sick. Instinctively bringing up his number, I pressed call without hesitation.

The phone rang, which I took as a good sign. He might not be answering Savannah or his director, but surely he would answer me. But after it rang and rang, never going to voicemail and never cutting off, I had to re-think my earlier thoughts.

Hmm. Well, if he wasn't going to answer my calls then I could at least go to him and check he was all right. I dashed to my bedroom and grabbed the spare key Sean had given me to his house and then swiped up my phone and handbag before dashing to the door.

Just as I was reaching for the door handle, I heard the sound of a key in the other side and pulled it open hoping to see Sean, but it was Cait who almost tumbled in on top of me and laughed. 'Ha! Thanks, that was good timing.'

Taking one look at my face, the smile fell from her lips and she reached out to touch my arm. 'You're white as a sheet, what's up?'

Grimacing, I tried, and failed, to get a grip on my emotions. 'Sean's missing. He's not turned up to work this week and he's not answering his phone.'

'What? Really? Oh God, no wonder you look like that.'

Thinking how he had turned up at here and spoken to Cait on Saturday – two days after our break-up – I suddenly realised something. 'Actually, you might be the last person to have seen him.' Today was Wednesday, so if Cait had seen him last Saturday, then he'd technically only been missing for four days. But still, four whole days?

Where the hell was he? It was probably nothing. Sean was no doubt just holed up at his beach house sulking. Hopefully, that was the case, but as much as I tried to convince myself, I still had a decidedly edgy feeling in my gut.

'I'm heading over to his place to see if he's there.'

'Do you want me to come with you?' Cait asked, dumping down her work bag and looking completely ready to drop any plans she had just to help me out.

'Nah, it's OK. It'll be a waste of your time if he's not

there, and besides, if he is then I think it's about time I sat down and had a talk with him.'

'OK. If you're sure?'

'I am, thank you though.' Pausing, I had an idea. 'Actually, could you call Jack and see if he's heard from Sean?' Seeing Cait blanch slightly, I winced but persevered, Sean was missing, I needed to follow up all possible links. 'Sorry, I know things are delicate between you two at the moment, but he's good friends with Sean. He might have heard from him.'

'How about I give you his number and you call him?' Cait asked, looking almost as frantic as I felt.

'No time for that, I want to get to Sean's house as quickly as I can. I owe you big time. Call me if you get any news.' And with that I was gone, dashing from the house with Sean's key clutched in my fist as I hurried off to find a taxi.

Chapter Thirty-Seven

Cait

Picking up my bag, I walked to my room and sat on the end of my bed worrying about Allie and flicking at my elastic band as a consequence.

Sean *had* been really upset when I'd seen him on Saturday, but I certainly hadn't expected him to go missing or skip out on work. It was concerning, to say the least. But was it concerning enough for me to consider calling the one person I'd been avoiding since our declaration of 'friendship'?

Squinting hard, I stared at my reflection in the mirror as I tried to think what else I could do. I almost immediately drew a blank and so dragged my bag over to pull out my phone with a nervy sigh. Allie had a good point – Jack was friends with Sean, so maybe he did know where he was.

I really didn't want to initiate contact with him – mostly because I still hadn't fully decided how I was going to progress things – but if Allie needed me to, then of course I would.

Drawing in a deep breath, I pulled up Jack's number and persuaded myself that this would be fine; I could keep it short and sweet, quickly check if he'd heard from Sean, and then bid him a polite goodbye. Simple.

Yeah, right. A dry laugh left my throat.

Nothing that involved Jack Felton and me had ever been

'simple'.

Pressing call, I tried to steel my nerves so that his voice wouldn't affect me and turn my senses to jelly. Unfortunately, my preparation was completely wasted, because as soon as his deep, rich tone resonated down the line I felt my fingers start to tremble as the breath stuttered in my lungs and my stomach filled with excitable butterflies. *Damn it.*

'Hello. This is a nice surprise …'

'Uh … hi, it's me. Uh, I mean, Cait.' I was such a blathering idiot. Kill me now.

I heard a soft chuckle down the line and closed my eyes as a warm sensation spread through my body. His laugh was so lovely that it seemed to warm me from the inside out. How was that even possible? 'I know, Caitlin, my phone has caller ID. How are you?'

Of course he had caller ID. I think all mobile phones had that these days for stored numbers, didn't they? I tried to engage my brain so I wouldn't make any more ridiculous comments, cleared my throat, and got straight to the point.

'I'm fine, thanks. I'm actually calling on behalf of Allie, she's worried about Sean. Apparently he's gone missing. No one has heard from him for four days now. She wanted me to ask if you've seen him.'

'Hmm. No, I haven't. I wouldn't worry too much, Sean often goes off and plays golf if he wants to get away from it all. It's a little strange that he didn't tell Allie where he was going, but I bet he's in a resort somewhere practising his putting or something. He won't want to be away from Allie for long, though.'

It wasn't really my place to discuss their relationship issues, but it did affect the situation, so I decided I needed to let him know. 'Actually, they split up. And he's missed work all week.'

There was a pause down the line this time and then another thoughtful humming noise. 'That's a little more concerning. He takes his job very seriously. They've really split up? When?'

'Yeah. Last Wednesday. Long story involving Savannah. But I think they'll work things out, I hope so, anyway. I know how much she cares about him, and she's really worried about his disappearing act.'

'I bet,' Jack paused as if wondering what help he could be. 'Tell her to check the St Almino Golf Resort, they're an exclusive club and boutique hotel, and they're really discreet so celebrities often go there because the staff never tell the press.'

Grabbing a sheet of paper, I scribbled the name of the resort down and wandered back towards my bed, still with the phone clutched to my ear.

'I'll try calling him, but tell Allie to try not to worry. He does this type of thing sometimes when he needs to think.'

'OK. I'll tell her. Thank you, Jack.' I was preparing to hang up when I heard Jack take a deep breath down the line.

'Caitlin, wait.' Swallowing hard, I felt my tummy quiver in anticipation as the butterflies upped their fluttering.

'Yeah?'

'Can I buy you a coffee sometime?'

Closing my eyes, I tried to control how wildly my heart was suddenly beating, but it was a difficult task because it was pounding like the bass line on a dance track.

'Jack …' His name whispered across my lips as a drawn-out breath. 'I really don't think …' My hesitation must have been obvious because Jack cut off my reply mid-way though.

'If it'll make you feel better we could just meet at the studio during a break?' Hmm. That sounded more feasible, and definitely less scary than a real 'coffee date'. Perhaps sensing that I was close to giving in – which even against all my better judgement, I was – Jack persevered. 'Just a friendly coffee between two colleagues. Just friends? Please?'

'Why me?' I asked, knowing it was a stupid question but blurting it out as a delaying tactic.

'Why do I want to be friends with you?' he chuckled, but I was so torn I could barely swallow normally let alone laugh. 'Well, if I really have to give you a reason, I'd say I like you, you're interesting, and I'd like to get to know you more and find out how you're settling in.'

'Do you see me as a challenge? Because I said I don't date?' I asked curiously. 'Is that why you're pursuing me?'

A scoffed laugh sounded down the phone. 'No, of course not. You're intriguing, but a challenge? No. And I'm pursuing you because I like you, Caitlin, no other reason.'

He knew my hesitation was because I was scared of something more developing between us, but would a friendly coffee between two workmates really be such a bad thing? He'd proved himself time and time again to be a gentleman, and I'd made it perfectly clear that I wasn't in the market to date, so really, it couldn't be so terrible to spend some time with him, could it?

Allie's words about me needing to start getting some male friends swam in my mind, but seeing as I'd kissed Jack, and liked it, he didn't exactly seem to be a completely platonic choice. 'I'm not sure it's a good idea,' I whispered.

'Why?'

Put on the spot like that, I suddenly couldn't think of a reason. Because … because what, exactly? Because he was the first man I'd found attractive in four years and I barely knew where to start with my feelings? Because I was terrified of how he affected me? Because I was scared to admit that I knew next to nothing about sex? Now I'd started to think of them, the reasons just wouldn't stop coming. Closing my eyes, I scratched at the back of my neck as I struggled to find an excuse I could say that didn't make me sound completely immature. I failed, and ended up staying mute, thankful that this conversation was over the phone and not in person so he couldn't see how badly I was floundering.

'If you're hesitating because of the way I kissed you, then don't,' he added softly, and even his casual mention of our kiss made my cheeks flame. 'I promise I'll behave myself from now on. Scout's honour.' I could hear the smile in his voice, and could almost imagine him holding three fingers aloft and touching his thumb to his little finger in the Scout salute while grinning down the other end of the line.

'I brought you bacon when you most needed it, didn't I? Surely that earns me a coffee in return?' he added, the humour in his tone making me smile. I suddenly got an incredibly vivid image of his face in my mind: his dark, intense eyes, floppy, brown hair, tanned skin, and gorgeous mouth. I imagined him grinning broadly at our teasing conversation. Little creases that made my stomach flip always popped up at the corners of his eyes, and I'd place money on the fact that they were there now. Gosh. He was so handsome when he grinned. Biting on my lower lip, I shook my head in resignation. He was handsome, full stop.

I needed to say no to coffee.

Agreeing would mean setting myself up for future torture, because being mates with a man that I secretly lusted after – but was too scared to pursue – was just asking for trouble. Not to mention heartbreak.

'Please, Caitlin?'

I needed to say no.

But honestly? I didn't want to any more. I was sick of fighting my feelings, and I was sick of deflecting him because it was obvious that Jack wasn't going away anytime soon. Closing my eyes, I wondered if I might live to regret the next words from my mouth as I sighed and nodded. 'Yes. OK. Coffee.'

Bugger. I really was my own worst enemy sometimes.

Chapter Thirty-Eight

Jack

I hung up and allowed myself a second or two to absorb the almost euphoric feeling buzzing around my veins. She'd said yes. Finally. It was a coffee as friends, but it was a good start, and I was so bloody happy that I could barely get the grin off my face.

Thinking back over her call, I shook my head and my smile faded somewhat as my thoughts turned to Sean and Allie splitting up. It didn't seem possible. I knew how crazy he was about her, and on the occasions I'd met her she had seemed just as smitten. I couldn't imagine either of them dumping the other.

Frowning as I recalled Caitlin's mention of Savannah, I made a disgusted grunting sound and shook my head. If that devious bitch was involved then I could only assume she was up to her old tricks and had somehow managed to poison the relationship between Sean and Allie.

I'd never seen Sean so into a woman, so splitting up with Allie was sure to have screwed him up. I wasn't overly worried about his disappearance because I knew from experience that he often liked to head off on his own to escape the pressures of fame every now and then. I was much the same, but whereas Sean would usually veer towards a mountain retreat or golf course somewhere, I usually liked a remote spot with sun, sea, and sand.

Even though Caitlin had said he wasn't answering his phone, I decided to give it a go anyway and searched for his name before pressing call.

It rang out without going to answerphone, so I sent a message just in case he was checking them.

To: Sean Phillips
Hey. I heard about you and Allie, and I get that you need some space, but people are worried about you. Especially Allie. Let me know where you are. Give me a shout if you want to grab a beer. Jack

I didn't actually expect an answer, so when my phone chimed a few seconds later my left eyebrow arched with curiosity as I quickly opened the new message.

From: Sean Phillips
Thanks. Allie tried to call me, but I didn't answer in case she just wanted to finalise our split. I miss her so much. I needed some space from Savannah and her bullshit, so I'm in Vegas at the MGM. Probably golfing tomorrow. Tell everyone not to worry. I'll be back soon.

Vegas? Although actually, that made sense; it was just a short hop on a plane from here, and seeing as his uncle ran The Mansion – the MGM Grand Hotel's exclusive suite of rooms and villas – it was often somewhere Sean headed for a break. Privacy was guaranteed at The Mansion, not to mention sumptuous luxury and service in style. If he wasn't going through such a shitty time right now, I might be jealous.

As desperate as I was to hear Caitlin's voice again, I was worried that calling her so quickly again would be too much for her. She was definitely fragile, and seeing as she'd just agreed to a coffee with me, I didn't want to push my luck, so instead I opened up my messages and sent her a text with an update about Sean's whereabouts. Once I put my phone down, I headed off to my gym session grinning like a Cheshire cat as I thought about the date we had arranged. It was only coffee, but I could not wait.

Chapter Thirty-Nine

Allie

Arriving at the gate to Sean's complex, I jumped out of the cab and walked up to the security hut. Thank god he'd moved to this place that no one knew about yet, because there was no way I could have turned up at his old house and its resident journalists without drawing attention to myself.

Handing my passport to the guard as ID I waited while he checked me over. I was on Sean's approved list of visitors, so it didn't take long for him to look at me with a nod as he handed my passport back. Leaning out the window, he frowned. 'You walking? You want a lift up the drive?' I flushed slightly. Everyone in LA seemed to have a car, so I was definitely in the minority as a pedestrian.

'Um, yeah, I got a cab over, but I can walk. It's fine, thank you.' Granted the driveway was long, but it wouldn't kill me to get a bit of exercise.

'OK.' He raised his eyebrows as if walking a few hundred metres was a marathon, then opened the gate for me.

'Actually, before I go, have you seen Sean around this week?'

The guard shrugged and took a sip from a mug. 'Can't say I have, but I just got on shift last night. Sorry.' Another dead end then. 'Remember to stick to the central driveway when they separate,' he reminded me. Nodding my thanks, I strode through the gate and started the hike towards his house.

By the time I reached Sean's house, I was sweating lightly from the heat of the day and glad when I stepped up into the shade of his porch area. Digging out his key, I opened the door and paused on the threshold, suddenly unsure. We had technically broken up, so should I really be entering his place unannounced?

Looking back outside, I couldn't see a doorbell. Presumably these places had an intercom at the front security gate, and there was no way I was trudging all the way back down there again. Hmm. What to do? I settled for knocking loudly and then poking my head inside and calling him. 'Sean? You here?'

There was no answer, so I entered and closed out the heat, glad for once that Sean favoured air-conditioning when I was surrounded by a refreshingly cooler temperature.

'Sean?'

I tentatively made my way through the hall calling out his name every now and then, but my voice dried up when I came to the lounge. There was no sign of Sean, but the coffee table and surrounding carpet was absolutely littered with beer bottles.

Shit. Doing a quick count, I got at least thirty bottles, but my stomach plummeted when I spotted two vodka bottles under the table too. Sinking onto the couch, I picked them both up, letting out a relieved sigh when I saw that one was full and the other had barely been touched. Thank God. Sean wasn't an alcoholic, but I knew he never drank spirits. His avoidance went back to the speedboat accident with his ex when she had died and he'd blamed himself. Apparently guilt and sadness had led him to six months of binge drinking, mostly hard spirits, and of course binging on women too, but I tried not to think of that part.

He might not have drunk much of the vodka, but thirty plus bottles of beer was still a hell of a lot. Certainly enough to make me seriously concerned for him. Mind you, I had no idea how many days he had taken to amass this collection of empties. He might have drunk four a night for the past week and just not bothered to clear up. Standing up, I headed off to check the rest of the apartment.

Sean was usually pretty tidy, so seeing the state the kitchen was in – dirty pans, two pizza boxes, and a pile of unwashed dishes – not to mention the bedroom with its unmade bed and clothes strewn on the floor, made my stomach twist with guilt.

Was this because of me? Had finishing with him caused Sean to go completely off the rails?

He clearly wasn't here, and from my limited detective skills, probably hadn't been for at least a day – the food on the plates was congealed and old, and the bathroom surfaces were all completely dry, indicating that no one had showered recently.

So where was he?

Wandering back to the lounge, I sank down onto the sofa again and stared hopelessly across the sea of beer bottles. Something caught my eye and I leant forwards and peered at the small square of paper propped against one of the bottles.

My breath stalled in my lungs when I realised what it was. The photo of us that I had seen in his wallet weeks ago when we'd first come here. We looked so happy in his picture, loved-up, and flushed from arousal.

So he'd been sitting here drinking himself into oblivion and staring at a picture of us. I definitely was the cause of his drinking, then. And probably to blame for his disappearing act. Shit. I couldn't have felt any lousier if I'd tried. Closing my eyes, I leant my head into my hands and tried to hold back the tears I could feel building behind my lids.

Regardless of how badly Sean had taken our split, I still felt justified in my actions. There was no way I could be with him while he was still supposed to be with Savannah, it would kill me, and I had more self-respect than to be his secret woman. I'd thought Sean would have reacted a little more maturely than this, perhaps get on his director's case about going to the press and get things sorted so we could be together, not drink himself stupid and vanish.

Suddenly feeling totally drained, I lay my head back and closed my eyes. Drawing in several deep breaths, I tried to calm myself and plan what I could do next. As I pulled in another lungful, I got a whiff of perfume and frowned. Sniffing again, I rapidly opened my eyes.

What the heck was that smell?

I was now sniffing the air like a dog, trying to work out where the sweet, floral aroma was coming from. It was nice, but definitely not my perfume. Twisting my head, my gaze landed on something pink tossed over the end of the sofa. I had been so distracted by the bottles that I hadn't seen it at first. Shuffling along the couch I picked it up and felt my stomach drop so fast that I thought I might puke.

It was a cardigan.

More accurately, a woman's cardigan, and definitely not mine.

Lifting it to my nose, I breathed in and got a stronger whiff of the scent. *Holy shit*. Why was there a woman's cardigan at Sean's apartment?

Was it Savannah's? She was the only woman I could imagine coming here, but she had said no one had seen Sean all week. My head was spinning, but my thoughts were coherent enough to recall that her perfume had been pungent and earthy, so unless she had changed fragrances and lied to me again, she hadn't been here. Besides, even in my panicked state I had to acknowledge that this scent was far too nice and light to belong to Savannah. Someone with taste had chosen this perfume.

So from the evidence, it seemed that Sean had completely reverted back to his old ways, drinking himself silly *and* entertaining women here.

Bloody hell. My stomach cramped at the thought of him with anyone else and I had to bend forwards to try and ease the pain spreading across my mid-section.

As much as I hated the idea of him with someone else, and I really flipping hated it, I had no one to blame but myself. I was the one who had agreed we were 'on a break'. As much as I had needed the distance between us I hadn't expected him to jump into bed with the first thing he encountered with a pulse.

Looking around the lounge for any other tell-tale signs, I spotted a multi-coloured scarf tossed over a chair and a pair of heeled boots casually discarded next to it on the floor. Seeing unfamiliar but obviously feminine things in his house was a surreal and unpleasant experience. Walking over in a daze, I picked up the scarf and examined it. It was lovely, soft and high quality and just the type of thing I would buy. Sniffing it, I smelt the same perfume and felt my stomach roil.

Gagging on a sudden wave of nausea, I dropped the scarf and dashed to the kitchen sink, where I heaved several times as my world seemed to crumble. What was worse was knowing that it was all my fault.

In the background, I heard my phone ringing, but I was too busy empting the contents of my stomach into Sean's sink to be able to answer it. Once I had finished, and rinsed both my mouth and the sink, I stumbled over to my bag and pulled out my phone to see a missed call from Cait. Listening to the message I frowned as she told me that Jack had heard from Sean and that he was in Las Vegas staying at The Mansion in the MGM Grand.

He was in Vegas?

Looking around the depressing evidence again, I weighed up what I should do. There was plenty of proof to suggest that my worst fears had indeed come true – he was on a bender again like when Elena had died, and was out there drinking and fucking himself into oblivion.

But even suspecting that Sean was quite possibly off his head on booze and balls deep in a random woman, I still loved him more than I had ever loved any other man, and every molecule within me was telling me to find him and shake some sense into him.

So really, the question was, did I fly to Vegas and fight for the man I loved, or give up and run away with my tail between my legs?

Chapter Forty

Cait

The very day after I'd agreed to a coffee with Jack, he had woken me with a text asking if he could pop by during the morning break to see if I was around. Talk about keen. Deciding there was no point delaying it, denying it, or avoiding it, I had agreed, and now, at just gone ten thirty, there he was in all his glory at the outdoor café area in the studio with a grin on his face and a happy twinkle in his eye.

Man alive, he was hot.

An appreciative sigh slipped from my lips, but I was too far away for Jack to have heard me. At least I hoped I was.

'Good morning.' Jack greeted me with a nod, holding the coffee jug in his hand as I took a seat at one of the high stools in the sun.

'Good morning,' I replied with a small returning smile. After initially berating myself about agreeing to meet him, I had spent the night considering it and decided that actually, this was a good step for me. I liked him, he'd somehow made me trust him, and most importantly, I felt safe around him.

What it really came down to was one simple fact. I *wanted* to be friends with him. Jack knew I was only capable of friendship, I'd made that more than clear, and yet he was still intent on sticking around, so why shouldn't

I indulge?

Now I had relaxed my defences, I'd come to work today with a totally new outlook. I was no longer going to be terrified of bumping into him around the set. Quite the opposite, in fact – I was looking forward to seeing him and getting to know him. Who'd have thought it?

'Any news on Sean?' Jack asked, his grin fading marginally as he spoke.

Shaking my head, I felt a tingle of worry in my belly, briefly covering my earlier happiness. 'No. I got a text from Allie yesterday saying she was heading to Las Vegas to talk to him, but I've not seen her and she's not picked up any of my calls so I don't know much more than that.' Her one text had been brief, thanking me for the information and giving me her flight number, but I had a strange feeling about it all and suspected there was more to it all than she had told me. I would certainly be sitting down and grilling her once she was back, that was for sure.

'I hope they work it out. He seemed OK in his text, but it was clear he's missing her,' Jack mused.

'Yeah, me too. They've certainly had enough drama in their relationship so far.'

Nodding, Jack raised the coffee pot and gave it a waggle, presumably his silent way of asking if I wanted one. 'Yes, please. I haven't had chance to grab a coffee yet, so I'm really looking forward to this.'

Jack looked pleasantly surprised by my more relaxed state and nodded as he poured out two cups. 'Me too.' I couldn't help but think that he was talking about more than just the coffee, but that was fine. I was looking forward to chatting with him too.

'I'm glad you agreed to meet me,' he added quietly. I decided not to answer, and gave a small, one-shouldered shrug and tiny smile instead.

Pulling in a deep breath, I turned my face towards the sun and felt my shoulders relax. Sharing a coffee with a man. Blimey. I'd come a really long way, and I was actually rather proud of the steps I'd taken. I was stronger than ever, more confident, and loved my work.

Considering we'd kissed and admitted to having feelings for each other we weren't acting on, it was slightly odd just *how* comfortable I felt around Jack. I had worried that it might be awkward with all that unspent sexual chemistry churning between us, but it wasn't in the slightest.

The buzz was noticeably still there though, hanging between us like static electricity making my skin tingle and prickle deliciously, but surprisingly I felt relaxed enough to just enjoy it and not worry that he would push my boundaries. I wondered if he felt it too.

It was a tantalising feeling, offering promises of something potent, powerful, and sinfully good, if only I would give in to it. But as much as I had decided to relax my defences with him, that was one limit I wouldn't be changing. Regardless of how good he made me feel, friends was one thing, but opening up about my history and explaining what a freak I was about sex was a whole different ball game I couldn't even entertain where Jack was concerned. Not yet, anyway. Maybe not ever.

I would allow myself to enjoy the thrill of being near him though and see where it led, and it really was quite thrilling. He emitted this strong calmness that simultaneously seemed to arouse me, calm me, and strengthen me.

Watching as he poured my drink, my eyebrows rose as he added just the right amount of milk, and topped it off with a dash of cold water. He'd remembered the way I took my coffee?

As he held out the beverage to me, I looked down and couldn't help the small smile that slipped to my lips. It looked perfect, and I was oddly touched by the gesture.

'Strong coffee, a splash of milk, topped up with cold water. Just how you like it, right?' Jack announced proudly.

'Yes.' Looking at the drink, I chuckled and grinned at him. 'Your stalker-like tendencies are still active, huh?' I couldn't help making the dig again, but I saw Jack's mouth twitch into a smile in response.

'Stalker?' He pursed his lips and narrowed his eyes as if deep in thought. 'I'd prefer to be called sweetly observant,' he concluded, watching me over the rim of his cup as he took a sip of his own drink.

I blinked several times and tried to hide my growing blush by sampling the coffee in my hand. Sweetly observant. He was actually rather accurate with that comment. So far in our acquaintance, Jack had proved his attentiveness time and time again. He'd spotted my dislike for contact and made every effort to avoid it, identified my elastic band habit and tried to alleviate it on several occasions, stuck to his promise that we could stay as just friends, and now had my coffee choices spot on.

Yeah, all in all, he *was* sweetly observant. But seeing as we seemed to be entering a new teasing dimension to our relationship, I wouldn't give him the satisfaction of rolling over and agreeing.

'A sweetly observant stalker then,' I concluded with a small smirk.

Jack threw his head back and laughed, the lovely raspy sound sending an answering grin to my own lips regardless of how much of a spin it had sent my brain into.

'Some compromise that is,' he grumbled good-naturedly, his eyes shining as he looked back at me with a wink.

His winks were so charming that they caused my heart to skitter in my chest, and this occasion was no different, as my heart leapt up several gears. After several moments of companionable silence, Jack glanced at me and tilted his head curiously. 'Can I ask you a question, Caitlin?'

Blowing the steam from my cup I gave him a measured look and smiled cautiously. 'Sounds serious. But go on. I'll retain the right to deny you an answer,' I joked, which elicited a smile from Jack before his face turned thoughtful.

'I was just wondering if you might tell me why you don't date?' Instantly the smile fell from my face as my mask slid back into place and I found myself firmly shaking my head. That story didn't get broadcast publicly, and I wasn't planning on changing that rule for Jack.

I saw a flicker of disappointment cross his face, his brown eyes clouding over with acceptance as he nodded glumly. A twinge of guilt twisted in my stomach and I realised that he obviously thought we were becoming close too. And we were. But could I extend that new friendship bond and take the huge step of sharing my past with him?

My fingers were trembling slightly, so I put my mug down and fiddled with the elastic bands at my wrist. Jack watched me ping them, but made no move to stop me this time as he had in the past. I almost missed his intervention.

The air between us suddenly felt strained, the playfulness of earlier completely vaporised and replaced with a tense, stilted silence. I hated knowing that it was me who had created that void, but I didn't know what to do to alleviate it.

Stilling my hand, I gripped my stinging wrist and stared at the concrete below my stool before making a decision to let him in. Just a little. I couldn't tell him the whole story, but perhaps a small nugget of information might ease the pressure between us and get us back to the relaxed friendship we'd been trialling.

'My ex …' Swallowing hard, I could barely bring myself to say anything else, but I managed to get past the painful lump in my throat and elaborate slightly. 'Let's just say he wouldn't have won any awards for boyfriend of the year. Can I leave it at that for now?'

Jack's focus on me immediately became intent as he nodded once and feigned casualness by sipping his coffee and sitting back in his stool.

'Thank you, Caitlin,' he murmured softly, and I nodded in response, my eyes feeling moist.

'I …' Jack started to speak, but instead he paused, dug in his jeans pocket and produced a crisp, neatly-folded hankie for me. Another one.

What man seriously carried real cotton hankies around any more? Did he do this for my benefit, or was it possible that Jack really was a gentleman in disguise, handkerchiefs and all? Maybe he wore braces with his suits and had a pipe and slippers sitting at home waiting for him too, like a true, olden-day, romantic hero.

His hand hesitated on mine as he passed the hankie over, our fingers caught in a not-quite-hand-hold for a second or two. The thin cotton was separating our skin, but it didn't reduce the thrill I got from his touch one little bit.

'Th … thank you.' I fingered the soft material and used it to quickly wipe under my eyes. I'd have quite a collection if he kept doing this, but it was yet another show of his sweetly observant nature and made my stomach tumble as I dabbed at my few stray tears again.

'You're welcome,' he murmured softly, his gentle tone

somehow making me feel OK about the fact that I was basically a sniffling mess. 'Our friendship means a great deal to me, Caitlin. I just want you to know that I would never jeopardise that. How we proceed, and what you choose to share with me, is all up to you, your pace, and your comfort.'

I couldn't help thinking that he was talking in terms of more than just friendship, but I didn't try and correct him, so I just nodded my agreement.

'You're safe with me, Caitlin. I swear it,' he added, almost so quietly that I wasn't sure I was supposed to hear it. But I did, and those few simple words meant so much to me that I could barely even comprehend the direction my thoughts were starting to take where this man was concerned.

Chapter Forty-One

Allie

What the hell was I doing? My body was trembling so badly that I would surely never be able to pull this off. Swallowing hard, I drew in a deep breath, straightened my spine, and tried to look haughty, confident, and rich as I approached the woman wearing the navy blue uniform.

I'd completely struck it lucky on my arrival at The Mansion in Las Vegas, and while waiting by the reception desk to try and find out what room Sean was in I'd overheard a cleaning woman talking to the manager about Mr Phillips in suite 6 needing a bucket of ice.

I hadn't stopped to let myself consider if there was more than one Mr Phillips staying here, or let myself dwell on why Sean would want a bucket of ice, (hopefully it wasn't to cool some champagne that he was sharing with a woman) and had instead put on my best attempt at a smooth, confident swagger as I made my way past the concierge and towards the rooms.

Miraculously, it had worked. No one had questioned me, stopped me, or even batted an eyelid, and I was now outside the door to suite 6 staring at it. How the hell I'd fluked that, I had no frigging idea. Perhaps my fake bravado had worked, or maybe my expensive dress and high heels looked convincing enough to fit in here. Who knew?

I'd come this far, but now I was stuck. I didn't want to just knock and hope he answered. If Sean was entertaining a woman, or god forbid, *women*, then I wanted to catch him at it so it might help to harden my heart against the pain I was currently experiencing. The only way to do that was to finish my fluky morning with one more blag.

Clearing my throat again, I prepared to put on my best posh accent and stopped by the cleaning woman's side before dramatically digging through my handbag, coming up empty, and sweeping my arm through the air. 'Excuse me, *daarrling*, but I seem to have left my key with Mr Phillips in the dining room. He's still breakfasting. You couldn't be a dear and let me into our room, could you?' I'd stolen the condescending tone, overly expressive arm flaps, and exaggerated *'daarrling'* from Savannah, but it had sounded just as revolting and patronising in my voice as it did in hers.

The cleaning lady looked me up and down and examined a list on a clipboard before her, presumably checking the name of the occupier of room 6, before nodding and pulling out a key card for the door.

Oh my god, it actually worked! But my glee was short-lived as the door swung open and I realised that I was just seconds away from confronting Sean and seeing what he was really up to.

Crap. Maybe this wasn't such a good idea after all. If I found him screwing another woman, the images would be burnt into my retinas for eternity. I wasn't sure I'd ever recover from something like that. Nerves were close to overwhelming me, my knees felt wobbly, my hands were shaking so much I had to bunch them at my sides, and I felt decidedly like I might throw up.

Inching my way inside the hotel suite, I closed the door

behind me and took off my heels as quietly as possible. If I was about to discover Sean shagging someone then I at least wanted to be able to run away with dignity, and not fall arse over tit because of my stupid shoes.

After a small hallway, the suite opened up into a huge lounge area and I immediately saw Sean crashed out on the sofa. He was alone, which was a relief, but there was an assortment of empty glasses on the table, his face was red, and he had an ice pack over his forehead. There was also a bucket next to him, which judging by the funky smell in the air was for vomit, and in addition to that, I saw that one of his hands was wrapped up in bright white bandages.

The cherry on the cake was the woman's coat I could see carelessly tossed over a dining chair behind him.

So he definitely wasn't here alone.

My stomach plummeted. Goddamn it. It would seem he had continued on his bender in significant style.

Was he hungover now, or still drunk? I had no idea, but as I walked closer and he opened his eyes to reveal a bloodshot, bleary gaze, I settled on the latter.

'Alllieee?' He slurred my name dreadfully, sounding at once confused and seemingly happy.

'Jesus, Sean, how much have you had to drink?'

'Nooott drunk.'

Yeah right. He looked as drunk as a skunk that had been on a week-long bender. Rolling my eyes, I put my hands on my hips and wondered what the heck I could, or should, do to help him. 'You're slurring, there's an ice pack on your head, and you've thrown up.' Pretty recently too, by the looks of it. 'You sure as shit look drunk to me. Where is she, Sean?'

'Eehhh?' He was making no sense at all. 'Bathooom.'

Which I took to mean she was in the bathroom. 'Oh my

god, you're not even going to try and hide it?' I don't know why I said that out loud, because sleeping with someone else *and* lying about it would be way worse than simply cheating. Not that either were acceptable, really. And I supposed seeing as we were on a break, I couldn't call it cheating either, could I? It was certainly a flipping slap in the face though, that was for sure. God, this was all such a monumental mess that I barely knew what to do. Maybe I should just leave.

'Whaaaa?' Sean seemed to try and get up for a moment, his arms pushing himself almost to sitting before he fell back with a groan. If he was still this drunk, then he was going to have a monster hangover once the booze wore off.

'You're drunk off your face, you have a woman with you, probably more than one, and you can't even be bothered to try and hide it?' I flung my hands into my hair as scalding tears began to pour down my cheeks. I was just about to launch into another tirade when a voice floated through from another room. A female voice. His other woman.

'I won't be a second, Sean. I'm just mixing you another drink.'

Another drink? Bloody hell, it was clear he'd already had enough – he could barely speak, he'd already thrown up, and wasn't even able to stand. Who the hell was this woman? Did she have no sense of decency at all?

I'd spent the entire hour's flight from LA to Vegas imagining what the owner of the scarf and cardigan might look like. All the images had revolved around a trollop with fake tits, bleached teeth, over the top make up, and a slaggishly tight outfit.

Unfortunately, with beautiful large blue eyes, sleek brown hair, an exceptionally pretty face, no make-up at all, and a relaxed jeans and jumper combo, the woman who walked into the room the next second looked nothing like that at all.

Scanning her from head to toe in case I had missed some slut-like quality, I paused, and had to grudgingly admit that this woman didn't look like a slut at all.

Goddamn it, I had been pinning my hopes on her looking trampy so I could persuade myself she was just a quick, convenient lay. But this woman actually looked quite normal and nice, and … sweet.

Steadying my resolve I told myself fiercely that it didn't matter what she looked like. She was here with Sean, they had obviously been drinking – and presumably screwing – and that was all I needed to know.

'I think he's had enough to drink, don't you?' I spat as I tried to push past her as my tears overwhelmed my vision. 'I hope you'll be very happy together.' My voice choked on the last word, but as I blindly reached for the door, a hand landed on my arm.

'*What?* Wait, are you Allie, by any chance?'

Pausing, I turned my tear-stained face toward her and swallowed loudly before nodding slowly. 'I thought I recognised you from the photograph. I'm not sure what you think is going on here, but I'm Evie. Sean's sister.'

She was his sister.

His sister?

What was Evie doing here, and why the heck was she letting him get so plastered?

Shaking her head, a wry smile curled Evie's lips as she looked over to Sean, who appeared to have passed out again, and then turned her gaze back to me. Gosh, now I knew who she was it was screamingly obvious that they were related because she had the exact same hair and eye colour as him, not to mention she was a younger imprint of their mother.

'I can only imagine what this must all look like.' Letting go of my arm, she smiled at me and jerked her chin toward the lounge. 'This was not how I pictured our first meeting to be. Will you come in so I can explain?'

Attempting to reel in all the thoughts speeding around my brain, I nodded mutely and followed Evie back inside the suite as I quickly wiped at my cheeks.

'There's a lot to explain, but let me start by saying, he's not drunk.' I opened my mouth to disagree, but she placed a full pint glass of orange liquid on the table and held up a hand to stop me. 'I know it looks that way, but he's got heatstroke. Pretty badly, too.'

'Heatstroke?' I choked, wondering if this was just a line from Evie trying to cover for her big brother.

'He got roped into playing some charity golf thing yesterday, but his mind wasn't in it. It was really hot, he was out all day and he obviously didn't hydrate himself enough. When he finished he said he had a headache, but within half an hour of getting back he was throwing up and talking absolute nonsense.'

My eyes narrowed with concern as I looked back to Sean and noticed the sweat beading on his nose and cheeks. He was sick?

'We just got back from the emergency room a few hours ago, actually. They kept him in overnight to give him some fluids, and now I have to keep him drinking those rehydration drinks every hour,' she explained, indicating the pint glass and other empty glasses collected on the table.

'Sorry it's such a mess, I haven't had time to tidy up since we got back.'

Wow. So he really wasn't drunk? And he wasn't balls deep in another woman fucking away his problems? This new, pleasant reality was taking quite a bit of getting used to. Although having heatstroke obviously wasn't pleasant for him, it was a damn sight better for me than the alternative I had been imagining.

A knock at the door made me jump, but Evie nodded and turned away. 'Hang on, hopefully that'll be the ice I ordered.' Coming back with a bucket of ice, she carefully wrapped some cubes in napkins and tucked them under Sean's armpits before looking at me again.

'The doctor advised I do this until he's more lucid.' Flopping down into an armchair, she wiped her hands on her jeans and gave me a hopeful smile.

'What happened to his hand?' I asked, noticing the bandages again.

'He bust two knuckles in his right hand when he hit a sign by accident after you two broke up.' Oh. I could remember him thrashing his arms and banging into the sign, but I didn't realise he'd done that much damage. 'He explained to me about the issues with Savannah and how you and he are taking a break. I'm sorry.'

Pulling in a deep breath, I glanced at Sean again and gave Evie a sad nod of thanks.

'So, I bet you're wondering what I'm doing here in the States, right?' she asked, a smile pulling at the corners of her mouth.

Wiping away the last of my tears, I nodded and returned her smile with a weak, watery one of my own.

'Basically, to cut a long story short, I was booked to come out and visit Sean last week, but when I arrived in LA on Saturday night I got to his apartment and found him drunk and distraught.'

'I saw the beer bottles … and the vodka,' I murmured.

'Yeah. Luckily, I arrived just after he'd opened the bottle so I managed to stop him.'

A thought occurred to me that made my shoulders feel ten tonnes lighter. 'So the cardigan at his house is yours?'

Nodding, she smiled. 'Yeah, and the shoes. I travelled in them but I never really wear heels, so when we decided to come here I just left them at his place.'

'You left a scarf too. I thought he'd had another woman there,' I admitted quietly.

'Oh God! No! I can't imagine what that must have been like. Sorry.' Evie laughed, but then she licked her lips and flashed me a sympathetic look. 'So Savannah's been playing up like a spoilt child?'

Nodding, I drew in a breath and pushed my hair back from my face, before bringing my feet up onto the sofa and hugging my knees to my chest. 'Yeah, she's a cow. It's so messed up.' Glancing at Sean's slumped form, I sighed heavily. 'God, this is all my fault.' Flopping forward, I rested my head on my knees, completely swamped by everything.

'No, it's not. I know Savannah and I can't stand her. Sean told me the pranks she played so I totally get your side of things. Having said that, you should know just how cut up about it he is. I've never seen him like this about a woman before.' Guilt slithered in my belly again, and I began to chew on my lower lip fretfully.

'Anyway, enough of my guilt trip. Our uncle runs this place, so we decided to get away from it all for a few days so Sean could clear his head and give you the space you had asked for.'

Looking at me curiously, she tilted her head. 'He really wants to make things work, you know. Before he left he demanded that his director bring forward the press conference so he can put everyone straight about Savannah and be free to date you.'

So Cait had been right. That was good news. A small relieved murmur fluttered from my lips, followed by a giggle. 'When I heard he was in Vegas I was thinking all sorts of things. I thought he was on a bender trying to forget me.'

'Nope. Just chilling with his sister. It was going nicely, until the golf tournament yesterday,' she added wryly with a shake of her head.

Beside us, Sean let out a low groan and fidgeted on the sofa, causing both Evie and me to jump up and go to his side.

'Eww. Let me empty this. I didn't know he'd used it again,' she said, grimacing as she picked up the sick bucket. 'Can you lightly waft him, please?' she asked, handing me a paper fan from the coffee table. 'The doctor said I'm supposed to fan him while he's sweating because it will help the moisture evaporate and keep his skin cooler.'

'Of course.' Taking the fan, I perched on the side of the sofa and began to gently swish it back and forth to create a breeze across his face. Sean shifted slightly, and his eyes fluttered, but didn't fully open.

Gazing down at him, I couldn't help gently cupping his jaw and stroking it with my thumb. It was rough from several days' stubble growth, and the prickly sensation tickled my skin until I was overcome with the urge to lean down and place the briefest of kisses on his chin.

I loved him so much. So much had happened in the last week that I was still struggling to comprehend it all, but I supposed the only important things I needed to know were that Sean hadn't cheated, and was demanding that his director sort out the mess with Savannah, which was music to my ears.

The rest we could sort out once he was recovered, and better yet, once he was officially single.

Chapter Forty-Two

Allie

Evie and I took turns fanning Sean and bringing him drinks, and by the time I'd been with them for just over ten hours, he was becoming more lucid when awake and starting to make a better recovery.

We'd moved him to a bedroom because he was still asleep most of the time, and so during some of his snoozes I grabbed the opportunity to chat to Evie and get to know her. She was just as lovely as I had expected, and we hit it off immediately, lounging together on the sofa and gossiping like we'd known each other forever.

'You guys better get back together,' she announced suddenly, offering me the packet of crisps she was chomping her way through. 'You're the best girlfriend he's ever had.' I grabbed a handful of the crisps and laughed, feeling a little embarrassed. 'Well, he's not really had any other girlfriends, but you know what I mean. You're lovely. I want you as part of the family!'

Evie's enthusiasm was charming, and her love for her brother was incredibly touching, but I still couldn't get past all the issues Sean and I had yet to resolve. Taking a deep breath, I decided to ask the question that had been burning in the back of my mind ever since I'd arrived.

'Evie, do you think I'm being awful telling Sean that I won't be with him until things with Savannah are sorted?'

Evie finished chewing her mouthful while looking at me thoughtfully, and then shook her head. 'No, I don't. I mean, he's my brother and I want him to be happy, and it's obvious that you make him happy, but I can totally see your side of things too. Going out with someone but not being allowed to be with them? That would be horrible.'

'You should try going out with someone and having to watch them touch someone else in public and pretend to be with them instead of you,' I added quietly, hoping I didn't sound quite as bitter as I felt. 'I kills me a little bit every time I see him with her,' I admitted, my voice cracking slightly.

Dumping the crisp bag down, Evie leant forward and patted my arm supportively as she nodded. 'Especially because it's Savannah the super bitch we're talking about,' she agreed with a sage nod. 'I get it. Sean does too. At first he was frustrated, but we talked about it a lot when I first got here. He knows what he needs to do, and I'm pretty sure that disappearing for a week will have shown his director just how serious he is about ending the farce.'

'I hope so,' I agreed softly.

Beside me, Evie tried to stifle her third gigantic yawn in less than a minute, so I turned to her and smiled. 'Look, it's late and you were at the hospital all last night. Why don't you go and get some rest? I'll keep an eye on Sean.'

'Are you sure?' She might have been asking, but from the way Evie immediately jumped up, she was clearly keen, and I couldn't help shooing her towards the bedrooms.

'Of course. My flight back isn't until tomorrow morning at ten. You hit the hay.'

Giving me a hug, Evie stood back and smiled fondly. 'Thank you so much. And thank you for caring about my brother, I'm so glad you two found each other. Goodnight,

Allie.'

My throat closed as I suddenly felt flooded with emotion: love, stress, desperation, hopelessness … you name it, it was there, forming a solid ball I just couldn't seem to swallow down.

After getting a grip on myself, I changed into my pyjamas and sat on the sofa for a few minutes, but I was worried I might fall asleep and miss Sean if he called out, so I ended up back in his room standing at the foot of the bed watching him sleep.

His trademark intense look was absent for a change, replaced with complete relaxation as he slept. He was so handsome, with his dark eyelashes fanning over his cheeks, lips slightly parted, jaw dark with stubble, and a chunk of his hair fallen messily across one eye. He looked like sexiness on a plate.

The ultimate temptation.

After staring for several minutes, I couldn't resist going closer and gently brushing the hair back from his eyes. His skin was cool beneath my fingers, a good sign that he was over the worst of his heatstroke, and I nodded in satisfaction.

Settling in the only armchair the room had, I tried to get comfy as I watched him sleep, but the chair was too small and boxy. Clearly finding out that your boyfriend – ex-boyfriend – was missing, and then suspecting him of being with another woman in Vegas was tiring stuff, because even in my stiff position I soon found my eyes pulling closed with exhaustion.

Luckily, every time I drifted off, my head lolled forward and woke me up by cranking my neck uncomfortably, until after the fourth or fifth time, I stood up with an annoyed grumble. Chewing on my lip, I briefly debated my options, and after a short pause, decided to crawl into the bed beside Sean. We were broken up, but it wasn't exactly like we'd never shared a bed before, and I knew he wouldn't want me to be uncomfortable all night. Besides, this bed was easily a super-king size, so I was miles away from touching him as I rolled onto my side and fell asleep almost immediately.

Sean

A lovely floral scent filled my nose as I woke up, and I felt my lips pull into a smile. Allie. That was definitely her perfume. She must be here. My eyes flew open and the smile on my lips grew even broader when I found her curled next to me fast asleep.

As much as I wanted to fill my vision with her, my throat was parched, so I took a long drink from the water on my bedside table and did a quick survey of how I was. Surprisingly, I felt fine apart from my raging thirst. I could remember the golf tournament, and the doctor telling me I had heatstroke, but everything after that was pretty fuzzy. I'd had mild heatstroke before, but it had been nothing compared to this. Finishing the entire glass of water, I placed it down and turned back to Allie with a grin.

My gorgeous girl. I'd thought she was here earlier, but my mind had been so foggy that I'd half suspected I'd conjured her up in my imagination.

My head was clear now though, and there was no doubt that she was real, and here. More than just being here, she was in my bed. Back where she belonged. I could only assume from her presence that she'd relented on her decision for us to be split up, and that realisation made me so bloody happy that I couldn't wait to get reacquainted with her properly.

Allie

The sharp, delicious rasp of stubble brushed across my inner thigh, and then, before I was barely even awake enough to know what was going on, the rubbing moved across to my clit and I found myself arching off the bed with a gasp of surprise. Sean often went a few days without shaving so he had a bit of a rough and ready look, but this was definitely longer and scratchier than usual, tickling and arousing in all the right places, just on the pleasurable side of painful, and it was hot as hell.

A chuckle from between my legs sent his warm breath fanning across my sensitive skin, and then the stubbly teasing was replaced with a hot mouth as he tongued urgently at my opening and sucked my clit into his mouth.

'Oh, fuck!' I couldn't help the curse that exploded from my lips, because he had used far more force than usual, and had nearly sent me spiralling straight into an orgasm. One of his hands pressed into my inner thigh to part my legs wider, and the other snaked up my belly, over my ribs, and then cupped my left breast before rolling the nipple between his fingers and tugging. *Hard.* Another curse left my mouth, along with a further jerky hip thrust, as my core clenched and eyes squeezed shut from the sudden onslaught of pleasure.

It felt so good I could hardly decide if I was awake or just dreaming. Either way, one thing was clear; Sean was on a mission. I was barely even conscious and that was twice he'd nearly made me come already!

The mattress shifted below his weight as he began to crawl up my body, his lips leaving a scolding trail across my skin as he went, my hands digging into his hair and urging him to hurry up. His head had only just emerged from beneath the duvet when I felt the solid, silky tip of his cock pressing against my opening, and a second later he surged upwards, his arms falling on either side of my head as he plunged into me in one long, hard stroke.

A garbled, nonsensical yell left my throat as I desperately struggled to accommodate him. I was turned on, but not quite ready enough for his size, and it took several shifts of my hips and some shallow grinding until if I felt my body give the extra lubrication we needed to allow him fully inside me.

As he slid in to the hilt, he gave a heated curse and paused for a second while he breathed raggedly by my ear. Now we were fully joined, I parted my thighs as much as I could to allow him the depth I knew he would want with his coming thrusts, a move that earned me a grumble of appreciation. My man liked his sex primal, hard, and as intimate – *deep* – as physically possible. I didn't know if it was a possessive thing or if he just liked to try and get as far inside me as possible, but over the next several seconds he followed tradition by repeatedly burying himself in a series of hard, fast, and deep thrusts of his beautiful cock.

This was full on and frantic, even by Sean's standards; there was none of his usual tenderness. Instead, his hips were pumping out an incredible rhythm as if attempting to charge us towards our orgasms in record speed. Gripping his shoulders and raising my hips in time with his thrusts was about the only thing I could manage to do, and then, barely a minute or so after we'd started, I felt my body flare with a rush of heat and fly into a huge climax, my muscles gripping him as I threw my head back and dug my nails into his back to ride out my orgasm.

Sean growled above me, his cock thickening as he continued to drive deep inside of me, and then he yelled, his hips bucking as I felt him come inside me in a series of hot, flooding spurts.

Holy hell. What a way to wake up.

We were both panting and sweating as Sean rested his head on my shoulder and nuzzled into my neck, placing a string of kisses along my raging pulse. 'I'm so glad you've come back to me, my gorgeous girl.'

'Mmmm,' I murmured, lifting my hips into his lazy thrusts and still dazed by the suddenness of that speedy sexing.

Wait a second. *Back?* He was glad I'd come back?

Hold on …

My sleepy, lusty fog began to clear, and my sated relaxation quickly started to turn into panic.

Oh crap … crap, crap, *crap*.

It felt so natural being with Sean, and I'd been so warm, sleepy, and comfortable that when he'd woken me with sex I'd completely forgotten everything going on between us. Blinking several times, I willed my drowsy brain to catch up with events, and then sucked in a breath and pushed at his chest in a panic. I couldn't believe I'd just let him have sex with me when we were supposed to be broken up!

'Sean, no, wait …' Wincing, I realised just how belated my request was. I should have shouted it at the top of my lungs five minutes ago before I'd clawed his back raw with my nails. Fuck, I was such an idiot.

'What is it, baby?'

His soft endearments weren't helping ease my guilt at all and I winced as my heart clenched with worry. Sean sounded so ecstatic because of my appearance in his bed that I was tempted to crumble, stay with him, and just demand that we hole up in this hotel room until Savannah went to the press and admitted her lies. But I knew that couldn't happen. He had to pretend to split up with her, and that would mean going back to LA and facing the journalists with her. Together. As a supposed couple.

If I gave in now he might not rush to clear things up, and for the sake of my sanity, I *really* needed him to clear things up. The last few weeks had been hell. I wasn't cut out for so much drama in my life. He needed to be with me, or not; I couldn't handle some secret in between relationship any more. I could be stuck as 'the other woman' for months on end.

'I'm not back with you, I just … *shit* …' Pushing at his chest again, I finally managed to shift his weight enough so I could scramble from the bed. Running my hands through my hair, I looked down and realised that while I was still wearing my vest top, my panties and pyjama shorts were gone and were nowhere to be seen.

How the hell did Sean always manage to undress me as I slept? He was like the flipping Houdini of sex. God, this was all such an incredible mess.

Sean pushed himself to a kneeling position on the bed, completely unashamed of his nakedness, or his semi hard cock, which was laid on his thigh glistening with a mixture of our climaxes as if goading me about what I'd just done.

'What do you mean you're not back with me?' he asked in shock, his tone causing my gaze to leave the sight of his manhood and raise to his eyes. 'What the heck was that then?' His voice rose as his hand gesticulated around the bed.

'You pounced on me when I was asleep, it's hardly my

fault!' I shot back defensively, guilt flooding my system and causing me to panic. It didn't help that I suddenly became hyper aware of the fact that I could feel moisture escaping my body and wetting the tops of my thighs. Goddamn it, where were my bloody shorts? It was hardly appropriate to ask, but Sean's post-sex cleansing routine would have been pretty welcome right about now.

'You were in my bed! What was I supposed to think?' His eyes darkened as anger replaced his shock.

His words were so justified I could hardly stand it. 'I didn't want to be far away in case you were still poorly and needed me in the night, but I was tired so I lay down for a while.' Stupid girl. I should have toughed it out on the uncomfortable armchair.

Thinking of the chair behind me, I sighed heavily and allowed my legs to give way as I collapsed my naked arse onto it, not even caring if I made a mess of the fancy fabric.

Dropping my head into my hands, I stared at the floor and tried to reel in my skittering emotions, but it was a battle I swiftly lost. 'I should have stopped you earlier, but I was sleepy. I wasn't thinking straight … I'm sorry.'

'*Sorry?*' he choked out. 'That sex was incredible. I felt so close to you, so connected, didn't that mean anything to you?'

'Of course it did. But it still shouldn't have happened,' I muttered. He was angry, but what else could I say? Nothing would make things better. I had seriously screwed up. Tears burnt at my eyes and began to run down my cheeks, dripping from the end of my nose and onto the carpet in a steady, seemingly endless stream of hopelessness.

'This is all messed up,' I murmured through my clogged throat. 'I came to Vegas because I thought you were with another woman, and I stayed because you were sick, but I still can't be with you until you can be properly mine.'

Sean let out a muttered growl of frustration that caused me to look up and meet his gaze. His eyes softened slightly when he saw my tear-streaked face and his shoulders slumped. 'It might sound dramatic to you, Sean, but I wasn't kidding when I said that a little piece of me dies every time I see you with Savannah. Just knowing that you're going to work with her where everyone thinks you're engaged is just … just … too much for me to handle. I need to distance myself from it until it's sorted.'

Standing up, I tried to ignore the incriminating wetness on my thighs and began to search for my shorts. 'I know it's not enough, but I really am sorry. I shouldn't have come here in the first place. Just forget this happened.' Finally spotting my knickers and shorts on the floor by the side table, I pulled them on and risked a glance at Sean. He was still frozen in the bed, but his expression had now morphed into weary resignation.

'Never, I won't forget this. It was too incredible to forget.' He stated with a defiant glance. 'And I'm glad you came. Thank you. I'm sorry I yelled, I just really miss you.' My heart broke a little at his words. I missed him too. So much, but it was a screamingly obvious fact so I didn't bother to say it out loud.

Shaking his head again, he raised both hands and ran them through his hair. 'Is there anything I can say to make you change your mind?' he murmured, his dark-ringed eyes looking so hopeful that I hated to be the one causing him pain.

'As soon as you're officially single, I'll be all yours,' I vowed softly.

He let out a long, low breath and closed his eyes on a slow blink. 'But not before then?'

As awful as it made me feel, especially after what had just occurred, I had to stay resolute, so I shook my head sadly. Sean's eyes flickered shut, but then eventually he nodded reluctantly. 'OK. I understand. I'd be the same if things were reversed. I will sort it, Allie. You're going to be mine again, that's a promise.'

A small, sad smile curled my lips as my tears continued to flow down my cheeks. 'I like that promise,' I whispered thickly. 'A lot.' Grabbing my handbag from the dresser, I slung it over my shoulder, trying to remember where the heck I'd left my clothes when I undressed. 'I need to go, my return flight leaves soon.'

Sean's face fell at my words, but then he nodded. 'OK. Thank you for coming, my gorgeous girl.'

I winced. It was amazing how painful it was to hear his nickname for me when all this tension lay between us.

Seeing me flinch, Sean's shoulders slumped. 'Sorry. I'll stick to my earlier promises. No calling you until everything's sorted. Just know that I will be missing you and thinking of you every single second, regardless of where I am or who I'm with.'

His words were low and rough and so full of emotion that my throat closed up, rendering me completely unable to answer verbally. Giving him one final nod and a loaded glance, I turned on my heel and walked away from him again, hoping with everything in me that he would be true to his word and sort things with Savannah sooner rather than later. Perhaps then we could get on the straight and narrow and I wouldn't ever have to do the walk of shame away from him again.

Chapter Forty-Three

Cait

My plan for the afternoon was to finish work and immediately meet with Allie and see how things had gone with Sean. I'd had a text from her this morning saying she was getting on a flight back and would be in LA just after lunchtime, and I'd been itching to get out of work ever since. I had five minutes left of my shift, and I knew exactly what I'd do when that time was up … run to the house to see if she was back.

Her text had been brief, so I'd assumed she didn't really want to talk about what had happened with Sean, but for once I wasn't going to be the quiet friend. This time I was going to push her for details about Sean's disappearance and make sure she was definitely OK.

Finally, my shift was over and I made my way towards the lockers so I could grab my bag and head off. I veered as far away from my manager's office as possible just in case she tried to grab me for some overtime, and then felt my shoulders slump with relief when I made it to my locker.

I tensed again almost immediately however, when I overheard a conversation taking place between two crew members beside me. 'Yeah, so apparently the fire closed down the entire stage. They've only just managed to put it out.'

That was a slightly alarming statement to overhear, so I

marginally slowed my movements and fiddled with my bag so I could listen for a little longer.

'I bet it was dodgy wiring, that stage has needed work for years. There was bound to be an accident at some point.'

'Yep. I heard a rumour they'll be moving the filming of *Fire Lab* to stage six, right next door to us.'

'Really? Just think, Johanna Stram within just a few feet of me … God, she is *so* hot. Those legs of hers drive me insane.'

'Not appropriate, dude, some of them are in hospital at the moment.'

'Sorry, but I'm just saying, she's got a decent pair of legs on her.'

As I absorbed their words, my stomach twisted with apprehension and I had to grip the locker to steady myself. Just a few weeks ago, the news that Jack's show might be moving right next door would have terrified me beyond belief, but now, that news paled into insignificance when coupled with the fact that there had been a fire on his set.

That must have been terrifying. As I processed the thought, a more alarming one sprung to my mind. What if Jack was one of the injured?

Studios were busy places and always packed with people, so the chances of it being him were quite small, but I found my breathing turning a little ragged. I couldn't allow myself to dwell. I turned to the two men beside me and cleared my throat.

'Did you say a fire? Who was hurt?'

The man who had been practically drooling over thoughts of Johanna Stram, who I happened to know was Jack's leading lady in the show, suddenly flushed bright red and averted his gaze as he realised I had overheard them.

'Yep, the *Fire Lab* stage went up in smoke about two hours ago. Ironic, huh, the stage of an arson drama burning down to the ground?'

Burning to the ground? Holy shit. I barely took a breath as I waited for him to elaborate. 'I don't exactly know about the extent of the injuries, but my pal is a gaffer over there and said that Brent, one of the cameramen, got trapped in a corner of the studio when the fire started. Luckily, Fiona, the line editor, and Jack Felton were nearby and quick to grab extinguishers. They managed to douse enough of it to get the guy out. I heard they've all got burns and smoke inhalation, but I don't know how bad.' He gave a shrug and slammed his locker shut. 'But I saw at least three ambulances arrive. Apparently, everyone else was evacuated safely. They've shut off the entire corner of the studio site at the moment.'

Everyone else was evacuated safely.

But not Jack?

My heart went from galloping to exploding, and I actually saw little white lights in front of my eyes for a second or two. Pulling in a long breath through my nose, I tried to calm my skittering nerves, but it was a bloody difficult task.

Nodding jerkily at the two men, I closed my locker and began to make my way towards the exit on jellified legs.

Jack had been hurt. And as a result I felt … what, exactly? Sick? Traumatised? Terrified? Blinking several times, I shook my head to try and shake some sense into myself, but it failed. I was a complete mess.

If he had been seriously injured then news would have spread around the studios … wouldn't it? Although from what the guys were saying the fire had only happened recently, so perhaps news hadn't had time to get out yet.

Pinging the elastic band around my wrist, I briefly considered getting my phone out and calling him. I had his number, after all, I could call him and see if he was all right. Or maybe send a text?

Stopping, I stared sightlessly at the ground, completely torn over what to do. Jack and I had unquestionably moved into the 'friends' category, and it was definitely OK for a friend to call the other if they'd been hurt, wasn't it? Nodding decisively, I brought up his number and dialled, listening intently as the call went through and gripping the phone so hard that my knuckles hurt.

As the first ring sounded down the line, my heart was absolutely pounding in my ears, but after ringing and ringing it went through to answerphone. What did that mean exactly?

Almost overcome with growing panic, I hung up without leaving a message and dashed out into the fresh air. Pausing to draw in several calming breaths, I realised I could smell a faint tang of smoke in the air, which only added to my dread.

I had to do something, but what?

Deciding that the best thing I could do was to ask at the information point to see if they had any news, I quickly set off towards the front of the site.

I tried to look calm and professional as I strode into reception and enquired about the well-being of those involved in the fire, but my voice had a definite edge of hysteria in it which I couldn't tamp down. The woman behind the reception gave me, and my identity card, a thorough look-over before she nodded her head, satisfied, and reached for a sheet of paper.

Pushing her glasses further up her nose, she skimmed over it before reading aloud. 'Three of the cameramen have been admitted for smoke inhalation but they're set for release in a day or two. Fiona is being treated for some minor burns, but is expected to be out later today.' I was literally bouncing from foot to foot as I waited for her to scan the rest of the sheet.

'What about Jack?' I blurted, unable to wait a second longer.

She raised an eyebrow and re-read the sheet. 'There's been no word about Brent or Jack.' No word? My heart sank. Why not? Apparently seeing my panic, she softened her features and gave me a sympathetic smile. 'They got it worst. All I know for certain is that they got taken away by ambulance about an hour ago.'

My emotions were so screwed up I truly wasn't sure what to do next. I'd spent the last few weeks feeling conflicted about just how much I felt for Jack, but one thing was certain – I would never in a million years want him to be hurt.

In our short acquaintance, I'd thought some dreadful things about him, wishing he would bugger off, leave me alone, and stop throwing my emotions into turmoil … but I had changed my mind. I liked him.

Really liked him.

Possibly in a 'more-than-just-friends' kind of way.

I'd finally got around to admitting it to myself, and now this had happened. I couldn't breathe properly, and had to bend forward to rest my hands on my knees for a moment as I tried to refill my lungs. What if he was seriously injured … or worse? Swallowing hard, I closed my eyes as nausea swirled in my stomach and one thing became vividly clear in my mind.

I had to get to him.

Author's Note

Thank you for reading!

Join Cait and Allie in *Undone*, the final instalment of the Revealed series, as they pursue their Hollywood dreams. Is Jack injured? Can Cait lower her defences and finally allow a man into her trust again? Will Sean go public about Savannah so that he and Allie can finally be together?

I write for my readers, so I'd love to hear your thoughts, feel free get in touch with me:
E-mail: **aliceraineauthor@gmail.com**
Twitter: **@AliceRaine1**
Facebook: **www.facebook.com/alice.raineauthor**
Website: **www.aliceraineauthor.com**

When I write about my characters and scenes, I have certain images in my head. I've created a Pinterest page with these images in case you are curious. You can find it at **http://www.pinterest.com/alice3083/**

You will also find some teaser pics for upcoming books to whet your appetite!

Alice xx

The Untwisted Series

By Alice Raine

Printed in Great Britain
by Amazon